Gifted Fae Academy

The Complete Collection

BRITTNI CHENELLE

Copyright © 2019 by Brittni Chenelle

All rights reserved.

No part of this book may be reproduced in any form or by any electronic or mechanical means, including information storage and retrieval systems, without written permission from the author, except for the use of brief quotations in a book review. Cover art and design Maria Spada for the set and the individual books by Silviya Yordanova of DARK IMAGINARIUM Art. Chapter headings by Molly Phipps.

BRITTNI CHENELLE

THE fae AND THE fallen

GIFTED FAE ACADEMY
BOOK ONE

THE fae AND THE fallen

BRITTNI CHENELLE

For my brother, Trey.
(Even if I mostly hated him <3)

Also Available in Audio

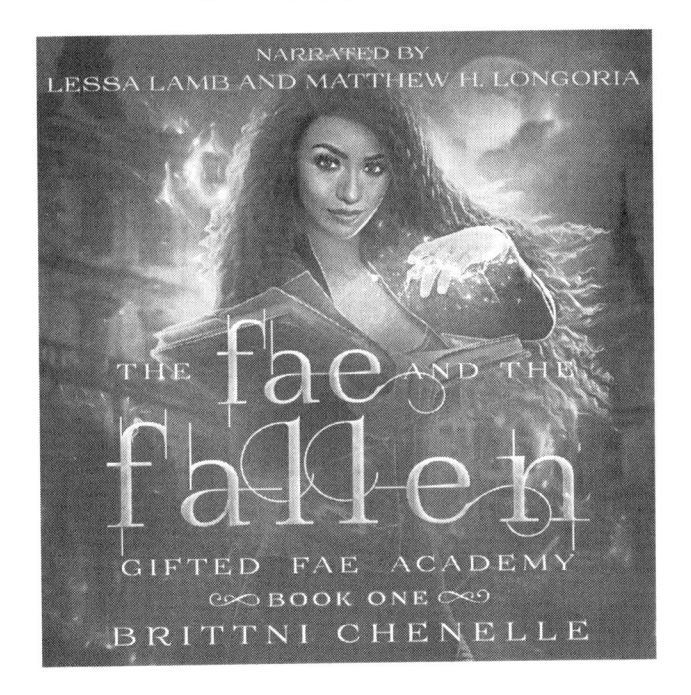

Narrated by Lessa Lamb and Matthew H. Longoria

The Fae and the Fallen

Gifted Fae Academy — Book One

Brittni Chenelle

Take advantage of the discounted price.

Reina

ONE

My first kiss nearly killed me—*literally*.

We had just entered middle school and most of our class had already received their gifts. It was the year that most people came into their abilities, and the ones who didn't—like me—were mercilessly tortured.

I wish I could say there had been strength in numbers, that by banding together, we ungifted Serfs could make it through the day in peace. The reality was that the Commons, those with useful but not extraordinary gifts, could still hurt us. The Elites were worst of all, but there were only a few of them around. They could knock all five Serfs out of school for a week with a touch, and as classmates, we were kept in frighteningly close proximity.

Still, we suffered *together*. But of the five companions I made, I grew closest to one boy in particular, Kaito. He was a transfer student from overseas, a couple of inches shorter than me and a little more than chubby, but every time it looked like I'd be targeted by the Elites, he'd do something to provoke them and draw their attention so I'd be spared their cruelty.

One day after school, we sat at our usual spot on the pier. The sun was setting, and the bright orange light splashed across the clouds.

"You didn't have to do that," I said, eyeing the sling that cradled Kai's right arm. "I could've kicked his ass."

He grinned. "If you're missing the rest of your friends, you can always just *visit* them in the infirmary."

I laughed. "It's faster just to let them knock me out." I turned away and absently watched the pink hues flicker on top of the waves.

"If only we had Fae at school."

I tilted my head. "Can you imagine the great Yemoja Roux cornering Westly in the hallway?" I laughed. "I'm sure she has bigger fish to fry than a few middle school bullies. She's out there with the rest of the Fae, holding this whole world together."

He nodded. "Things will be better once our gifts come in… *if* they come in."

I punched his shoulder, forgetting his sling. He winced.

"I'm getting my gift," I said. "And when I do, I'm going to Gifted Fae Academy just like Yemoja Roux."

I let my thoughts drift to the rhythm of the waves as I recalled my few encounters with the Fae. Sure, they were all over the news, using their powers to stop the criminal Elites from tearing society apart, but seeing them in person was like seeing the ocean for the first time. They were more than beautiful. They were infinite. Only the greatest and most morally incorruptible Gifted were selected by the government to become Fae and protect the rest of us. They were like celebrities, worshipped by the public and paid crazy amounts of money with tax dollars for their services. And from the moment I caught a glimpse of Yemoja Roux fearlessly dashing into harm's way, I knew I would follow in her footsteps someday.

"Don't move," Kai said, lifting his phone to take a picture of me. "The light is perfect." He smiled down at the screen. Without looking away from it, he said, "Don't forget about me when you go to GFA."

I tucked a curl behind my ear. "I'll never forget about you."

He looked up, his serious expression stirring a torrent of nerves and butterflies inside me. He looked down at my lips. *Is he going to kiss me?* I'd never kissed anyone before. *Had he?* I felt panicked as my mind raced my heart for top speed.

I looked down at his lips, trying to decide if I'd imagined the whole thing, but he leaned closer. I froze, squeezing my eyes shut with the hopes that he'd do the rest. His lips were soft against mine, but looking back, it was more like our lips bumped together than an actual kiss. Still, I felt a tingling sensation rush through my body and stop at the tips of my fingers. A feeling of weightlessness overcame me, like I was floating through the air.

"Reina!" Kai shouted.

My eyes snapped open to the distant voice, fear tearing through me. Stunned, I looked down—*way down* at Kai—reaching out to grab something. *Anything.* Too afraid to even scream, I floated twenty feet above the pier for twelve seconds before I plummeted down, my leg buckling under me with a snap. I was rushed to the infirmary, and after they put a cast on I was sent back home. Kai came to visit once, asking how I was, sounding very sorry. That was the last I saw of him.

It took eight weeks for the bone to heal and, by the time the cast came off, I realized Kai was no longer friends with us Serfs. He'd unlocked his gift, a rare power that allowed him to make what he touched weightless and, in a matter of weeks, teachers and students alike were tossing around words like "genius" and "prodigy." He may not have bullied us himself, but he certainly didn't stop his new friends, either.

I was very certain my time would come someday. With eighty percent of the population possessing some uncanny ability, odds were high I would at least become a Common, but then the year passed. And the next. And the next. When the time came to begin high school and I was still a Serf, I started to lose hope.

Foolishly, my crush on Kai lingered for too many of those years before I got my head on straight. I was finally over him… At least I thought so until I returned to school for our sophomore year. In one short summer, he'd sprouted up to six feet tall, was lean and muscular, and with his high cheekbones, dark eyes, and brooding good looks, he made my heart stop. He'd gone from a genius to a high school god, and inevitably, as the last remnants of our friendship died, and the new semester began, he became a bully.

Kaito

TWO

I nearly killed the first girl I ever kissed, *literally*.

But that was the moment when my gift awakened. It was like I was suddenly someone new, someone with a gift, someone who was Elite. Reina was just a Serf and still talking about going to the Gifted Fae Academy like it was a foregone conclusion. It drove me crazy. Life wasn't fair and you couldn't get where you wanted in life by believing you would. You had to be destined for it, so I made new friends among the Elite who were more like me and when they tormented her, I just stepped back. I figured maybe that was the way for her to learn and to accept that she was never getting a gift.

But no matter how many beatings she took, she never learned. Before I knew it, I was starting to hate her. Mob mentality. Why didn't she get it? She was lesser. Lesser than Elites, lesser than Fae, lesser than me. The way she provoked us was just begging to get seriously hurt. I might've started out wanting her to accept her fate and stop pushing, to protect her and to shatter those delusions of hers. But, after awhile, I found that I enjoyed tormenting her. I had new friends, a new life. She was on her own.

It was our sophomore year and we had a little less than three years of high school left. I couldn't believe Reina was still walking around telling people that when she got her ability, she'd transfer to Gifted Fae Academy. But that was the least of my worries. I was more worried about getting myself into the Academy. If anyone at our school deserved to get in, it was me, our school's most Elite student. But I'd failed the Academy's brutal entrance exam— twice.

I strode through the hallways, feeling the pull of every female gaze I passed. It had been that way since my power had come in, but this year the look in their eyes was different. I wasn't sure if it was my sudden growth spurt, or that my private combat training had turned me lean and muscular, but the looks I got now were far more pointed than just from my power, and I planned to enjoy this level of attention. Attention was one of the reasons I wanted to become Fae. To be as respected and loved as Yemoja Roux. Bathe in the glory and wealth that came with the job. Bigger pay days for taking down high-level criminal Elites meant there was no dispute who was the strongest among them. Yemoja Roux had held the title my whole life and I wanted to be just like her. There was no other job worth having.

Across the hall, I could see Westly looming over a terrified freshman girl. I heard the crackle of ice beneath her feet, and with a gentle shove to her shoulder, her legs flew out from under her and she landed hard on her ass. I smirked, but it quickly faded as Westly stumbled back.

Reina shoved him back with two hands. "You don't have to

be such a dickhead," she fumed, helping the girl to her feet. The freshman backed away and took off down the hall, leaving Reina to square off with Wes alone.

Fuck. Why did she always have to get involved?

I tried to hide my increased pace as I rushed over to them, throwing my arm around Wes before he could freeze her solid on the spot. "What do we have here?"

"The Serf is back for more," he said, pushing a handful of sandy brown hair out of his eyes. "I was just going to teach her a lesson."

I looked up at Reina. Her skin was rich and dark in color, kissed a few shades darker, from her summer exploits no doubt. Her curls had grown out to reach her lower back and today she wore a plaid skirt that stopped just above her knees. My gaze lingered over her curves. I guess I wasn't the only one who changed over the summer. I'd hoped to intimidate her with my appraisal, but she looked unfazed.

I rolled my eyes. "What, you think if we hit you enough times with magic you'll get some?"

"Reina!" a red-headed girl said, pushing through the crowd. She stepped between us and dropped forward in a deep bow. "She's very sorry," the girl said. "Please, just let it go this one time."

Wes grinned and shoved me. "Oh look, two for one." He raised his hand to attack, but I stopped him.

I spoke slowly. "If we let you go now, you'll think this kind of shit's ok."

The girl straightened, fear pooling in her eyes. She dropped to her knees. "Please," she begged, her face nearly at my feet. "That's better," I said, moving my gaze to Reina. "Your turn."

"Fuck you, Kai," she spat, helping Red to her feet.

I nodded. "Thought so." I reached out and brushed Reina's face. She slapped my hand away, but it was too late. The moment my skin touched hers, I felt her weight slide in range of my gift. It passed through my body, mimicking the sensation just before pins and needles, and she began to rise into the air.

Wes craned to get a better look as Reina scrambled to cover herself, her skirt already rising up along with her body from my magical energy. Wes shot me a wicked look. I nodded and, with a turn of my wrist, I flipped her upside down, exposing her black lacy underwear to the crowded hallway. Within seconds, there was a huge crowd, snapping pictures and video.

I wanted her to scream, to beg me to let her down and end the humiliation, but she hung there, silently, glaring at me defiantly. So I left her there.

Reina
THREE

I dangled in the hallway for an hour and a half before Kaito's magic finally wore off and I came crashing down. Thankfully, it was during a class and there was no one to watch me cry on the floor while I waited for my body to recover. I let my limbs go limp as my blood evened out, taking deep breaths. When I was up there, all I could think about was the pressure on my lungs. I was certain I'd suffocate—a corpse suspended in the hallway as teachers and students passed below, occasionally snapping pictures of my bare ass. An unfortunate end to a ridiculous life. At least I'd saved that girl, and more importantly, I'd worn good underwear.

I didn't have long before the bell sounded and I didn't want to be in the hall when the students made their way through. I peeled myself from the floor and pushed open the front doors of the school. I was sure they wouldn't miss me, at least for my first few classes. I needed to pull myself together. There was only one place that cheered me up when I felt this bad. I headed out into the streets, my home whenever I sprung myself from the orphanage.

An elderly lady crouched on the street near the bus stop raised her tired gaze to me. "For eight dollars, I'll change your hair color to a lovely shade of orange. Lasts almost twenty minutes."

Things were getting worse. If even Commons like her were having trouble finding work, what chance did I have as an orphan Serf? Of course, orphan and Serf went hand in hand, as any kid with a gift was quickly adopted. I waited at the bus stop for the 747 bus to take me to the edge of Ancetol City. Only Serfs took the bus; there were more efficient ways for the rich and Gifted to travel, but I didn't mind it. I felt safe there, unlike at school.

An hour later, I exited the bus. When it pulled away, I found myself outside the large gated lawn of Gifted Fae Academy. This had always been my go-to place to imagine a better life, but the competition to get into GFA went from regional to international two years ago when Yemoja Roux took a first-year from GFA as her personal apprentice for the summer: a green-eyed heartthrob named Oden Gates. He appeared beside Yemoja Roux in several of her interviews that summer, and ever since, my spot had become overrun with fangirls vying to get a look at him—not that I blamed them. Regardless of your type, chances were you were into Oden Gates. He was on track to become a Gold Tier Fae, just like Yemoja Roux, and he was just a sophomore like me. Talk about putting life into perspective. Luckily, with school starting up again, the coast seemed clear.

I ran my fingers over the iron crest, the owl insignia on each side, framing the letters GFA, as I'd done so many times.

"Please," I whispered, tears springing to my eyes. I wasn't sure if I was still upset from the incident, or if I was just worn out from fighting for my life day in and day out.

"Back again, Miss Reina?" a voice called from behind me. I spun. Professor Greene had his gray hair pulled into a bun. I wiped my face quickly. "Yes," I said. "Just getting ready for when my gift comes in."

His smile faded. "You've been crying."

"No, no, no. I just have... I just..."

"Have allergies?" He grinned. He opened his briefcase and pulled out a small bag. As he held it out, I could see there was a small piece of candy inside. "Did you know that I'm a confections professor?"

GFA was the home I'd never had. My dream of going there was the only thing I had left after my parents died last year. I'd stood outside that beautiful gate and traced the lines of it with my fingers so many times I could draw the crest with my eyes closed. I'd never been inside though—only the gifted were permitted to enter and only the staff and students who'd passed their notoriously rigorous entrance exam. But everyone knew the subjects taught in the top magic schools and the names of the retired Fae who taught there. I nodded. "Of course."

From my frequent visits, I'd met at least five of the professors, but the students rarely left campus. I'd never been fortunate enough to see Oden Gates in person.

"Give this little treat to whoever... gave you allergies."

Drug someone? I shook my head. "No thank you, professor," I said. "I don't want to hurt anyone."

He motioned to the gate. "Do you see the F on the crest? Do you know what it stands for?"

I nodded.

"Fae deliver justice. All this one does is suppress hatred for a short time."

I hesitated but, unwilling to insult him, I took the bag with the morsel. "Thank you, professor."

Whatever happened, however bad Kai made me feel, I knew I'd never give him the magic-infused confection. If anything, I would eat it to stop myself from hating him. Maybe then he'd stop being so damn… important.

The professor winked at me, and I held my breath as he squared his shoulders to the gate and it opened. I craned to see what lay behind those bars but, as usual, the image was blurred with magic. I was running out of chances to get in. Since I'd missed this year's exam, I only had my junior and senior years. If my gift didn't come by then, I'd age out of my group home and be thrust into the streets again.

Every year the likelihood I'd gain a power dropped. There was only a 7% chance left that I ever would—but that was more than enough. All I needed to do was survive until that day—the day when my life would really start and I'd finally get my chance to go to my real home, GFA.

Kaito

FOUR

I had those lace panties on my mind during every class, but I didn't see Reina again until lunch. She was chatting with the redhead at her usual lunch table, laughing. *Laughing.* What was with this girl? Why couldn't I break her? And worse, her nonchalance about the whole situation made the other students stop rubbing it in her face. I'd watched as several of them showed her pictures of her ass midair on their phones and she smiled and shrugged at them. There wasn't much fun in tormenting her if she wasn't going to be tormented. I wasn't sure if she was brave or just stupid.

Wes walked over and put our lunch trays down in front of me. "What are you looking at?"

He traced my gaze to Reina. "You still thinking about that ass? Me too, bro. I wasn't expecting all of *that*." He laughed. "I swear the Serf girls are the biggest freaks."

I sat down, pulling my tray toward me as my table filled up with several more of the school's Elites, although I was the only one at this school who could truly wear the title. Out of the corner of my eye, I saw Trevor, my number two, approach Reina's table. *He wouldn't fucking dare.* He smiled at her and her hand shot up to the charm on her necklace, the tell-tale sign she found him attractive.

My body moved, and before I knew it, I was right within earshot of their conversation. I walked up and gave Trevor a friendly pat on the back to remind him I could toss him into the air at any moment.

"Kaito," he said, "I was just telling Reina that I enjoyed her performance this morning."

I didn't like the sound of her name in his mouth. I sighed, turning my gaze to her. "I'm surprised you're back so soon. Perhaps I didn't leave you there long enough."

Reina's hand dropped from her charm. "It's actually kind of impressive that you managed to hold me up that long while you were in class. Not bad, Kai."

I hated when she did that. It was so much harder to torture her when she acted nice. I clenched my jaw to keep from smiling. "Whatever," I mumbled.

Trevor leaned closer to the redhead. "So, are you a Serf too?" he asked.

The girl nodded. Her eyes moved to me and widened. "Kaito, can I see your tattoo?"

I held my arm out to show her the black markings that snaked up from my wrist to my elbow on one side. She traced over the lines with her finger and I was surprised someone so vulnerable would be willing to touch me, knowing that she'd put herself in my magical range. It could have been a sign of surrender; after all, if I wanted to hurt her, there was nothing she could do about it.

"I had one for a year, but it wore off. I was thinking about getting another one myself because the Common in my neighborhood is pretty good at them," Trevor said. He nodded to Reina. "You going to get one?"

She shrugged, tugging on her necklace.

"But a tattoo might cover the lovely bruises." I smirked.

Reina frowned, looked up at me and asked, " What bruises?"

"The ones you got when I dropped you on your ass, of course," I laughed.

"Oh, there were no bruises. I just sort of, floated down, no problem," she lied. I knew she was lying but there was no way I could call her on it.

"Reina," I said, suddenly. "Do you ever think about that day at the pier?"

Her mouth dropped open.

A smile crept onto my face. "I do. You know, I still have the picture I took—" I snatched my arm away from Red. How *dare* she.

I leaned into her and she leaned back, fear flaring in her eyes.

"That was a huge fucking mistake," I hissed. "Who do you think you are? Yemoja Roux?"

Reina shot between us. "Wh-what happened? What's going on?"

Trevor stepped forward. "So Red's not ungifted?"

Reina shook her head. "She is. Trust me. She didn't do anything."

I crossed my arms. "Are you telling me you didn't know?"

Her gaze snapped to Red. "Emma. Tell them."

"It's true," she said, mystified. "I didn't do anything. I'm a Serf."

"Wow. That's a bald-face lie if I've ever heard one," I spat.

Reina leaned closer to Red, her voice dropping to a whisper. "If it's true, you can tell me."

She shook her head. "I didn't do anything. I swear, Reina."

She was certainly lying. I wasn't sure, but her gift seemed to purge secrets. My mind raced at the implications. It was incredible. With a single touch, she could coerce confessions out of criminals. Or gather secrets from the underground organizations that ran this city. Forget Elite, forget GFA—if I understood her gift correctly, she could have a one-way ticket to become Fae. So why was she hiding it? As the four of us looked around in confusion, I was grateful no one was asking the important question: what her gift actually was. If they did, they might think more carefully about what I'd said. I needed to make a quick exit.

I eyed the trays that lay in front of the girls. Red had a cold slice of pizza and Reina had an untouched sloppy joe which was the only option for free lunch—clearly one she didn't like much. Reina had been stuck with free lunch ever since her parents were killed, and she ended up in the group home. On the corner of her plate was something not from the cafeteria. A delicious-looking piece of candy. I tapped the trays and swiped the candy before using my gift to dump the remaining contents on the girls.

They gasped.

"Adios, ladies," I laughed, and I popped the candy into my mouth.

Reina

FIVE

I'd be lying if I said it never got to me. If that were true, I never would have put that magical morsel on my tray for Kai to find. I'd originally planned on eating it, and I could have hidden it until I got the chance, but something dark inside me wanted him to take it, most likely the part of me that he'd scarred. I scooped a handful of sloppy joe from my lap and dropped it on the floor. "That was weird, Em," I said. "He really seemed to think you used a gift on him." I nervously picked at the food on my lap. "But what else could make him say all that stuff?"

"But, I didn't," she whispered.

"Did you see anyone else touch him?"

She scrubbed at the pizza sauce with her dry napkin, no doubt guaranteeing her a stain. "Just Trevor."

"And it couldn't be him because his gift is paralysis and that can only last a few seconds."

Emma stopped dabbing at her shirt. "Do you think someone tried to frame me?"

"Like, without touch magic? It's impossible. Yemoja Roux isn't here. Unless..."

Emma's eyes widened.

"Unless Kai was trying to frame you. I mean... maybe he was pretending." I smiled at the unlikelihood of it as I pushed more lumps of meat off my lap.

Emma nodded with a weak smile, and I scanned her face for any sign of deception. She was telling the truth, I was certain of it. Yet, somehow, I had just witnessed a gift being used on Kai.

A gasp sounded behind me and I turned to see a girl gaping at the table of Elites. Kai stood on the table, drawing the attention of the entire cafeteria. He nodded to Vinny, a muscular jock with a sound manipulation gift. Vinny opened his mouth wide and put his hand on his cell phone. Music filled the cafeteria, pouring from Vinny's mouth like amplified speakers. The lyrics rang out.

I wanna be honest, I can't hide it.
Anyway, I don't care.
My eyes are already on you.
Come to me
Let me lay my feelings bare.

That's when Kai began to move. One spin and the thrust of his hips was all it took to send every girl there into a frenzy, crowding around his table like fangirls at a concert. But Kai didn't stop there. He loosened his tie.

Down, down, let's fall
I wanna fall together.

My mind went immediately to the magical morsel. He'd eaten it and there was nothing I could do now but watch the show. I sat on my table, crossing my arms with a grin as I soaked in the glory of my victory. I had to admit, I felt the leftover shreds of my former crush stir inside me as his gaze met mine. He pointed to me and smiled—actually *smiled*—and I gulped with uneasiness as he bit his bottom lip. *I'm glad I'm over him.* I felt my daydreams mix with the spectacle, stirring feelings I'd thought long dead.

Down, down Let's fall
I'll fall only for you.

My stomach sank when Kai didn't stop there.

One by one, he popped open his buttons, his muscular chest coming into view inch by inch. Heat tore through me, but was quickly extinguished by dread when the other girls spun into near hysterics. This was getting out of hand. Before I could think about it, I was fighting through the crowd. Kai's gaze followed me as I elbowed my way through, reaching up for his hand. I had to get him out of there. I searched the cafeteria for an escape route and noted that if I could get him away from his table, we could make a break for it—preferably before his pants came off. His hand closed around mine, but instead of pulling him off the table and through the crowd, an all too familiar sensation tore through me and I rose into the air.

We ascended together, spinning slightly as if suspended on an invisible carousel.

"Oh my god, Kai. I'm so sorry."

He smiled. "Why? Don't be sorry. I'm glad I finally got your attention."

"No, you don't understand... That candy on my tray, it was gift-infused."

He tilted his head back. "Well, it feels great—"

The music cut. My hair stood on end as every person in the

room besides Kai and me were completely immobilized. They were a mausoleum of statues, timeless and horrifying. Was it some extreme form of Wes' magic? No, I saw no trace of ice. There wasn't a single student at our school who had that kind of power, or teacher. Which meant...

"Ms. Bennet, Mr. Nakamaru, to my office immediately. And put on your shirt," Principal Angora said. Her words were sharp, but they were nothing compared to the spectacle of the entire student body rooted in place.

Kai reached for my hand but I pulled it away. I wasn't used to being in trouble; in fact, no one was. In all the years I'd been bullied, I'd never seen a teacher intervene, much less the principal. I knew it was bad, but I wasn't sure why this incident in particular garnered so much attention, or what the consequences would be.

Even as we moved into the hallway, we saw more ensnared students. One girl reached for her locker but could never touch it. A guy with a contorted face looked like he'd been mid-sneeze when Principal Angora's gift hit. They were frozen in place and I shuddered that a gift so strong could live within someone I'd passed every day. A glance at my cell phone told me that time was still passing—even if it seemed like the three of us were the only ones who were able to continue our lives.

As we stepped into Principal Angora's office, I heard the slam of lockers behind me and I exhaled the relief that all had returned to normal. Even when the door closed, I could hear the chatter of nosy students that caught a glimpse of Kai and me being marched to our fate.

We sat across from Principal Angora, her dark dingy office littered with books and files, some stacks partially covering the only window at the back of the room behind her desk. The light behind her head shadowed her face, but I could see her well enough to know I hadn't given her a good look before. She had half-moon glasses that hid a beautiful face, though she was at least a decade beyond her prime.

"Excuse me," I said, without thinking. "You don't use touch magic. How'd you freeze everyone?"

She folded her hands together and I tried to ignore the way Kai's gaze was burning my cheek.

Principal Angora sighed. "I shake everyone's hand on their first day of school. Don't you remember?"

I gaped. "That's amazing. How long can you keep them frozen?"

"Just a minute or so," she said blandly. She got up and started filling a glass of water at the bubbler in the corner as a surge of questions flooded my brain.

"How long can they stay in your range after you touch them?"

She dug through her desk drawer and pulled out a small blue packet. "A few months. But I make appointments to check in with students who have fallen out of my range."

I blurted, "Why aren't you Fae? With your power, you could easily—"

"Summer vacations, holidays, home by five, not to mention this is a much safer profession than Fae. I'm not the showy type. But we're not here to discuss me," she said as she emptied the contents of the packet into the water, giving it a slight glow before it settled back to looking like ordinary water.

I eyed the glass absent-mindedly. "Sorry, yes. I know. You're just so amazing."

"I'm flattered," she said, but her dry expression said otherwise. "You," she barked at Kai, who finally tore his gaze away from me. "Drink this," she said.

He took a sip and his smile slowly faded. He turned to me, fire blazing behind his eyes. He stood. "What the fuck?" He turned to Principal Angora. "I'm sorry for the language, but...but...she fucking drugged me!"

I slouched in my chair, pulling my arms to my body to avoid letting him touch me.

"Sit down, Mr. Nakamaru."

Kaito sat slowly.

"Ms. Bennet, is this true? Did you drug Mr. Nakamaru?"

"No, ma'am." Technically, I didn't. But Kai deserved whatever happened here. After all, if he hadn't decided to throw my tray of food on me he never would have noticed the confection, and I had to admit the thought of him embarrassed for a change felt good.

"Mr. Nakamaru, how did this infused confection end up in your system? You are claiming Ms. Bennet drugged you. Would you care to elaborate?"

"She had a piece of drugged candy on her tray and I ate it. She should have stopped me! She just let me eat it knowing it was drugged!"

"Did she offer you this candy?"

"Um...no. I...um...well...I took it from her tray. But she knew! She should have stopped me! It's one hundred percent her fault!"

A big part of me wanted to laugh watching as Kai scrambled to get out of this one. I hadn't wanted any of this to happen, but I did have to admit it was funny as hell. I struggled to keep a smirk off my face.

"Mr. Nakamaru, as I see it, you saw a piece of candy on Ms.

Bennet's tray, and without her permission, you took it and ate it. I'm certain Ms. Bennet knew it was drugged, but she could not have foreseen that you would steal it. The blame is entirely yours," the Principal told him. "However, Ms. Bennett, you brought drugged candy into this school which is in direct violation of our rules."

Well, I couldn't argue with that. That part was true enough. But the look on Kai's face when the Principal blamed him was worth it.

"The administration has been told to stay out of the affairs of the students. A little competition in the hallway teaches the Common or Serf students how to survive after graduation as well as encourages Elite students to improve and hone their gifts. But we have a strict policy against child pornography or drugs of any kind including infused confections, and our school has been flagged for both."

Kai looked down at his unbuttoned shirt and began to frantically button up.

Principal Angora went on. "As you know, we have a zero-tolerance policy for such extreme situations."

As if he hadn't heard a word the Principal had said about him being to blame for his being drugged, Kai nodded. "Thank you, Principal Angora. Kick her out."

I clutched the arms of my chair so tightly I felt my fingernails cut the wood. Would she really do that?

"Actually, you are both expelled."

Kai stood. "Both? What the hell did I do? She was the one with the drugs."

The principal held up her phone, my bare ass floating across the screen. I winced but was pleasantly surprised by the nice shape in the image.

Kai pressed his lips together. "But you can't expel me! I'm your best student."

"Then I imagine you'll have no trouble getting another school to take you."

Kai sputtered and spun to me. "And why are you so quiet?"

"I don't care," I said. "Besides, we *are* both guilty."

"You think that orphanage is going to pay for a private school? This is the only public school in the district. Good luck with your two-hour commute." Kai was so angry he was practically spitting. But I knew where I was going.

"You can save your concern. I'm going to GFA."

Kaito

SIX

I stormed out of the school, slamming the door behind me. *Fuck this school and fuck Reina.* My stomach sank as I imagined my parents' reactions when I told them the news. It would likely be worse than when I was rejected from GFA for the second year in a row. My mom had gone into a full-on episode, screaming at me about how I'd brought shame to the family and how much I'd embarrassed her. She cried as she smashed various objects around our townhouse. But my father's reaction had been much worse. He stared at me for a long time, shook his head, and hadn't spoken a word to me since. Not that we were ever a happy family to begin with. My parents had sacrificed a lot to move us here, all to improve my chances of getting into GFA. And now I'd been thrown out of the second-rate public school that I attended.

I was so caught up going through my options that I'd reached for the door handle of my house before I realized Reina was following me.

I spun on my heel. "What the fuck do you want?"

"I've been calling your name for like five blocks, you didn't hear me?"

I sighed. "Obviously not."

"What are you going to tell your parents?" she asked. I unlocked my door and pushed it open.

"They won't be home for two more weeks." I nodded her in. "Shoes off."

She kicked off her shoes and looked around the foyer, her gaze landing on the crystal chandelier we'd added a few years after she'd last been here. "I see you're still rich," she said and her voice carried down the hallway.

She followed me to my bedroom, the muscle memory still unbroken after all these years. "Sure am. Why aren't you?"

"My parents died," she stated flatly.

"Yeah, I heard, but like… didn't they leave you money or something?"

She shrugged off my question and I wasn't about to push. I opened my bedroom door and, out of the corner of my eye, I saw Reina hesitate before crossing the threshold. The fraction of a second that she'd paused was all it took to remind me we were no longer close middle-school friends.

I scanned my room self-consciously, but when she jumped onto the foot of my bed, I relaxed. I lay in front of her and noticed she pulled her arms to her chest to avoid being touched. It was for this exact reason that most Serfs wore long sleeves and gloves. Extra protection from touch—it was also how they were so easily targeted.

"No Pokemon sheets?" she asked, trying to move the comforter to get a peek.

I smiled. "Got rid of those when I started having sex—" I

almost caught myself, but the last word came out clear as a bell. My thoughts jumped to the video clip our former principal had shown us in her office. The black lacy panties broadcasted on screen.

She pressed her lips together and a silence settled between us that set my nerves on edge.

I raised my eyebrows and she turned her face away. Even with her dark skin tone, I could see her blush.

My eyes bulged. "Are you serious? You're *still* a *virgin?*"

She covered her face with her hands.

"What about… what's his name? The Serf."

She crossed her arms over her face. "Can we talk about… anything else?"

I settled back on my bed, pleased with my investigative skills. After a few seconds, my mind returned to my parents and the fucked-up situation I found myself in. "This is all your fault," I said. "My parents… they're going to kill me."

"You started it," she said.

"No," I said, tossing a pillow at her. "You started it by getting involved in a fight that wasn't yours."

"You did the exact same thing."

I sighed. "Rei, you have no gift. You're going to get yourself killed."

She rolled onto her back and put the pillow under her head, her gaze fixed on the ceiling. "I didn't know you cared."

"I honestly don't." We lay in silence my mind wandering to why I mentioned she was going to get herself killed. I didn't care…did I?

"Kai, can I ask you something?"

I gulped, terrified of what she might ask.

"Will you come with me to GFA?"

I scoffed. "No. And I don't know why you still go there. It's pathetic."

"I'm going to convince them to let me take the entrance exam, so I need you to tell me everything you can about the test."

I rolled my eyes. "Exams are done for the year and you have no gift."

"Why do you keep telling me I don't have a gift? I know I don't have a gift! I think about it every second of every day. You don't need to remind me." She sat up. "And, honestly, it doesn't matter, Kai. Being Fae isn't about your gift. It's about being there to help people when they need you so no one dies before their time."

I knew with her last statement she meant her parents, but there wasn't the faintest sign of emotion in her voice or eyes when she said it.

"Without a gift, *you'll* die out there. I'm not going to help you get killed. If you're suicidal, there are quicker ways." I picked up a pillow and pushed her over, pressing the pillow to her face. I heard her muffled laugh as she squirmed free. "Are you dead yet?" I teased. She pushed me off, but her thumb touched a piece of my neck, yanking her into my magic range.

She stiffened.

"Relax. I'm not going to do anything."

She leaned forward. "Don't you think if anyone could pull a gift out of me, it's the greatest Fae academy on earth?"

I looked up, ready to answer—ready to shut down her delusion—but the way she looked through me told me she wasn't actually asking but trying to convince herself.

I sighed. "Ugh. Fuck... let's go," I said, hopping off my bed.

Her face lit. "Reina and Kai, back in action."

I stopped and turned to her. "Let's get this straight now. We are not friends. We're not teammates. This is a last resort because you totally fucked me over. We go to the school, we ask to get into the test, and when they say no, I go back to hating you for ruining my life."

"And if we get in?"

"*If* by some miracle they let us in, I'll continue to educate you on your place, until you learn it."

Reina

SEVEN

Oh my god, what an asshole! Well, I wasn't going to let him ruin this with his nastiness. He said he'd go with me and I wasn't going to lose this chance.

I insisted to Kai that we take the bus to GFA. He, of course, was rich enough to travel through Gemini Gates, but I needed the long bus ride to formulate a plan for getting into the school and didn't want to draw any more questions about how I'd spent my inheritance or why I'd landed in a group home.

But I couldn't formulate a plan, not with my mind racing. *Holy shit. Holy shit. Holy shit.* My skin felt as if it would burst into flames the moment Kai lay beside me on his bed. I'd practically lived there in middle school, but in a few short years, everything changed. It wasn't the room where we used to sneak tastes of liquor from his parents' stash, or where we'd researched the top Fae and debated over whose gift was strongest after Yemoja Roux. Now it was the place where Kai had sex with the girls who fawned over him. I mean, of course, he wasn't a virgin. *Look at him.* Ugh. And now he knew I *was* a virgin. I chewed my lip wondering which of the girls from our school he'd been with.

"So what's the plan?" Kai asked. His gaze moved across the scattered passengers. Despite the summer heat still lingering this first week of September, many of them wore long sleeves, gloves, and scarves to prevent, as much as possible, being touched. Kai's collared shirt was rolled up and pushed behind his elbows, exposing his hands and arms—a silent warning to anyone who passed that he was a force they'd be stupid to mess with.

"I-I'm still working on it." And I was because, even if I didn't exactly have a plan for getting in, I knew I wasn't going back to my old life.

Kai grabbed my hand, setting me on edge. "You better know what you're doing."

When he let go, I could still feel his magic gripping me. It always reminded me of the feeling just after running on a treadmill when my body was moving both too quickly and slowly at the same time. Some intangible force had ensnared me and I had no gift of my own to counter it.

I gritted my teeth, resenting that I didn't have the good sense to wear gloves.

When I stepped off the bus, I felt my nerves surge with every step toward the school's front gates. I heard the scrape of Kai's shoes on the sidewalk behind me but didn't wait for him to catch up. This was my moment. But, as I neared, I could tell *something was going on*. There were at least thirty people standing in a semi-circle outside the school. I increased my pace, curiosity tearing through me. Then I saw him standing at the center of the circle—Oden Gates. My heart leapt in my chest as I craned to get a glimpse of his smile. Dark skin, green eyes, and a smile that nearly knocked my knees out from under me and sent heat straight to my face. While Kai had been a god of sorts at our school, Oden was as close to being an actual god as the world had after the Fae; an apprentice Fae and leader of the Noble Four. He wasn't even just an apprentice; he was the apprentice for none other than Yemoja Roux, the greatest Fae who ever lived.

I joined the crowd, straining to hear what Oden was saying. "No, really," he said. "She's as awesome as she seems. I swear."

I wiggled my way through the crowd, bringing my exposed hands to my chest. It was an even mix of Commons and Serfs based on who was wearing gloves and who wasn't. So I knew who would let me pass them to avoid touching me.

I got to the front, my mouth gaping at his muscular arms that were completely exposed as if he'd intentionally cut the sleeves off his uniform. I was mesmerized. As an apprentice Fae, he'd already saved people. He'd already made the world a better pla—

My thoughts were disrupted when Kai pushed passed me, reaching his hand out to shake Oden's.

The crowd gasped.

Kai smirked. "You're Oden Gates, right? I'm Kaito Nakamaru."

The entire earth seemed to freeze as if our former principal's magic lingered over us as we waited to see how Oden would react to such a blatant challenge.

I held my breath, but a moment later Oden's shocked expression dissolved back to his bright smile and he shook Kai's hand. They sized each other up, waiting to see if the other would dare use their gift, but after a few seconds of inaction, the crowd all seemed to exhale at the same time.

"Kaito Nakamaru? Yeah, it sounds familiar. You failed the GFA entrance exam twice, right? Heh, and they say you're a genius."

"They also say the third time's the charm."

Oden shrugged, his sculpted shoulders a treat for the crowd. "Well, I definitely don't see a genius, but I don't see a coward either."

"Is that a challenge?" Kai asked.

I knew where this was going. I'd been on the wrong side of this kind of confrontation my whole life, but Kai hadn't. He hadn't been a weakling in quite some time. I had no doubt that Oden could destroy Kai. Without thinking, I sprung between them. I grabbed them both by the wrist to part their extended handshake. "Let's go, Kai," I said. But then I felt it, the dizzying magical energy of both guys at once. I sucked in a sharp breath as I released their arms and turned to Oden to beg his mercy.

"Who's your friend?" Oden asked, his green-eyed gaze burning me as it dragged down my body and back up to my face. I knew what it looked like. Like I had some kind of delusional complex where I thought I was Yemoja Roux and could challenge multiple Elites at once. The only thing I had going for me was the fact that no one knew what my gift was, or that I had none. But now that was shot to hell. It would only take a moment for him to sense the absence of my gift the same way I could sense the presence of his. I wanted to run, but the instant I touched his skin, I belonged to him just as I did to Kai.

"Leave her out of this. This is between you and me," Kai said.

Oden smirked, his dimpled cheeks sending a flutter to my gut. "I don't know. She's kinda cute."

My stomach flipped and I wasn't sure if I was going to cry or jump into his arms and tell Kai to get lost.

"She's a Serf," Kai said. "Just let her go."

I was dead. Fucking dead. Killed. Dead as fucking shit. I knew I shouldn't have trusted Kai. That was the absolute worst move. One which guaranteed me at least a beating. I dropped my gaze to the ground, ready to accept the punishment for willingly touching an Elite. And everyone knew Oden's gift. Strength. Unfathomable strength. He was going to smash me into dust right here and no one would bat an eye.

I felt Oden's gaze on my face, but I didn't dare look up. Then I heard laughter burst from him, sweet as honey. I looked up and he asked, "Are you serious?"

Kai's brow furrowed.

"You can't feel that? No, I suppose not. She's definitely gifted."

"What?" I said, drawing his attention.

He stepped closer, his green eyes burrowing into me, sending every nerve on edge.

"How do you know?" I asked. My heart raced as he smiled down at me. My legs jellied.

"I know because you feel just like she does—like Yemoja Roux."

Kaito

EIGHT

If Reina hadn't been in range, she probably would have dropped to the ground right there. But just as she swayed back, I suspended her weight on my gift like a puppet caught in my magical strings. Oden couldn't have possibly known what a cruel prank he'd played on her, getting her hopes up like that. I'd known her for four years. She was a Serf through and through. If she'd had any hint of ability, I would've caught it.

I faked a laugh. "Whatever man, we're leaving."

But as I grabbed for Reina's wrist, Oden grabbed the other. "I'm serious," Oden said. "Headmistress Tricorn will want to meet her."

I thought exposing Reina as ungifted would force away Oden's interest in her, but I should've known he would torment her before letting her go. I flinched when Oden slung his arm around her and guided her toward the gate, but I didn't fully understand what was happening until the gate opened and

Oden walked with Reina over the threshold. The threshold that no Serf had ever crossed.

"Hurry up," he called back to me, and I scrambled after them. I thought about tossing Reina into the air and holding her out of Oden's range to make a getaway, but once the gate closed behind me, the blurred image of the school cleared and I saw GFA for the first time.

The school sat at least five hundred yards back from the gate. Long stretches of green grass framed the cobblestone path that split down the center. There were several fountains that spurted clear blue water, with hedged mazes winding through the flower-arched courtyards. All those things were eclipsed by the school itself which resembled something between a mansion, a castle, and one of the wonders of the world.

I'd imagined it all wrong, the grounds and the secretive school. I couldn't have been further off. There wasn't so much as a thumbnail image of the school online. I'd hoped to catch a glimpse of it when I'd taken the test my first year, but the tests were held off-campus. Standing transfixed, I drank in the excellence.

Reina's hands moved to cover her mouth, her eyes glinting with tears. I gaped. Reina didn't cry. Not ever. Not when I bullied her, not even when I'd seen her after her parents died. As I watched her, I wasn't sure what enthralled me more, GFA or Reina crying. I couldn't let myself believe she was gifted, not after what I'd seen her go through without fighting back. Still, she'd promised me she'd get us an opportunity to take the entrance exam and she'd already gotten us much farther than I thought. If I found out that, after all this time, she'd been lying about being a Serf, I would have no reason to pull my punches.

Oden paused for a moment to let us take it all in before

leading us around a fountain and back to the main path where two staircases parted, wrapped around, and came back together in front of the large maroon double doors.

"Where are all the students?" I asked as Oden pushed the door open.

"Class," he said over his shoulder, and his hand dropped to Reina's lower back.

My throat tightened while he continued. "This building is just where the professors keep office hours, host parties, and where the headmistress's office is."

The floors were made of warm hardwood but mostly covered by the golden-trimmed maroon carpets that stretched across the foyer. At the center was the school's crest with its signature owls embroidered in jeweled tones on each side. Reina slipped her phone from her pocket and tried to snap a picture of the crest, but from over her shoulder, I could see the image come up blank on her screen.

"It's enchanted," Oden said. "One of the school's protections."

I bit back a smile. "Rei, stop being a tourist."

"Shut up," she spat.

A dull tapping sent the three of us spinning to investigate. A tall, gray-haired woman stood on the half flight of stairs. Her sleek hair twisted into a bun at the back of her neck. She looked no older than eighteen, but everyone knew that the ageless form in front of me was the very first person gifted, more than two hundred years ago. It was nice to know the internet trolls had something right. Even in her retirement from Fae, she looked formidable.

"Oden, why did you bring this riff raff in here?" she said, her voice as stern as her high-set nose.

Oden seemed to shrink several inches under the headmistress's gaze. "It's not what you think," he said. "This girl is—"

"I know very well what *she* is. Why did you bring this Academy reject into my school?"

All the air was sucked from the room as the three of them turned to me. What kind of parallel universe had I fallen into where Reina was welcomed in GFA and I was considered a reject?

"I'd like another chance to take the test," I said.

"You failed not three months ago. Why should I give you another chance?"

Had she been there? It seemed as if she knew me before I even spoke. I wasn't sure why, but she seemed interested in Reina, so I took a shot in the dark. "I brought Reina here."

The long-legged headmistress turned to Reina. "Is that true? Are you here together?"

Reina's gaze met mine, a glimmer of the love-struck daze present as it was with all the girls in our old school.

I smirked as Reina turned to Headmistress Tricorn. She said, "I've never seen that guy in my life."

Oden snorted and my mouth dropped open. Like a reflex, I flung Reina into the air. Oden's fist collided with my ribs and I slid back across the room, catching myself with my gift. With one leap, Oden crossed the room, catching Reina before she hit the wooden floor.

Headmistress Tricorn sighed. "Enough. You may both take the exam tomorrow morning." Her gaze locked with mine. "However, if you should fail, I don't want to see your name on another test application. I don't care how much your parents donate to this school."

"What if she fails?" I said with a nod.

The headmistress's gaze moved to Oden and they exchanged a loaded smile.

"Eight AM tomorrow. If you're late, don't bother coming," she said. "And Oden," she said, her red lips pursed, "remove them from my campus."

"Yes, headmistress," he said.

Reina threw her arms around Oden. "Thank you so much."

Ms. Tricorn turned the corner and her footsteps grew fainter as she ascended the stairs.

Oden turned to me with a grin. "So I guess she's not your girlfriend then," he said.

"Fuck no," I spat as I spun and headed for the doors.

Reina's voice shot out from behind me. "Don't be such a cry baby. You got your test, just like I said you would."

"No thanks to you," I called.

"*All* thanks to me."

Even ungifted, she'd always thought she was better than me, and now I come to find she's been lying this whole time. If she thought I was hard on her before, she had another thing coming.

"You better watch your back at the test tomorrow," I said, and I meant it.

Reina

NINE

The door slammed in my face as Kaito stormed out. Revenge was kind of sweet. It was one little lie and it didn't even hurt his chances. If anything, it gave him an excuse to show off his gift in front of the headmistress. Yet out he stormed like the victim. Like he hadn't *deserved* a kick in the ass after how he'd tormented me over the years.

"Sooo... " Oden said, drawing my attention. "There's a history there, huh?"

I clutched the owl charm on my necklace. "Not really," I said, and it wasn't a lie. I would hardly describe our little rivalry as history.

"Can I walk you out?"

I nodded and, as we stepped back into the sun, I was startled by how beautiful he was. He almost looked like a sculpture, his green eyes sending waves of shivers through me.

"Got any pointers about the test?" I asked, slowing my pace. I wanted to spend every second on the school grounds that I'd attempted to imagine every day and failed so immeasurably. Rows of pink and red flowers lined the hedge mazes. The fountains filled the air with the sputter of falling water. It was as if we weren't near the city anymore, like the magical barrier that protected the school from prying eyes also blocked out the sound from beyond the walls.

"I'm afraid it's different every time."

I nodded. I heard the gate shut and wondered if Kai had used his gift to flee the school grounds so quickly. "I figured. Can you tell me about the gift you seem to think I have?"

"And rob you of the joys of figuring it out for yourself?"

Our hands bumped together and I wondered if he'd done it on purpose to renew his hold on me.

I smiled. "Obviously I'm not great at that. How'd you discover your gift?"

"One day, I broke the shit out of just about everything I touched."

I laughed, my stomach tightening. "Seriously?"

He nodded. "My parents were so proud."

I chuckled and my thoughts moved to my own parents, but no sadness came.

"Why did you and your boyfriend decide to come today?"

I slowed to a glacial pace as we neared the gate. "He's not my boyfriend. I actually come here all the time." I turned back to the school. "But I couldn't have imagined..." My breath came short.

"Take a long look, this is going to be your new home."

I turned to him, his yellow-green eyes like precious gems in the sunlight. "You seem pretty confident I'll pass. Why is that?"

"Because..." I froze as he leaned in and kissed my cheek. I

touched my hand to my cheek as if I could feel his kiss there. "That was for good luck."

It was strange to be touched and kissed, and I liked the ease with which Oden touched me. He had no fear, when all my life I'd come to know touch as the surest way to be hurt.

He smiled and turned back to the school as the gate swung open to let me out. I stumbled through, replaying the kiss in my mind again and again, my cheek tingling with the memory.

As I stepped over the threshold, Ancetol crashed down on me. Sudden flashes of piercing white light, a slew of cameras and reporters all huddled around the gate. They held microphones out with their gloved hands, hurling questions at me. The thrum of traffic assaulted, horns blared to scold the cars who crept past, craning to investigate the commotion. "Miss, can you tell us about the school?" a mousy reporter asked.

Another reporter asked, "Will you be attending?"

Overwhelmed, I backed into the already closed gate. The questions were endless. "Why did Oden Gates allow you to enter the school?"

"Will other visitors be allowed to—"

Before I could settle on one to answer, my thoughts flung back to my first kiss as my body lifted from the ground. My mind slingshotted through each memory I'd retained where I'd felt the magical pull of Kai's gift. The same strained surrender pulsing through my limbs, the energy escaping through my fingertips. I once again flailed to cover my butt from being exposed on camera as I floated over the crowd. *Fucking skirt. Never again,* I thought when I was finally able to see Kai on the other side.

"Is that Kaito Nakamaru?" I heard someone say. "Is he transferring to GFA?" Kai must've been stopped by the reporters just as I had, but they must not have known who he was until they saw his gift.

"Mr. Nakamaru!" someone yelled from behind us. I landed right behind Kai and, with a nod, we started running down the hill. We sprinted past the bus stop, along the outside of the school's walls that seemed to go on forever. We slowed to a jog and then a stroll as the footsteps behind us grew faint.

"Thanks," I said, finally. "For pulling me out of there. That was… a lot."

He smiled. "*That* was a lot?"

I looked up, confused.

"We just broke into GFA, met the world's most promising apprentice Fae, got in a fight, and won a spot in the entrance exam. Oh!" he said, his eyes widening. "And let's not forget we found out that you've been gifted this whole time."

"I'll give you that other stuff, but that last one I'll believe when I see it."

He stopped walking so I turned to face him. "You seriously didn't know?" he asked, scanning my face.

I shook my head. "Did you?"

He sighed. "No. You still seem like a Serf to me."

Kaito

TEN

Reina and I took separate ways home. I thought I could convince her to take the Gemini Gates with me, but she insisted on waiting for a bus. I popped open a soda around the corner, not so close for Reina to know that I was there but close enough for me to make sure she got on the bus safely. It wasn't that this area was any worse than the one we lived in, but a block away was a street filled with bars that sold magic-infused elixirs that often caused things to get out of hand. Alcohol and magic didn't mix well, but that never seemed to stop anyone.

As we neared happy hour, the bus stop, which was more of a multi-bus terminal, began to crowd with all manner of people. Most seemed to be arriving, no doubt headed to drown out their day with an elixir of contentment and lime or confidence gin and tonic.

There was a Gemini Gate nearby, its travelers a stark contrast to those coming by bus. For starters, the richer group wore less clothing, their gifts offering most of them adequate protection. They also seemed to have bright, multicolored hair while the bus riders mostly had their natural colors. Magical dyes wore off quickly unless you had the more expensive ones. I checked around the corner, and Reina sat unbothered, scrolling away on her phone. To pass the time, I amused myself by mentally sorting the Elites, Commons, and Serfs based on appearance alone.

Across the room, I noticed a man with blue hair and round-framed glasses smirking at me. His exposed arms were crossed over his chest and he was leaning against a vending machine. I went back to my game, but a few minutes later I noticed he was still staring.

I locked my gaze on him, narrowing my eyes in warning, but he didn't look away. The crowd rushed between our silent standoff, and I noticed an arrow tattoo that ran across his arm in the same place where I had my own. It started at his wrist and met at a point that faced his elbow. What was this dude's problem?

He nodded toward a television screen that hung almost directly between us that, as ever, was silently playing the news. Red headlines flashed across the bottom of the screen one after the other. I thought I'd misunderstood his nod, that he might have been drawing my attention somewhere else, but an older woman stopped suddenly amidst the crowd, her gaze transfixed on the screen. She put a gloved hand over her mouth. I didn't think much of it, until one by one the other passengers stopped to read the headline. There were police gathered on the screen but I couldn't tell from the image what had happened, and the headline was too small from where I stood. I squinted, stepping closer to get a good look.

Raphael Mazarin found dead. Investigators have no leads.

Impossible. Raph was a Silver Tier Fae. No one could have taken him down. The Fae were unbeatable. I'd seen Fae get injured. I'd seen them retire early, but never had such a high profile Fae fallen in combat.

My gaze snapped to the stranger across the room and he hadn't moved a fraction. His smirk deepened as he lifted his closed fist to the side of his cheek. I swallowed hard, as in that position the arrow tattoo on his arm pointed down. I wasn't sure what it meant, but I had a sneaking suspicion he knew something about Raph's death.

I walked through the crowd and they parted like a river around a stone to avoid my touch. But the man with blue hair had vanished. I spun with the sudden realization that I might have been in the presence of someone genuinely dangerous, which meant so was Reina.

My pulse deafened me and, as I dashed around the corner back to Reina, there was a pressure in my ears and in my throat. The bench where Reina had been sitting was filled with new occupants.

Then I saw her, lifting her phone to the scanner before she stepped onto the bus. I exhaled my relief. She was safe, and it would be a quick trip through the nearest Gemini Gate for me. But no matter how hard I tried, I couldn't shake the image of the man with the downward arrow and menacing smirk.

Reina

ELEVEN

I didn't hear the news until I returned to the group home. I walked into the common area, my mind preoccupied with the possibility that I might be gifted and the sudden pressure of the test I was about to face. If I had been paying attention, I would have been alarmed by the silence coming from an area where the other orphans usually argued about whose turn it was to watch TV. As I watched the twelve others huddled around the TV in stunned silence, I felt the uneasiness in the room.

"What's wrong?" I asked, but no one responded. I moved closer and heard a sniffle coming from Jerome. He was the youngest in the home, just eight years old. I looked up at the screen and in blood red, the caption read, *Raphael Mazarin found dead.* I sat down on the edge of the armrest, the only place I could squeeze myself in without blocking someone's view. My stomach tightened as Yemoja Roux stood in the frame. I held my breath as she spoke. "I just don't know who would do such a thing. Raphael was a good man and a great Fae. And whoever did this will be found and brought to justice."

"Yemoja!" a reporter shouted. "Are there any leads?"

She leaned over to a police officer and whispered something. He nodded, handing her a slip of paper. She turned back to the camera holding up a drawing of a simple arrow. "This image was found at the scene of the crime. If anyone has information that they think could be relevant to this case, please call the authorities."

I reached out and rubbed Jerome's back as I watched the news in disbelief. My thoughts moved to what Principal Angora had said about Fae being a dangerous position. I guess I always knew it was. But only the strongest were chosen as Fae, which meant they were pretty untouchable. I shuddered to think that someone out there had a gift strong enough to take down a Fae as well known as Raphael Mazarin.

Jerome squeezed my hand, a gesture that was only safe within our home. All thirteen of us were Serfs. But it meant we could touch, in moments like this, and fight like regular siblings. My life had not thus far been kind, but I felt grateful that I'd somehow found a little peace and landed here of all places. Others had it much worse. The presence of gifts had turned the foster system into a game of roulette, for ill-intentioned people looking for helpless kids with gifts they could use, but that system collapsed long before I became an orphan.

Once we aged out, all of us would be at the mercy of the gifted for the rest of our lives. I needed to become Fae. I needed to find a way to protect the Serfs. The only way to do that was to pass tomorrow's exam, and I didn't have the faintest idea how to prepare.

The TV shut off and Alyssa, the oldest of us, held out the

remote somberly. We spun to her for an explanation. "She'll be home soon. We'd better head to our rooms and stay out of her way."

There were many things we argued about—who spent too long in the bathrooms, who ate more than their share of dinner—but one thing we all agreed on was that it was best to be in our room and out of the way when Vivian got home. She had a particularly cruel brand of touch magic and a nasty temper to match. There was a sort of electric energy that she could emit through her fingertips. It was a dull sort of pain, as she wasn't very strong, but she could hold it for long stretches, and on two at a time.

I lay awake that night thinking about Raphael. And how Yemoja Roux had, for the first time, seemed shaken. I wondered if they knew each other well, or even if she was afraid of the killer. I'd only seen her in action for a moment, many years ago. Just a flash of magenta hair and a bright smile. Of course, no one believed me, but my parents were there... *my parents*. I held their image in my mind, my mother's tender gaze and knowing smile. My father's quiet strength and optimism. They'd been gone a full year now and I felt numb to it. I'd made a huge mistake, one I couldn't take back. I learned the hard way that the only thing more dreadful than grief was indifference. And with that thought, I let myself drift to sleep.

Kaito

TWELVE

It seemed just a moment after I shut my eyes, my alarm woke me. I walked like a zombie through my empty house as I got ready. I was used to the silence, brought girls back when I felt lonely—but that morning I wanted my parents there to wish me luck. I'd almost called them to tell them about the test, but I couldn't bear the thought of disappointing them. Not for a third time, and I worried that if they knew and I didn't pass, they might stop coming home altogether.

Even though I hardly slept, my adrenaline would be enough. Surely no matter what opponent they pit me against or what they put on any written test, I could solve it. But I'd learned that this test wouldn't be like the first two, so I willed myself to push aside my expectations.

My nerves got the better of me when I arrived at the school and Reina was already there, tracing over the school's crest with her finger. "Couldn't sleep, huh?" I said.

She turned. "Hey, Kai. No, I slept just fine actually."

I clenched my jaw. I hated her tough guy act.

"How are you?" she asked as she fiddled with her necklace.

The gates to GFA crept open, the magical barrier stretching thinner until the school beyond it came into focus. It was just as striking as the first time I'd seen it, if not more so, as the grounds were covered in the silver sheen of morning dew. The top of the red-tiled roof glistened in the lazy yellow hues of the early morning sun that stretched out over the wall.

As we walked toward the school, I wondered if under her calm exterior Reina was nervous about the test. "Did you hear about Raphael Mazarin?" she asked.

I nodded.

"They have a lead. There was this arrow at the scene."

I stopped walking, my mind halting on the image of the man who'd smiled as he silently urged me to watch the news at the bus stop yesterday. "What do you mean, 'arrow?'"

She reached for my hand and turned it over, drawing the symbol on my forearm. It didn't seem like Reina was worried we'd have to face off in combat, otherwise she wouldn't have opened herself up for my attack by touching me. But as her fingers swept over my arm, I couldn't deny that it was at least similar to the man with the blue hair. *It had to be a coincidence.* "Hmm," I said dismissively. It wasn't my concern. The only thing I needed to worry about was passing the test.

We walked up the steps in silence and, just before I pushed open the door, Reina stopped me. She took my hand and took a deep breath, a warm smile on her face. "Good luck, Kai," she said.

Those were the exact words I craved that morning. I should've known she was still like this, that I couldn't beat it out of her. Not wanting to appear weak, I ripped my hand away. "Save it. You need it more than I do."

The door swung open and a large woman appeared. She was at least a hundred pounds overweight, her deep curves layered onto a wide frame, and every inch of her stunning. *Veranda Yarrow*. She was a known teacher of GFA, but there was little to no information online about what her gift actually was, only speculation. Her beauty was well known, though, undeniably so, but seeing her in person was a new experience altogether. Her blood-red hair flowed over her shoulders like lava over a volcano, her red lips plump, and her eyes had the warmth and kindness of a beloved relative. She wore thick black gloves that met her sleeves at the elbow, a rarity for Fae of her caliber. I'd rolled my eyes at the web debates about her size, but now that she stood in front of me, I knew firmly where I stood.

"You're so beautiful," Reina blurted. "Even more than your pictures online."

I bit back my smile, as she beat me to it, but it was all you could say after seeing Veranda.

"Thank you, darlin'," the red-haired goddess said, waving us through the door. "Your test will be held in exam room six. Please follow me."

We followed and my gaze was drawn to her wide hips as they swayed back and forth. *Back and forth.* Reina hit me, causing us both to chuckle.

Veranda stopped outside the door. "They want Miss Bennet first."

I nodded and the two women walked into the room, locking the door behind them with a click. I wasn't sure how long I'd be waiting outside, but every second was an eternity. Now that I'd met a few of the teachers and Fae, the stakes really sunk in.

Veranda Yarrow, I gulped. And no doubt her gloves were meant for the protection of others and not herself. I existed in a society where the amount of clothing reflected your power— where less coverage always meant more power. But now I was among Fae so Elite, their gifts so intense, they needed to protect others from them. It was almost too much to fathom. Of course, the most famous Fae, like Yemoja Roux, were not teachers. They were in the field, but the school had many gifted teachers and apprenticeships worth killing for.

My nerves flared as the lock clicked and Reina stepped out. Her gaze met mine and I wished I had the gift to know her thoughts.

"Enter," said a voice I recognized as Headmistress Tricorn. I stepped through, closing the door behind me.

My breath skipped as I walked toward the center of the room. There were five retired Fae seated at a long table— three more than either of my other two exams—and I knew every single one of them.

Veranda sat on the left, and beside her was Maxim Tuberose, a retired seer. The headmistress sat at the center with a displeased look on her face. To the right of her was the professor of confections, Mr. Greene, and finally, all the way to the right was Dr. Havier Azul who had a healing gift. Havier Azul's presence told me I could expect some form of combat in this exam as he'd also been at one of my other exams, the one where they'd tested physical combat. I shuddered at the memory—how the flat empty terrain and my quick-footed opponent had prevented me from being able to use my gift. It was a disgraceful performance that I promised myself not to repeat.

"Hello," I said, my voice cracking. "I'm Kaito Na—"

"We know who you are," Headmistress Tricorn said. "We contacted your old school, we know about your expulsion."

I swallowed hard, my throat tightening.

"So before we continue with this exam, we'd like to ask you some questions."

I nodded.

"In your own words, what was the nature of your expulsion?"

I took a deep breath. "Reina and I have a sort of…" *What word was I even looking for?* "rivalry."

She pursed her lips, pushing me to continue.

"Our pranks got out of hand."

She folded her hands. "Do you think it would cause a problem if I admit you both to my school?"

"No, ma'am," I said, too nervous to meet the gazes of the other teachers.

A strained smile touched her mouth. "If we were to select only one of you, who do you think deserves the spot. And why?"

"I do," I said. "My gift is far stronger than hers—if she even has one. I'm certain I'll have a greater chance of becoming Fae post-graduation."

The teachers exchanged glances but their faces told me I'd misspoken.

"What is it?" I demanded.

Professor Greene said, "We find it interesting because Reina also said she believed you should be given the position."

My pulse raced. "She did?"

The headmistress leaned forward. "One looking out for himself, the other striving to protect others…" She tilted her head. "Which of those sound like Fae to you?" She pressed her lips into a line and I dropped my gaze to the floor. Fuck. I was failing *again*.

Reina
THIRTEEN

The door swung open and Kai stormed through. "This is *bullshit*," he said, pushing past me.

I gripped his arm and pulled him back into the room. "Look, whatever he said, you have to read between the lines. He's not great with words."

"I don't need your help," Kai said under his breath.

Maxim Tuberose spoke, his voice velvety smooth. "He's not the type of temperament suitable for Fae in training."

"You're wrong," I said. "I know him. I've been ungifted my whole life and in middle school Kai and I were always targeted by Elites, but Kai landed in the clinic much more than me. He always did what he could to—"

"And how about after middle school?" Veranda asked. "Your former principal gave us the impression he bullied you quite regularly."

I dropped my gaze. He certainly did, and I wasn't sure if it was our past that compelled me to speak on his behalf, but we'd gotten into this mess together and I had also been to blame for our expulsion. "He doesn't want me to get hurt. That's it. It's his messed-up way of protecting me."

Headmistress Tricorn spoke, "You admit it's messed up."

"All he needs is a great teacher. That's why we're here."

The room fell silent and, after a moment, the headmistress nodded to Veranda.

She said, "Then let the exam begin. But be warned, there will be no talking your way through this time."

The teachers leaned forward with anticipation as Veranda stood in front of me. I shook, my legs going weak beneath me.

Headmistress Tricorn said, "Miss Yarrow will use her gift to determine the potential of your gifts. This was chosen mostly for Reina, as she does not yet know her gift, though we can sense a hint of its type. Kaito, if you're as strong as you think you are, you should have no problem passing the exam."

Veranda pulled off her black gloves, her perfectly manicured hands yet another show of her beauty.

"May I, baby?" she asked, holding her hands out. It was strange to see someone so powerful ask permission to touch. I nodded quickly. She had the answer I needed. She could tell me if I had any hope of becoming Fae.

I slid my hands onto hers, her head rolling back and her eyes snapping shut. I held my breath, willing any power within me to her hands, but of course I felt none. She lifted her head and opened her eyes, a deep sadness in them. She teared, putting her hand to her heart.

"What is it?" Maxim asked, but she ignored him. Instead, she looked at me, as if in search of something. "Your parents…" she said, sending my heart into a frantic race. "I know what you did," she whispered.

I felt Kai's gaze on my face and I hoped Veranda wouldn't say more.

She held her hands back out. "Let's try again."

I hesitated before putting my hands on hers. She'd uncovered my darkest secret in an instant and I was afraid of what else she might discover. Just as before, her head rolled back, her breaths became labored, and I resisted the urge to rip my hands away. Finally, she lifted her head with a gentle smile at the corners of her mouth.

"It's as we thought. Just like her."

I shook my head. "Like who?"

"Yemoja Roux," she said.

My gaze moved to Kai as a rush of emotions flooded me. I was *gifted*. I was gifted like Yemoja Roux. I clenched my teeth to suppress every emotion swirling through me because Veranda had already moved to Kai, her hands held out for him to touch.

"Your turn," she said with scarlet lips. He put his hands in hers and I found myself nearly as nervous for him as I'd been for myself. My heartbeat raced, to a new rhythm, one that echoed "Yemoja Roux, Yemoja Roux."

Veranda's breaths deepened. She began to shake, then convulse. *Something was wrong.* Her breaths grew more erratic. I gasped as blood shot from her nose and she collapsed onto the floor. Kaito stood stunned as Dr. Azul leaped over the table and ran to Veranda. Blood-red tears dripped from her eyes as the other teachers encircled her in a panic.

"What happened?" Kai asked, staring at his hands in horror.

Dr. Azul dropped to his knees and placed his hands around Veranda's throat. In seconds, her shaking stopped and the flow of blood from her ears and nose slowed. I stared down with a mix of terror and awe as Dr. Azul's gift took over, easing her convulsions.

The headmistress' gaze moved to Kai. "Maxim…"

Without another word, the gray-haired elder stood and forcefully grabbed Kai's hand. The time for asking permission had come and gone. I'd never seen a seer work in real time. But just as it looked online, his eyes lit up a radiant blue that filled the room. We all held our breath as he spoke. "The path is not set. There is greatness here, but it is not yet determined whether it will be nurtured by the Fae or their enemies."

Havier Azul looked up. "I need to get her to my office." The four teachers worked together to lift Veranda, a task Kai could have managed with a touch. But Kai was terrified. I understood why he didn't volunteer. In fact, I'd have understood if he never touched anyone again.

"Stay on campus, but speak of this to no one," the headmistress said as they carried Veranda out of the room, her consciousness dimming as they went.

Kai stared down at his hands, his mouth open. Veranda's blood was smeared across the floor.

He turned to me. "I… I didn't—"

"It's okay, Kai. No one thinks you did."

"You know my gift. It's levitation… I… couldn't have…"

My skin prickled when a clear streak fell down his face. "Let's go get some air," I whispered. He said nothing for a long time as he continued to stare at his hands.

"It's okay, Kai." I wanted to reach out and touch him. I wanted to pull him in for a hug. But the memory of Veranda's bleeding eyes was fresh and I was afraid. I took a deep breath, thinking of something my mother used to say: *Never let fear stop you*. I reached out for him, but he hovered and slid himself back out of reach, his heels never hitting the ground.

"Let's go outside. We need some air," I said again. I opened the door and felt him follow silently behind. We burst through the front door, where we'd come in, and rushed back to the courtyard as if fleeing the school we both longed to enroll in. I turned into a hedge maze and wove through the floral labyrinth. The sun's rays warmed the top of my head, soaking into my dark curls as I turned a corner and spotted a bench that was tucked away. I didn't want anyone to see us. I didn't want Kai to feel ashamed to cry.

I sat first and Kai sat on the opposite end, taking extra care not to touch me. We didn't need words. The quiet of the morning in the garden calmed us both after a long while, and when he was ready, he spoke. "Thank you for what you did in there."

I shrugged. "It was nothing."

"Not to me."

I chewed on my lip.

"You know, none of that was really true. That stuff you said about me protecting you."

"I figured," I said, but the bite of disappointment lingered. I had, of course, made the mistake of thinking he cared. That's what I wished was true. "Can I ask you what it is that you hate about me?"

He shook his head, rubbing his hands on his knees. "I don't know. I guess I hate that it never gets to you."

"Wh—"

"You just come into school every day with a smile, as if the whole world hasn't gone to shit. I mean, all those years you thought you were ungifted. What the fuck did you have to smile about?"

I let my hand drop to the bench between us.

"I had this amazing gift and everything still hurt. So… I guess I wanted to hurt you. Or for you to, I don't know, understand." He chuckled, but it was a sad sound and the corners of his eyes glistened. He turned his confused gaze on me, "Does that sound like Fae to you?"

"Kaito." I reached out but froze before I touched him, a flare of fear halting me. "Maybe you're being a little hard on yourself." I half smiled, "I used to spend a lot of time with you, you're not so bad."

He sighed, but his expression softened. "You're too nice, Rei. You don't recognize a monster when you see one."

I grinned, "No, you're right. You're a total asshole."

His face brightened, "And yet here you are, as ever, trying to rescue me."

"Well, yeah, you're hot now so…"

He laughed and nudged my shoulder with his.

I shook my head. "It would be such a waste."

I realized we'd been inching closer, growing bold in our desire to touch.

"You've always been beautiful."

His cell phone floated from his pocket and he swiped through before holding up the image of me he took at the pier.

I took a shallow breath, "You did keep it… So why did you stop being my friend?"

He sighed, "It's complicated."

I glared.

He rolled his eyes, "Well, everything changed and…" His gaze moved to me, "I don't mean just me getting a gift. I figured the gap in our abilities would separate us eventually. Besides, at the time, I thought I'd get over it." He slipped his phone into his pocket and stared down at his hands. "I almost reached out to you when I heard about your parents, but I chickened out."

Stunned, I whispered, "I wish you had." I thoughtlessly touched his arm. We froze, staring at our touching skin, my heartbeat turbulent in my chest.

A sudden heat burned me and I wasn't sure if I would soon meet the same fate as Veranda, or if my body's reaction wasn't gift related at all.

His gaze rose to mine.

A wave of his gift pulsed through my blood and I was weightless, hovering ever so slightly off the bench. My breath caught as I felt myself move closer. My thoughts dimmed, leaving me with a burning hunger, though I wasn't sure for what. Kai reached for me, his warm palms on my cheeks. I gripped his tie, losing myself as I pulled him in. His lips were hot on mine, his tongue numbing any thoughts of stopping. His hands slid over my body as I gripped his hair. He bit down on my bottom lip and I whimpered. He pulled away slowly, his eyes wide. He stood so quickly that, if I hadn't been hanging in his gift, I would have toppled to the ground.

"I'm so sorry," he said, running his hand through his hair.

I felt myself lower to the bench, a riot still raging in my chest. "No, it's okay. I was the one who... pulled th-the..."

"No, it's me, I shouldn't have--" he pressed his lips together. "I'm sorry Reina."

I stood. "It's okay Kai. It was just a kiss."

"Was it?"

I swallowed a lump in my throat, my pulse racing. He was right. It was anything but just a kiss.

He took the silence as my response and nodded before jogging back into the maze of hedges without another word.

I sighed, was walking not fast enough? I was left alone to wonder who Kaito really was: the sweet boy from my childhood, or the bully. I was an idiot. His excuses were flimsy at best, and I spent years in pain because of him and I still went for it. Even worse, I still wanted to.

Kaito

FOURTEEN

The funny thing about momentum was, once it started, no matter if it was positive or negative, it was hard to stop. First, I practically murdered a legendary Fae, though I have no clue how. I botched my entrance exam. And worst of all, I kissed Reina.... *Again*. At least I didn't break her bones this time. I don't know what I was expecting. For her to push me away and slap me for all the things I'd done to her, I guess. But she pulled me closer, and if I hadn't suddenly remembered she was a virgin, I might've taken her right there. Why didn't she stop me? And why did it take me so long to stop myself?

I'd been horrible to her. If she felt something between us, she was an idiot too. I felt sick. I was the ultimate dickhead, *a failure*, and possibly a murderer. I understood why my parents never came home. I understood why I was always alone. Something was broken inside me. There was a darkness I couldn't seem to keep at bay. If I let myself slip up again with Reina, eventually I'd break her too—just like I'd wanted to.

My reeling thoughts were interrupted by a figure coming down the stairs. Professor Greene spotted me on the lawn. I scanned his face, half expecting to be arrested on the spot, but his shoulders were relaxed, his bun bouncing on the back of his head in time with his bow-legged gait.

"Veranda will be fine. She's resting," he said, and I felt a wave of relief crash into me.

"Do you know what happened?" I asked. I wasn't sure I wanted the answer.

He sucked in a breath, as if he were unsure if he should tell me what he knew. "We think that your potential may have been greater than her body could handle."

A pang of nervousness hit my stomach. "Does that happen a lot?"

He shook his head.

I swallowed a lump in my throat. Too much power? Was there such a thing? I knew my gift was exceptional, I'd discovered levitation had many uses, but it also had limits. I'd completely botched the physical entrance exam. I wasn't even strong enough to be admitted. My thoughts were interrupted by the professor's next words.

"The headmistress has decided to admit both of you. Pack your belongings and come at the same time tomorrow to move in and start orientation," he said, his gaze moving past me.

I spun to see Reina a few yards away. "Thank you, professor," she said, and coldly turned away without so much as a glance at me.

Professor Greene eyed me, as if he understood everything

that had transpired with our body language alone. He nodded at Reina, a gesture that to me seemed to say, *Go get her.*

I smirked and jogged after her, the news of our acceptance surging through me like a great light driving away my dark thoughts and apprehensions. I threw my arm around her. "Hey, classmate!"

"You know we were classmates before, right?"

"Not at GFA," I cooed. "Look, Reina, about earlier... I'm sorry. I-I promise I won't do that again. I was overwhelmed and just kind of lost control. Let's just pretend it never happened."

"*That's* your explanation? Seriously?"

"Let's celebrate tonight."

She raised an eyebrow and it looked like I might get the slap I was looking for earlier.

I laughed. "I mean dinner."

She moved my arm off her shoulders. "I don't know, Kaito."

"Please, let me do this. I have to thank you for getting us both in GFA."

She grinned. "So you admit I got us in?" She pulled out her phone and held it up. "Can you say that again for the camera?"

"I will. After dinner."

She sighed. "Fine."

"Great, come to my place at 8."

"You're not taking the bus home?" she asked.

I floated my cell phone out of my pocket and into my hand. "Nah, I'm going to call my parents and stuff. You know, tell them the news."

She smiled and headed for the gate.

"Don't forget, Reina," I called. "Eight o'clock."

She called back, "I'll never forget about you."

The sweetness of the memory of that day at the pier, echoed

through me. Back then, I'd been looking for the right moment to kiss her for weeks, and by the ocean that day I wanted to go for it. My nerves got the best of me and I was going to chicken out until she said those *exact* words.

Today I'd once again stolen a kiss, and it surprised me as much as it must have done her. It was a mistake I wouldn't repeat, but I was too excited to spend the night at my empty house. My "friends" would no doubt be jealous and hateful about it, and how could I explain to them that ungifted Reina and I had taken the exam together? I chuckled at the irony, that after all the years of torture I'd dished out, Reina was still all I had.

Reina
FIFTEEN

It was official. My crush on Kaito had returned with a vengeance. All I wanted was to go to GFA and leave my old life behind, but no. My stupid heart made me fight on his behalf to get him in. Kaito… the freaking master of my torment. Never mind that aneurysm or whatever happened to him earlier. Now we were going to have to live on campus together. My mind shouted in distress, but my stomach was in knots and jumbled with butterflies. My heart raced. Kaito *kissed* me… then he promised never to do it again.

My skin stung with disappointment as my mind replayed that promise on loop. Why? Didn't he want to do that again? I didn't even want it to stop that time. It was a far cry from our first kiss, and I felt… *hot*. I scrambled to crack open the bus's window, but it didn't help much. I heard the whipping of the wind but didn't feel it.

I pressed my forehead to the glass. In all the times I'd imagined what it would be like to kiss him, *really* kiss him, I'd certainly never imagined *that*. The exam, GFA, and my newly-discovered gift had taken a back seat to the kiss I could still feel on my lips.

The bus hit a sudden bump and my head slammed against the glass with a smack and, before I could react, it happened a second time. *Ouch*. That was karma one hundred percent. I took a deep breath, willing all my butterflies to drop dead. I could control my emotions. I'd gotten over Kai before, I could do it again. Instead of dwelling on the kiss, I thought of all the times Kai had humiliated or hurt me. I thought of how many nights I cried myself to sleep. And by the time the bus stopped to let me out, a few blocks from home, I had worked myself up enough to cancel our dinner plans.

Instead of going straight home, I decided to walk a few laps around the block. I found myself check-listing what I had to do rather than deal with such a weighted day. First, I had to pack my things. That would be easy enough; I hardly owned anything since I'd sold it all. Even with my inheritance, I had to sell everything to have enough for... I sighed. I hated the empty feeling that popped up when I thought about it. It was a void where something important belonged—something I'd given up. I debated whether to tell Vivian that I got into GFA and was moving out. *Fuck that*. There was no universe in which that conversation went smoothly. Finally, I needed to cancel my date. I mean *dinner*. It would only take a second to send the text, but... I could squeeze that in later. I saw something move out of the corner of my eye and spun.

I gasped. William Citrine, a Bronze Tier Fae, jutted past on the far side of the street, fire spurting from the bottom of his shoes. His trademark golden hair was almost reflective in the orange glow of the low sun, his gift blazing from his feet like he were wearing rocket boots.

"William Citrine!" I called, fumbling for my cell phone in hopes I could snap a picture, but in a flash he was gone.

It was a sign. Everything would be okay. I felt a little bit cheerful as I rounded the corner. After all, my dream of going to GFA had come true. I was finally *gifted,* and I wasn't sure how, but they said it reminded them of Yemoja Roux. I almost broke into a skip. The sun was setting and streetlights had already clicked on. I pulled open the door to my house, imagining what my roommates would say when I told them. No doubt they wouldn't believe me. I was delighted. I froze as Vivian stood at the base of the stairs. She shouldn't have been home yet. She stood with her hands on her hips, nodding as if we were having a silent conversation.

"Your school called," she said. "Why didn't you tell me you got expelled?" My gaze was drawn to movement at the top of the stairs; several of my roommates peeked around the corner.

"You don't understand. I—"

She grabbed my hand and the electric pain shot up my elbow, spreading to the rest of my body. "I got into GFA," I said through clenched teeth. "I'm *gifted.*"

She chewed loudly on her gum. "You're a fucking liar, that's what you are."

My body screamed for release. "It's true," I spat, feeling vomit rise to my throat. "I start tomorrow."

"The fuck you are," she said.

Tears swelled in my eyes, her gift twisting each cell in my body. I writhed. *I'm gifted.* Tears spilled down my cheeks. *I'm gifted.* Something snapped inside me. If I was gifted, I wouldn't take another moment of this. I gripped her second hand and pushed my gift to my hands. She stared back at me stunned, and after a moment's delay, she burst into a fit of laughter.

Veranda Yarrow was wrong. I was not gifted. Not at all. And Vivian held me in torturous pain for a full hour, but I'd already cried myself dry by then.

I splashed my face with water, my bloodshot eyes and red nose an accurate reflection of how I felt on a day that was meant to be triumphant. My cell phone buzzed in my pocket.

Kai:

My parents were so excited about the news they came home early. Reschedule?

I sent a thumbs up and felt my eyes begin to water again. Of course. I was happy for him, but the ache leftover in my chest told me how much I'd actually wanted to go.

Later that night, I was violently shaken from my sleep by one of my roommates. I sat up. "What's going on?" I asked, squinting through the dark to see who'd woken me.

"Another Fae died," she said, and I knew it was Alyssa by her voice.

"Who?" I asked, and I internally begged for her to say anything besides Yemoja Roux.

"Will Citrine."

Kaito

SIXTEEN

As I stepped out onto the fourth floor of the boy's dormitory and the smell of stale sweat hit me, I regretted my decision not to commute. My parents had encouraged me to give dorm life a try, but I couldn't remember, for the life of me, why I thought it would be a good idea. It was nice having my parents back. We'd spent the whole night discussing the circumstances of the entrance exam, all of which I fabricated and they fell back into their parental roles like they hadn't given me a debit card and abandoned me for the last two years. They were finally proud of me and I'd do just about anything not to mess that up… except live in this disgusting dorm.

I dragged my suitcases through the empty hallway, observing that the size of the rooms didn't appear to be much bigger than jail cells, but found relief that everyone appeared to be in class already. I wanted to get my bearings before I was forced to defend myself against the most Elite students in the country.

Then I heard it, the thrum of a guitar pouring out of a room at the end of the hallway. *For the love of god, please don't let that be my room.* As I read the numbers on the doors and moved closer to the end, I began to give up hope. "Fuck," I said as I arrived, double-checking that the room I'd been assigned was in fact the one with the guitar-playing douche in it.

I stepped in and my eyes were immediately drawn to the huge posters on the right side of the room, which prominently displayed a familiar pop idol. *Oh god, what the fuck?* My concern quickly changed to a cringe as my gaze lowered to the guitar slung guy with unmistakable blonde curly hair. I had to press my lips together to keep from laughing. "Carter Mason?" I asked. "Seriously?"

He brushed his curly blonde hair out of his eyes only for it to fall back into place. He grinned up at me without missing a note on his acoustic guitar. "The one and only."

Sure enough, splayed out in his desk chair with his bare feet up on the bed, was the once legendary pop star who dominated the charts in his early teens.

I turned back to the door. "I'll just get a transfer."

"Wait, bro," he said. "Listen to this part." I sighed, debating whether I should use my gift to smash his guitar. The melody switched to a slower more soulful tempo. The notes danced through the air and lulled me into a sort of involuntary calm. I gaped, but the shock I felt was instantly wiped away with every pluck of his strings.

"Chill, man. Just chill."

I pulled my luggage into the small room and sat on the empty bed to the left as my new roommate played on. A few moments later, his hands stopped and he coddled his guitar down on his bed as if it were a baby he was putting into a crib.

I ran my hand through my hair. "What was that?"

"My gift allows me to help people relax."

I swallowed. "But you didn't touch me."

"Sound waves, man."

It was unfathomable. Only Yemoja Roux could use magic without touch… This was a strange exception. "What else can you make people do?"

He shook his head. "Just relax. It may sound lame, but the last thing your opponent wants to be during an attack is relaxed. Plus the teachers allow me to use my gift outside the classrooms and training zones since I can't really cause harm with it. As your mentor, I should mention that using your gift willy-nilly is a big no-no. If you use it outside of the designated areas, you will get thrown out of here fast as shit."

I crossed my arms. "How do you know who's the strongest if you can't fight?"

"Dude, relax. You can fight all you want in the designated zones, plus there's the class ranking. I suggest you learn quickly what everyone's gift is before you go challenging people. I guarantee everyone here will know yours, although it's been impossible to get any intel on the new girl, Reina." He raised his eyebrows. "You know her, right? What can you tell me about her?"

I shrugged. "No idea. I don't think she even knows what her gift is."

"Alright, man, well get unpacked. I'm supposed to show you the campus."

I unzipped my suitcase and started pulling out my clothes. The prison cell-sized room was symmetrical with twin-sized beds pushed to the side walls. A desk and chair for each of us at the back with a window above them and an impossibly small dresser on either side of the door. My gaze drifted to the posters on the opposite walls. "Why do you have posters of yourself hung up? That's so weird."

He crawled out of his chair and lay in his bed. "Just reliving the glory days, my friend."

An odd thought popped into my head. "Wait, did you use your gift when you were on stage and stuff?"

He beamed. "You think they liked me for my pretty face?"

Reina
SEVENTEEN

When I woke up, I felt a new sense of purpose surge through me. I was finally going to begin attendance at GFA and leave my old life behind, along with my past mistakes. I found a moment to pull each of my roommates aside to say goodbye, but most of them didn't believe my story. I'd visit when I could, but I knew moving on to GFA made keeping in touch unlikely.

Considering this was my fresh start, I was certainly bringing a lot of baggage to it. I'd literally only packed a backpack full of belongings, but emotionally I carried a lifetime of expectations, along with newly-invigorated feelings for Kai.

On the bus ride, I decided to lay low at this school. I'd fly under the radar and sharpen my skills without drawing the wrath of the school's Elites. Even with all my thoughts consumed with daydreams about my new life, none of it sunk in until I was standing outside my usual place at the school's gate. I reached out to trace my fingers habitually over the crest when the doors opened.

I stepped through the magical barrier, revealing the school that sat tucked away behind it. I nearly choked with emotion, as I'd so often imagined what it would feel like when those gates opened for me. I walked through the gardens toward the front building and climbed the stairs as I'd done the day before. This time, at the top of the stairs stood a girl who looked about my age.

She had long, enviable legs, a tight blush pink ponytail, and a heavy black eyeliner that winged out from the sides of her ocean blue eyes.

"Hurry up," she groaned.

I skipped up the stairs. "Hi, I'm Reina."

She rolled her eyes. "Pleasure. I'm Miranda Callix, your mentor apparently."

Oh great. She hated me already. "Oh, well if you're busy, I'm sure I can figure it out on my own."

"And disobey Headmistress Tricorn? No, thank you. Just move quicker and don't ask me any questions. I'll tell you what you need to know. By the way, where's your shit? You were supposed to bring your stuff today."

I lifted my engorged backpack. "In here."

"That's all you have?"

I nodded. "I'm an orphan, so…"

She tossed her ponytail over her shoulder. "Luckily we wear school uniforms here, so no one will really notice you're poor. Except at the end of the term is the Winter Ball and you'll need a dress for that."

I followed her into the main hall, secretly screaming with delight as I observed the iconic maroon blazer with the school crest on the left, black gloves, collared shirt, and black, maroon, and white plaid pants. I couldn't wait to get my uniform, and I couldn't believe I was actually a student.

Instead of heading up the stairs, she led me down a different corridor. There were large portraits of high achieving Fae who had once attended the academy. I stopped at one in particular: *William Citrine*. It was hard to believe that a Fae so great he had his portrait hung in his alma mater could be dead. He wasn't even twenty-five.

"Keep up," Miranda bellowed, and I followed as she turned into an enormous ballroom. The vaulted ceilings were painted with clouds dipped in pastel colors and went up at least four stories. The entire south end of the room was made of glass that poured the light of the morning onto the hardwood floors. And just on the other side of the glass lay the rest of the campus.

"Eeeeep!" I squealed and ran to the windows to get a better look, my voice carrying through the gold-trimmed ballroom. "This is amazing!"

Miranda nudged me out of the way and pushed open what I'd previously thought were glass windows, but they must've been doors because she stepped out onto the balcony.

"Okay, left to right," she said, pointing to the closest building to us. It was a basic shape made from sand-colored stones, but had expensive looking moldings around the windows and the front door, and lush green ivy crawling up the side. "That's the girl's dorm, Pink House. You can get your room assignment and key from the security desk in the foyer. Usually you'd be assigned to a room with your mentor, but I happen to have my own room." She smiled brightly but it dimmed when she looked back at me, as if she'd only just remembered she was mentoring me.

She pointed to an identical building on the far side. "That's Blue House. We can totally sneak in and hook up and stuff, but don't try it unless you know what you're doing. If you get caught, they'll throw you out." She looked me up and down. "Not that you'll need it. You're obviously a virgin."

My gaze bulged. "You can tell that by my face?"

She tilted her head. "I don't know, it's more about how someone carries themselves."

I started fiddling with my charm as she continued her pseudo-tour. "That big building in the back is the class hall. Obvi, it has all the classrooms."

I gulped. It looked more like a mansion, with its huge windows and ivy-covered stones, than a school. In the back right of the campus was a modern-looking building that appeared to be made of mostly iron, concrete, and glass.

"That's the student center. It's got a cafeteria, ping pong tables, a movie theater, clinic… I don't know, maybe a library. I don't spend much time there, obvi."

I wasn't sure what was supposed to be obvious about it. Or if she just liked the word.

On the far right were two massive snow globe shaped buildings that seemed to capture the sunlight and shoot it through the iridescent walls. "And what are *those?*" I asked.

"Those are the combat zones. One is for physical training, you know like weapons and stuff. It's for upperclassmen, so you won't use it this year, and the other is for gift training. At some point you can meet with Professor Cordovan to figure out how they can accommodate you in the gift training arena, since everyone is different." She put a hand on her hip, and she looked a lot like the fashion models plastered all over social media. "By the way, what *is* your gift?"

"I... I don't know."

She raised an eyebrow. "Playing it coy, I see. It's not a bad strategy except I'm fifth in our class and you don't want to make an enemy of me."

"Who's first?"

"You're so new it hurts. Oden Gates, obviously. And just so you don't do anything you might regret, he and I are kind of a thing."

I put my hands up in surrender. "Got it."

"In fact, the Noble Four are all sort of off limits to you."

I nodded. "I just came here to study."

"Atta girl," she said.

"Let's hit the Pink House first so you can drop off your little homeless lady bag. I also seriously encourage you to start wearing gloves. You wouldn't want to be seen as conceited."

I bit back a laugh. "You're right. That *would* be the worst."

"I mean, the students can use their gifts on objects and stuff around campus, but not on each other outside of the training zones. I don't mean to tell you this to make you feel safe, I just want you to know that when you step into those domes, prepare yourself for a brawl."

It was a blatant threat. So much for laying low. *Still*, as I followed Miranda down the stairs of the main building balcony, down to the GFA campus, I knew there was nothing that could mess up my day. Then, like clockwork, across the way I saw Kai.

Kaito
EIGHTEEN

I saw Reina coming down the stairs from the building with the headmistress' office. Her gaze was locked on me, giving me a rush of whatever was left over from our kiss. Though Carter was on my heels and I'd practically begged him to show me the gift training arena first, I was curious how Reina was doing on her first day. That's when I noticed the bombshell showing her around.

She was all legs with pouty lips and a checklist of features that looked like they'd been strategically picked from a catalog.

"Good spot, bro. That's Miranda," Carter said. "And you already know the new girl."

We met up outside the girl's dormitory, my gaze transfixed on Miranda. Reina cleared her throat. "Hey, Kai, how's your first day going?"

"Just started," I said half-heartedly. "Who's your friend?"

Miranda interjected, "Mentor, actually."

Okay, rude. With two words she'd lost my interest. It was a clear shot at Reina, and no one messed with Reina but me.

"Rei," I said, shifting my attention, "this is my mentor slash roommate."

"Carter Mason," Reina said, her eyes bulging just as mine had when I'd first seen him, but then she touched her necklace charm and I felt a touch of jealousy flair. Carter unslung his guitar from his shoulder to give Reina a better look, but her gaze was locked on his face, like a young child meeting a mall Santa.

Miranda patted her gloved hand on the top of Reina's head. "Good girl. Stay in your lane. These are your people," she said.

I half expected Reina to jump in and defend herself, but her face beamed with suppressed amusement. I relaxed, realizing I'd felt defensive for no reason. Reina would probably be okay. Of course someone as basic as Miranda wouldn't actually get to her. Still, I was certain there was an insult for me in there and I wasn't going to let that slide.

I smirked. "I'll be one of the Nobles by the end of the day."

She rolled her eyes. "Aren't you the guy who failed the entrance exam twice?"

I gritted my teeth. "Well, it's been a pleasure," I said, hoping Miranda heard the bite in my tone.

She grinned menacingly. "Right. You better get to it if you're going to rank up by the end of the day."

Without another word, I turned away and headed for the arena while Carter slung his guitar back over his shoulder. "Man, that was intense," Carter said when the girls were out of earshot.

"She's a fucking nightmare."

Carter shrugged. "She's like some high-budget porn star mixed with a sex cosplay goddess. I don't care if she's a bitch."

"You have issues, man." But I had to admit he had a point.

"Honestly," he said, "the students here are the best in the world. The elite of the Elite. Don't let my charm fool you, I've already interviewed with a hostage negotiation Fae division and have a contract to do my apprenticeship with them next summer. Everyone here is going places, and their egos match. I suggest you get kind of used to it." He put a hand on my shoulder. "You might've been a big deal at your old school, but now that you're here, you're all the way at the bottom with a nasty rumor about failed exams to boot."

I shrugged his hand off. "Let's go," I said, dismissing him as my attention was drawn to a familiar face inside the arena—Oden Gates.

"Wait! Stop," Carter said. "I didn't realize there were students in there this period. We better come back when the area is free."

"Relax. I'm not going to do something stupid."

"That's what someone whose going to do something stupid would say." I heard him, but his words hardly processed because I was already on the move.

I pushed open the translucent door and stepped into the arena. Once inside, it reminded me of the giant greenhouse at our local zoo with panels of partially filtered light pouring through. The stadium had gift-sealed panes that were reminiscent of the seal around the school's outer wall. I recognized Oden right away, but my attention skipped over him as I sized up the three other guys in his little crew. They were the school's Nobles. I knew this because I recognized every one of them. Starting on the left was the 5'5'" prodigy from New Valand,

Enzo McCain. He had slick brown hair and a smirk that insisted he was too cool to be here. He made a name for himself at the bi-annual World Varsity Tournament last year for possessing a gift that was hotly debated. Like most who were trying to become Fae, he never gave any direct answers about his gift in interviews, but one thing was certain; when he touched his shoes, he ran quite a bit faster than what should be humanly possible.

Next was Prince Finn Warsham, the actual fucking third prince of the four Zalmian princes, and the only of them invited to attend the academy. Like his photos online, he was a tall black man whose hair always looked like he'd just come from his barber and whose posture was so straight it made me want to loosen my tie and slouch. There was almost no information at all about his gift, but I had the feeling I would find out soon enough.

The last of Oden's stooges was Quan Levout, the legend who used his doppleganger gift to fix the Varsity Tournament. He'd been disqualified, of course, but the subsequent lime green hair trend lasted an entire year.

I was admittedly starstruck seeing them all in one place but knew what I needed to do to earn their respect.

"It's a little reckless for you to step foot in here on your first day," Oden said.

Carter grabbed my arm. "Come on, man, let's get out of here."

I yanked my arm away, steadying my nerves. "Actually, Oden, I came to challenge you."

Reina

NINETEEN

The number of celebrities at this school was insane. I could distinctly remember swooning over Carter Mason as a middle schooler. In fact, Kaito was there for that phase. He'd seen my bedroom walls plastered with pictures of the blonde pop star. I cringed at the possibility that my little crush might find its way into the conversation.

Miranda and I headed to the girls' dorm and, besides Kai and Carter, the rest of the campus seemed deserted. It didn't seem like students skipped class around here. I almost dreaded how I might feel when the bell rang and students spilled into the courtyard. Oden Gates was somewhere around here, along with royalty and some of the most gifted people on the planet. The more I thought about it, the more I felt like an imposter.

I felt my nerves soothe when a familiar face smiled at me from outside the dorm. Professor Greene perked up. "I'll take it from here, Miranda. You may return to your morning classes."

"I haven't shown her to her dorm yet," Miranda said.

"She won't be needing it for a while."

She shot me a worried look, brushing a stray wisp of pink hair out of her eyes.

"Thank you, Miranda, for the tour and the advice."

She gave a half-smile before heading toward the back of campus where the mansion-like class hall was situated.

Professor Greene sucked in a sharp breath. "How's your first day going?" he asked.

I smiled through gritted teeth. "It's a little overwhelming. Did you know *Carter Mason* goes here?"

He nodded, but his expression didn't imply he shared my excitement. "There are many celebrities in attendance here. You'll get used to it." He shifted his weight. "I… I think we need to have a discussion."

I swallowed hard. First he stopped me from moving in and now this? "Are you kicking me out already?" I said with a smile I hoped would break his grim expression.

"That's entirely up to you." With a wave of his hand, he motioned for me to follow him back to the front building and it sent a new wave of dread beneath my skin. By the time we reached his office, I was almost in tears.

"Take a seat," he said.

I sat like a woman condemned. I felt my posture slump as I tried to disappear into the chair.

"As you must know by now, the first term for every student here at GFA is a probationary period. If you don't show significant progress on your midterm, you will be dropped from the program."

I shook my head, my throat constricting too tightly to form words. *Dropped from the program?* I shuddered at the idea of returning to the group home and how long Ms. Vivian would torture me when I returned.

"Since you and a few others have transferred this year, that means you'll need to have your skills up to par for the winter midterm."

I nodded. Three months wasn't a long time for me to pull it together, but it was a chance and that was all I needed. Still, I doubted from his tone that he was sharing the worst of the news.

I held my breath as I waited for the gavel to drop.

"I've spoken to Ms. Yarrow and she told me what you've done."

I gulped, tears pricking my eyes as they threatened to spill out.

"I'm only going to ask this once. Why did you do it?"

I straightened in my chair. I'd made many mistakes in my life, but the one Veranda Yarrow found inside me was the greatest. If I got thrown from GFA to answer for it, I'd accept it.

"My parents died a year ago. I had no one, the grief was overwhelming and I thought it was the only way to move on."

"I see," he said, lifting his nameplate and turning it over in his hands. "Ms. Yarrow thinks your gift may be tied to your emotions as a sort of way to focus and aim them. You can't reach them, let alone fully master them, if you've taken a confection to dull your feelings of loss. You need the full spectrum."

"So you're kicking me out."

He tilted his head. "I have to ask how you came to find such a rare confection. Unlike what I gave you, which might only last a few minutes, this could only be made by someone as powerful as Fae and would be expensive and extremely difficult to locate."

Despair pooled in my stomach. "I received a large inheritance."

"That's quite a sacrifice. You must've been in a great deal of pain."

"Yes, I must've." But I didn't know for sure. Even the memory of that time seemed drained of emotion.

"I can make a confection to counteract the one you took, but I need to know if that's something you'd be open to."

I stood. "Yes." I put both hands flat on his desk, leaning into him. "Please," I begged, my voice cracking. It was a miracle. A second chance at life. In less than a day, GFA was offering me everything I'd ever wanted.

Professor Greene looked down. "Before you agree, I must tell you that this will be an agonizing experience. Every emotion you've suppressed over the last year will hit you at once. You'll have to spend the week in the infirmary because the sudden burst of grief and despair often leads to thoughts of self-harm."

I sat back in my chair, but the professor didn't look at me, and I wondered if he was afraid of what he might see.

"You are not the first case I've seen. I've seen that particular confection used after a breakup or after losing a great deal of money. I fear the amount of grief you will need to process at once may be too great for you to overcome. So I'll give you the choice—leave GFA with grief suppressed, or risk your life to undo it, to unlock your full potential."

Fear tore through me so quickly that it pushed the breath from my lungs, and that's how I knew I'd already made my choice.

Kaito

TWENTY

I wasn't a fool. I knew I couldn't take GFA's top student in a fight. He was probably the most Elite teenager on earth. It may have seemed like a death wish to some, and the grin on Oden's face told me he might be of that mind, but I didn't have to beat him to earn his respect. I just had to put up a good fight.

He beamed. "Well, that's perfect because I thought I'd have to give you a few days to settle before I could kick your ass."

His goons laughed, smiling at me like I was a meal they were poised to consume.

"One on one?" I asked.

Oden stepped forward. "You think I need help to beat you?"

I shrugged.

I heard Carter mutter under his breath, "This is a bad fucking idea."

"Training zone two is open," Quan said.

Oden gestured to the back of the domed arena. "Is that cool with you?" Oden asked.

"Wherever."

The four Nobles practically squealed with excitement as I followed Oden through the greenhouse-like arena. They shook Oden's shoulders and whispered to each other as if their bodies might explode from sheer adrenaline.

The dome was separated into different zones that seemed to house a variety of environments. The one closest to where I'd entered was filled with trees and lush plant life, but as we made our way through to the neutral plane between zones, I saw that there were seven. My attention was drawn to one in particular that seemed to somehow have snow accumulating in it—the flakes falling from nothing and perfectly contained in the borders of the zone without any visible walls to contain it.

I wondered which zone was number two, and if Oden had chosen one that would play to his strengths.

The second zone from the left was a flat and empty dirt patch of land that reminded me a lot of the physical exam I'd failed. Without any materials to grab onto, I'd been unable to use my gift. However, the second zone from the right looked like a city block complete with skyscrapers and industrial construction sites. There was so much to touch there, so much to use. Oden banked left and I knew I was about to receive the ass kicking of my life. But I fought to hide it from my face. I was a great deal more gifted than I'd been a year ago. Maybe I could win.

We stopped outside the flat zone. "You go in from that side," Oden said. "The duel starts when we're both in."

I took my position, Carter following close behind me like a

puppy. "You can't be serious, man," he said. "You're going to get yourself killed." His words chipped away at my facade.

I spun to him. "I need to do this," I said. "You're either Elite or you're not."

"You're either alive or you're dead," he mocked.

I faced the zone and saw Oden near the center pacing back and forth.

Carter's voice shot out beside me in an angry whisper. "Look, man, I wish you the best. But I can't watch this. I'll be in our room if you somehow make it out of here."

I swallowed a lump of nerves and stepped through the barrier to zone two. As I entered, my heart beat like a drum marching me to war. Like I'd expected, there was nothing loose to touch, so my only option was to get close enough to touch Oden. The problem was, one touch from him and his strength gift could break every bone in my body, and the easy grin on his face told me that was his intention.

I sprinted towards Oden, the howls of his goons ringing through the zone from the other side. I was a slightly faster runner because my gift could propel me, and speed would be the way to beat him.

If I could touch him and escape his counter attack, I could drop him from a great height and his strength wouldn't be a factor.

He took a defensive stance as I charged him. I leapt into the air and used my gift to hold me. My manipulation of gravity threw him, as he incorrectly anticipated my fall. Reaching down, I swept my hand through the air to catch a piece of him. The tip of my finger hit the top of his ear. I pushed myself away with every ounce of power my gift could muster, hovering out of his powerful reach.

I have him. The onlooking Nobles went silent as I thrust Oden into the air. Higher and higher until he bordered on the edge of my range, nearly fourteen stories up in open space. Then I dropped him.

Oden plummeted head first toward the solid dirt. I gulped, suddenly aware of the possibility that I might kill him. Still within my range, I had time to save him. I lifted my hand but froze. He cocked his arm back, ready to strike the ground with a punch.

No fucking way.

The zone exploded into a dark dusty hell as his fist collided like a bomb. The ground shredded, crunching into shards of rock and dirt that scattered through the air. *This wasn't over.* Bombarded with debris, I squinted through the dusty air, searching for my opponent.

Had I been on the ground when he'd struck, I'd be finished. Suddenly, Oden shot through the dust, nearly reaching me several yards above the rocky terrain. I shot back, barely missing his blows. How was he getting this high up? His momentum cleared some of the dust, and I saw his gift gather energy in his legs as he leapt once more, swinging his fist to kill.

I narrowly slipped it when I noticed my advantage. We were no longer in an empty zone. The shattered rock was ripe for my gift and I felt a few that had hit me in the explosion still in my range. I shot myself back toward the surface, touching as much of the surface as I could before Oden charged me. I felt some large sharp stones enter my range. Oden sprinted at me and I sent one boulder after the next at him, hoping one might slow his speed. He punched through one after the other—each crash like a bomb growing closer and closer. Dust flew, but through it I saw Oden's bloody fist blast toward me, a dark streak of blood across his face. I pulled myself back through the air, but I was too slow—his hand collided with my cheek with a crack and everything went black.

The next thing I remember was a bloodcurdling scream, but the voice was not mine, it was Reina's.

Reina
TWENTY-ONE

I clutched the sheets of my hospital bed and screamed my throat raw. Professor Greene had not exaggerated the agony. All those years of bottled up grief were coming out with a vengeance. I writhed through a cycle of screaming and vomiting, my body unable to handle the avalanche of emotion, as one memory after the next tore through me. My parents were dead. My parents were *dead*. My heart ached as I fought to come to grips with this new sensation.

I'd been there when it happened. I watched them die—their blood froze and their faces settled into this...empty expression that told me their souls had fled. It was just a touch to the backs of their necks in a crowded street. I hadn't seen who did it, just saw the life drain from them as they quietly slipped away. They were both Commons, and law enforcement officers with gifts that wouldn't have saved them even if they had seen their attacker coming. I too was helpless. I held their hands and screamed for help, too afraid to let go, and I rarely brought forth the memory since I'd taken that grief confection. I certainly hadn't felt it. Now it looped through my thoughts endlessly as if in punishment for denying the heartbreak due.

They were gone. I felt selfish as I choked on the thought that I still needed them. I still longed for their guidance, the warm sound of their voices. There were so many things I never got to ask. My shoulders shook as a wave of fresh pain cut through my chest. "I'm so alone," I whispered into my pillow.

My eyes burned from all the tears I shed, my chest so tight I couldn't breathe. The pain and loneliness were overwhelming in the intensity. Dr. Azul stood over me, trying to look encouraging. "You'll make it through this," he said, "You are *not* alone." But his healing gift did not extend to emotional pain, and all he could do was say soothing words and hope I pulled through it whole. In my haze, I heard the door slam open and another student rolled in on a gurney with a squeaky wheel. But it didn't register.

My mind was trapped on a hamster wheel. *My parents were gone. My parents were dead. I am alone.* Just when my body finally relaxed, a new wave of grief crashed over me. I curled into a tight ball as the pain swept through me in an emotional torrent so brutal that it was like a sharp electrical current shooting through me. The pain was unrelenting, draining me to a point I thought I just might die. I reached for the doctor, but Dr. Azul was no longer beside me. He had moved on to another student with injuries more pressing than mine.

Mom. Dad. I sobbed quietly into my pillow, knowing this pain was never going to end, and it was almost enough to make me regret the bitter morsel Professor Greene had given me. *Almost.*

Dr. Azul's voice cracked through the room. "Who is it?" he asked.

"Kaito Nakamaru," I heard a voice say. That seized my attention as I clenched my teeth to hold in the tears. *Why didn't he know it was Kai?* Dr. Azul *knew* Kaito. He'd seen him just yesterday. I couldn't imagine what could cause him not to recognize him.

"Is he alive?" someone asked.

"Just barely."

I held my breath, hoping to bottle up the emotional assault that awaited my next breath. But it finally broke through and my heart seized up until, inevitably, my consciousness blinked out.

I awoke slowly, my tears breaching my eyes before I could even remember why. My gaze lifted to the empty end table beside me, and then to the bed on the other side. Kaito lay bruised and bloodied on his back, his eyes open as he stared at the ceiling.

I sat up quickly, dizziness seizing hold of me. "Just like old times," I said, my throat burning with pain. It had been a few years, but back in middle school we spent a good amount of time together in an infirmary just like this one. He looked beat to hell, but that was the kind of joke he usually jumped at. He must've been in pain. "Kaito, what happened? Are you okay?"

His eyes moved to me before his head. "You were the one screaming."

I lay back down, biting my bottom lip to keep from crying.

He asked, "Are you going to tell me what happened?"

I shook my head, turning my gaze to the ceiling as I fought to suppress the sound of my sobs.

"It's about your parents, isn't it?" he asked. "I heard you call for them."

I pulled my blanket up to my shoulders as if it could somehow shield me.

"What I don't get is, you've been so calm about what happened all this time. What happened? Is it the new school?"

I took a steadying breath but it caught in my throat. "I took something," I wheezed through my sore throat. "A..." I cupped my face in my hands. "A grief-numbing confection."

Kaito was so silent I couldn't hear him breathe.

"I s-spent my inheritance," I said, the sadness overtaking my words. "So I could stop hurting."

"Veranda felt it."

I nodded and we fell into silence as I turned to muffle my cry in my pillow.

"Why did you have them undo it?"

A slew of reasons popped into my head. Because I'd be kicked out of school if I didn't. Because I regretted that decision. But only the most prominent reason came to my lips. "Because..." I sniffed, "the inability to mourn their loss felt like they were never here." I fell apart again, but as bad as the last few days had been, I was happy to finally mourn. I was happy to feel my parents' connection to me. Every wave of grief reinforced how much I loved them and, if I survived it, I'd be able to carry them forward with me.

I dared a glance at Kaito and I thought I saw his eyes get glossy. He reached out a trembling hand marred with purple flesh and lay it out across the end table. "Are you going to tell me what happened to you?" I asked. He didn't bother to answer but, knowing him, he probably picked a fight with the wrong person. His palm rested on the edge of my bed. I buried my face in it as a new wave of grief rolled over as Kai rubbed his thumb up and down the side of my face.

When I awoke again, my body felt heavy and stiff. My gaze moved to Kaito's empty bed, and a panic flashed through me before I felt his warmth along my back. My head was resting on his right arm, his left arm draped around my waist. I traced my fingers over it to find that what was purple the last I'd seen was now a blotchy yellow. I wasn't sure if I'd been sleeping for a long time or if Dr. Azul had been every bit the healer as reported by his reputation. I wondered what he'd gotten himself into to get so battered, or why the bully who tormented me relentlessly not three days before had rushed to hold me when I needed it most. I would have faked sleep for the next ten years to be held like this for a little while longer, but I had to pee. So I slipped out of bed, cupping a hand over my mouth as Professor Greene's morsel kicked back in, reminding me once again that my parents were dead and, even if Kai was here today, tomorrow I'd again be alone.

Kaito
TWENTY-TWO

I never felt more helpless in my life. Reina had always been strong. It was one of the reasons I'd been friends with her in middle school, and one of the reasons I tormented her when we got a little older. When I looked back on this past year, I suppose I always thought it was weird how casually she spoke about her parents, but I couldn't have imagined that she'd be desperate enough to blow her inheritance on a grief curber. How did she even find one that powerful? That was some deep black market shit. I shuddered to think of Reina in the kinds of places that sold that sort of thing, and all the time she was going through that, I was trying to teach her a lesson. I sighed. Now she was in the infirmary, a place I'd once taken pleasure in sending her, but I took no pleasure seeing her here now, so broken and fragile.

The infirmary was well lit and cozy with no more than ten recovery beds. I'd looked out the window to find myself across campus, somewhere in the building Carter called the student center. The past few days Dr. Azul had worked wonders on healing me, his gift like ice pushed into each cell, numbing the pain as they thawed into regenerated flesh and bone. He ran out of stamina after a while and needed long rests between treatments, but I couldn't deny that his gift was both fast and effective, so I was not surprised that Reina and I were the only patients he had. I stifled a laugh. We'd both made a hell of an impression.

I listened for the doctor's footsteps while I put together the sequence of events from the last few days. I was pretty out of it when I'd first been wheeled in and only remembered flashes of pain and voices. Enzo had rushed me here using his speed gift. I felt a pang of embarrassment about my defeat. I should have listened to Carter. I reached to search through another blurred memory, one of Oden getting his arm patched up, but I couldn't be sure if those were real or something I dreamed up in my recovery. When I came to, I found a text from my parents.

Dad:
I heard you were defeated in combat and are in the school's infirmary. This was not the kind of fresh start we were hoping for. Your mother and I have decided to leave town for a while.

I considered smashing my phone in frustration over my parents when Reina screamed out for hers. What different lives we led.

It was difficult to watch my wounds heal drastically day after day while Reina seemed to suffer to no end. I knew Reina's condition couldn't be fixed with the doctor's gift, but the worst part was his attempts to comfort her. He kept telling her that she wasn't alone which only made it more apparent that she was. She even cried when she slept, as if even her dreams wouldn't allow her peace. On my third night, there she was shaking so violently that I leapt out of bed, forgetting about the doctor's orders to rest my newly healed bones, and lay down beside her. But as I pulled her in, I found myself repeating the doctor's soothing mantra to her. "You'll make it through this," I said. "You're not alone." She calmed a little and, before I had time to think better of it, I fell asleep beside her.

I awoke to find Reina had moved to my bed on the other side of the bedside table, and I worried that my attempts to comfort her had only freaked her out. What was I *doing*? Even I had to admit I was all over the place lately. I'd bullied her so hard we got expelled from school, then I kissed her, now this. Why had she become such an obstacle all of a sudden? Reina rolled toward me and I noticed she was awake.

"You seem a little better today," I said.

"So do you. Your bruises are healing."

"Bruises." I scoffed. "I broke like fifteen bones."

Her eyes widened. "Oh my God, Kai. How are you even alive?"

Dr. Azul pushed open the curtain that separated the recovery beds from the rest of the infirmary. "That would be me."

"It's true," I said. "He's pretty strong."

Dr. Azul scoffed and froze suddenly. "Did you two switch beds?"

Heat rushed my face.

"Alright, Mr. Nakamaru, you're good to go. Focus on your classes for a while and try not to pick another fight."

I didn't like the idea of leaving Reina by herself, but if I spent any more time with her, she was going to continue to infect me with her woman magic. Still, I considered asking him to let me stay, but he'd just announced I was fine to leave, in front of her. It would look weird. I was just trying to be a good friend. Right? Fae helped people. It was nothing more than that.

I gathered my tattered clothes, grabbed my cell phone that somehow wasn't cracked, and changed from my hospital clothes to a school uniform Dr. Azul had laid out for me.

"Kai," Reina said before I could slip out. "Thanks… you know. For last night."

I half smiled. "See you around, Rei."

I felt flustered and couldn't get out of the hospital fast enough. I took an elevator to the first floor and stepped out into the hallway which passed by a bustling cafeteria with glass walls. I felt the sting of a hundred pairs of eyes on my face as I focused desperately on the door ahead. Finally, I stepped out into the cool autumn air and inhaled a mouthful of it. GFA had already proved to be a little more than I'd expected. I probably should have laid low.

"Hey," a voice shouted from behind me, drawing my attention. "Kaito Nakamaru." I turned to see Oden Gates and his three backup dancers approaching. *Fuck.* I had half a mind to flee into the infirmary until I remembered he couldn't hit me outside the combat zone.

The foursome walked over and I felt the soreness of my bruised ego flair. Behind him, I could see the prying eyes of the other students pressed against the glass.

"Have you come to gloat?" I asked.

He reached his hand out, the antiquated gesture I'd previously offered him more frightening than anything else, but I shook it without hesitation. I felt him move into my magical range and considered tossing him over the wall. It would almost be worth the expulsion. "That was one hell of a fight," he said. "I misjudged you."

I nodded, turning my face away with discomfort.

"When you get settled in, come find me. I'll show you the ropes."

Quan said, "The Noble Five. Sounds badass."

I smiled and the four guys patted me on the back before they turned back the way they came.

Reina
TWENTY-THREE

By the time I was cleared to leave the infirmary at the end of the week, I barely recognized myself. My eyes had dark circles around them, I'd grown pale, my cheeks were a little sunken in, but the biggest change was the glossy sheen of defeat in my eyes. *My parents were dead*. I couldn't bear the repetition of it. My heart ached and I clenched my stomach to keep from crying. A year of grief packed into one week had left me with an emotional hangover complete with a splitting headache. Dr. Azul had said he was proud of me for enduring it so well, but I hadn't felt proud of any of it. I was broken and I deserved every bit of it.

I put on my plaid pants, collared shirt, and blazer. I'd always imagined how I'd feel the first time I put on those burgundy uniforms, but it wasn't this. I never thought I'd feel like such an imposter. I hadn't even been strong enough to face my parents' deaths, so how could I become Fae? It felt like the entire week I'd been there was some kind of nightmare; the only reprieve from the agony was Kai. One familiar face. In the moment, I didn't care how badly he'd treated me in the past. He was there when I needed him, even if it was by pure coincidence.

As I stepped out of the elevator on the first floor, I realized I didn't know where I was or where I was going. There was a large cafeteria to the left of the hallway where students chatted and ate on maroon trays. It was separated by a glass wall that reminded me a little of a zoo or a fishbowl. Then, from inside the fishbowl, someone saw me and, like a viral disease spreading to each cluster of prying eyes, the cafeteria fell silent. I pressed my tongue on the roof of my mouth, willing myself to hold it together, when I was rescued by the person I least expected.

"Good, you're here," Miranda said. "I'm supposed to show you to your— Woah! You look like absolute shit."

"Thanks," I said, wiping my nose with the back of my hand.

Her eyes lit. "Did you hear the news?" she asked, but she didn't wait for my response before she gushed on. "Kaito Nakamaru challenged Oden Gates and, like, he lost obvi, but apparently the fight was *crazy* and like now Oden let him into his group and they're calling them the *Noble Five*." She thrust her chest out. "Gah, I can't believe I brushed him off the other day. I mean, he was obviously gorgeous but I didn't know his gift was *that* strong. I mean, didn't he fail the entrance exam twice?"

I envied her energy. "You were showing me somewhere?"

"Right," she said, flipping her rose-gold hair over her shoulder. "Your dorm." I followed her out and the students returned to their lunches.

"So," Miranda said over her shoulder, "is Kaito like *single*? You're not together or anything, right?"

My mind flickered to the past few days. *The kiss*. Waking up in Kaito's arms. He was the biggest train wreck I knew and my fractured heart was not ready to take a risk like that. Part of me wished the world was different. That my parents were still alive. That I was as gifted as Kaito so we could explore whatever was going on with us without the outside world using the gap to end it. If what Miranda said was true, and Kaito had become Elite at GFA, I could guarantee I was about to get middle school deja vu. Now that Kaito fit in again, he didn't need me to be his safety net. "No, we're not together," I said. "I don't think he's seeing anyone."

I wish I could say the pep my reply put in Miranda's step didn't bother me, or her giddy grin, or her confident gait. I wish I didn't notice her daydreaming as she twirled her silky hair around her polished finger. I wanted to lie down and forget I ever knew Kaito Nakamaru. I wanted to sleep until I remembered why I wanted to go to this stupid school to begin with.

kaito
TWENTY-FOUR

I must've picked up my phone a hundred times to message my parents and tell them I'd turned things around, but every time I tried, I saw the last message my dad sent me, the disappointment ringing through every cold word of it. Why get their hopes up only to let them down again? Once I became Fae, they'd be proud. I was sure of it.

Since I arrived at GFA, I had no luck connecting to the internet. It seemed like all I could do was call or text and download ebooks from the library. It wasn't so bad when I was in the hospital, but now I was out and desperate to know what was going on outside the walls of the school. I made a mental note to ask Carter about it as I headed to Blue House.

I had almost made it back, while partially dreading Carter's remarks, when a very specific shade of blue caught my eye. I spun to investigate and my body pulsed. Round glasses, blue hair, and a sharply pointed nose. *The bus stop guy.* He was a few yards away, but I could have sworn it was the same guy I'd seen last week at the bus station, the one with the tattoo that matched the mark at the scene Reina described. It most likely circulated the news and internet by now, so why wasn't this creepy guy in jail? He was chatting up a girl with purple hair tied into two ponytails. *Mind your business, Kai.* I planned to hurry past, but he turned to me and shot me the same malevolent smile he'd given me the day Raphael Mazarin died.

"You," I called without thinking.

He grinned as I approached, dismissing the purple-haired girl with a wave. "Kaito Nakamaru," he said with a nod.

I gripped his gloved wrist and yanked his sleeve up to check his arm for the tattoo. He yanked his arm back in alarm, but it was too late. I'd already gotten a good look; his arm was completely blank.

"What the hell?" he spat.

"I-I-I'm sorry," I said, my mind fogged with confusion. "I thought I saw you at the bus station the other day, like a week ago."

"So what, crazy? You think I stole your lunch money or something? You have issues. Besides, I've been on campus for the last few months since I wasn't offered an internship this year," he said as he pulled his sleeve over his exposed arm. "Man, how bad did Oden rock you?"

I shook my head. "My bad, man. I'm a little off today." It was a piss poor excuse.

He nodded. "Well, no worries, bro. It happens. I'm Zane Blaque, by the way."

Zane Blaque? I hadn't heard of him, which meant it must've been true that he hadn't scored an internship worth media attention or even done well at the Varsity Tournament last year.

What was wrong with me? I literally just got out of the infirmary and I was going around picking fights?

I smiled sheepishly. "Nice to meet you. I'm sorry about that."

"Not a problem. See you around," he said graciously and headed back toward the class hall.

I pulled out my phone and mindlessly tried to connect to the internet, hoping to dig up a little more information about Zane Blaque, but when I reached Blue House, I still hadn't been able to connect.

Carter stood, moving to his desk to get his guitar. "You're alive," he said, pushing a handful of blonde curls from his eyes.

"Surprise."

"I heard they're calling you a Noble now. Mission accomplished." He sat on his bed and began to strum something mellow.

"You don't seem happy about that," I said, but the calm of Carter's gift soothed me.

He shrugged.

I sat on my bed, noting how much harder the mattress was than the one in the infirmary. "By the way, how did you hear about the whole Noble thing? I can't seem to get onto the internet."

"Ah, yeah. The school barrier blocks the connection. They say it's to help us focus and keep our minds off the status and stuff and on our studies, and to keep the privacy of the school, but there was a breach using the connection like ten years back by some bum looking to cause trouble."

"Fuck, this place is like a prison."

His fingers danced over the guitar strings and I laid back on my bed.

"There are a few ways around it. You can leave campus, but

the area around the school isn't the best. There's a fort where some students go to hook up. That gets wifi, but it's slow and spotty. Or if you're friends with Briara, her gift has some kind of workaround, but she's a total psychopath—voodoo witchcraft and such."

I stared at the ceiling and let myself float in the grasp of Carter's music. I felt a rush of gratitude that I'd been assigned him as a roommate.

"Can I ask you something?" he asked, cutting through my serenity.

"Shoot."

He paused, finishing the chord progression before he timed his question with the next. "Why is being Elite so important to you?"

I sighed. He wasn't going to let this go. "Because it's a one-way ticket to a great apprenticeship and ultimately to becoming Fae. Why isn't it important to you?"

He strummed a little louder so we could still feel every note as we spoke. He looked out our window, and when his next question came, I wasn't sure it was directed at me. "Is it really heroic if they pay you a million dollars to do it?"

I opened my mouth to respond, but my answer caught. He had a point. "If you don't want to be Fae, what are you even doing here?" I asked.

"I mean, of course I do. Everyone does and everyone has their reasons. Just think about it. Have you actually thought of your reason for trying to become Fae? Is it money? Status, perhaps? I wonder why your new friends want to be Fae. How many of us are actually trying to help people?"

My fingers tapped to the rhythm. "Did those guys do something to you?"

He shook his head. "Nah, man, I think I just... don't like what they represent."

"And what I represent."

He leaned back against the wall without missing a note. "Nah, man. You're cool. I just hope they don't turn you into one of them. I hope you find a good reason before you sort of adopt one of theirs. The last thing we need is a new generation of camera-obsessed Fae."

I suppose I understood where he was coming from. Still, without the Fae, society would have collapsed ages ago. Why shouldn't they be paid well to risk their lives for us? "Don't be so naive. The system may be broken, but that's the way the world works."

He sighed his disapproval. "Personally, I think it's a Fae's job to fix what's broken in the world. Don't you?"

I didn't know what he expected me to say. "Whatever, man."

Reina
TWENTY-FIVE

Miranda stood in front of my dorm room with a smirk that said she knew something I didn't.

"I'll let you settle in," she said. "Cheer up," she added.

I forced a half smile and opened the door to find myself smack in the middle of some bizarre ritual. My nose was assaulted with a spicy aroma I couldn't place. The layout of the dorm was plain enough, but the left side of the room was draped with black webbed fabric and littered with lit candles. It looked like Halloween threw up in there. On the free bed, the one that was supposedly mine, stood a girl with two purple pigtails tied up with black ribbon. She was wearing a school uniform but her blazer was slung over her bed—a pop of red in a sea of black. It looked like she was burning scraps of paper and releasing them into the air above my mattress.

"Uh... hi," I said sheepishly.

She spun, nearly losing her balance. "Oh good, you're here," she said, "I thought I'd smudge the place for you before you got here. I thought I felt something nasty pass through earlier."

"Smudge?"

She looked more confused than I was. "Yeah. Smudge, to rid this room of evil spirits."

I nodded. "Oh. Of course," I said, too tired to inquire further. "Thank you. I'm Reina, by the way."

"Briara," she said, hopping off the bed. She threw her arms around me and held me like a long-lost relative.

"What's that smell?" I asked as a strong whiff of spice hit my nose.

She pulled away. "Sage. You have so much to learn."

I walked over to my bed, collapsing onto the bare mattress. I didn't believe any of that spirit stuff, but I wasn't going to let something so harmless bother me. One less thing to worry about. I was too tired for pleasantries and too emotionally drained from my hospital stay to put together more than a couple of words.

"Are you okay?" she asked.

I groaned. "I have to pee."

"The bathroom is at the end of the hall."

I dragged myself back up and out the door, slogging toward our floor's communal bathroom. As I walked, I sorted through my odd first impression of my new roommate. Rituals and spirits. Eh, she had her own style. Miranda's smirk insinuated I was in for a ride, but she should have considered I was a tad offbeat myself. It wasn't until I returned to my room that my opinion of Briara was cemented. While I was gone, she'd put a spare sct of black sheets and blankets on my bed. I felt a wave of regret for not hugging her more sincerely the first time, but I hugged her again this time with every ounce of gratitude I could muster because my drowsy mind could not find the words.

She patted my back and watched me lay on my new bed, pleased with her work as I snuggled in, gripping my charm. I felt something hard beneath my pillow and reached under to find the smooth object. I held it up to the candlelight. It was some kind of crystal or stone. I looked over at Briara and she shrugged. I smiled as I shoved it back under my pillow. *It couldn't hurt.*

When I awoke, I felt like a new person. The bulk of the year's sea of suppressed sorrow had ebbed, I found myself feeling grateful that I'd gotten time with my parents at all and that they'd continued to guide me. Wherever they were, they must've pulled some serious strings to get me into GFA.

"Ah. You're awake." I sat up, and Briara sat on her bed, sipping a cup of tea that steamed in front of her face.

"Oh, you have a heat gift?" I asked.

She shook her head. "Hot pot." She pointed to a silver pot that had a black base and a wire that was plugged in beside her laptop. "I can mess with radio waves, you know, if I'm touching something already connectable."

My eyes widened. "Can you, like, intercept messages?"

"Really? That's where your mind goes first? Most people here call me wifi girl because I'm the only one on campus who can connect."

"Oh," I said, brushing the sleep from my eyes. "But that's so cool, though. You must be one of the most powerful students here."

She shrugged. "So glad you think so. But that's not the general consensus. Elites are chosen mostly by flash. I'll easily get an apprenticeship, but I'll likely be in some office intercepting waves instead of smashing bad guys like Oden Gates."

I moved back to lean against my wall. "Briara, right? Can I apologize for yesterday? And possibly thank you for... just everything?"

"Don't mention it," she said. "I put your class schedule on your desk, there."

I jolted forward. "Class? Fuck!" I hopped out of bed. "Oh my god, I'm going to be late on my first day."

"Uh... Reina, it's Sunday." There was a yarn spider web pinned to the wall above her bed and a sudden memory of her seance slipped through. I smiled to myself and exhaled my panic.

"Do you want to hang out today?"

She lowered her teacup. "Really? I didn't freak you out last night with all my... you know... ritual?"

I scoffed. "As far as I'm concerned, your ritual was being exceedingly kind and forgiving of my poor manners."

She walked across the room and sat at the edge of my bed, her face turned away like she was trying not to say something. "May I ask what your gift is?"

"You can, but I don't know what it is yet."

She shook her head. "What do you mean?"

"I haven't figured out what my gift is. Ms. Yarrow said—"

"You've met Ms. Yarrow?"

I nodded.

"Beautiful, right?"

I chuckled. "Stunning."

"So they let you in without knowing? I have to admit your schedule is... a little strange. Even for a sophomore, you have too many studies. They probably don't think you'll learn much in regular class without a gift. What about the new guy?"

"His gift is levitation," I said, Kai's kiss shooting back into my mind.

She spit her tea, snapping my attention back to her. "Sorry," she said with a grin. "Everyone knows his gift. I guess I was asking how well you know him."

I swallowed a lump in my throat, burying an ache in my chest. "Hardly."

Kaito

TWENTY-SIX

I didn't know why, but I couldn't get Zane Blaque out of my head. The more I thought about it, the more I knew I wasn't mistaken. He was the guy I saw at the bus station, the one whose tattoo was somehow linked to the death of Raphael Mazarin. It didn't make him a killer per se, but his chilling smile had me convinced he was involved. That theory was shot to hell when a few minutes after I'd last seen him, rumors began to circulate that another Fae was found dead on the far side of Ancetol. The only teleportation gifts were through Gemini Gates. So, unless he had a twin across town, he was most certainly innocent. Still, it couldn't hurt to look into the guy.

A knock at my door halted Carter's guitar, which had become such a fixture in my life in a few short days that I felt uncomfortable in the silence. I even felt myself craving the calming effect of his gift. I opened my door to find Prince Finn

Warsham. It was hard not to be starstruck. I didn't care much about his title, but last year in the Varsity Games, he'd picked up a spear and pinned his opponent to the wall, just two inches from the finish line. *Two inches.* I knew specifically because after the games they measured the exact spot. He'd swept the round but didn't fare as well in the other events. Still, that moment had always stuck with me as the most exciting of the Games that year. Now that I was at GFA, I'd get my chance to compete in next year's games which was the biggest perk GFA had to offer.

I stared blankly. "Uh… Your Highness?"

He grimaced. "Just Finn, please."

Quan Levout stepped between us, wrapping his arms around me. I froze while he gave me a tight squeeze, nearly pulling me off my feet as his lime-colored hair tickled my chin.

"Uh… okay," I mumbled.

Quan dropped me and stepped back, beaming. "Man, you were awesome in that fight. Oden's arm was pretty messed up. You were just like BAM BOOM! And he was all like whaaaa?"

Finn rolled his eyes. "Oden wanted me to check to make sure you're going to the fort this afternoon."

"I don't know what that is."

"Carter knows," he said, nodding to my seemingly uninterested roommate. "Bruh, will you show the new guy to the spot?" he said, his voice smooth and low.

"You got it, man," Carter said without looking up.

Carter was a homebody and therefore seemed a little apprehensive about leaving the dorm to help me get on the internet, so these guys were my best shot. "Do either of you know how I can get online?"

Quan nodded. "You trying to check your new status? It's all over the internet, man. You're officially one of us. No doubt you'll get a sick internship next summer."

He rattled on and I turned to Finn for help.

Finn shrugged. "There's wifi at the fort, but we don't go out there until nightfall. If you want to get online now, Quan's really the only one with a workaround for security into Pink House."

"I'll hook you up, man! It's going to be so dope. I'll, like, get you in and then you can, like, make me fly and shit in front of Miranda and you know, like, she'll be all into me and whatnot."

I rubbed my hands together, mimicking his enthusiasm. "Let's do this."

Quan's eyes lit and I followed them outside, giving Carter a quick nod before I went. Quan pulled me to the side of the girls' dorm, away from the front entrance and security desk. He pulled off his gloves and slid them into his pockets. He took a nervous breath before he reached for my hand.

"Are you afraid?" I asked, trying to read him.

He laughed. "No man. I mean, you're cool and we're friends and stuff. You wouldn't… you know, like toss me around or anything."

It amused me, but the moment he took my hand I regretted not giving his gift more thought before it was upon me. I felt my form shift along with his. My body bent and contorted in his power. I felt my hair reach my lower back and new unbalanced weight on my chest. Before my eyes, Quan changed into the girl I'd seen earlier with Zane Blaque. He now had a delicate face with purple pigtails, his skin paler, his waist smaller until there wasn't a trace left of his real self. I was suddenly wracked with anxiety when I realized he'd transformed me into Reina. This was so messed up. Panicked, I tried to yank my hand away, but he tightened his grip.

"Relax, man," he said. "It's no big deal."

"Pick someone else for me to be. Anyone else," I said, but Reina's voice came out. "It's too weird to be Reina." I patted my new body, unable to reconcile its appearance with how I felt. "And I don't think her ass is this big."

Quan held up his phone and Reina's black lace underwear moved across the screen.

My eyes bulged. "How did you find out about that?"

He laughed. "As soon as she got in, this video went viral on campus. I'm pretty sure every guy here has it saved to their phone."

I swallowed a lump in my throat. "This is so pervy."

Quan smirked. "You have no idea."

I yanked my hand out of his and wiped it on my pant leg. "Hard no on this mission."

He grinned. "Don't act like you wouldn't do it."

I turned to head back to my dorm.

"Wait, wait, while we're on the subject, what's it like to have sex in zero G?"

I bit back a smile. It was a question I'd been asked by guys and the occasional girl a lot in the last couple of years. I sighed, leaning in so I could whisper my answer. "It's terrible."

His face lit. "Really?"

I nodded. "Gravity is one hundred percent necessary."

He shook his head. "Damn. Way to ruin the fantasy."

I shrugged.

"Look," he said, "nothing weird. We're just going to disguise ourselves as the girls, sneak past security, and ask Briara to connect you to the wifi."

I sighed in resignation and reached out for his outstretched hand. Reina's form once again formed on my body. "Kaito, you're so strong," I said with Reina's voice.

Quan snickered. "Who's the pervert now?"

Reina
TWENTY-SEVEN

I eyed my schedule warily. There were so many teachers I'd hoped to see on it, but Briara was right, it was nearly empty. I supposed you couldn't infuse confections with an ability if you had none, nor face-off with classmates in combat, but I hoped to have something.

All I saw listed on it was a general studies class with a professor I'd never heard of, a history class with a professor listed as "To Be Determined," and Gift Defense, which I immediately deemed my most interesting one. The rest of the day was a blank sea of independent studies with no professor at all broken up only by a lunch break. I was confident that GFA, with its incredible reputation, knew what they were doing. If anyone could bring out the gift in me, it was the greatest Fae academy in the world.

A knock at my door put me instantly on edge. I looked up to Briara who seemed to ask with her gaze if I'd been expecting someone. I shrugged and stood, hoping it wasn't Miranda as I reached to open the door.

I sucked in a sharp breath as I stood face to face with myself and Briara. Their hands were clasped together, a strange gesture that surely meant a gift was to blame. Stunned, I eyed my clone closely, the image slightly older than how I thought I looked. Briara's clone was spot-on accurate, which made me believe that mine must've been too.

"What the hell is this?" I said, trying unsuccessfully to cloak the uneasiness in my words. I backed away.

"Oh," Briara said. "Let them in, they're here for me." She put down her cup of tea. "Close the door."

I obeyed, but my mind seemed dead set on the possibility that we were about to be murdered and replaced with our unexpected doppelgangers.

The two silent girls stepped in and dropped their hands. Their features melted away, the deformed mixture giving way to their true forms. I nearly squealed when I saw Briara's purple hair change to the most famous green. "Holy shit," I said, practically hyperventilating. "You're Quan Levout." Duh, it was obvious. Everyone knew about his transforming ability after the stunt he pulled at the Varsity Tournament. Still, I hardly expected him to visit.

"Sup, girl," he said with a nod.

I blushed, but that was nothing compared to the heat that rushed my face when I realized that the clone of me was actually Kai, who now stood inches from my bed. I gulped. What was more horrifying, that Kaito was just in my body or that he was currently in my dorm room? With the dorms separated by gender, I'd completely let my guard down. Of course, Kai's new crew had a way into Pink House, but what were they doing *here?*

Kai watched my mental flips with a satisfied grin then turned to Briara. "Hi," he said. "I'm sorry to barge in like this. I'm Kaito Nakamaru."

My mind got foggy and Briara also seemed to lose her words until finally she uttered, "Yeah, I know. Are you here for wifi?"

Quan looked around, unsettled by Briara's spooky decor. "He's new. You know, wants to check his status and stuff. I was thinking that after you hook him up, you and I could grab lunch or something."

Briara rolled her eyes.

Kai tilted his head and gave a Prince Charming smile that turned Bri's face a deeper shade of crimson than Veranda Yarrow's hair. I couldn't help her. I was frozen, half a second from burying my face in my pillow until they left.

"No problem," Bri said. "Give me your phone."

Kai held out his phone and, even with gloves on, she hesitated to take it. Then she sat back in her chair and pulled off her gloves, resting Kai's phone on her palm.

We all waited for something to happen, but Bri's gift wasn't flashy. It hardly looked like she'd done anything at all. A moment later, she put her gloves back on and handed the phone to Kai.

"That's about twenty minutes. Use them well."

Out of the corner of my eye, I saw a weighted look pass between Kai and Quan.

Quan leaned in and began to whisper to Briara. I bit my bottom lip to stop my nerves from spilling as Kai's gaze moved across my side of the room.

Briara's voice shot out, "But she sa—" Her voice cut and Quan leaned back into her, making her giggle. She looked up at me, her eyebrows raised and her lips pressed together.

What? What was she trying to say? I unfortunately didn't know her very well, certainly not well enough to figure out what was going on.

"Fine!" Briara said, loud enough for us all to hear. "I'll go to lunch with you." She turned to Kai. "If you stick around, I'll charge your wifi one more time when I get back."

"Wai—" Before more of my objection reached my lips, they left, or should I say Bri left with a clone of me. I turned to Kaito, my stomach knotted with butterflies, my mind screaming scenarios.

I wasn't sure if Quan was trying to get Bri alone, or if Kai was trying to get me alone, but either way I found myself alone again with Kai. My instincts told me to run, but I was too curious to obey. Kai smirked at me and lay in my bed. My breath caught in my throat.

"Oh, relax," he said, laying back. "We both knew I'd end up here eventually."

"What are you doing?"

He inhaled slowly, delighting in the torment of his delayed response. "I just came to use the internet."

I nodded, crossing my arms.

"Have a seat," he said, tapping the bed. "You've been in my bed a hundred times."

I nodded. "But this is the first time you've been in mine."

He laughed. "Your parents would have—" His smile dropped. "Sorry."

I shook my head, taking a seat at the end of the bed. "It's okay. I'm feeling a little better today."

Sensing my need to change the subject, he sat up and leaned against the wall. "Do you remember the day Raphael Mazarin died?"

"Yeah, you walked me to the bus stop."

"Yeah, well… before I left, I saw this weird guy. He had blue hair and a tattoo similar to the mark they found at the scene. He had this creepy smile and he kind of drew my attention to the news." He shook his head and looked down at his phone. "I don't know, Rei. It was like he was bragging about it or something."

"You should report that, Kai."

"Thing is, I saw him again here. His name is Zane Blaque. I confronted him and he had no tattoos and acted like he never saw me at the bus station."

"Are you sure it's the same guy?"

He nodded. "I'm at least 50% sure."

I bit back a laugh. "Well, 50% may as well be 100%."

He smiled. "Don't be a jerk, Reina."

I took a deep breath and crossed my arms. "Just admit you wanted to check out what the internet is saying about you."

He lifted his phone and the screen read *Kaito Nakamaru joins GFA Nobles after duel with Oden Gates.*

"Catchy. Maybe, just this one time, you can just chill out and enjoy your time at school. You know, be a normal high school boy for once."

He leaned closer. "Really? And what would a normal high school boy do in this situation?"

A sweet scent filled my nose as he inched closer. It reminded me of cinnamon and made my mouth water. *Deja vu.* I felt Kai about to strap me in for another go at the emotional roller-coaster. I stood breathless and flushed. Was this some kind of joke? Why was he hitting on me? It could only be a trick. "I think I prefer your old way of bullying."

"What do you mean?"

"You're confusing me," I said.

He smiled and stood. "I don't know, I like seeing you like this." As he stared down at me, I could scarcely see the boy I knew so well. This one was a mystery, a dangerous one. He was going to hurt me, and this time would be much worse than the others.

"Like what?"

"Just, the look on your face. I can't tell if you want me or if you're scared."

"Neither can I."

A knock at the door broke the silence. I opened it and my stomach dropped to find Miranda at the door. "Where's Briara? I need wifi," she said. Her gaze lifted to Kaito and her expression brightened.

"She's not here," I said, but she pushed passed me like I wasn't there.

"Are you here for wifi too, Kaito?"

"Sure am," he said. And I felt a twinge of regret that I hadn't seized my moment with him. It was like Miranda had boy radar.

"I'll wait with you," she said, pulling him to sit beside her on my bed.

She giggled and whispered something to him that made his eyebrows shoot up.

I heard him say back, "Everyone always asks that."

The urge to flee slammed into me. "I don't need wifi. I'm going to go grab some lunch," I said, moving to the door.

But instead of a response, Kaito leaned into Miranda and whispered something else.

Fickle, unreliable asses—they were perfect for each other. And that's what I told myself as I swallowed my jealousy. I went to lunch alone, reminding myself every chance I got that he wouldn't have been worth the tears.

Kaito

TWENTY-EIGHT

Carter gripped the strap of his guitar as we made our way through the school's underground tunnels. He explained, "This is all within the barrier of the school, but back when Lannon Gainsboro was a student here, he cloaked the memory of this part to everyone but the students who attend here, so we can pretty much do what we want."

"Does that include him?"

He shrugged. "Probably. I mean, he hasn't returned to undo it. Maybe when he graduated his gift cloaked his memory of it too."

We'd been walking for some time and there was still no end in sight. The tunnels were well lit and cheerfully decorated with spray-painted murals of famous Fae and line art.

I stopped when I got to the image of Yemoja Roux. "Why do they call this place the fort? Do people fight there?"

"Chill, man. I hope you're not planning on starting something. I mean… didn't you prove yourself or whatever to Oden? You're not going to try and get revenge or something, right?"

I shook my head and continued walking when I noticed several more murals starred Yemoja Roux. It was no surprise that she was so popular among the other students. She was popular around the earth.

Carter continued. "Most people are just glad we have a place to hang out unsupervised that they don't risk starting anything at the fort. The combat zones are enough to keep people who need to battle it out satisfied. The fort is mostly for parties and hooking up."

"You didn't answer my question about the name," I said, but he only smirked. Thirty minutes later, when the tunnel finally let out, I understood why.

I stood before a grassy plain filled with students and music. It had huge slates of broken gray walls that rose and fell through the uneven hill. There was an inner wall with a tower and a labyrinth of open air paths which held the bulk of the forty or so students, as well as a table with bottles of liquor and rainbow-colored mixers. My gaze moved to the larger wall that ran along the edge of the ocean, where several couples sat together and gazed out at the sea. Even in their poor condition, I could tell it was made of the ruins of some forgotten coastal fort whose better days seemed long since passed. The sun had just begun to droop low, reaching out across a turbulent ocean and rigid hostile environment. I tried in vain not to notice that one of the GFA students was missing from the night's festivities.

"Carter!" We followed the voice to see a petite blonde girl in a knotted spaghetti strap top hustle over, her bare stomach and low-cut shirt a delightful alert that no one here was in uniform.

I technically was wearing mine, but the way I'd rolled up my sleeves and kept it mostly unbuttoned could hardly be considered uniform. The girl grinned. "Oh my god, Carter, I can't believe you're here!" she said. "You *have* to do the music."

He turned to me and nodded with a satisfied smile that I understood completely before he followed the girl to the fort's only tower. I didn't want to wander around the party looking for someone I knew, so I turned my sights to the outer wall. I walked up the slow incline as the uneven rocks beneath me were nearly five feet wide. Even with the waves crashing against the wall, it was completely solid and, with such a wide width, it was hard to imagine someone being dumb enough to fall off. I threw a hand in my pocket as I walked easily past a couple who were so engrossed in their conversation they didn't even notice me pass. The ocean seemed alive and wild, as if in warning of a storm, but even though the clouds grew darker, no one at the party seemed to worry about rain.

I continued to the highest point on the wall, the furthest corner from where I entered, and I could see that the school's boundaries didn't extend far into the ocean. I estimated it to be about twenty feet, based on the usual movement of the ocean's waves at that exact point, on the far side of the wall. To my left, the wall turned back and sloped to the inner fort on the opposite side, where I spotted another couple who leaned in for a kiss. The salty air reminded me of the days I spent with Reina at the pier. I wished I could go back to that first kiss and redo everything, but I wasn't sure what I would do differently. Surely, if I'd protected her and made a spectacle out of her situation, she would have been targeted more. I sighed, but perhaps I didn't need to enjoy tormenting her. It was obvious she found me attractive. I could see it in her face. But lots of girls did—

even Miranda. Why then did the prospect of messing around with Miranda seem so simple and easy and with Reina seem so consequential? Why did my mind linger on her, despite knowing it would be a terrible idea?

My gaze was drawn to a fleeting movement in my peripheral vision. I snapped my eyes to the water just in time to see a black object break the surface of a wave, just on the other side of the school's barrier. I leaned forward and squinted. What was it? Some kind of claw? A hand touched my shoulder. I yelled, nearly jumping from my skin. I slipped off the edge of the wall. Stunned, I caught myself in my gift and rose to face a stunned Oden who looked like he'd accidentally murdered me.

"Dude," he said. "I'm so sorry. I didn't mean to scare you. I just came to say hi."

"I saw something. There," I said, pointing to the black mass.

Oden leaned forward, squinting. "What is it?"

"I don't know."

He turned to me. "Maybe seaweed on a rock or something. In any case, it's on the outside, so don't worry about it."

I nodded, shaking the worry off my face.

"Glad you could make it," he said. "Let's get you a drink."

Reina
TWENTY-NINE

Briara clung to my arm as we walked through the party, and I didn't mind one bit. It was also my first real party, and it was nice to have someone around who shared my apprehension. It was much warmer at the fort than it should have been for the season, and I wondered if someone was somehow regulating it. More than anything, I wanted to avoid the first awkward moments of mingling, so instead, I took in the coastline and the beautiful gray structure that hosted the party.

There was a good collection of students standing around with red cups in hand. "Okay," Bri said, "if I don't leave here with a boyfriend, you've failed as a roommate."

I grinned. "Okay, so if you see a guy you want, say dibs. That way we both know he's yours and I know to help you snag him."

"Got it."

My attention snapped to a quick movement that sent my heart fluttering. "*Enzo McCain,*" I said in a daze.

At the base of the wall, Enzo zipped from one group to the other, distributing something that was too far to see. His speed was even more impressive in person than it was when broadcasted in the Varsity Tournament. He occasionally bent down to touch his shoes to keep them in range. I sighed. If only I had a gift that special. The high I'd been riding from learning that I had a gift that was somehow similar to Yemoja Roux had worn off in the week that had passed. I still felt unremarkable—more so when in the presence of students who would certainly become Fae.

Briara laughed. "At some point, you're going to have to learn not to be so starstruck. They're ordinary boys."

I smiled, eyeing Enzo's slick hair and confident smile. "They are anything but. They are literally going to save the world."

She squeezed my arm. "Trust me. They're just boys," she said, following Enzo with her gaze. "They'll hook up with you and never speak to you again like all the rest." She turned to me, her purple eyes cutting. "Don't fall for it."

"I mean… I'll do my best, but like… just *look* at them."

In a flash, Enzo was standing beside us and I nearly choked on my breath. He held out two multicolored shots. "Sunset shots."

I lifted the shot to examine it. "What's a sunset shot?"

"Reina, right?" he said, and his eyes flickered to Briarā, sending a pink tinge to her cheeks. "When the sun hits the horizon, everyone here will take the shot to kick off the party."

"The party hasn't kicked off yet?"

He put his arm around me, like we were old friends. "Not by a mile." He pointed up to the barrier that domed the entire area.

"You see the protection? Notice anything different about it than back on campus?"

I eyed it. "It's see through?"

He beamed. "Yep. We can see out to the ocean, the temperature is regulated, and when it hits sunset, it'll light up in wild colors and patterns, shifting the theme of the party as it goes."

"No way."

He leaned closer. "Way. Students have been infusing this sector of the barrier for years with their gifts, kind of like the professors do with the main campus."

He had an ease about him, a confidence and familiarity I envied. I wanted to ask a question about the barrier to keep him for another minute, but before I could, he turned to the next group. "I gotta make sure everyone has a shot in hand before sunset. I'll catch up with you ladies a little later."

Briara cut in, "Hope so."

Before he left, Enzo pointed to two figures walking toward us. I gulped—Kaito and Oden Gates. Kai seemed at ease, engrossed in conversation with Oden, a halo of red cups floating around him, and one in his hand that he sipped on every few steps. *Subtle, Kai.* Oden strutted around like Kai was the finest jewel in his crown. The two of them were such a sight that I had no hope of tearing my gaze away.

Briara leaned in and whispered, "Starstruck."

"Bri... LOOK AT THEM."

We burst into laughter, nearly spilling our shots, when the two high school gods made it over to us. "What did we miss?" Oden asked.

But one exchanged glance between me and Bri and we erupted back into a fit of laughter.

I straightened, mustering as much confidence as I could.

Perhaps if I mimicked Enzo's attitude, I'd feel more comfortable. "What's up guys?" I asked.

Oden's face teemed with delight. "Why are you two all the way over here?"

"We hadn't made our way in yet," I said.

Briara added, "We just got here."

Kai smirked. "First party, Rei?"

Damnit, Kai. I nodded, shyness wiping away my attempts at confidence.

Oden leaned forward. "Really? That's adorable. Okay, you girls need a drink."

I lifted the multicolored shot. "I have one."

"You can't drink that until sunset." He turned to his friend. "Kai?"

Two of the cups floating above Kai drifted down and hovered in front of Bri and me. We exchanged a glance then took the cup from the air.

"Thanks," Bri said.

Oden grinned. "Bottoms up."

I lifted the drink to my lips. After one gulp, the sting burned the back of my throat. Bewildered, I dropped my hand, but the cup remained in Kai's grasp, pouring into my mouth. It leaked from the corners of my mouth and I swallowed hard, my eyes watering until the cup was empty.

What the hell, Kai? I opened my mouth to scold him but Bri beat me to it.

"You're such a dick. I almost spilled on my shirt," Bri said.

Oden and Kai laughed. "It's all in good fun," Oden said. "Now you guys are ready to party."

Enzo rushed passed us and Briara's gaze followed. She leaned into me and whispered, "Dibs."

"Dibs?" Oden said, looking around. "On who? I was just telling Kai here that I had dibs on Reina."

I choked on nothing. My face burned with heat and I wasn't sure if it was from the drink I'd just downed or Oden's comment. I thought I'd drop dead on the spot, avoiding eye contact at all costs.

Suddenly, the barrier burst into a cascade of colors sparkling down from the top like fireworks. I gaped, half impressed and half happy to escape the awkwardness of the moment before. The color swirled around me, the alcohol hitting my stomach.

"Cheers," Oden said, and I looked up to see the three of them holding up their shots. I looked down at mine. I had no clue what was in it, nor what was in store for me that night, but just this once it didn't matter. I wanted an adventure. I deserved a night of fun. So I raised the rainbow shot and clinked it with theirs before I downed it.

Kaito

THIRTY

I awoke with a sharp pain cutting through my head and a ringing in my ears that had me disoriented. I felt a weight on my chest and peeked my eyes open, but the light slipped in and my head flared with pain. *Fuck*. After several minutes of trying to convince myself that if I was in pain, I must be alive, my headache dulled enough for me to realize how thirsty I was. My throat tightened with dryness and I waited until my desire for water overtook my pain, and ventured to open my eyes again. This time, I saw Miranda laying on my chest. She had a face full of fresh makeup and was peeking through her eyelashes to check if I was awake. *Water*. Nothing mattered but water.

I moved up to my elbows, taking it slow, and Miranda pretended to wake up. I looked around the room; we were in my dorm room, but there was no sign of Carter.

"Good morning, sleepy head," Miranda said, her chipper voice confirming my theory that she was already awake. "You were great last night. That whole thing you said about zero gravity wasn't true at all. Maybe you just haven't had the right partner before me." She dropped my blanket, exposing her chest.

I gulped. "Water."

I stepped out of bed, my memories moving back to me at a glacial pace. I stepped on a used condom and jerked my foot back, scanning the ground where I saw another. *Ugh*. I felt the alcohol slosh in my stomach and threaten to surge. I was slimy, naked, and looked down to see I was still wearing a condom. At least we were safe, though I couldn't imagine how I ended up with Miranda. Then the memory slammed into me like a truck. Oden's tongue practically down Reina's throat on the dance floor. So much from the night before was unclear—lost—but not that. That one memory rang clear as a bell. I remembered the pain that assaulted me and found no release as they spent the night holding hands and exchanging secrets.

A wave of nausea threatened to splurge out on my floor.

"Are you okay?" Miranda asked.

I stood and slipped on a pair of shorts before wordlessly moving to the hallway toward the men's bathroom. I turned the faucet and splashed a handful of cold water on my face. I hadn't been the only one grinding my teeth at the sight of them. Miranda had been too. When they approached us, hands clasped together like an actual couple, Miranda and I got the same idea. I slung my arm over her in hopes of returning the feelings of jealousy Reina had caused, and Miranda played her part splendidly for Oden. I sighed and knew exactly where that led. The running water became the background music to my thoughts as a sickening thought occurred to me. What if Reina woke up this morning in Oden's bed? I turned, desperate to reach the toilet before the vomit spewed from me. I felt a gentle hand on my back.

"Are you alright, man? Can I get you something?"

I turned to see Oden looking well-rested and composed in his unwrinkled uniform, a backpack slung over his shoulder.

I wiped my mouth, hoping I could rally what had already become an awkward morning. "I'm fine," I said.

"Quan just walked Miranda from your room. He said she was naked as shit when he knocked. Nice, bro."

I had a hundred questions of my own in regards to his night, but none I wanted the answers to.

"You better pull your shit together, though. Class starts in thirty. I'm headed to Reina's dorm to walk her."

I clenched my jaw, but it was no use; the words spilled out. "Oh yeah. I forgot you were with her. How'd that go?"

"Good, good. I'm taking it slow. You know, she's a virgin." He shrugged and I hoped he'd stop there, but he didn't. "I really like her. I think she may be the real deal. You know, like, a good person and all that. She has no idea how special she is."

I wanted to vomit on him, to douse the joy and excitement from his face, but before I could he hurried out of the bathroom, leaving me to my recovery and my thoughts. It was supposed to be my first day at GFA, which was everything I'd ever wanted. I'd spent my night having sex with the hottest girl at the school, so why did I feel so hurt?

Reina

THIRTY-ONE

I lay awake, practically holding my breath until the sun rose. What a night. What a beautiful, perfect night. The moment I entered the party, Oden did nothing but give me his full attention. He was gentle, attentive, and unfailingly kind—all the things Kai was not. How had I been so mistaken? How had I spent so many years confusing misery with love? My time with Oden had been a dream, and I lay awake all night with the fear I'd wake to a new reality. We talked, we danced, we kissed, and when the night was over, we walked hand in hand back to the dorms where he said his goodbyes. It was a perfect night. One I knew I'd relive in my imagination again and again.

I'd been so caught off guard by his attention that I asked him why he was interested. And he responded that he had been from the moment we met. Looking back, I remembered how he'd been the reason I got into GFA to begin with. How he'd kissed my cheek. He explained again, though not in any great detail, that my gift felt like Yemoja Roux and that he knew I'd be great one day.

Oden was everything good. I was crushing hard, and why not? He was so unlike Kai, who was virtually made of warning signs. Yet I found my mind continuously comparing the two.

"My fucking head hurts!" Bri said. I rolled over to see her also awake. "Last night was awesome. Thank you for making me go."

"Thank you for going. You and Enzo looked cozy."

She sat up and winced, bringing her hand to her head. "Right? I think he might like me." Her eyes bulged. "You and Oden were like… *in love.*"

I smiled, turning back to the ceiling.

She continued. "Neither of you spoke to anyone else. Are you guys, like, official?"

"What do you mean?"

"Did he ask you to be his girlfriend?"

I shook my head, but inside I was delighted by the thought. "I hardly know him."

"Look, normally people like each other and then they date. Don't try to mimic whatever you had going on with Kai. I mean… like each other, and then go to war for ten years. Maybe this Oden thing will be good for you. Besides…"

"Besides what?"

She lay back. "Nevermind."

I furrowed my brow. "No, what is it?"

"I'm ninety-nine percent sure he had sex with Miranda last night."

I rolled over toward my wall and pressed my forehead against the cold surface. "Sounds about right," I said, but I swallowed a lump in my throat as fresh tears pricked my eyes.

Later that morning, I put on my school uniform, a flutter of pride and fear swirling inside me. I wondered what my parents might say to me on my first day.

This was it. My chance to see what I was made of. This was my only hope of reaching my dream, and I found myself equally afraid that they wouldn't be able to make Fae out of me, and that they would.

I walked with my arm hooked around Briara's as we made our way to the front of Pink House. I was glad to have her, an ally in an otherwise uncertain world. We stepped out into the morning air, which was cold and wet, and Briara lifted her eyebrows, dropping her arm from mine. "I'll see you later," she said, hurrying off before I could protest.

Confused, I looked up to see Oden standing with a smile. He was a solid ten on a normal day, but in his uniform, he was easily an eleven. "Can I walk you to class?" he asked.

I nodded and walked over to him. He leaned in and kissed my cheek like he had the first time we met. Any lingering thought that his affection last night had been alcohol-induced vanished. I fell into stride beside him, hooking my thumbs on my backpack straps to avoid the awkwardness of whether we would hold hands or not.

"You look nervous?" he said.

"I am. I'm shaking," I said with a smile.

"Me too."

I recoiled. "You're the top student. Why are you nervous?"

He wrapped his arm around me. "You."

I rolled my eyes. "Cute." But it *was* cute. *He* was cute and *I* was in trouble.

"Look," he said, "you're going to be great today. I know for a fact that this will be the best day of your life."

"Oh? And who's going to make it so?"

He pressed his lips together and a dimple cut through his cheek. "You'll see. When the moment comes, when you're so happy you could cry, I want you to think, 'Oden was right, I should kiss him.'"

We laughed. A throat cleared and I looked up to see a sickly Kaito leering at the pair of us. His eyes had dark circles, his cheeks were a little sunken in, and his skin was so pale that he looked like a sexy vampire. The memory of Briara's update ran through my head. Kaito and Miranda. I sighed, hoping to exhale the pain of it.

"Alright, well," Oden said, drawing my attention, "good luck today."

"Yeah, you too."

Kai passed without a word and I felt a pang of guilt that Oden's smile dimmed when he saw me looking at Kai. *Let Kaito go.*

I walked into the class hall and found it's interior looked similar to the front office building. It had wooden floors and maroon carpets, only this building was packed with students in their distinctive GFA uniforms. I would have given anything to get a picture, but I remembered the first time I tried, how nothing but a black screen showed.

Across the room, a girl with one long, yellow braid stared at me. Her arms were crossed, her face expressionless, but her demeanor was unkind. I ventured to wave, but she didn't move. I passed through the hall, my eyes searching the classroom numbers for mine, when I saw a second girl with a similar scowl. Then another and another, until it felt like every girl at GFA had a bone to pick with me. Was it in my head? Had my nerves gotten the best of me? I rushed through the hallway in hopes that my classroom would offer salvation and hurried in, although most students seemed to be chatting outside the classrooms, waiting for the bell.

The classroom was ordinary in size and shape, but had a row of large windows on one side that stretched from the floor to the incredibly high ceilings. The morning light that poured in instantly quelled my nerves. I sat at an empty desk by the window. There were four other students already seated, a girl who doodled in her notebook and three guys who seemed half asleep. My stomach dropped when the girl with the yellow braid walked in, her eyes immediately locking on me. I turned and looked out the window with the hope that she'd leave me alone, but to my dismay, she sat down beside me.

Ignoring her, I scanned the courtyard outside, watching late students jog toward the school's front steps.

"So you're Reina?" a voice said.

I turned to the girl. "Yes, and you are?"

"Not impressed."

I shook my head. "Have I offended you?"

She grinned as if she'd been hoping I'd ask. "I guess it's your sense of entitlement."

"What?"

"This school has a hierarchy, and you completely disregard it."

Oh boy. "I can actually feel myself getting dumber from this conversation."

"Oden Gates is an Elite Noble. First in our class and king of the school. You're just a Serf. If you know what's good for you, you'll back off."

"And he'll realize you're more his speed."

I could see the wicked retort brewing in her smug face.

"Actually," she said, "I feel inadequate because, even without a known gift, you've captured the attention of my crush who I know will never want me, especially when I do petty shit like this." Her eyes bulged.

What the fuck? I couldn't say I expected that, but the look on the girl's face said she wasn't expecting to say that either.

A tall figure walked into the classroom. "Please refrain from using your gift outside of the assigned zones, Ms. Bennett. Even if they're well deserved by your victim."

kaito
THIRTY-TWO

I tapped mindlessly on my desk as my history professor droned on. It wasn't that the topic itself wasn't interesting, it was. It was boring because, as the most perplexing time in human history, it was the era that every history class always focused on. It was like the time before gifts never even happened. Everyone knew that gifts first popped up nearly two hundred years ago, that the government had been struggling ever since to reform the laws to accommodate the vast variety of them, and that gifts in highly populated areas tended to be stronger, but what irked me the most was the syllabus outlined the Fae who emerged and the enemies they faced like they weren't already such legends, that every man, woman, and child knew the stories inside out.

"Kaito Nakamaru," the professor said, drawing my attention. "Your thoughts?" I searched the screen behind her for clues, which read only Population: 8 million.

"I'm sorry?"

"Why do you think the gifts are usually stronger in areas of high population?"

"The official consensus is that there is no connection between the higher population and the gift a person receives. The higher population gives proportionally more opportunity for powerful gifts to emerge."

The class giggled.

"We've already been over the official consensus. I'm wondering if you have another theory?"

I scanned the class. "Why me?"

"Mr. Nakamaru, if you're not going to participate, I wonder why you bothered to come."

A hand shot up and I turned to see Zane Blaque in the back row. His blue hair looked brighter against the maroon of his blazer. "I think it's like a disease," he said, without waiting for the teacher's permission.

The professor raised an eyebrow. "Interesting. Do elaborate."

Zane smiled. "Although humans, and especially Fae, enjoy and benefit greatly from their gifts, they have similar properties to a disease. They develop slightly different symptoms person-to-person, not everyone catches it, and the effects are stronger in highly populated areas."

She nodded. "I see, but our bodies don't reject this 'disease', as you've called it."

"Yes, they do. They reject other people's gifts when touched."

A knock sounded at the door before the professor could respond, and Zane looked pleased with himself. I had to admit it was an interesting theory, and the approving glances of the other students seemed to suggest they agreed. A gasp and shriek make me whirl to the front of the room. My heart slammed into my chest and, without thinking, I stood as a figure entered the room. *No fucking way.* Yemoja Roux. She was tall and muscular, with her trademark magenta hair and a slitted bodysuit that left little to the imagination. Her shoulders were broad, her legs thick and muscular like vine-wrapped tree trunks. Beneath her gloves I could tell her hands were small and dainty, while the rest of her form was nothing but a show of unequaled power. Her expression was calm but I could see laugh lines around her eyes and mouth, no doubt from the smile I'd seen in every one of her advertisements and interviews since I was born. A girl in the front row began to cry with reverence and I had to will myself not to follow.

Any doubts that I had about GFA being the greatest Fae school on the planet died the moment Yemoja Roux walked in. "Good afternoon," Yemoja said. And I held my breath.

"You may sit down, Mr. Nakamaru."

Yemoja Roux's gaze met mine and I dropped into my seat.

"And what are we discussing today, Mrs. Opaline?"

"Mr. Blaque here was giving us his theory about the effect of proximity on the potency of gifts."

Yemoja Roux nodded.

"Would you care to share your theory?"

She smiled and a wave of excited whispers echoed through the room. That smile was her signature, the one you could always see on her face when in battle. Even in the face of unspeakable evil, it never wavered. Even I felt dizzy from the sight of it as I contemplated just how lethal she actually was. I could hardly fight the urge to throw myself at her feet or praise her for her deeds. But what merit would my words be to someone like her?

"Certainly," she said, turning to the students. She spoke and her gaze was directed at each student for a short time before she moved to the next. "The more I observe varying gifts in battle, the more I come to believe that all humans tap into a shared energy. Closer proximity allows those connections to strengthen the connection we have with that energy. Since we all interact with the world in our own way, we also access the energy in our own way and thus evince different abilities." I hung on her every word, drinking in the inflection in her voice, fueling my dream to become a great Fae like her.

Zane's voice shot out. "Sounds like a bunch of religious mumbo jumbo to me."

All the air sucked from the room. Had he just openly disrespected the most beloved hero of our time? Nobody dared to move.

Yemoja Roux tilted her head with a playful grimace. "And what's your name, sir?"

"Zane."

"Zane what?"

"Zane Blaque."

Her eyes narrowed. "Blaque with a Q-U-E?" It was oddly specific.

He nodded.

"What's your gift, Mr. Blaque?"

"Shield."

She lowered her chin and put a hand on her hip. "And would you say you go through life defensively?"

"You don't know me," he spat.

I laughed too loudly, drawing the attention of the room. Yemoja winked at me. She'd made her point, though the rest of the room was too still for me to read if they found it as amusing as I did.

I tried Yemoja's theory on my own gift. I made things float… I didn't exactly float through life. In fact, I always found myself battling against my feelings. I did that with my parents, with my desire to attend GFA, to improve my rank, and now with Reina.

"It stands to reason you would battle gravity as well," Yemoja said.

What the fuck? I exhaled a shaky breath. Did she just read my mind?

"I'm not reading your mind, you're just thinking so loudly I'm sure everyone here can hear you."

My face burned, but I relished every second of attention from Yemoja Roux. I could only imagine how many lives would be lost just from her short visit.

I stood. "Sorry. Thank you. I love you. Do continue," I said. I threw my hand over my mouth. *Fuck. I just told Yemoja Roux I loved her.*

I held my breath in my seat as if that would somehow pass the moment faster.

She giggled, and I felt the sense of accomplishment that I had making my parents laugh as a kid. In those days, I would have done anything to amuse them. "Anyway," she said, "I'm here on official business as well as to speak with you about the Fae murders."

I shot a look back at Zane, half expecting to see a satisfied grin, only to find him as attentively listening like the others.

She continued. "Through anonymous tips and whispers online, we've discovered a connection between the murders—a terrorist group that are calling themselves The Fallen." She waved her hand in front of the screen, drawing a downward arrow. "This is their calling card. I would like to stress how important it is to report anything that you know to a teacher or the authorities. There are now six Fae dead."

Impossible. I had been so caught up with the party and my new status that I hadn't checked the news. Six Fae dead. It was impossible.

"Since they are targeting Fae in such close proximity to the school, and you're all such promising Fae in training, it's not out of the realm of possibility that they'll attack GFA."

"What? Are you serious?" a girl from the front row said.

Yemoja Roux nodded and continued. "There's no need to panic. We have Fae reinforcing the school's protections, but as a precaution, whether you're on campus or off, it's best you stay with a group. All of six of the deaths were from Fae who were working independently. Be vigilant and aware of your surroundings until we can take The Fallen out."

A guy at the front of the room shook his head. "That's crazy."

"One more thing. Based on the injuries found on the victims, sharp cuts and punctures, we have reason to suspect The Fallen are using non-human allies."

"Like attack dogs?" another student asked.

She shook her head. "We couldn't identify the species."

Zane leaned back in his chair. "So monsters then."

When Yemoja Roux didn't correct him, the room erupted into panicked conversation. This was a whole new kind of evil.

She only let the conversation go for a minute before she raised a hand to silence the class. "The government would rather I not share any of this information. I understand your concern, but if you're really here to become Fae, than your job is to overcome fear in order to protect those who can't protect themselves. Everyone in here is Elite gifted, but imagine being out there without the protection of a gift. Imagine the fear and helplessness of those less fortunate. I can't protect them forever, and the burden will fall to you. It is under these trying times when we learn who we really are. Only in tragedy can we rise to become great."

We sat in stunned silence as Yemoja watched us one by one. Zane Blaque clapped his hands loudly, jogging us from our daze. "Great speech. Really inspiring. Can I ask one thing?"

Our professor intervened. "Mr. Blaque, please see Headmistress Tricorn directly after class. And I'd appreciate it if you'd show Ms. Roux some respect for taking the time to speak with you today."

He looked both amused and shocked. "It was just a question. No one's allowed to question authority around here, apparently."

"Go ahead," Yemoja said, challenging him.

"How do you know The Fallen or whatever are terrorists?"

I slammed my fist down on the table, disgusted by his blatant disrespect. "She just said they killed six Fae," I barked through gritted teeth.

His glasses gleamed, and I'd never been more certain he was up to no good. Ignoring me, he turned back to Yemoja Roux, looking her dead in the eye. "So, you're saying you've never taken a life."

Silence filled the room.

I raised my hand but didn't wait to be called on. "I'd like to report a member of The Fallen," I said, pointing to Zane. "That guy."

The classroom giggled. "Settle down," the professor said. "Settle down."

Yemoja Roux shook her head, an easy smile on her face. But

it didn't reach her eyes. "Unfortunately, I have a lot of classrooms to hit before lunch. Thank you for your time, and Zane, thank you for your particularly enthusiastic participation."

She nodded to me, a gesture of gratitude, before she stepped out of the classroom.

Reina
THIRTY-THREE

The sudden shock and thrill of being reprimanded for using my own gift after a lifetime of being a Serf felt like an emotional floodgate opened. I sat in my classroom wondering what happened. I hadn't touched the girl with the braid, so why did my professor seem to believe I'd used an ability on her? And why did the girl's scowl confirm she agreed? Was it some kind of embarrassment gift? Then I remembered another misunderstanding that also occurred without touch at my old school. Kai began to say strange things before he got angry and dumped my lunch on me. At the time, I thought Emma had done something to him, since she was touching his arm when it happened. Could it have been me? Is that how my gift was like Yemoja Roux?

My thoughts were interrupted when someone came into class late exclaiming that Yemoja Roux was not only at the school but visiting each classroom. My new ability could not be overshadowed by anything except Yemoja Roux. I could think of nothing else. Yemoja Roux the Great Fae was *here*. My heart leapt whenever a student came through the door. I hoped she would grace one of my classes with her presence, but as my third class came and went, with little more than going over the syllabus, I began to think that my sparse schedule didn't give me enough chances to meet her.

I went to lunch feeling deflated. The rest of the students glowed with excitement, their presence altered by beholding the greatest of all Fae. I wondered, what would it feel like to stand in her proximity? What did it feel like to witness greatness?

I feared I'd never know beyond the glimpse I'd gotten of her so many years ago.

"Reina," Oden called, waving me over to his lunch table. I sat down, putting my tray next to his. "How were your morning classes? Did you get to meet Yemoja Roux?"

"No, she didn't come to my class. But something weird happened."

He leaned forward.

"I… I think I used my gift."

He lowered his voice. "And you had those gloves on?"

I nodded. Of course, he knew. It seemed like he knew from the first moment we met.

"What's your gift?" he whispered as if unwilling to share the news with anyone else.

"Well… I think it's—"

Oden leapt up. "You're the man!" Oden said, throwing his arm around a stunned Kai. "I heard you told Yemoja Roux you loved her. You aim high, man. I'll give you that."

I gaped. *He did what?* The thought of competing with Miranda for his attention was one thing, but Yemoja Roux was something else entirely. Not that I was competing. *Ugh. What's wrong with me?*

Kai humored him with a smile and said, "She wants me."

"You're insane. Have a seat, man."

What? No, not here.

Oden gestured to the table and my stomach dropped when Kai's gaze fell to me. "Hey, Kai," I said sheepishly, but he couldn't have looked more eager to escape—no doubt in search of Miranda.

Kai turned back to Oden. "Sorry, guys, I promised my roommate I'd sit with him and stuff. See you around."

Phew. Dodged a bullet there.

Oden sat down across from me with a goofy grin that said he was still thinking about Kai hitting on Yemoja Roux. I was struck by how handsome he was, the green of his eyes, dizzying when he was in his uniform. It's almost like his status as king of the school and his rare gift overshadowed his looks, but not that day. Only now, as he sat eating his lunch, he wasn't a king or an apprentice Fae at all. He was just a high school boy. *A hot one.*

He took a bite of a burger. "So what did you say your gift was?"

I fiddled with the charm on my necklace. "I didn't."

"Well, you'll work it out in your independent studies."

I leaned forward. "How do you know about those?"

He lifted an eyebrow with a devious smile that was so alluring, if my virginity had been an object, I would have tossed it at him. "Still not talking, huh?"

"I can be bribed."

I leaned across the table and kissed him, taking far more

delight in his surprised and elated expression than even the kiss itself. He leaned in and groaned, "More."

I laughed. I wasn't sure how I got so lucky, or how after so much sadness and grief I could feel happy and excited for what lay ahead. Either way, if the wheel of fortune was spinning back, I wasn't going to waste it.

Kaito

THIRTY-FOUR

I grabbed my tray and made my way through the line, tossing bowls of lukewarm food onto it. I eyed the Common that stood behind the counter, Yemoja Roux's speech ringing through me. They were gifted, only enough to keep the food relatively warm. What chance would they have if The Fallen attacked? The sensor scanned my tray and I waved my school ID over the scanner which blinked red and three-dimensional letters appeared in the air in front of me that read Kaito Nakamaru before blinking out.

I appraised the tables that were half full with students engrossed so deeply in conversation, it didn't seem like anyone was eating. I looked for Zane Blaque, prepared to give him a little talk about respect, but there was no sign of him.

As I weaved between the tables, I could hear that the entire cafeteria could speak of nothing but The Fallen and Yemoja Roux.

An arm landed on my shoulders. "You're the man!" Oden said, shaking me. "I heard you told Yemoja Roux you loved her. You aim high, man. I'll give you that."

I grinned. "She wants me."

"You're insane. Have a seat, man."

He gestured to the table and my stomach dropped when Reina was seated there. "Hey, Kai," she said. The sudden memory of my night with Miranda hit me, followed closely by the memory of Reina's kiss with Oden, and I couldn't offer her so much as a smile.

I gulped, doing a quick sweep of the cafeteria, looking for an out. The last thing I wanted was to sit through their little date. I caught a glimpse of Carter. *Perfect.*

"Sorry, guys, I promised my roommate I'd sit with him and stuff. See you around." Before they could protest, I darted through the crowd.

Carter's face lit when he saw me. "Good timing, man. I was about to have a seat outside."

"It's a little cold, isn't it?"

He tossed his blonde curls out of his face. "A little, but that just means we'll have the place to ourselves. Or do you want to look at that?" He nodded and I turned to see Reina lean in and kiss Oden across the table.

I clenched my jaw. "Good point."

We headed outside and Carter inhaled his burger in no more than three bites before he pulled out his guitar and began to play. "Bro," he said, "I hear Zane Blaque was questioned by police."

"You're kidding. I just had a class with him." I shook my head. "He was rude to Yemoja Roux."

His brow furrowed. "So she had him arrested?"

I shook my head. "No... not exactly. He sounded crazy, though. He was supporting these terrorists, or whatever."

He looked puzzled, so I recounted the conversation as closely as I remembered it.

Carter strummed thoughtfully before he spoke. "You know… he kinda had a point?"

"What do you mean?"

"Well, the Fae kill people all the time."

I nodded. "Bad people."

"Who decides who's bad? I mean, what gives one person the right to kill and not another, and who has the power to make the choice?"

My thoughts reeled. I didn't exactly know how to answer him.

He continued. "Normally, when the Commons or even Serfs are attacked, and Fae protect them, we all kind of agree that's what's fair. But now that The Fallen are attacking Fae, it seems… I don't know, like an even playing field."

"You think Yemoja Roux is a bad guy?"

"Of course not. But if you *really* think about it, without the Fae the strong would survive and maybe the weak would die out. But at the end of the day, what's more fair and just than natural selection?"

I didn't disagree. I couldn't. Carter's soothing melody extinguished any spark of rage or defense that rose. There was something to his theory, something powerful that Zane Blaque thought was worthy enough to question the great Fae Yemoja Roux.

The idea that Fae might not be all good had never occurred

to me. They were the darlings of the media. Of course, they had to kill their enemies from time to time to protect the rest of us. Yet, for some reason, once the idea had found its way into my head, I couldn't get it out.

Reina
THIRTY-FIVE

I looked down at my afternoon schedule which was comprised of three hour-long independent studies. Well, this was going to be fun. All I could imagine was sitting in a training room, punching a dummy in the hopes that my gift would manifest. On top of that, it seemed like my gift made people say things—personal things. I was sure a dummy wouldn't have much to share. Under the location, it read Combat Zone One. I remembered exactly which of the two domes the combat zone was in from my tour with Miranda, and also her warning that the moment I stepped in there I could be attacked by any student. Had that girl with the yellow braid exaggerated? Were there other girls who felt slighted by me spending time with Oden? I reached out to touch the barrier around the dome. It reminded me of the one at the fort which I'd desperately wanted to touch once it started lighting up the party. This one didn't seem to have as many cool properties, but I was surprised to find the surface ribbed instead of smooth.

It took me a moment to realize I was procrastinating going in because I was afraid. I'd been a few days without a beating and already I'd become soft. I promised myself I'd never let fear stop me, but I stood frozen with my hand on the door. My heart raced. My breath became shallow. *What is happening?* My legs began to shake and buckle beneath me when I realized I was caught in someone's gift. I looked around, but the courtyard was abandoned mere seconds before the bell. No one but Oden had touched me recently, I'd even worn my gloves today to be sure. Anger tore through me. I would not be a victim, not again.

I ripped open the door to the combat zone, ready to face my attacker. When I saw her, my knees gave out and I toppled to the ground still caught in the wake of her gift.

Yemoja Roux stood at the center of the entrance, hands on hips, a victorious grin, and her unique magenta hair streaming to the side despite the virtually windless dome.

I gasped. "Yemoja Roux. I… I love you."

She winced. "I've been getting that one a lot today."

She walked over and held out her gloved hand. I took it, unable to believe my good luck that I happened to be assigned to this exact spot for my independent study.

"Good work overcoming my gift to come in here. You have spirit. I've released it now. Can you stand?"

I gawked as I scrambled to get my feet under me. "Yemoja Roux, I can't believe it's you."

"You're Reina Bennett."

I shook my head. "No. I mean yes, but it doesn't sound cool like Yemoja Roux."

She leaned in and winked. "They let you change it when you become Fae."

"Right," I sputtered, "Of course." The bell sounded and I looked around for combat zone one. It was to the far left, a silver one above a door to a smaller dome that encased some kind of jungle.

"I'm sorry," I said. "I have an independent study that I'm late for."

She flipped her gorgeous hair. "Class is already in session, honey."

My heart stopped in my chest. "You're going to teach... me?"

She furrowed her magenta eyebrows. "They didn't put my name on your schedule? Heh, they probably didn't want this place swarming with curious students." She slapped her hands together, startling me. "Anyway, we're wasting time. Tell me about your gift."

I gulped, uneager to deliver the bad news. "I'm not sure I have one. Well... I made this one girl say weird things, I think. Veranda Yarrow seems to think we have something in common... which is crazy. I mean, obviously I don't have anything in common with you, you're like a goddess and I like—"

"I was chosen to mentor you for that exact reason. You see, both your gift and mine can be cast without touch."

My body numbed.

"It's probably why you know so little about your ability. Since it works differently than ordinary gifts, casting it by touching someone wouldn't have yielded results. Can you identify what my gift does based on what you felt before you entered?""

"Make people dizzy?"

"Want to try again?"

I took a deep breath and replayed the moment in my head. I felt weak, uneasy, and ultimately, "Fear," I said. "But… your gift can't be fear. I've seen you use it to strike an enemy, even block attacks. You can't block an attack with fear."

"You'd be surprised how crippling fear can be if you learn to understand and wield it."

I nodded. "Okay. So how do I get from here to there?"

She sat down on the ground and patted the spongy turf beside her.

I looked around. "Here?"

She closed her eyes. "We have the place to ourselves."

I sat down, mimicking her posture and closing my eyes.

"Take a deep breath," she said in a voice that was smooth like a glazed sunrise. "Meditation is essential regardless of your gift, but more so for ours. This type of ability requires an understanding of the gift itself in order to control it."

I'm off to a great start.

"Banish those negative thoughts. Now I want you to take ten deep breaths and, as you do, reach inside and differentiate your body from your gift."

"How will I know what to look for?"

"You'll find what it is you're searching for."

I cursed the school for not letting me get a selfie with Yemoja Roux, like anyone would believe this. *Focus, Reina.* I wanted to learn from the best, and who would know better about this stuff than Yemoja Roux? I took my first three breaths and felt a tingling sensation in my arms and fingertips. I wiggled my toes and took another.

"That's it," she said. "When you find it, assign it a color in your mind. Visualize it spreading through your body."

Nothing. That's what I felt, but it didn't matter. I was sitting beside my lifelong hero. I'd gotten into the school of my dreams and suddenly everything seemed possible. Then I saw it, a fleck of light in the darkness. It grew and I thought it looked like a pale purple glowing white as it ran through my body like sand over my skin. Its shape was fluid, and I saw the currents push through my extremities. It ran down my neck, shoulders, chest, stomach, legs then out the bottoms of my feet to the center of the earth, only to swirl back into my body. I blinked through closed eyes as the purple glow hung above me like luminous stars. Each breath strengthened the light, the image burning more clearly in my mind.

Excitement overtook me and I opened my eyes, whipping to Yemoja to explain what I saw. I froze. Yemoja gaped at me, her trembling hand covering her mouth, tears sliding down her beautiful face. She stood quickly and I tried to follow but lost my balance and crashed back to the floor. "Wh-what's wrong? What happened?" I asked.

"That's enough for today," she said. "You did well." Without another word, she left and all I could do was wonder if that beautiful light I saw inside me somehow hurt the world's most powerful Fae.

Kaito
THIRTY-SIX

I hung out in the hedge mazes across from the Blue House. Every now and then I peeked over a prickly hedge to see Miranda pass far too many times, no doubt hoping to run into me. I owed her an explanation, but that wasn't a conversation I was ready to have. If I was being honest, I wasn't so much as hiding from her as looking for Zane. Unless I'd somehow missed him, he'd been in the headmistress' office all day.

The sun began to hang low, giving everything an orange tint and dropping the temperature low enough for me to see my breath. Finally, I saw him headed down the stairs from the front office, no sign in his gait that he'd been the least bit shaken by the interaction. Based on his speed, I calculated how long it would take for him to get to Blue House and timed it so our paths would cross.

His glasses glinted as he turned to me, an air of delight in his charmed smile.

"I see you didn't get arrested," I said, hoping to purge a real reaction.

"No thanks to you," he said, but if he was upset, there was no sign of it on his face.

"I just said what everyone was thinking."

"Look," he said with an easy hand gesture. "You can go and be brainwashed by the media about the Fae or whatever, but don't fault me for criticizing the entire hypocritical system."

"Why are you here if you don't like or believe in the Fae?"

"To change it."

I gulped. It reminded me a bit of something Carter had said a few nights ago.

He continued. "If the only way to have my voice heard is to become Fae, so be it. I'm just not surprised that someone else discovered a way to do it."

Another way to have their voice heard? Is that what he thought these murders were? "They're killing Fae."

"And what do you think will happen to The Fallen if the Fae find them?"

"If? You honestly think the terrorists have a chance?"

He shrugged. "The Fallen are 7 and 0."

"Six."

He nodded, a half smile on his face. "My mistake."

I shuddered. This guy knew something. Why then did the headmistress let him off? Surely one of the professors had a gift that could purge it out of him. The seer, perhaps. I shook my head. "You're one of them, aren't you? The Fallen."

"Look," he said, "I feel like we got off on the wrong foot. Do you want to grab a coffee at the student center? It's cold as balls out here and I imagine you've been waiting for me for a while."

Damn. I wasn't nearly as slick as I thought. Still, it was a peaceful gesture. It couldn't hurt to hear the guy out.

Zane said very little to me on our walk to the student center. It wasn't until we grabbed coffee and took a seat in a corner away from the bulk of the foot traffic that he began to talk.

He took in a deep breath, the only sign of apprehension I'd seen him give all day. "My family's really poor," he said flatly. "My parents are both Commons and their wages are minuscule. There just aren't any options for the Commons or Serfs, no opportunity to rise up. The only people who have a shot of making something of themselves are the Elites." He exhaled slowly and I wasn't sure if he was waiting for a response.

I sipped my coffee to fill his pause.

"Somehow, my parents got it in their head that if they had enough kids, eventually one might be born Elite and be able to deliver the rest of us out of poverty. Can you imagine? The Fae's pay being so unequal that they lounge in mansions and make their talk show appearances while the rest of us starve…" The last word was a hiss through gritted teeth, his free hand balled into a fist on the arm of his chair.

I had no response. I'd always had money, a legacy of wealth left from a Fae who died five generations ago. All these years later, we still lived off his earnings, and I hadn't given much thought to the unfairness of that situation until now.

He took a sharp breath in. "I have eleven brothers and sisters. I had thirteen, but two didn't make it. I guess my parents' plan worked, though, because I was born Elite and was accepted into GFA. If I can become Fae, I can help them." He looked up to me. "Maybe I can help more than just them." He gestured to the state-of-the-art student center, his voice cracking with emotion. "There's more than enough wealth to go around."

I nodded, my thoughts racing through his story.

"Every day I lived in fear that my parents would call and tell me another one of my siblings died. And I knew when the call came, it would be my fault for not becoming Fae sooner."

"So what happened?" I asked. "How'd you make the leap from desperate to become Fae to hating them?"

His glasses glinted, hiding his eyes. "My parents called."

My stomach sank and I wasn't sure I wanted to hear the rest.

"They received a donation. The only indication of who sent it was a downward arrow. Inside the parcel was ten years of my parents' salary, clothes, and possessions, all of which were the stolen property of Will Citrine."

I gaped at him. "So you're saying the—"

"The Fallen saved my family, and who knows how many others. They kill the greedy, media-hungry Fae and help those who weren't lucky enough to be born Elite."

The lines had blurred and Zane kept talking.

"I used to use my shield gift to sneak cafeteria food to my family out through the school's barrier and a gap in the wall, but they don't need it anymore."

He looked down at his hands. "I imagined I'd be relieved, but now it's been a while since I've seen my family." He smiled at me. "Go figure."

"Zane, I… I should have known you had a good reason to—"

"Don't sweat it."

"Seriously, I misjudged you."

He sipped his coffee. "Do me a favor and don't spread any of this around. My confrontation with Yemoja Roux has given me a reputation as a badass and I'd like to uh… cash in on it for a bit."

I held out my fist and he bumped it with his. "You got it, man."

Reina
THIRTY-SEVEN

I walked back toward Pink House feeling deflated. In one day, I'd gone from Serf to gifted like Yemoja Roux, and then to someone who unintentionally attacked my most admired idol. Her face was plastered in my head. *I hurt her.* GFA was so much more intense than I imagined and, after one day of classes, I was drained. But where I expected to be physically exhausted, I found myself emotionally so. I wanted to call my parents, to tell them what happened. I wanted to hear their voices—to listen to their comforting words.

The campus seemed deserted, as everyone was still in class. I headed straight into Pink House to my room, with the thought that if I made it there, nothing else could hurt me and I couldn't hurt anyone else.

When I awoke, the sunlight that was streaming in when I'd fallen asleep was replaced with the dark of night. I was confused and disoriented, unsure how long I'd been asleep. Briara's bed was empty, but I saw a piece of paper on my desk that told me she had been to our room at some point during my nap. Her note read:

I didn't want to wake you, but I went to the library.
    -Bri

My stomach twisted. *Ugh*. I missed dinner. I couldn't think of anything worse but then my mind drifted back to my afternoon with Yemoja Roux.

How was I supposed to use my gift after that? I sighed and pulled myself out of bed and headed for the student center to see if I could grab something before the cafeteria closed.

The outside air bit my skin through my blazer. I'd vastly underestimated how cold it was. Why couldn't the rest of the campus always be warm like the fort?

The student center had groups of students clumped together. One group was playing cards and laughing so loudly that I couldn't help but smile as I passed. I spotted the fishbowl, the glass cafeteria that had a few scattered students hunched over books, half the lights on that it normally did, and no obvious staff. I walked to the buffet line and was relieved to find a few leftover burgers wrapped up like they were from a fast food restaurant. I took two and eyed the third one that was leftover in the heated tray. "Yep, doing this." I grabbed the burger and had to balance it against my chest on the other two. When I got to the scanner, I couldn't reach my student ID.

I heard a laugh behind me. "Tough day?"

My gaze snapped up to Kai who reached for the ID card that

hung from the lanyard around my neck and held it to the scanner.

"Thanks," I said shyly.

He took a burger and led me to a table. I wasn't following him, I was following my burger, and I didn't give much thought to him as he took a seat beside me.

"Do you want to talk about it?"

I unwrapped the paper around my first burger and took a huge bite. I didn't even wait to swallow it before the words flew out between chews. "There was this terrible girl and she was being mean and stuff and all of a sudden she started saying weird stuff." I took another bite, and Kai flashed an amused smirk. "And then the teacher was mad that I used my gift on her."

He leaned forward. "So you do have a gift? It makes people weird. Nice."

I shook my head. "It's not nice. Because I was sad I didn't see Yemoja Roux and then she was my mentor and my gift was purple, and she told me to use it and she cried."

"That barely made any sense at all… Wait, what? You made Yemoja Roux cry?"

"And now I don't want to use my gift ever again because I can't get her face out of my head."

He reached out and rubbed my back. "Don't feel bad. It's not like Yemoja Roux is a saint or anything."

"What do you mean?" I asked, polishing off my first burger and unwrapping my second.

"I mean, she has hurt plenty of people in her time. Not to mention, she's the richest person in the world."

What did that have to do with anything? I wanted to argue

or at least ask what the connection was, but I didn't want him to stop rubbing my back with those calming circles.

"I've missed you, Rei," he said, and I froze mid-bite.

He raised his hands defensively. "I know you're with Oden and stuff, but does it mean that we can't hang out from time to time?"

"Isn't that going to freak your girlfriend out?" I asked. I was obviously fishing, but I wanted to hear him confirm or deny it himself.

"I won't tell her if you won't."

So it was true. *I knew it*. That settled that. I needed to make an escape immediately. Kai leaned in and his devilish smile brought me right back to our kiss in the courtyard. My budding romance with Oden was a spark, but whether from years of suppressed feelings or shared history, my feelings for Kaito were a raging inferno. I was a moth to the flame and I always got burned. I felt dizzy. So dizzy that I put down my burger and stared into Kai's dark eyes. Maybe if he wasn't so messed up. Maybe in a different life we could—

My thoughts were cut short as Kai put his forehead to mine. "Reina," he whispered. "I can't seem to—"

"Kaito," a voice called from across the fishbowl. We looked up to see a blue-haired boy waving him over. "Are you ready?" the boy called.

"Is that Zane Blaque?" I asked.

He nodded, his gaze dropping back to me. "Yes."

"Why are you hanging out with him?" I asked. "Didn't you say he was somehow connected to Raphael Mazarin's death?"

Kai said, "I should go. See you around?"

I nodded and, to my dismay, he grabbed my third burger off the table before following his new friend out of the cafeteria.

Kaito

THIRTY-EIGHT

I leaned back in my chair, pulling on my hair in hopes that the pain might drown out the sound of Quan bouncing a tennis ball off the wall, or of Enzo trying to snatch it between bounces by running across the room at super speed. I groaned, turning to Finn. "Why does Oden even call these meetings if he never shows up?"

Finn grinned. "Give him a break, Ace, he's super into his new girlfriend."

"They're not like official or anything," I said.

Quan interrupted, "They looked pretty official to me the other night at the fort."

I shot him a glare, but he seemed not to be bothered by it. Enzo shot into my line of sight. "But let's not forget about your night with Miranda."

I shook my head. "How do you even know about that?"

Quan said, "I snuck her out, remember? Plus, she told

everyone and, by the way, I can't believe you lied to me about zero gravity."

I put my palm to my face, letting out an exasperated sigh. "I should talk to her."

Enzo zipped over to me, his hand held up for me to high five. "Yeah, you should."

"Not what I meant."

Oden rushed in the door, half out of breath. His face was red, his shirt misbuttoned, and his lips smudged in the corners. "Sorry I'm late guys, I was with Rein—"

"We know where you were," Finn said, cutting him off. I shot him a thank you with a glance. His royal highness wasn't as bad as I thought. Of the other Nobles, I'd expected to like him the least, but it was the opposite. Unlike Quan and Enzo, he sort of kept to himself, he extinguished conflict, and he seemed to communicate on my non-verbal frequency. As for Oden, I thought that guy was a dick. Green-eyed devil was right. He just took whatever he wanted. Somebody had to teach that guy a lesson.

I stood. "Actually, I was just saying to the guys that I owed Miranda a little chat."

He nodded. "Yikes."

"Do you mind if I meet up with you later?"

Oden said, "I just got here, man."

"I've been here for an hour. It's not me that's been absent lately, bro."

Finn stood. "Oden, he's right. Just let him go. He'll meet us later."

Oden stepped aside and I made my escape. I headed down the hall toward the exit when I ran into Carter. "Hey, buddy," he said, cheerfully. "Did you hear the news?"

"No, what's up?"

"They're letting me do a set at the Winter Ball."

I patted his back. "Well done, man. Congrats."

He swung his guitar around and began to play. "Where are you headed?"

"I was actually looking for Miranda."

"Good thinking, better ask her to the ball. All the hot girls get asked first. I just saw her in the cafe."

I nodded my thanks and headed to find her. When I entered the cafeteria and saw a swarm of girls hanging on her every word, I knew exactly what they were talking about. Heat burned my face as I stormed over. "Miranda."

"Hey, sweetie," she said.

"Can I talk to you…" I scanned her captivated audience. "Alone?"

She followed me across the cafe. I stopped just outside of earshot of her little crew. "I need you to stop this. Stop telling people we hooked up. You're a beautiful girl and everything, I'm just—"

I stopped as Miranda began to laugh, her eyebrows raised with pity. She bit her bottom lip. "You don't remember that this was your plan?"

"What do you mean?"

"You were upset about Reina and I was upset about Oden and we decided to date to make them jealous."

"That's ridiculous. I would never agree to it."

She shrugged. "How else would I know how into her you are?"

"I'm not into her."

She pressed her lips together, stifling a smile. "We didn't plan to hook up or anything, we just… drank a little too much I guess. I mean you're hot and I wouldn't be opposed to another night with you at Blue House, but did you really think I liked you for your personality? No offense, but next to Oden... you're just—"

"Whatever," I said, to shut her up. Each word was colder than the last. It wasn't that I cared what she thought. It was that some of those sentiments kept me awake at night for the last few years. "I don't care about what I said when I was drunk. It stops here." I turned to leave.

"Too bad, it was working."

I stopped. "Why do you say that?"

"Well, Oden has asked me about our relationship. Has Reina asked you? Has she mentioned me in conversation to see your reaction?"

Actually, there was last night in the cafe. She'd asked me if "my girlfriend" would mind us hanging out.

Miranda leered at me, analyzing my reaction, and when she found what she was looking for she tossed her ponytail over her shoulder and said, "But if you want to stop, it's your call."

"Wait," I said, without thinking. "What do I have to do?"

"Take me to the Winter Ball."

It was a trap. Scheming wasn't going to win Reina. "Nice try, Miranda. You'll have to find someone else. Besides, I don't think this Oden and Reina thing is going to last. The ball is two months away. I'd rather be there alone just in case."

I left the cafe while Miranda headed back to her table of friends, but instead of relief, I left the conversation feeling dejected. Miranda was the most awful girl I'd ever met, and even she thought I was a monster.

Reina
THIRTY-NINE

I never thought there would be a circumstance where I would dread seeing Yemoja Roux, but as I walked toward my second day of independent study, fear spread through my bones and settled on my ribs. What if she was angry about what I did? What if she didn't show up at all? I felt so nervous that I grew increasingly suspicious that she'd already ensnared me in her gift.

I opened the door to the combat zone and felt immediate relief. Yemoja Roux stood at the center of the entrance, as she had the day before, with the same bright smile I was used to.

"Uh.. good afternoon?" I said.

"Welcome back! Let's get to work." She sat and I took my place beside her.

She looked at me, her gaze sympathetic as if to tell me she understood my apprehension.

"I won't cry again. Promise," she said with a wink.

"I'm so sorry," I said, but she raised her hand to stop me.

"It was my fault. I dropped my gift's defense in the hopes of bearing yours so I could help you understand the nature of it. I prepared myself for pain, and wasn't expecting such a unique and dangerous power to emerge from you. It's an atypical gift, and no wonder you've had so much trouble discovering it."

I shook my head. "So you know what it is?"

Her dark eyes stared solemnly into mine and I could see the glint of yesterday's memory lingering behind them as she nodded. "Your gift is truth."

Truth. I sat staring down at my hands. "I don't understand. You seemed so hurt yesterday."

"There are truths we hide from ourselves. Everyone has demons they're not ready to confront," she said, turning away, but the smile returned to her face. "Maybe we don't always trust our ability to cope." She tucked a strand of magenta hair behind her ear. "I suppose the things I've been hiding were difficult to face."

"But... you're Yemoja Roux. You can do anything."

She grinned. "And you're Reina Bennett and I have to thank you. Your gift has given me a lot to think about."

"It seemed to make you sad."

She laughed. "It's the trials in life that make us grow."

I nodded. Of course she was right. I didn't necessarily like that growth required so much pain, but I was far from the girl who once numbed her grief. I understood how important it was.

"Reina, I must urge you to be very thoughtful about when you use your gift. Unless you're in the field, you must never force the truth on someone without their consent."

The idea that I even had a gift had barely sunken in. Not to mention the obvious pain I'd caused Yemoja Roux had me far too nervous to attempt it on another person. "Of course."

"You'll be tempted. But it's just the kind of power that could corrupt even the most heroic Fae."

She took my hands in hers and said, "Promise me."

"I promise."

Her intensity softened to a gentle smile that reminded me a little of my mother and my chest ached. As I looked at her, I was surprised to see a much older woman than the posters. She appeared tired, and there was a faint scar that ran along her jawline. Despite the countless interviews and documentaries I'd seen about her, she felt like a stranger.

I spent the next few weeks fighting desperately to catch up to my peers. I'd lost so much time thinking I was ungifted, but having the greatest Fae on earth as a mentor meant my progression was swift. Yemoja Roux's presence soothed me and it pushed our training into overdrive. I'd visualized a color for my gift, but learning it was truth gave it a distinctive shape during meditation. After the first full week of private lessons, I could pull my gift out of my body at a radius of a few inches, which was more than enough to start participating in my other classes. After several failed attempts in Professor Greene's class, I successfully infused a bit of truth in a confection, but the taste was so bitter he spit it out before my gift could take effect.

By the second week, I could block a strike defensively with my gift but only in a small area and only when I could correctly predict where I would be touched. Yemoja Roux said that was the exact reason why her Fae costume had pockets of exposed skin. Her enemy always went for those areas, so they were easiest to defend. In a way, she lured them into attacking her where she wanted. If I had a thousand lifetimes to absorb all of Yemoja

Roux's knowledge, it wouldn't be enough time, but I only had the luxury of training with her at my scheduled times, a minute past and she'd jet back to her patrol like Cinderella from the ball.

By the third week, I began to understand the corruption Yemoja Roux had warned me about. Before I went to sleep, I imagined things, *dark things*. Sometimes I imagined using my gift to purge the truth from my wicked orphanage guardian, Ms. Vivian. Why had she tortured me and the other orphans without remorse? Was there more to that story? I daydreamed her responses, but in my imagination, she wasn't my only victim. I wanted to know the truth of how Kai felt about me, if for nothing else than so I could put my feelings for him to rest once and for all and fully give my heart to Oden, like I wanted. Especially since things were heating up with him.

One weekend we were tucked away in one of the dark corners of the fort. A late-night picnic turned into a heavy make-out session. The friction of his jeans against mine sent chills through my body. We were both caked in sweat, our mouths unwilling to part even to breathe. Oden grabbed a handful of my shirt in frustration as I wrapped my legs tighter around him. We separated only long enough for him to move his mouth to my neck and I strained for release. "Just tell me when to stop," he whispered, sliding his hand under my shirt.

"Don't stop," I said in a stupor.

He froze. "What? Really? You want to have sex? Are you sure?"

His questions sobered my daze, but I still felt a tickle at the back of my neck that radiated down my whole body. I had no reason to hesitate. I really liked him. He was good for me. I could see myself falling in love with him. I wanted to fall in love with him, and I was sure these make-out sessions were starting to frustrate him as they were me.

Sensing my hesitation, he pulled me in for a hug. "Don't worry. There's no rush," he said, taking my hands in his.

"But I want to, it's just… I've never—"

He leaned in and kissed me. "I know. Miranda told me, or was it Kai? That's why I wanted to make it special for you."

The mention of Kai was unwelcome. Why the hell did that guy walk around telling people about my sex life anyway? I felt a pang of guilt for being here with Oden while my thoughts still lingered on Kai. Oden and I were dating. Kai was nothing. Why couldn't I get that through my head? I just needed more time with Oden. I'd known Kai since middle school. That history was already being overshadowed by my new relationship. I felt my gift press against that thought.

"Any time with you will be special," I said, and his green gaze made me melt back into his arms.

"What about the Winter Ball?"

"What do you mean?"

He looked up at me shyly, a foreign expression to his usually confident face. "Will you go with me?"

"Of course. I've never been to a dance before."

"Then maybe we can plan something special for after… you know… if you're ready."

I grabbed his shoulders and shook him. "But it's two months away."

"I know." He groaned with a smile. He kissed me softly. "But you're worth the wait."

My thoughts were consumed with the pending loss of my virginity. I knew it was a normal part of life, but I wished I had someone to talk to about it with. I wished I could ask my mom questions. I didn't know why, but I wanted permission.

I'd begun to grow closer to Briara, but that only meant I was aware that girl talk for her mostly consisted of seances with spirits and ouija board chats. We chatted about crushes a little, but when the conversation got a little more personal, she always changed the subject. Still, I thought I'd give her a try. Who else did I have in my life?

Briara's eyes bulged. "You guys haven't had sex yet?"

I shrugged. "Well actually, I haven't had sex with anyone… ever."

"You're a virgin!"

"I don't like that word."

"Not even with Kai?"

I shook my head and her posture went rigid. "I'm probably not the best person to talk with."

"Right. Of course. Sorry," I said.

"Do you want to ask the spirits?" she asked in earnest.

I shook my head. "I think I'm good. Thanks, though. I'm sure I'll… you know… figure it out."

I lay back in bed and crossed my arms over my face to block out the sensation that I was alone. I had no woman in my life that I felt comfortable enough to ask about this sort of thing. Except maybe Yemoja Roux.

Kaito

FORTY

As if the ranking of the students wasn't already a huge point of contention at GFA, the headmistress installed a giant digital board that displayed the top 100 students in every building. The class rank of the top 100 was updated in real time as the professors voted students up or down based on their performance in class. Everyone was obsessed. There was a steady camp of students around every board, and friend groups were shattered by shifting ranks among the Elites. I'd even heard the list was streamed online for the public to access. If I wasn't training to the brink of collapsing every day before the list went up, I certainly was afterward, endlessly pushing the number of objects I could hold, and their duration. Since both combat zones always seemed to be booked, I had to find creative ways to test my limits, like touching every book, pencil, backpack, or scrap of paper that crossed my path during the day and holding them in range until I fell asleep.

The Noble Five were alright because, aside from Quan

thinking he should be ranked above Finn, the rest of the rankings were as we expected. Oden on top, followed by me, Enzo, Finn and then Quan. Still, Oden and I had been tense ever since he started dating Reina.

It was no surprise that Miranda was ranked sixth, but I was shocked to see Carter in seventh. I wouldn't have thought he would even make the list, let alone the top ten. I wanted to be the type of guy who didn't care about the list, the type that only knew his rank from being congratulated by other students, but I watched it like a hawk.

I searched for Carter to congratulate him on such a great rank, but when I found him in the student center, he was playing an impromptu concert to about twenty girls all of whom looked like they were a few songs away from throwing their bras at him. He caught my eye and smiled, nodding to me. *Way to go, roomie.*

I had a meeting with the Nobles coming up, but since Oden never showed up on time, I wanted to make sure I was later than he was. Since I had time to kill, I decided to head to the library to see if I could dig up any information about life in the world before gifts and before the Fae, a topic Zane and I discussed at length that week.

I hadn't spent much time at the library since I transferred to GFA, just a few hours after I first discovered it, but I'd since made use of the database of books that I could access from Blue House with my ID card. But since I was set to meet the guys at the student center anyway, it didn't make much sense to head back.

The library was well lit and clean, like the rest of the student center. It had snack machines and nap pods tucked away on one wall. There were always a dozen or so students hanging around its various desk types and couches, which made it feel more like a cozy home than a school library.

The least popular area was the one with the stacks of books. Most students preferred the digital versions, if for no other reason than because they were much faster to find and access. But something about physical books always charmed me, so I made my way through the seemingly endless rows that stretched twenty feet up and went back further than I cared to explore. I walked through the rows of books, going deeper until I found the history section. Most appeared to be biographies of famous Fae or Fae collections from a specific time period, but I didn't immediately see anything from before. It must have been further back. I moved quickly along, the dates moving back month by month, so I picked up my pace. The shelf wrapped around the corner, like the hedge mazes in the courtyard.

I turned the corner and froze. Reina was pressed against the bookshelf by Oden, her neck craned back as his mouth devoured her neck, his hands lost beneath her shirt. Her gaze snapped to me and I spun as fast as I could to flee.

"Wait wait," I heard her whisper.

"What's wrong?" Oden asked.

What's wrong? I seethed, already reaching the end of the stacks, my feet never touching the ground. What's wrong is that bastard. I was certain when they started dating that it wouldn't last long, but this was ridiculous. I was losing her. I didn't realize things between them had gotten so serious and now it felt like every second that passed was one where Reina was slipping away from me and into the arms of Oden. To think he'd been touching her like that all this time made me sick, and I glided out the front door of the student center, hoping the cold air would numb the pain. I felt the cold reach my bones, and my teeth began to chatter. How many books had I touched on my way through the library? I pictured the tidal wave of books crashing down on Oden as he tried to scramble free from the falling tomes. I had to win her back. I couldn't lose her, *not like this*.

Carter walked by, strumming his guitar as two girls I'd never met followed him and Quan not far behind them. If Quan was being dragged into this, I knew where they were going. He caught a glimpse of me. "Oh, bro, I need you to stay out of our room for the next..." he eyed both girls who were already undressing him with their eyes, "minute and a half."

I bit back a laugh. At least someone was doing well with women. I nodded to him, and my appreciation for him lingered long after he entered Blue House with the two transformed guys and Quan, who headed back towards the student center a minute later.

Quan grinned at me. "Meeting in five," he said.

"Don't think I'll make it," I said, trying not to let my anger into my voice.

He shrugged and headed back inside. I shook as the image of Reina with Oden replayed in my head. I clenched my fists, looking for an outlet for my fury. He was a better man than me, but I wasn't ready to let her go. I wanted him to hurt.

My chance came the next day, when our combat professor, Mr. Cordovan, unwittingly paired me with Oden.

Oden grinned at me across the arena like we were friends. Like he didn't know how much danger he was in. I wasn't being overconfident either. Since he'd been dating Reina, he'd been too busy to put in extra hours of training like I had. He was slipping and this was the perfect opportunity to dethrone our school's king in front of everyone.

Zone six, where our battle was set to commence, was a city block packed with sharp metal that I was eager to make use of. I wanted nothing more than to smack the smile off his pretty boy face. A guy like this, Elite with something flashy and good looks to match, was on a one-way train to become Fae from birth. Riches and fame all showering on him along with a license to kill. There was something unjust about how his dice were loaded, and I was going to set it right.

Professor Cordovan's voice shot through the speakers, "You may begin."

I took off running away from Oden until I had no breath to spare. It wasn't a manly move, but I needed to buy some time. I leapt into the air and let my gift carry me. I slipped in and out of vacant buildings until I was sure he didn't know where I was. A crash rattled my bones as Oden smashed the glass on a building he thought I was occupying. I used every second to touch loose objects on the ground. A steel pipe, a plank of wood, anything that my gift could pull free as Oden mindlessly created more debris. One building after the next, I clouded my gift with all manner of objects which I left undisturbed in their various locations in the arena.

When I was nearing my limit, I closed my eyes to catalog my haul. It was the largest number I'd ever captured and I felt the strain of every one. It was time to make my move.

"Don't be a coward, Kaito."

Now. I propelled a shard of glass from the far side of the zone at the sound of his voice. He deflected it with ease. "Good. I was worried you weren't even going to put up a fight today," he said. "Look, man, I didn't know how much you liked Reina. But I like her too. I'm not going to mess it up."

I seethed.

"No one is forcing her to be with me. We just like each other."

I stepped out into the street and he turned to me to finish his speech. "Can't you accept that?"

I chuckled.

He smiled. "What's funny?"

"What's funny is you're out here lecturing me like some arrogant prick, and I've already won."

With a clap of my outstretched hands, I hurled every object ensnared in my gift at him, but instead of striking, I swept them into a whirlwind around him and watched as one of the pipes scraped him. I spun a thousand objects into a tornado, with him at the center. He crouched, using his gift to shield himself from the blows. The objects that struck him bounced off and it took almost no effort to yank them back to the cyclone and tighten its twirl. I walked toward him and felt the shudder of his gift as his endurance gave way. Nails, glass, metal, wood, thrashing at his skin, whittling away his strength. Then I saw the first cut draw blood. He yelled and started frantically punching the objects, but there were too many, moving too quickly, and each time he swung he left an opening for me to strike another blow.

I bared my teeth as he fell to his knees, his eyes pleading at me with terror and surrender. I pushed the objects tighter and he yelled in pain. Nearly satisfied, I walked up to him and all at once I let the objects drop from the air around him, the severity of his injuries on display for the first time. I cocked my arm back and punched him across his jaw, the pop echoing through the zone. He stared up at me with alarm as blood dribbled down his cheek.

Professor Cordovan's voice shot out through the speaker.

"Congratulations, Mr. Nakamaru. That was very impressive. You didn't even get a scratch on you. I've called Dr. Azul for you, Mr. Gates. Can you stand?"

Oden never broke eye contact. Not until the zone was overrun by our fellow classmates. Only then did the weight of what I'd done settle in. Whatever kindness he'd shown me in the past, including me in the Nobles and vouching for me on the media, was gone.

By the end of the day, my name had jumped to number one in the school ranking and I had eight missed calls from my mother. Unsurprisingly, it seemed they wanted me as a son again.

I could barely move without being swarmed by students wanting to hear the story of my victory, and no one seemed more proud or supportive than Carter and Zane. The adrenaline from the battle stayed with me all day, and it was almost enough to help me forget about what I'd seen in the library.

Even Quan congratulated me before he urged me to visit Oden in the hospital. Oden would be there for a while. Today was for celebrating and tomorrow for apologies.

After a wonderful day filled with positive attention, I headed back to Blue House. I walked with my head held high as if there wouldn't be consequences. That's when I saw Reina.

"What the fuck, Kai?" she said. She had on a jacket but was shivering enough for me to guess at how long she'd waited outside Blue House. "That was messed up, even for you."

I scoffed. "I didn't break a single rule. It was a battle and he lost."

"That's not what I heard. I heard it was personal. I heard it was frightening."

I pushed past her. "You're ridiculous."

"Why are you even here?" she asked. "This school is for future Fae. You seem much more suited for The Fallen."

"Those are pretty harsh words for someone who went from a shy virgin to banging in the library in zero point two seconds."

Her mouth dropped open. "You don't know what you're talking about, Kai. We were just kissing, and it's none of your business anyway."

I ran a frustrated hand through my hair. "It didn't look like just kissing to me."

"Well, it was. We're waiting for—" She stopped herself and silence grew thick between us.

"For what?" I whispered.

She stared down at her feet, fiddling with the charm on her necklace.

"For the dance?"

She shook her head. "He wanted it to be special."

"Yeah, because that's not cliche as fuck."

"You know what, Kai," she said, her voice heavy with emotion. "You're awfully invested in my personal life. Do you want to tell me why?" She stepped toward me, her chest nearly against mine.

My breath caught. My heartbeat dashing.

"There are only two possibilities here. Whichever it is, tell me and I promise I'll believe you." A tear slipped down her face and I felt my misplaced anger break. She continued, "Either you have feelings for me or you can't stand the thought of me being happy."

I was paralyzed by her obvious pain. It seemed like no matter what I felt for her, I always ended up hurting her. I looked up to the glow of the half moon and felt the cold seep through my jacket. I didn't want to hurt her anymore. My heart beat, *Please be with me instead.* She was only a few words away from knowing the truth, and the weight of that kept me suspended. She was right about one thing—I was no Fae. How could I ask her to choose me when I'm so unworthy? She had the chance to be with someone whole. Someone who was programmed for kindness, and I was planning on asking her to wreck it. For me. I was asking her to choose her tormentor over her savior. I clenched my fist. *Reina, I promise this is the last time.* "You're right," I said. "I don't want you to be happy. I can't stand the thought of a Serf like you sailing through life."

"You're lying," she said, tears pouring down her cheeks. "Tell the truth."

Her eyes turned angry as her gift struck me. I saw a purple glow in them and on the tips of her fingers. We hadn't even touched, yet I felt the truth surge to my lips. She was strong and everything I couldn't say to her was desperate for release. *I don't think I'm good enough for you. You're the only one who understands. Please don't go. Don't give up on me. I love you, Reina.* The urge to say the words was intolerable, but I fought it, leaning on my own gift as my final line of defense. I was losing. Tears pricked my eyes as my will gave way. Desperate for a way out, I bit down on my bottom lip hard, until it split, blood running down my chin.

I must've been a sight because Reina cupped her hands over her mouth in fear. Her gift let me go. Then, as if resigned, she wiped her face. I swallowed hard and she shook her head, her gaze slipping between sad and angry. "Okay, Kai. Message received."

Reina
FORTY-ONE

I never told Yemoja Roux that I used my gift on Kai. I was ashamed that I broke my promise and how quickly my ability corrupted me, and I knew, if she ever found out, that would be the end of my training. October gave way to November and Kai and I could barely look at each other when we passed in the halls. My anger from our last conversation burned hot without any sign of abating. He was still in the same place in my heart he'd always been, but now his presence was a dagger that on some days made it hard to breathe.

I visited Oden in the infirmary as often as he'd allow, but it took longer than Doctor Azul predicted for him to get well again. It was as if losing his rank had broken his spirit, and I missed his sunny disposition. I didn't care how long it took him to recover, I would be there for him, and not because my mind endlessly reminded me that I was responsible, because I cared. He was surprised when I first came to see him and seemed to think that his rank had anything to do with how I felt about him. Like I'd jump ship to Kai now that he was the new top student. But even the thought of Kai made me sick. I wanted nothing to do with him.

By mid-November, Yemoja Roux had me in decent fighting shape. Defense was well enough, but the day she taught me to use my gift offensively, I finally felt like I could become Fae.

"Concentrate on your arm," she urged. "Let the truth swallow it."

As the purple shade of my gift engulfed my arm, I was alarmed to discover that it felt heavy, like it was encased in metal.

"Good, now sharpen it," Yemoja Roux said, pacing around me.

I visualized its edges coming to a point. With just a few swipes of my arm, my muscles grew fatigued, but I pushed through. I slashed at the practice dummy and felt delighted when the edge of my blade sliced into it. Losing my concentration, I gaped at my ordinary hand. My troubles with Kai felt minuscule compared to the satisfaction of raw power. I whipped back to Yemoja Roux. "Let's try it again."

She smiled at me proudly. I reveled in the chance to show her my progress, or even talk about life. In a short time, she became a fixture in my life—something I hadn't had in some time. One day, when I was on a high from spreading my blade to my elbow, I worked up enough courage to ask her if she'd ever been in love. Her eyebrows rose in surprise but her expression softened, and her voice came out as a whisper. "Yes, I have, once."

I watched as her gaze turned distant and she appeared to transport to a memory she wasn't ready to share. Then she turned to me. "Why do you ask? Are you in love?"

To my dismay, my thoughts went to Kai before Oden. I threw my hands up defensively. "No, I don't think so. I mean, how do you know exactly?"

She pulled back her hair and started to work it into a braid. "I think it's different for everyone."

My heart squeezed in my chest as the next question escaped my lips. "Do you think love is a choice? You know, something you go into with both eyes open? Willingly? Or is it something that happens to you? Like an intense feeling you get swept up in?"

She pursed her lips. "It seems you already know the answer to that, Reina."

I didn't, but it was nice to have someone to chat with, someone who never pushed me but always listened when I was ready to share. She was making me better, a guiding light brought in when I needed her most and mended things I thought broken forever.

I saw those improvements reflected in my battle skills as well, and when I could sharpen the truth into a blade and cut with it for more than a few minutes at a time, I began to excel in my defense class—a class that had deemed me helpless from the start and took turns sending me to the infirmary.

Some of the classmates who delighted in tearing me to shreds a month ago turned green in the face as I deflected the attacks of my class's best Elites, and my unplanned trips to Dr. Azul's office stopped altogether.

Then, on a cold autumn day, my name slipped to the bottom of the class rank. Reina Bennett, 100.

Ever since Kai took the number one spot, I scarcely dared a glance at the board, but a sudden rush of attention alerted me that my name had made the list. Despite my rapid progress, Yemoja Roux never reported. It wasn't until my skills started manifesting in other classes that my name rose to it, and the moment it did, I understood why Yemoja Roux had avoided putting my name up. After two days of my name on the list, moving from 100 to 94, someone discovered and leaked that I'd been training with Yemoja Roux. The combat zone was swarmed with students. I had to admit that I enjoyed the release of the secret. I was tired of it nearly slipping during conversations with Briara, and the stronger my gift grew, the more difficult it became to lie. In all the years I dreamed of becoming Fae, I imagined liking the attention that came with it, but it was so polarized between being admired and hated, I longed for the days when I was invisible. I even saw pain in Oden's eyes when he congratulated me, and I wondered if he felt I'd hijacked his spot by his mentor's side.

The one lighthouse in a stormy sea of uncertainty was that Yemoja Roux began to take me with her on actual missions in the city. I wasn't ready for combat, but was instructed to protect civilians in the vicinity when Yemoja was stopping a crime. On my first day, I had never been more excited in my life, or more nervous. The only thing that kept me going was Yemoja Roux's faith in me. Even if all I was allowed to do was guard civilians while Yemoja Roux handled anything dangerous, this was Fae work. As it turned out, I was born for it—enamored by the whole process. It was the first time I felt like Fae and even had a public stage to do good. I may have been new to my gift, but I had enough power to help and protect alongside the great Yemoja Roux. For a few short weeks, it seemed like everything would be okay. I should have known that my mentor was keeping me far from any real danger. I should have accounted for my luck running run out because, the moment I got too comfortable, everything changed.

One night, the air dropped below freezing. Yemoja Roux and I were patrolling the east side of Ancetol—covering a wide area, waiting for the local precinct to call in—when we heard the chilling scream of a young child. We exchanged a glance and tore into the direction of the sound.

We slipped down an alley when the creak of deformed limbs crackled and from behind a dumpster a black-pointed claw shot out of the darkness and slammed down onto the dumpster with a rattling crash that made my hair stand on end.

The dark mass stepped into the open alley, its body clinked as if made of shards of black glass, the pieces shifting as its form grew before us. "Go," Yemoja whispered, but my legs were locked with fear.

One pointed limb after the other sprouted from its largest heap, like barbed lances ready to impale us. I didn't know what it was, but I was certain it was responsible for killing the Fae. Without thinking, I lunged forward, sharpening the purple truth into a keen blade and slashing at the enemy. The magical edge caught and the faceless beast devoured it into itself. The glass demon thrashed, and I barely slipped out of its range before a new barb lurched forward to impale me.

I doubled over. Gasping for air. Reaching inside myself to find my gift, which felt weak and weary, like on training days when I overexerted myself.

Yemoja Roux slid in front of me. "Get out of here! Now!" she yelled.

"I won't leave you here."

"You're just a student. This is my job. Now go, or you'll put us both in danger."

With the last word, her gift filled me with such fear that I cried all the way home. I pulled out my phone, desperate for comfort.

Me:

Kai? I was on patrol and something happened.

Kai:

Are you okay? Where are you? I'm coming.

Me:

I'm almost back to campus. We were attacked by some kind of monster. Yemoja Roux made me leave. She's fighting it alone. Kai, I'm so afraid. If anything happens to her, I'll never forgive myself.

Kai:

It's going to be okay, Rei. Whatever happens. We'll get through this.

I was too panicked to respond again.

Kai:

Let me know when you're back.

. . .

His words only comforted me for a second and, by the time I reached campus, I was panting as I tried to explain what happened to the headmistress.

Ms. Tricorn surprised me with her response. "You're foolish," she said.

I wiped my eyes, looking up at her in confusion.

"You think the Great Yemoja Roux will be defeated so easily?"

My stomach swirled with shame and relief and I waited eagerly in her office for nearly an hour before an exhausted Yemoja Roux limped through the door.

I ran to her, throwing my arms around her. "I'm fine," she said, rubbing my back.

The headmistress said, "I'll call Doctor Azul." She hurried back in a minute later and asked, "Did you kill it?"

Yemoja Roux nodded. "But when I broke through, it turned to ash."

I took her hand. "How did you kill it? It… absorbed my gift."

She touched my face. "By refusing to lose."

I texted Kai that I was back and that Yemoja was alright. I told him we didn't need to meet.

He replied, K. I didn't want to dwell on the fact that I'd texted Kai instead of Oden, nor did I want to explain it to Oden when Kai inevitably brought it to his attention. But Kai never mentioned it.

My independent study was suspended after that. I was moved into the classes I'd been missing, including Professor Cordovan's Combat Training with Kai and Oden. I was also allowed to visit Yemoja Roux in the private infirmary during her recovery, a privilege I took advantage of whenever I could.

"So," she said one afternoon, "things are getting pretty serious with you and Oden, huh? Are you being safe?"

Heat burned my face and I narrowly resisted the urge to flee. I'd been waiting for an opening to ask some questions and, if this wasn't it, I wasn't sure what was.

"I... uh... well. Safe?"

She smiled. "Oh my, do we need to have a talk?"

"Well, he's my first boyfriend and we haven't... you know." I fiddled with my necklace, too afraid to make eye contact. "We were thinking after the Winter Ball."

She nodded. "Big step."

"How do you know if you're ready?"

"I suppose it's different for every person, but if you care for each other and you trust him, it can be a meaningful way to express your feelings. Sex is a part of life. It can complicate and intensify things."

I tucked a curl behind my ear.

She continued. "As you grow, you face more difficult obstacles. If you think you're ready to face the ones that come when you're sexually active, and if you understand how to be safe, then it's your choice to make. However!" she said, with so much intensity I jumped. "If you can't say the word, chances are you're not ready."

I grinned. "I can say it. It's weird to say it when I'm talking to you."

She tossed a pillow. "Sure."

"You know, this is a little off topic, but there's something I always wanted to ask you."

"Shoot," she said, gesturing for me to fetch her pillow.

I handed it to her. "On our first day training together, what truth brought you to tears?"

She paused for a long time and I wasn't sure if she would answer, but then she said, "I don't want to be Fae anymore. I'm afraid my chance to have a family has passed."

"What? You can definitely have a family. You're only twenty—"

"Sixty."

I knew it, technically. She'd been saving people long before I was born. But she looked nearly identical to the images of herself when she was twenty. She was so strong and youthful it was hard to think of her as old or ready for retirement.

"Being Fae means putting others before yourself. How would they feel if I just abandoned them to pursue my own goals? Especially now."

I shook my head. "So what are you supposed to do, die in the field?" Her silence and kind gaze confirmed that theory. "You don't owe us anymore."

"I'll tell you what, train hard and take my place so I can retire."

"You got it, Roux."

Kaito

FORTY-TWO

The night of the Winter Ball arrived and I knocked back several drinks at the fort along with a ton of other students while we waited for the event to start.

I looked for Reina, but she wasn't at the pre-party. Many of the girls were still getting ready while the guys drank and bragged about their dates. However, Miranda was there, strutting around in a pink skin-tight gown that trailed behind her and left nothing to the imagination. There was some kind of furry dead animal draped over her shoulders, and her expression was pleased as she drew the lust-filled gazes of every guy there. Quan looked like he might spontaneously combust.

"You alright, buddy?" I asked.

"She's a goddess, I say. A real live goddess."

I patted his back and took a swig from my cup.

I had kept my distance from Reina over the last few months because I knew I'd have a chance to see her at the midterm exam that marked the end of our first term at GFA, but since

Reina and I both ended the term ranked in the top ten, Headmistress Tricorn waived it.

My suit didn't feel much different from my school uniform, except thank god it was a nice charcoal gray instead of that horrible maroon color.

The only one who seemed more nervous about the dance than I was, was Carter. How could a famous pop star be so wary about performing at a small high school function?

On the other side of the fort, Zane caught my eye. He raised his cup and took a sip. He was a good guy and I felt guilty for being virtually a shut-in this past month while I tried to let go of Reina.

The ballroom glowed with lights that hung mid-air like snow, and everyone looked so different than how they normally looked in their uniforms. Even Carter had taken the time to slick back his hair, though his shirt was just a long-sleeved mesh monstrosity that proudly showed his nipples. I thought he might've been wearing eyeliner too, but I didn't get a good enough look at him to know for sure.

He took his place on stage and I held my breath as I shared in his nervousness. The moment he began to play, the party boomed to life and his voice sailed through the arched ceilings strong and angelic. My chest warmed. Even though I lost Reina, I'd been more than fortunate to leave this term with some new friends. Carter, Zane, Finn, even Quan. If I got nothing else from GFA, I got them. Things weren't so bad.

When Reina arrived at the top of the stairs, my breath caught and my mouth fell open as she glided down the steps in a dress that glimmered the same iridescent purple that I saw when she used her gift.

Fuck. I was not over her.

The world crashed back to me as Oden took her hand and led her onto the dance floor. Why had I even come tonight? For Carter? With the number of crazed women who reached for him at the bottom of the stage, I was sure he'd be just fine. Wait. Why were the women crazed when they should have felt relaxed by his music? In fact, even I felt a sort of involuntary mania coursing through me. Was Carter's music causing it? He could only calm, right? Unless he lied.

Reina and Oden danced into my line of sight, Oden's hands running up and down her body.

I turned away. Reina was with Oden. I had to let her go, and I refused to stay here and risk wrecking her special night.

I'd wrestled with the idea and finally made my mind up to leave. Then I heard her voice behind me. "Kai."

I spun. "Oh, hey, Reina. You… you look beautiful. I mean, obviously… like for Oden, because you're his girlfriend and not mine." *Oh god. Shut up. Shut up.*

She smiled. "Thanks." She reached up and started fiddling with her necklace. "I uh… I just wanted to thank you for being there for me that day, when Yemoja Roux and I—"

"It's no problem. I'll always be around if you need me." I gulped. "I'm so sorry about everything I said. It's your life and I've been terrible."

"It's really okay."

"Can I ask a favor?" I asked before I panicked and turned away. Across the hall, I could see Oden carrying two glasses of punch and scanning the crowd for Reina. "Uh, never mind, it's stupid."

She tucked a curl behind her ear. "What is it?" She grabbed my arm and turned me back to her.

"I wanted you to use your gift on me one more time, so… you know I'm not a monster."

She took a step closer. "I know you're not a monster, Kai."

"Please?"

She smiled. "You're not going to make yourself bleed again, are you?"

I felt the blush sting hot on my cheeks but, before I could respond, her eyes flashed purple and I felt her gift take hold.

Reina
FORTY-THREE

Kai looked down at me, the truth on his lips. I felt wracked with nerves. What could he possibly say? I knew whatever was coming would hurt, even if that wasn't his intention, yet I couldn't walk away. I was sure Oden would be looking for me now, but when I saw Kai across the dance floor alone, I knew the least I could do was come over to thank him. A moment ago I believed myself to be completely over him, but now, as he stood in front of me, I wasn't so sure.

"Reina, I know I'm not good enough for you."

"That's my choice to make."

"But you won't. You never do. No matter how I hurt you, you always end up back here. Choose better. I mess up everything in your life and most days I can't see any good in myself. I'm afraid I'll never meet anyone else who can believe in me like you do, but you're wrong about me." His eyes began to tear and mine mirrored them. "I think I might be in love with you, which is why I'm going to let you go be happy. Even if that means being with Oden."

My heart raced, and I wanted nothing more than to touch him, but I didn't. "Kai, I—"

A shrill scream filled the air as the glass wall separating the ballroom from the balcony shattered and rained down on us all. My gaze snapped up and three shadowy figures crept into the room. *Glass demons.* The students scattered into a panic. A sharp whistle shot out and in an instant Oden, Enzo, Quan, and Finn were assembled in formation.

"Run, Reina," Kai said, and he dashed to Oden's side.

Oh, fuck no. I sprang into action behind the guys, taking licks at the creature from a safe distance as the guys tried wounding it from close range. Behind me, Professor Greene and Professor Cordovan took on a glass demon of their own, its barbs shooting out and retracting with no predictable pattern. The shrill screech of glass on glass echoed through the ballroom while most of the students sprinted for the exit.

The third demon was headed for Carter, whose expression showed no trace of fear as he strummed his guitar, no doubt lending his assistance in our battle. Kai shot audio equipment from the stage at the demon, and it seemed to hardly affect the faceless creature at all. Oden was slower than usual, no doubt from his injuries, but still kept his body in front of his team as they slung their attacks futilely at the monster. But the demon absorbed Oden's punches and his fists had already begun to bleed. He slipped. A barb flew toward him. I slashed at the monster to deter it, but it was no use. Quan leapt between Oden and the glass demon, only to be run through his chest with black demonic glass. Stunned, Quan turned back to us before he collapsed on the floor in a pool of his own blood.

I screamed with horror as the boys charged in recklessly. We were all going to die here. A flash of magenta shot through. With an arm encased in magic shaped like a sword, Yemoja Roux sliced through the demon. It burst to ash and smoke so I sprinted to Quan, pulling him onto my lap and pressing his wound. Kai grabbed my shoulder and slid Quan and me out of the way as a second demon attacked. As if thirsty for more of Quan's blood, the demon charged me, and my gaze moved to Yemoja Roux who was busy blocking attacks from the third demon. Too far to help. I dropped Quan and stood to block the attack, but its powerful limbs broke through my gift. The demon's talon slammed into my head as Kai's gift yanked me back and tossed me into the air.

My ears rang as my vision blurred. I hung suspended over Quan as he bled out, but the darkness stole the scream from my throat and everything went black.

Reina
FORTY-FOUR

I awoke in a haze, feeling the warmth and familiarity of Kai's gift wrapped around me. It had been some time since I was held by him, like this. The memory of the attack on the school dance slammed into me, jogging me fully into consciousness. Suspended above a shattered ballroom, I resisted my urge to scream. Below I saw Yemoja Roux, Headmistress Tricorn, Veranda Yarrow, and some police officers standing around a body-shaped lump under a black blanket. They whispered sharply and their voices carried just enough for me to catch bits of their conversation.

Ms. Tricorn said, "I understand, Yemoja, but a student is dead."

Yemoja Roux shook her head. "I know how it looks, I just think we should take a moment to consider other possibilities."

Veranda Yarrow held out a large screen, but the headmistress blocked my view of it. Veranda said, "This was obviously orchestrated by The Fallen. But how did these students get involved? And what was their end game?"

Yemoja shook her head. "If he wanted to betray us, why did he try and rescue Reina? Why is he still holding her?"

The three turned, noticing that I was awake. Yemoja walked over and I felt her gift slip between me and Kai's gift. It broke and she caught me like I weighed nothing at all.

"Are you okay?" she asked, and she reached out and touched my forehead where a sharp sting flared beneath her touch. "We'll get you to Dr. Azul," she said.

I looked at the lump on the floor, tears springing to my eyes. "Is that Quan?"

Yemoja Roux nodded, putting me down before pulling me into her shoulder.

"W-why did they attack here?" I said, my voice breaking. I reached instinctively to touch my necklace charm for comfort, but it was gone. I must've lost it in the battle.

Veranda Yarrow stepped forward, a harsh look on her beautiful face. "We think it was a recruiting mission. A message to the students to pick a side." She turned to Headmistress Tricorn, who nodded at her, before returning her gaze to me.

Yemoja Roux said, "I'm not sure this is a good time—"

"This is a crime scene. I'm sure for Mr. Levout's sake, Reina would like to help in any way she can," Ms. Tricorn said, her words pin sharp.

"I do," I said, and Veranda Yarrow held out the screen. I held my breath as a video played. Zane Blaque stood at the school's barrier. He cast his gift, a shield that seemed to be concentrated on his left arm. He reached out and held it to the barrier, the glossy wall bending around his gift like a crowd of Serfs around an Elite. My pulse rose as one demon creature after another crept through the gate.

"Oh my god. Zane Blaque let them in," I said.

Veranda Yarrow said, "Just wait." She swept her finger over the screen and the video sped up. She slowed it as two figures approached Zane's gap in the wall. My heart stopped as Carter walked cheerfully toward Zane, his ever-present guitar slung on his back. Beside him was Kai. *My Kai*. The guy who had apparently saved my life. No. *It was impossible*. Kai didn't have anything to do with it. He and Carter fought with us. Carter stepped through the barrier and Kai looked back at the school dance as if reconsidering his choice. Then, of his own free will, he walked through the gap in the barrier—and Zane followed before closing it for good.

"It's a mistake," I said. "Kai isn't involved."

"You never saw him spend time with Carter or Zane?"

"I... I mean of course. Carter was his roommate."

"And Zane?" the headmistress asked.

"He..." My breath skipped as I exhaled. "He's not involved."

Kai seemed to become more unhinged these last few months. Was it possible I'd missed the signs? Was I so blinded by our history and his pretty words to know he was saying goodbye? No. *I knew him*. I balled my hands into fists, grinding my teeth. I knew with certainty that someone had set Kai up.

The evidence was damning. Which left me with only one option: find him and clear his name. There was no one left to believe in Kaito Nakamaru but me.

Read The Brave & The Broken

BRITTNI CHENELLE

the brave and the broken

GIFTED FAE ACADEMY
∽BOOK TWO∾

THE brave AND THE broken

BRITTNI CHENELLE

Also Available in Audio

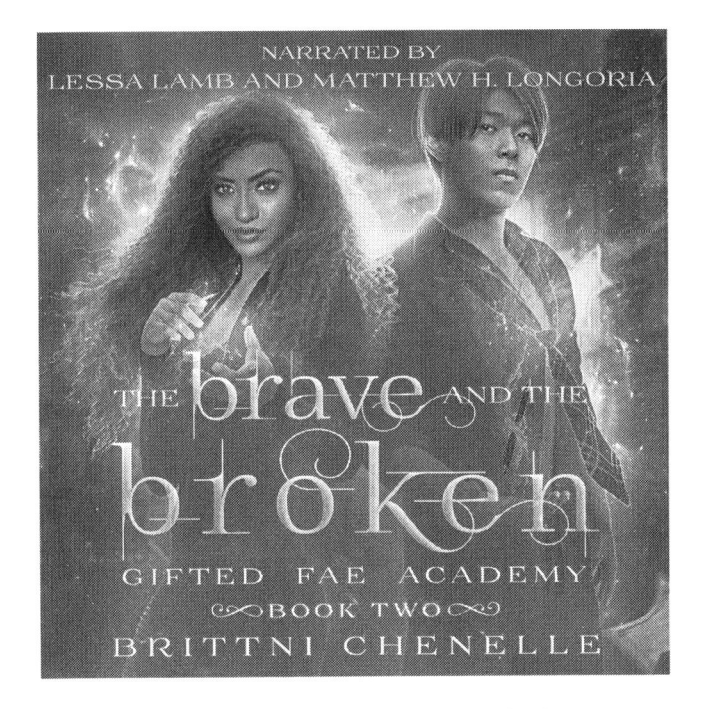

NARRATED BY LESSA LAMB AND MATTHEW H. LONGORIA

The Brave and the Broken
GIFTED FAE ACADEMY
BOOK TWO
BRITTNI CHENELLE

Take advantage of the discounted price.

Reina

ONE

Lightning crackled through the courtyard as the last of the students filed into the auditorium. Though midday, the clouds blocked the sun's rays and threatened a storm like a knife at our throats. The thick mossy smell of the impending rain filled my nose as I stepped out of the cool air and into the auditorium, only to regret it a moment later. The sobs of the broken-hearted students reverberated off the domed ceilings, and the air was so thick I thought we might suffocate in each other's grief. Dressed in black, the room was guarded by a host of Fae ready to jump into action at a moment's notice. We were no longer safe. The walls of Gifted Fae Academy had been breached, and with them fell one of our most beloved students.

I took my seat beside Briara, my head pounding from a night spent crying, but unlike her I had no more tears to shed. It was as if I'd cried myself dry. My roommate, however, seemed to have an endless supply. I wanted to reach out and hold her hand, but she was so fragile I worried she'd shatter at my touch. I traced her gaze past the rows of students to the stage where a large portrait of Quan Levout sat, grinning brightly. Bri choked on her tears, and I turned my face away, clenching my jaw to the point of pain at the sound of her agony. I reached for the owl charm on my necklace only to remember that it, too, was gone.

There is nothing so senseless as a murdered kid, and at a school filled with aspiring Fae, where we should feel safe, we instead felt helpless. As I replayed the night of the winter ball in my head, I kept coming back to the same thought: *What was all this training for if I couldn't even save a friend?*

The big screen above the stage lit, and a close-up of Veranda Yarrow filled the space. Although I could see her on stage just fine, the live feed intensified her expression. Her wide hips and fierce red hair swayed as she stepped behind the podium, her eyes glistening with pain. "Quan Levout was kind and brave," she said, her words slicing into the crowd. "He died defending his friends and his school, an act worthy of the title Fae." Her voice broke and she stepped away from the mic while Yemoja Roux took the stage.

I leaned forward at the sight of my mentor. Her magenta hair was dulled, her skin ashy, and her eyes sunken in and dark. When her gaze flicked up to the crowd, I saw in her vacant expression that she'd been asking herself the same questions I had. Her slumped posture implied she blamed herself. She lifted the mic. "I'd like to present the honorary title of Fae to Quan Levout for his heroic actions during the recent attack."

A flare of sniffles and sobs filled the air, and my vision began to blur. I was no stranger to funerals. I'd been to my parents' just over a year ago. The only thing that got me through back then was the hope that I would one day get into GFA, and things would be better. Only now, behind the walls of the institution I had admired all my life, I found myself walking toward the same despair but without the comforting vision of a better future.

I snapped back to attention when the next speaker took the stage. Oden Gates—my boyfriend, and Quan's closest friend—stepped behind the podium, looking much worse than Miss Yarrow or Yemoja Roux.

He hadn't returned a single call or text since the attack, and I'd imagined he was in bad shape. I just wanted to be there for him if he needed me. Dread flared inside me at the sight of him. Unlike Yemoja's dulled appearance, Oden's eyes blazed such a vivid green that he hardly looked human. His skin was waxy, his plump lips chapped. Rather than broken, he looked frightening, dangerous, ready to kill at the slightest provocation. Just from looking at him, and everyone else for that matter, I feared that if the school and the local Fae could be so defeated by a decimated spirit alone, The Fallen had already won. Robbed of my usual nervous habit, I smoothed out the folds in the black fabric of my dress as I waited for Oden's first words.

Finally, Oden tapped on the microphone, his green eyes glazed over like he forgot the whole school was watching.

"I can't believe he's gone. Just like that." He snapped his fingers as he shook his head. "Quan didn't deserve to die." He gritted his teeth, his jaw clenching. "What's the point of these Gifts if we can't protect the people we care about? What's the use of all this training?" he asked, a low growl in his voice.

I swallowed; there it was. I bit my bottom lip and shut my eyes. Oden was unraveling, and it was painful to watch. Professor Greene and Veranda Yarrow exchanged a look, as if debating whether to put an end to his speech. I hoped they would, but I supposed they were giving him leeway since he knew Quan best.

Oden sputtered, "When I find Kaito Nakamaru, I'll make him fucking *pay* for what he did!"

Veranda snatched the microphone away and the room sat in stunned silence.

I dropped my head, the heat of fresh tears streaking my face. *Kai*. I placed my hand flat on my chest where the owl charm used to rest. My heartbeat raced against it as I swallowed the urge to defend him.

Miss Yarrow spoke, "Emotions are running high. There will be grief counselors available to any who feel the need to talk. Please join us in the cafeteria for refreshments, if you wish."

The screen above the stage flipped to static. Taking it as a sign that the ceremony was over, some eager students stood and prepared to move to the cafeteria. I didn't blame them. The sorrow in the auditorium was palpable. Thunder crackled outside as the first few students filed out, then the screen lit up again. My stomach dropped, my heartbeat racing as I gaped at the screen. Kaito Nakamaru stared back, and before he spoke his first words, I feared trusting him had been a terrible mistake.

kaito
TWO

I glared into the blackness of the camera lens and took a steadying breath before I shattered my former life. Willing myself not to think about who would be listening, I interweaved my fingers to keep my hands from shaking. I felt DT looming over me, heard the scrape of his boots as he paced behind the camera, his eyebrows raised and his head cocked at my hesitation.

I sighed, knowing I'd agreed to this, as the camera's static red light urged me on. I spoke, "By now you know of The Fallen's involvement in the attack on Gifted Fae Academy. Now that we have your attention, we'd like you to know why. This unwarranted hero worship must end. Wake up! The Fae's hands are covered in blood. Their power has been absolute, their victims slaughtered without a trial. Why should some be praised for these violent acts and others punished? As a society, we've been brainwashed by the media, taught to love and trust the unchecked Fae as we reward them for their violence.

They grow richer, while the rest starve on the streets. We die, they profit. According to the Fae, there is no benefit in financially assisting the poor or ungifted. Gifts alone determine whether we starve or thrive, with no merit given to any other aspect of our being. The Fallen merely seek to correct this injustice. To take back the wealth and power that belongs to the people. We are driven by the ones we couldn't save, the fallen among us. We have grown in numbers, gifts, and strengths, and we will purge this city of the corruption that has placed the Fae upon pedestals, allowing them to play judge and jury. The leaders of this city have turned violence into an exalted enterprise—paying the Fae with the funding that should be helping the less fortunate. It's time to stand up and rise against the Fae.

"My name is Kaito Nakamaru, the leader of The Fallen. Join us, and together we'll build a better world—one where your gift won't define your life."

The red light on the camera blinked out but the tension in my body didn't ease. DT stepped in front of me. "Very good, Kaito. Very good. Your sacrifice is going to help so many people." He turned back to Zane. "You were right about him. He's perfect."

I stood. "Forgive me for not being flattered," I growled as I headed for the door, making sure to knock shoulders with Zane on my way out.

It was supposed to be a threat, but Zane's clumsy footsteps behind me said he hadn't gotten the message. "Kai," he called. I froze. "This really is for the best, you know. I know you're not happy about how it all went down at the school but—"

I turned on him so quickly that I felt his gift flicker to life between us. He pushed his glasses up on his nose.

"A kid is dead, Zane. He wasn't Fae, he wasn't part of the system. He was a high school kid, like us."

"And more kids like him starve on the streets everyday and they don't get a shred of the news coverage he did. They don't get a fucking honorary title. It's one thing to be the face, man..." He stepped toward me. "...to say the words verbatim, and to even sound committed to the cause, but if that's not how you feel, what are you even doing here?"

I ran a hand through my hair.

His mouth tensed. "Don't forget about the bigger picture."

I glared at him. "I didn't ask for this."

He shook his head, his blue hair glinting in the stale light of the office hallway. "None of us did."

DT walked out from behind Zane and my hair stood on end.

"Is everything okay?" he asked, his voice teeming with sincerity and concern. I'd met with him on several occasions but I never quite got used to the look of him. He was, in a word, transcendental. His skin looked ceramic, like carved marble, his polished features delicate and almost feminine. His white hair further emphasized his youthful, almost ethereal appearance. But it was the ease with which he moved through the world that unnerved me. He was all things pleasant, gentle, and charismatic—hardly the type I would have thought capable of masterminding The Fallen. Alongside DT, Zane wilted like a flower exposed to too much sun. He leaned away as if his body instinctively fled DT's dark gift.

Before Zane could get out of reach, DT draped his arm over his shoulder like an old friend, but Zane's panicked gaze snapped to me so quickly I could tell we feared the same thing. My breath caught as I waited to see if Zane would drop dead, then and there. The last thing you wanted was to be touched by the harbinger of death. Instead, DT grinned and said, "Be easy on him, Zane. Kaito is burdened by what he lost today. Give him time." His gaze moved to me, but he spoke to Zane as if I weren't there. "In a few short minutes, he accomplished more for our cause than our entire enterprise. He's a hero."

I felt like many things: a traitor, a liar, but certainly not a hero. Without a word, I turned and headed for the elevators, leaving Zane to fend for himself. I wanted nothing more than to hide out in my new apartment. DT was right about one thing, I did need time. He knew that by making me the face of The Fallen, I would be sacrificing my reputation and any chance at a normal life. That was certainly true enough. But as I moved into the elevator and the doors closed in front of me, the sick pang in my stomach said what I lost that day was much more precious. I reached up and ran my thumb over the owl charm on the chain around my neck, the one that once belonged to the girl I finally realized I loved. *I'm sorry, Reina.*

Reina
THREE

The screen blinked out and with it the last semblance of faith I had in Kaito. My skin seared as the collective student body's attention turned on me. I trembled, my mind so caught between a web of emotions that I couldn't settle on one. Then slowly, like a feather drifting below the breeze, it landed. *I was fucking pissed.*

"Reina," Bri whispered, but words just swirled in the tornado that raged inside of me.

How could he do this? I believed in him. All that bullshit about his feelings for me, all those games. Every memory I had of Kai was suddenly filtered through a new lens; the lens of a traitor. Tears pricked my eyes as I ground my teeth together. He'd hurt me for years and I'd defended him. My breath caught. He was nothing but a fucking pathological liar.

Briara touched my arm and I snatched it away instinctively.

"Reina," she said more sternly, "you're glowing."

I looked up at her, a purple sheen reflected on her face. Her gaze moved beyond me and I turned to find a museum of frightened statues. Desperate to flee, I planned to push my way through the crowd, but they parted so quickly that I made it to the door in a few clumsy strides.

I burst out into the courtyard, where the sky had already opened up to rain, and slashed a glowing hand through the air in frustration. The rain split as the purple blade sailed through the mist before dissolving. I placed a quivering hand to my chest, as if I could slow the race of my heart with a touch. The rain soaked through my clothes, and I heard the shuffle of students as they started to file out of the auditorium behind me. There was nowhere I could think of to be alone, so I fixed my gaze on the hedge maze. I headed for the entrance, the icy rain seeping into my shoes. I shivered, though my skin felt hot, sweat mixing with ice on my forehead.

I blinked, and standing between me and my escape was Yemoja Roux.

"Let me pass," I ground out through my clenched teeth.

She raised her hands defensively. "I know you're hurting right now, but if you stay out here, you'll get sick and you won't be able to help anyone."

I pushed past her. "I don't care."

"Oh, so you thought being Fae was only about fame and glory, then? Good to know."

I spun. "What are you even talking about?"

Her tone hardened. "Did you think it would be easy? This, right here, is what it feels like to be Fae. Bad things happen—horrible, unspeakable things—and those are the moments when you need to hold it together. When things are the darkest, the Fae step up. They don't fall apart, or put their lives at risk because they're upset."

"You don't understand," I said as hot tears spilled down my cheeks.

"Then tell me. I'm here for you. Let's get out of the rain, and you can share the story. We can talk about why this is hurting you so much."

I stumbled over to her, my strength draining from my legs. Her voice was a mix of firmness and tenderness, a sound that was so like my parents. It soothed me, so I moved towards it like a flower towards the sun. I collapsed into her arms and cried while she carried me inside. "I got you," she whispered.

Bri dashed after us with no regard for the rain. "Can I come along... please? I... I think I should come," she said, her gaze moving between me and Yemoja Roux, her dark makeup already running down her face.

Later that afternoon, after I'd dried off, I sat with my hands cupped around a gold-rimmed teacup and held it to my face as the steam warmed my nose. Yemoja Roux sat on the far end of the L-shaped couch, wearing a similar t-shirt and sweatpants combo as the one she'd given me to wear while my clothes dried. She looked so human in normal clothes, and I realized I'd never thought of her that way before. I was reminded of the time she cried when I used my gift on her. Bri was smudging the apartment, burning sage in every corner, and Yemoja Roux didn't seem to mind in the least. As I scanned the penthouse apartment, with its high vaulted ceilings and arched windows, it was hard to imagine that Yemoja Roux lived here. While it was every bit, if not more, the flashy and expensive place I imagined all Fae to live in, it was something else—something I hadn't expected. It was cold... lonely.

Bri took a seat beside me and rested her head on my shoulder. She looked different without her makeup, and even after living with her for months, I'd scarcely seen her without it. The makeup suited her, but the ease of her features without it seemed to capture her good nature. I was glad she'd come along. She'd always told me how bad she was in emotionally charged situations, but I don't think she gave herself enough credit. She was here. What more could I ask?

Yemoja Roux's gaze moved to me, but she didn't say anything. She smiled softly and turned her attention back to the muted TV screen. She was waiting for me to be ready. I was grateful for what she'd done, how she'd rescued me from myself; and though I wanted to say so, the ache inside me was so strong I knew that a single word would set me off again. I focused on the steam rising from my tea, because I was safe in the home of Yemoja Roux, beside my best friend, and the silence suited me just fine.

Kaito

FOUR

I didn't know I was asleep until a knock at my door jolted me awake. I dragged myself across my apartment and swung it open. Carter stood in my doorway, his guitar at the ready. "Nice digs, man."

Oh, fuck no. I swung for his face, but with a quick run of his fingers his gift soared through the musical notes, halting my fist. I strained against it, but as he strummed through a smooth melody, each note was a new layer of his gift to push through.

He smiled brightly. "Whoa, what's with all the hostility? Not happy to see your old roomie?"

"You killed someone," I hissed.

He raised his hands in surrender. "Hey, I didn't work alone. Besides, I'm just an underling. You're the leader of The Fallen."

A fist collided with Carter's jaw, and I felt his gift drop along with his body. Zane stood over him. "Back the fuck off, man," Zane said, adjusting his glasses. "DT won't be happy if he finds out you're messing with Kaito."

Carter ran a hand through his blonde curls and adjusted his jaw, clearly taken off guard, but a smile soon followed. "I was just congratulating him on being chosen." He stood, checking his guitar for damage as he slunk back down the hall. "We're on the same side, man," he muttered before clicking the button for the elevator.

I turned to Zane. "I don't need your help." I tried to shut my door, but he caught it.

"I know, I just hate that guy. He takes everything too far."

I sighed and headed back into my apartment, leaving Zane the choice to come in or leave. He followed, and I prepared myself for the lecture he had cooked up.

I slumped down on my couch and watched as Zane took a quick scan of my apartment. I had to admit that the open floor plan and black furnishings suited my taste much more than my parents' house. It was the kind of place I would have chosen after I graduated. It was situated in a skyscraper in a crime-riddled part of Ancetol, perfect for a new Fae. I swallowed... but I would never be Fae—not now.

Zane's voice broke me from my pointless thoughts. "Look, I'm sorry. I didn't know the whole story. I knew you came with us to save the school, but I thought once you spoke to DT that you'd come around to our cause. I should have realized when he postponed the rest of the assault that you'd worked out some kind of deal."

I pressed my fingertips together, trying to get a read on him. I wasn't worried that DT had told him about our deal, but about what Zane might've let slip during their conversation.

"But you know, Kai, the Academy will have to fall eventually. It's a big part of the system we're trying to—"

"I know. I just need some time."

Zane nodded. "So, it's not about the school then."

I stood. "DT needs to believe that it is."

"And you're hoping to drag this out until she graduates? It's a bad plan, Kai. She'll become Fae and be an even bigger target than she is now."

He'd always been weirdly observant, but his accuracy about Reina was unsettling. How many other people knew? Did Carter? Fear licked at me like a flame reaching for dried wood. They'd target her if they knew. They could use that information to control my every move. I tried to remember my time with Carter. How much had I told him? I have *never* been so grateful for not being the type to share my feelings. Still, I had to know. "Who else knows? Does Carter? Did you mention it to DT?"

He shook his head. "I didn't mention it, and I won't. I'm not trying to screw anyone over, I just… believe in what we're doing here. I don't know about Carter. Maybe…" He tucked his hands into his pockets. "Never mind."

"What is it?"

"Maybe we should hang out with him."

I sighed. "Like, keep your enemies closer? Don't you think that'll just give him the same opportunity?"

He shrugged and rustled his blue hair. "I actually came here to show you something."

"You mean you didn't stop by just to punch Carter in the face?" I asked. I felt a slight tickle running up my arm between my wrist and my elbow.

He smiled. "That was just a bonus. Come with me."

I stared at my arm as my tattoo vanished, the gift's time running out, returning to my unmarked skin.

Zane eyed it. "Bummer. You going to get a new one?" he asked, opening the front door to my apartment.

I followed. "You mean like The Fallen arrow you had at the bus stop?"

He grinned. "I needed to get your attention somehow."

I bit back a laugh. "Yeah, that fucking did it all right."

Reina

FIVE

Bri gaped at me, her purple locks bobbing in the messy bun on the top of her head. "He... he said that?"

I mindlessly stirred my tea. It seemed like every time I told my version of what happened at the winter ball, it made less sense.

Yemoja Roux leaned forward, her magenta hair pulled into a braid as she sipped her tea. "That *is* strange," she said. "I think it's all too fresh for us to see clearly."

"What do you mean?" I asked, sipping my tea.

"He actually *said* that?" Bri said.

I nodded.

Yemoja's gaze drifted up to the left. "Well, I didn't know Kaito, really. But he once accused Zane Blaque of being a member of The Fallen during a lecture I gave."

I said, "But... Zane *is* a member of The Fallen."

Her expression hardened. "Exactly. The two seemed to be at

odds, and yet you say they spent a lot of time together after that."

I nodded, enjoying the objective analysis because it hurt so much less—helped me gain perspective.

She continued, "It's possible that he became involved with The Fallen at that point, but by then they were already an established group with the capability of killing Fae. Perhaps he joined to sabotage them, not help them."

"So you're saying he lied about being the leader," I added.

Briara rubbed her face with her hands. "Well, if he lied about that, he could have lied about that other thing."

I shot her a playful glare... although she had a point.

Yemoja said, "I hardly think he would have said those things to you, fought alongside his friends, and protected you, if he was part of the plan. It's just too... odd."

I dropped my gaze to my teacup. "Unless... he was saying goodbye."

A musical sound rang out and Yemoja Roux lifted a finger and mouthed, "Excuse me."

She sat up straight, lifting her phone to her ear. "Mhmm. Okay," she said, and I strained to hear the other half of the conversation. "What can I do? I'm on my way."

She stood so quickly it startled me. Her gaze whipped over to me. "I have to go to the school."

I sat stunned as Bri asked, "Is everything okay?"

She nodded. "Do you two want to come with, or stay here?"

Stay here? I looked around her apartment. "Would that be okay? Can I stay?"

"Of course. You both can. I was thinking you could crash here for a couple of days to maybe rest, after... everything." She pulled her hair out of her braid and it fell back into its usual waves.

"Yes. I would love that. Thank you," I said.

"Me too," Bri chimed in. "I'll catch a ride with you so I can grab my stuff. I *need* my makeup."

Yemoja smiled then rushed out of the room, and when she returned she had on her pastel uniform. She was every bit the image of the idol I'd admired my whole life, with one small difference: I knew her. I knew that the waves in her hair came from her keeping it braided when home; I knew that she loved tea, and had fears just like everyone else; and I knew she was kind, because, when the walls of the Academy had been breached, she offered me a few days of sanctuary.

"Alright. I'm headed out," she said. "Ready, Bri? We should be back in a few hours. Make yourself at home."

In a flash she was gone, and Bri along with her. Yemoja's last word echoed through her beautiful apartment. *Home.* My thoughts drifted to the orphanage that technically warranted the word, then moved to GFA where I resided, and finally it moved to Kai.

I was angry, but Yemoja Roux had planted doubt inside me. I knew there was some truth to what she said about Kai, but I was tired of having faith in a guy who always let me down. *Not this time.*

I sipped my tea when a flash at the corner of my eye drew my attention to the muted TV. I scrambled for the remote when I saw the reporter standing outside GFA. This must be why Yemoja Roux was called in.

I frantically clicked at buttons on the remote, unable to turn on the sound. The scene changed to a limousine, and I watched in anticipation as the door swung open and a tall man donning a golden crown stepped out.

He was broad shouldered, his posture rigid. He had a peppered goatee that stood out against his dark skin. And with his handsome but serious face, I instantly recognized the similarities he shared with his son. There was no doubt he was the father of Prince Finn Warsham—the King of Zalmia.

The headline flashed red:

King of Zalmia pulls son from GFA due to recent attack.

I stared and wrapped the blanket tighter around me, but the next headline caused me to leap from the couch and head straight for GFA.

Could GFA be closing its doors permanently?

kaito

SIX

Since I'd arrived, I hadn't spent much time exploring the tower where The Fallen operated. Despite his lethal power, DT was a soft-spoken leader, and only asked that I read his speeches and stay in the tower. He made sure I was accommodated with a nice apartment, and gave me access to the company cafeteria. But I wasn't an idiot. I knew our partnership couldn't last forever. GFA would have to fall for their plan to be complete, so I needed to find a weakness in their organization before it was too late. My best bet was to embrace The Fallen to gain their trust so I'd be in a position to counter them when the time came. But seeing how committed Zane was to the cause had me worried that I'd get in too deep and not be able to find my way back.

I also knew the moment I turned on The Fallen, I was a dead man. There were no Fae coming to rescue me, and I wouldn't last long as an enemy to both sides. Though I was sympathetic to some of The Fallen ideology, the choices I made were to protect Reina and the other students. The moment Quan was skewered, my body moved into hyperdrive. And, although it was a snap decision, it was one I didn't regret. Once I crossed DT, I'd have no allies to rely on… except maybe Reina. I knew it was a long shot that she wouldn't hate me forever, but it was that foolish pipe dream that pulled me through. Even if I lost my life in this battle, I wanted her to know, somehow, that my intentions were good.

No matter how defeated I felt, I could no longer spend every spare moment in my apartment alone, trying not to think about all I'd lost. The fight wasn't over.

Zane pushed the button marked B1 on the panel, and my mind shuffled through the horrors that might lay in the underground floors of a criminal organization. Then, as the elevator lowered, I remembered the glass demons that attacked us at the dance. I knew there was someone gifted that was responsible, but I shuddered to think that those things could be nearby.

We stepped out of the elevator and Zane tossed me a mischievous smile before leading me to a pair of double doors. He nodded for me to enter.

"Okay…" I pushed open the doors and threw my hands up in front of me defensively. After a stunned pause, cheers burst through the room. I gaped as I scanned the crowded hall. There were about two hundred people all turned to me, smiles plastered on their faces. Zane patted me on the back, ushering me further into the room. Despite the cramped, windowless room and low ceilings, it was a cheerful party. Most of the occupants had drinks in their hands, and the walls were covered in screens with colorful lights dancing and shooting around the room. At the back of the room, DT strode out onto the stage. He wore a white fitted suit with a purple scarf slung over one shoulder. His musical voice flowed from the microphone. "Welcome, Kaito!" he said. "We've thrown this party as a token of our appreciation for your bravery and sacrifice."

Heat burned my face as I waved off their attention. A party? It was literally the last thing I'd expected. DT left the stage and the crowd resumed their conversations, but I couldn't shake the feeling that they were all waiting to talk to me. I turned to Zane, hoping to give him shit for setting me up, when a petite girl with a bright grin and a lavender pixie cut walked over to us. Two beer bottles were floating beside her as she motioned them to our hands. I raised an eyebrow. *Impossible.* "Levitation?"

She shook her head. "I wish. It's more like strings and a puppet… plus I can only do it with glass."

I nodded. "Ah."

"Mr. Nakamaru," she said, her words jumbled together.

"Kai."

She gulped, and I could practically see her struggling to form her next words.

Zane cleared his throat. I turned to him and nearly laughed as his face turned beat red. With the tiniest nod of his head, I knew what to do. "Do you know Zane?"

She barely glanced at him before turning her attention back to me. "I'm Ensley and I just wanted to thank you personally. You're a hero."

Zane leaned in. "I helped."

Ensley and I both turned to Zane as an awkward moment passed. I sipped my beer. Oh boy, he wasn't going to make this easy. "Yeah, well, Zane did convince me to give The Fallen a chance." Ensley's gaze brightened. "Well then, I guess I owe you thanks too," she said.

She turned back to me. "I'm supposed to give a speech. Do you think we can chat later?"

Zane blurted, "I'd love to."

Ensley gave a pained smile before pushing through the crowd toward the stage.

I grinned, patting Zane on the back as he turned his attention to the floor. "Smooth," I whispered.

It wasn't until Ensley reached the stage, and I took another sip of my beer, that a chilling realization dawned on me. *Glass? Puppet strings? No.* I had to be wrong. There was no way that cute, bubbly girl was the one who killed Quan Levout. Was there?

Reina

SEVEN

I wasn't able to catch Bri and Yemoja Roux before they left, so by the time I made it to the school, there was a mob of media outside the gates. Camera flashes, waving microphones, and gloved reporters were all being kept at bay by four Bronze Tier Fae. I dropped my head, so my curls could hide my face, and snuck my way toward the front of the crowd. I scanned the Fae; they were familiar, but I didn't know them by name. I hoped they'd recognize me from my meltdown that morning, and I waited until one of them made eye contact. His face lit with recognition, and I lifted a shy hand to confirm. He whispered to another Fae, and the two ushered me through the gate and the school's new barrier.

It might've been that the school's reinforced barrier was thicker so less light shone through. Or maybe it was the clouds refusing to lift the ominous gray blanket the sky had become. Either way, the school that had once captivated me with a single glance now looked haunted… ghostly. The sheer number of Fae lining the halls of the main building, and the speed with which they ushered me to the back where the campus was located, told me that the King of Zalmia was still present.

I came to a halt when I noticed Miranda shuffling through the hallway toward the balcony stairs that led down to campus. We weren't exactly friendly, and I didn't want to engage in any unnecessary battles, so I slowed to match her pace. I didn't immediately notice that she was dressed more casually than usual, with sweatpants, an oversized t-shirt, and a puffy jacket that didn't look like it belonged to her. I didn't even register the dullness of her usually sleek ponytail. It wasn't until I heard her sniffle that I realized she was crying. "Miranda," I called as I hurried over, and she slowly turned, her watery eyes fixed on me as if she was waiting for me to set the tone of our interaction. Even with a pink nose and no sign of make-up, which I'd never seen her without, she was stunning—maybe even more so.

"Are you okay?" I asked.

It was as if those three words broke her, because fresh tears spilled out onto her cheeks as she wrapped her arms around me. Stunned, I rubbed her back as she shook. Her cheek brushed mine. My body went rigid as both my gift and hers awakened. What had Oden told me about her gift? She was a seer? I didn't see any immediate danger in that, but I didn't want to take any chances. We were at each other's mercy. Noticing my tension, she pulled away, wiping her nose with the back of her hand. "Don't worry," she croaked. "I won't do anything. I was thinking we could..." she sniffed, "be friends or something."

It wasn't what I expected, but I was in no position to turn down a friend. We'd had a complicated start at GFA, but everyone seemed to be affected by losing Quan. I nodded. "Yeah, that would be... nice." I didn't want to push, to mess up whatever we'd just agreed to, but my curiosity overtook me. "Were you close to him?"

She shook her head. "I always kind of thought he was a perv, you know?"

I was confused. Looking at her, it seemed like she'd lost a beloved friend, but that obviously wasn't the case. Was grief just some accessory she was trying on?

Her eyes widened. "Oh, you mean why am I upset?"

"Kinda. But if you're not ready—"

"No, it's okay," she said, seriousness and dread seeping into her delicate features.

My anxiety rose to meet hers in anticipation.

"So, like... now that we know for sure that Kai's betrayed us, I just keep thinking..." Before she even finished, I regretted asking. "I had sex with him. Like a few times, and I really *loved* it. Why am I always attracted to these bad guys, you know?"

I sighed, unable to mask my annoyance.

She shook her hands like they were on fire. "Like, I told everyone about it, too, and now they probably think I'm a traitor... and like when we were doing it—"

Lord, please just strike me the hell down. "Miranda, I'm sure nobody thinks that."

I fought against a wave of nausea as she pulled me in for another hug. I patted her back. "You're such a good friend," she said.

Desperate to change the subject, I asked, "Have you heard anything about the school? Is it really closing?"

She shrugged. "I'm waiting here for updates but they've been kind of tight-lipped about it. Finn might know, since... you know."

I nodded. "I'm going to ask around."

"Okay, bestie," she said.

I wasn't jealous. I was angry. As if I needed more reasons to be furious with Kai. As if it wasn't enough that he was tearing the whole city apart, I had to get a play-by-play reminder of how toxic our non-relationship had been, via Miranda, of all people. Before today, it was as if Kai's little confession at the dance had given me amnesia about all the crap he'd put me through, his escapades with Miranda included. Since I had proof that Kai's declaration was real, I held onto a shred of hope that it was all a mistake. That is, until the video this morning stamped it out, making the betrayal that much worse. Now Miranda seemed genuinely upset, but I couldn't comfort her. I was barely holding it together myself.

As I stepped onto the balcony stairs that led down to the campus, I could see students wandering around the misty grounds... aimlessly... like the undead... and a shudder shot down my spine as three began to move quickly toward me. I couldn't see them through the fog, but whoever they were, they might have information about the academy.

I made my way toward them, and the shapes grew more defined. I recognized Oden's first. A flutter of nerves wracked my body as he approached, Finn and Enzo at his sides.

"Rei?" he said.

"How'd you know it was me?" I said, moving closer as the three figures finally became clear.

"You're glowing," he said.

I looked down at my hands. "Shit. I don't know why it does that."

A half-smile slipped from his face so quickly I almost missed it. I could practically hear his thoughts remind him that Quan was gone.

He took a deep breath. "Everything's so fucked up."

I nodded. "I heard they might be closing the school."

Prince Finn Warsham stepped forward, and I stepped back from sheer intimidation. Then I noticed a gruesome slash across his forehead that looked straight out of *Frankenstein*. My mind raced to the dance, the attack, the monsters. I didn't remember when Finn got injured, but it suddenly made sense that his father was here.

Despite the rawness of the injury, it only seemed to add to his rugged good looks as he said, "That's not decided yet," his baritone velvety smooth. "My father is furious about the attack, and so the administration is trying to calm him down… but he's a powerful man."

Enzo snorted. "No shit, he's a fucking king."

"Is there anything we can do? Can we talk to him?"

Oden took my hand and ran his thumb across it, no doubt trying to dim the glow of my hands. Instead, the light flared, and we all squinted in the brightness before it dulled to its usual lilac glow. Oden said, "We did. They've… altered the terms. They're talking about suspending all internships or any other off-campus training."

They were taking an axe to my life, and my internship with Yemoja Roux. And worse, they were destroying any chance I had of finding Kai and taking him down. "No, they can't do this! I need to find Kai! I need to—"

I shook as a new wave of rage pulsed off my body, whipping my hair. Oden pulled me into his chest, and the warmth was as comforting as the tea I'd been downing all morning. He buried his face in my neck, and I saw Enzo and Finn exchange a look before wandering a few feet away to give us privacy. "I'm so sorry, Reina," Oden said into my neck. My heartbeat stuttered as his breath on my skin sent a shock through my body. I'd missed him. He loosened his grip but still held me in his arms the way he used to. "I just... with Quan—" His voice broke.

Cupping his face in my hands, I whispered, "I know, Oden. Don't worry. I know this has been a horrible experience for you." Taking his hands, I brought them to my mouth to place a gentle kiss. "I just want to be there for you... if you need me."

He sighed and looked down. "There was something else." When he looked up, his green eyes were glassy, the threat of tears as prominent as the threat of rain. "After the dance, I just got the feeling that you didn't, I don't know... blame Kai for what happened."

Words caught in my throat so forcibly I couldn't breath.

He continued. "But now that I see you like this, I know that we all have the same goal. To avenge Quan."

"Of course that's what I want! He fooled me most of all!" I spat, tears sliding down my cheeks.

He wiped them. "I know, baby," he whispered as he leaned in and kissed me, sending a tingle through my limbs. I tightened my grip and he followed, the kiss deepening as his tongue slid between my lips. I used all my strength to hold his body to mine as his fingers danced along the back of my neck. With his free hand, he lifted me, wrapping my legs around his waist. A new hunger awakened. I didn't want to stop, because, for the first time since the dance, something felt good.

A new presence surged through the fog. I screamed as fingers clutched a handful of my hair and snatched me out of Oden's arms, slamming me to the ground.

Kaito

EIGHT

*E*nsley practically squealed with excitement before she got a single word out. Even from the far side of the room, I could see DT's lanky form awaiting her speech. The two shared a similarly pleasing temperament, both likable and friendly. Why then could I easily imagine one as a killer and not the other? The way Ensley was so starstruck differed from DT. She didn't share his quiet confidence, or the unsettling calm within which he operated. I settled on the possibility that I was wrong about her involvement. She was more likely the friendly hostess for parties, not the ruthless killer that had been offing Fae and attacking schools.

She spoke, "I'm very happy to be here. For years, The Fallen have been trying to give a voice to those passed over by the system. But this morning, Kaito delivered our message to the world beautifully."

She gestured to me with a bright smile, prompting another round of cheers. I shifted, my face hot from the attention. I just didn't understand why I was getting any praise at all. I hadn't joined willingly, and I'd read the speech verbatim. It was a safe bet no else but Zane knew that, though.

When the cheers died down, Ensley continued, "The response has been far more positive than expected; Ancetol's major news outlets went so far as to refer to Kaito, and The Fallen movement, as visionary and thought-provoking. Just this morning, we've received over thirty thousand dollars in anonymous donations!"

Her eyes glittered. "What makes Kaito such an excellent candidate to be our voice is that he was the top student at GFA. He was already drawing media attention and a following, and has a seriousness to his personality that aligns with our cause. He's the perfect representative, both delivering speeches eloquently, and inspiring the youth to follow his example and question authority. He's the ultimate rebel, willing to sacrifice for the greater good."

I winced. Well that solved that little mystery. She obviously didn't know about my deal with DT. I was sure it was better for him to let them believe I was who they needed me to be. Perhaps DT's plan was to win me over with the acceptance and praise of his members. Ensley's theory as to why I was chosen, I suspected, was a little off. If I had to guess, I'd say it was because DT figured I was attention starved and emotionally vulnerable enough to be easily manipulated, but being underestimated could work in my favor. I only needed to play the part.

Someone near the stage said something to Ensley that I didn't catch and her eyes moved over to DT. He gave an approving nod, and a few seconds later all the television sets flicked on. I cringed the moment I heard a clip of my voice mixed in with a chorus of news reporters and talk show hosts.

The TV sets all muted with the exception of the one at the back of the room. Luckily, it didn't show my speech, but rather a set of middle-aged Bronze Tier Fae chatting on leather couches.

"It's ridiculous," one said. "If the Fae couldn't attack with lethal force, we'd lose every fight."

The other man seemed reluctant to agree. "I mean, obviously you're right, but we're putting a lot of faith in our government."

"What do you mean?"

"I mean, what if someone from The Fallen gets elected? Technically, they could order us to target whoever they wanted, and we'd have to obey."

The man shifted, his features lined with frustration. "They're killing Fae."

"And the Fae are killing *them*, too, they have been for years. Surely you know this has never been one-sided."

I felt Zane's hand pat me on the back. I turned to him, his gaze locked onto the screen. He had the same pleased grin as the rest of the people in the room. A pang of guilt hit me as it dawned on me just how important their cause was to them. And here I planned to derail it the first chance I got.

My attention snapped back to the broadcast as an off-screen voice read, "Next up, an exclusive interview with the parents of Kaito Nakamaru."

It felt like all the air was sucked from the room as every TV screen blinked out, and the entire room's attention slammed onto me. I froze. I'd be lying if I said I never thought about how my parents would react to my speech, or if I said I wasn't curious what they would say in an interview, but the last thing I wanted was pity, and if I didn't pull it together quickly, everyone here would start treating me like I was defective. I sucked in a shaky breath. This was nothing new. Even before I got mixed up with The Fallen, my parents hadn't approved of me. I knew what they would say. I wasn't their son. I've always been a fuck up. It didn't hurt less, but I was used to faking it. I swallowed a lump of grief, lifted my beer, and flashed my most convincing smile. "To the cause! Let's *party!*"

Reina
NINE

I scrambled to my feet as Enzo and Finn ran over. Their gifts flickered in my periphery as they prepared to intervene.

"Oh shit," Enzo said as I lunged for Miranda's smug face.

Before my fist could connect, Oden grabbed me. Turning to her with fire behind his eyes. "What the fuck Miranda?"

I shook, purple waves brimming off my skin. Too enraged to speak clearly I barely managed to choke out my words. "I swear to fucking god if you don't let me kill her, I'll kill *you* first," I said to Oden, but Miranda looked unfazed. My gift pushed against Oden, but he used his own to maintain a grip. Each thrash to free myself only made him tighten his hold.

Enzo's hands shot up. "Girl fight!" His smile was bright as his gaze darted between me and Miranda, while Finn looked only mildly intrigued.

Miranda tossed her ponytail over her shoulder. She cleared her throat to draw our attention, and paused to revel in it before she dropped the bomb. "This bitch is going to be with Kaito."

I strained against Oden's grasp. "You fucking *bitch!* You don't know what the fuck you're talking about. I'll kill you!"

"Dude, Reina's crazy," Enzo whispered, half under his breath.

Oden's grip on me tightened as my gift began to win the battle against his. "Reina hates Kai, Miranda. She's going to help us get him. Can't you see that? Look at her!"

Her expression grew somber as she shook her head. Her next words no longer carried a victorious edge and instead came out regretfully. "No. When the time comes, she's going to choose him. I *saw* it."

"You're a liar," I seethed. "You lied about wanting to be friends just so you could read me, and now you're standing here telling another Goddamn lie! Why would we trust anything *you* say? Fuck you, Miranda!" I screamed as I leaped for her again.

She glared at me, her voice soaked with emotion. "It wasn't an act. I genuinely wanted to be friends with you. A few minutes after you left, the vision hit." She sighed. "I've heard about your gift, Reina. I know that it has something to do with the truth. If that's the case, you tell me if I'm lying."

There was a coldness in her eyes but no lie in her voice. Well, I didn't care what she saw, I didn't care if she was the highest ranking seer in the school. As far as I was concerned, seeing was the most useless gift the world could offer, because without a doubt you make your own destiny, and mine was to stop Kaito. I took in a shaky breath before my rage tore through me again. I felt Oden's grip on me loosen.

Miranda turned to Oden. "It's okay, let her go." He obeyed as my gift spun truth and fury around us, but I didn't attempt to attack her again. Doubt seeped through the cracks in my defenses. *How could that be the truth?* She smirked. "It's too bad we can't use her gift on her. But you know my gift, Oden, and how strong I am. With all this purple shit everywhere, I bet she couldn't force a lie if she wanted to."

Finn and Enzo were so quiet as they watched, and Miranda's gaze was locked on Oden. "I'm telling you she's going to be with Kaito." She pursed her lips before strutting closer to him. She brushed his arm with her fingers. "Who are you going to believe?"

I had no words to offer. Instead my focus waited to feel her lie, but she didn't.

She gestured to me, as I remained frozen with rage. "Ask her if she thinks Kaito is a traitor."

Oden's gaze was so full of sadness that I turned my eyes away. "Don't you hate Kaito?"

"Yes, of course!" I said through furious tears. I balled my fist. That they doubted me at all was painful, but knowing Oden did was almost more than I could bear. The words flowed so smoothly, mixing with my gift as all truths did. I felt a tiny pang of relief.

Miranda rolled her eyes. She moved triumphantly toward Oden, her hips swinging with each step. "Come on, Oden," she whispered, egging him on.

Oden's sorrowful green eyes bore into me. A tear fell before he even asked, "Do you love Kaito?"

My heart raced as the air left my lungs. I bit my bottom lip, just as Kai had, the metallic taste of blood filling my mouth. I choked, "I would do what I had to—" But when I looked up, Miranda, Oden, Finn, and Enzo all had the same doubting expression. "You're wrong about me," I bit out. "I will kill Kai if he is what we think he is."

Oden's gaze turned cold as he turned to Miranda and said, "If."

They turned and began to walk away. "Wait! I said I'd kill him. It's the truth!"

Oden spun. "Are you fucking serious? He admitted it himself! You saw the video, yet you still have doubts?"

I dropped my gaze, and even from a few feet away I could feel his body heat swell. "He is nothing but a fucking criminal, Reina, and that you still have doubts just shows how fucked your loyalty to him is. You know better than this. You *are* better than this."

I spat out blood as I watched the four figures walk out of view. Furious, I swiped at my eyes. I was so angry my heart hurt. Once again, someone I counted on turned on me. Dammit! I didn't love Kai. I wanted justice for Quan, but did that mean killing? Why was everyone so ready to take a life? I didn't want to make enemies of the Nobles, and I envied their conviction. One way or another, I needed to prove to them that I would do whatever it took to bring Kai down. And, mostly, I needed to prove it to myself. Lost in my introspection, I spun as the scrape of footsteps startled me.

Professor Greene walked toward me through the fog. If he'd heard our argument, it didn't show in his carefree expression. He inhaled sharply when he saw me. I must've looked a mess with my frizzy hair, blotchy face, and swollen eyes, not to mention the blood dripping from my chin.

"I don't know what you heard," I said hesitantly. He pressed his lips together. Got it. *Everything.* "They're wrong about me, Professor."

He nodded indifferently. "So, Reina, you remember that confection I gave you, the one that got you expelled?" I nodded, though I'd never blamed him for what happened. "It wasn't exactly by chance. You know of Maxim Tuberose? He was at your exam."

"Yes, sir. He's a retired seer, right?"

"That's correct. He never mentioned why, but he told me to make sure that particular confection found its way into your hands. I felt quite a lot of guilt when I heard you'd been expelled from your old school because of it, but then you turned up here for the exam and I understood."

I paused to consider his meaning. "So you're saying you believe Miranda? You believe in seers and their glimpses?"

"I suppose I'm suggesting you seek a second opinion." He nodded toward the main building where the teachers kept office hours, and gave a half smile before walking away into the fog.

"Professor," I called, "can someone change their path? I mean… as far as you know, has Mr. Tuberose ever been wrong about a prediction?"

"Once," he said, and without another word, he was gone.

kaito

TEN

As a perpetual failure, there was nothing more bizarre than being at a party thrown in my honor. I was used to everyone trying to take me down a notch, and all this positive attention left me feeling out of my element. Each person I met was eager to tell me how The Fallen movement had impacted them or their family. The owl charm that brushed my chest with each small movement reminded me that The Fallen murdered the Fae, but that's not what anyone was talking about. They all focused on the redistributed wealth and the families who desperately needed it. While I sympathized with their plight, I'd been present during a Fallen attack. I watched a friend die and knew that if I had become Fae, the very people toasting my contribution would be first in line to toast my death.

I'd already worked up a nice buzz when I caught a whiff of something fried coming from the banquet table. I made my way over to it, thankful for the quick break in socializing, and eyed the trays loaded with finger foods. On the far end of the table, a young girl no older than eight grabbed a handful of cake and shoved it directly into her mouth. I bit back a laugh, but she caught me. She licked her fingers and grinned through missing front teeth. "Did you try the cake?" she asked with wide eyes.

"I was going to, but it seems like you beat me to it."

Her hair was sandy brown and her features were a little familiar, but I couldn't place them.

"We never could afford cake," she said, licking each finger and smearing her face with frosting. "I didn't know it would taste this good."

"If you eat too much, you'll get sick," I warned as I began to fill my plate with savory foods.

"Are you kidding? I'm never eating anything else again."

"Well, would you like me to cut you a slice? Or..." I eyed her slimy hands, "get you a plate?"

"No thanks. I think if I take handfuls the other people won't want any. This way it's all mine."

I nodded. "Good plan. But you know, since it's my party, it's kinda mine."

Her mouth dropped open and a little cake fell out. "Are you Kaito?"

I smirked. "You don't recognize me from the news?"

She shrugged. "Uh uh. No one lets me watch news stuff. I'm only seven. I just came for cake."

"Well have at it, kiddo," I said. "Before your parents see you over here."

"I'm here with my brother," she said, pointing a frosted finger to the far side of the room. I followed it to Zane.

"Ah. Well, that actually makes a lot of sense. What's your name, kid?"

"Wendy Blaque."

"I know your brother."

"Don't tell him about the cake," she whispered.

Across the room an icy gaze caught my eye.

"Why don't you bring a handful of cake to him," I said to the girl. "I'm sure he'd love it."

"Great idea!" she squeaked. I took the opening to make my way over to DT.

The crowd parted to let me pass. At the back of the room stood The Fallen's mastermind, his stark-white suit rolled up to his elbows, exposing his lethal arms and hands. DT's eyes brightened when he saw me approaching. He smiled, his teeth almost unnaturally white. He held out his beer. "Kaito," he said.

I tapped it with mine. "My friends call me Kai, actually."

His eyebrows raised. "Friends, huh. You want to be my friend?"

I shrugged. "Why not?"

He sipped his beer thoughtfully, an impish glint in his icy blue eyes. "What do I have to do?"

I suppressed a laugh. "Uh... for friendship? I don't know, what do you got? Let's hear your sales pitch."

He scratched the back of his neck, then pushed a handful of white hair out of his eyes. "I... don't know what to say."

I shook my head. "Well, what are your skills?"

"Um... I'm pretty good at baking."

There was no way to suppress the laughter this time. "A baker, huh? Can you make something with coconut? It's my favorite."

He grinned. "Is that it?"

"That'll do it." I patted his shoulder and hyper focused on not touching his skin. He seemed taken aback by the gesture. I couldn't imagine many people risked touching him. He always seemed to have at least a few feet around him even in a crowded room. He was a wild card, each interaction a game of Russian roulette—more so because he was unpredictable and unreadable.

But I liked the uncertainty and welcomed it as I awaited his response. His gaze turned on me as he said, "Kai then."

It was a strange move to offer DT my friendship. He seemed satisfied with letting me stay at an arm's length from his organization as long as I kept my end of the bargain. Not to mention he asked very little. But I felt oddly drawn to him, like we were two oppositely charged magnets. His sweetness masked the monster inside, while I fought to prove that I wasn't the devil everyone thought.

The music changed and I winced. It was the same song that Reina had dragged me into dancing to. It felt like a lifetime ago but the embarrassment still felt fresh. "What is it?" he asked.

I smirked. "This song."

"Not good? I kinda like it."

"Last year someone slipped me an infused confection and… I did a striptease for my whole school."

DT slipped his phone out of his pocket. "Looking it up."

"Don't you fucking dare. I'll kill you."

He looked up from his phone, a smile beaming from his every feature.

It was ridiculous, like threatening the grim reaper, and there was no denying the immense pleasure it gave him. He nodded. "I better not look it up then." He smirked. "You're not really what I expected."

I took a swig of my drink. "You either." He raised an eyebrow.

"I've been thinking you look a little young to be the leader of a movement."

He nodded. "As do you." He tilted his head in appraisal. "You're not afraid of me," he said matter of factly.

Well, he was dead wrong about that, but it was a comfort that he couldn't read me. I shrugged. "Should I be? We're friends."

His sly gaze was enough to guess what he'd do next. He held out his hand for me to shake.

"You sure?" I asked. "I'm pretty powerful."

He chuckled. "Why not? We're friends. I trust you."

But that wasn't why. He wanted to know for sure if I trusted him. I wasn't sure that I did, but I wanted to give him what no one but Reina ever gave me—the benefit of the doubt.

The moment his hand met mine, my gift awoke and I tossed him into the air.

Reina

ELEVEN

All I needed was a chance. If a famous seer like Maxim Tuberose could be wrong even once, I was sure Miranda could be too. As I walked along the maroon carpet that ran through the office hallway, I was surprised to see it so deserted. The professors must've all been in the meeting, as they would decide the fate of the school. I expected that Maxim Tuberose would also be in attendance and I was fine with that; I wasn't sure what I wanted to ask him, or if there was even any merit to his gift at all. To my dismay, the door beside the name plaque that read *Professor Maxim Tuberose* was ajar, and I could tell from the shuffle of objects that he was inside.

I took a deep breath.

"I can't help you," a weathered voice said from behind the cracked door, "but I fear you're going to come in anyway."

I wasn't certain he was talking to me or if someone else was inside, but a glimmer of light on the other side of the door compelled me to push it open. I stopped in the doorway. There were a thousand mirrors of every shape and size packed into the small room. Some had golden frames and looked old, some were simplistic and new. Some hung from the ceiling and walls, but most were packed into the small space, leaving only a small path to a wide redwood desk that sat at the center of the room.

On the desk was a single picture frame turned towards the maroon armchair. Sitting motionless in the center of the desk was a snow-white rabbit.

The back of the room had windows that tossed natural light off each of the mirrors. Mr. Tuberose arranged a mirror by his desk then sat. If I was a seer non-believer before, I was now convinced that the whole lot of them were mental cases. I took a step in and my reflection multiplied through the room.

At the center of the dizzying display was Maxim Tuberose. He was white-bearded, his face heavy with wrinkles, his gaze tired and light blue in color. I started when the rabbit moved toward him, nuzzling beneath his hands. "Uhm... nice rabbit," I said.

He glared at me. "Badgering an old man for answers because you're unable to see the thoughts in your own head. Typical... so painfully typical."

"I'm sorry. Should I come back?"

He stroked the back of the tiny white fluffball, whose nose twitched at his touch. I stood awkwardly without an answer, trying to catch a glimpse of his framed picture.

He looked up vacantly and sighed. "Rampant blindness," he muttered.

"Look," I said, "I'm not sure if I even believe in seers or whatever, but—"

"I wonder, then, why you bothered to come."

I stared blankly. For an old guy who looked so much like Santa, he was awfully harsh. "Did I do something to upset you?"

He straightened. "Not at all. I just find humanity to be a disappointment in general." He tapped on the far side of the desk and the rabbit scampered to his other hand. "So many wasted opportunities."

"Professor Greene said you're the whole reason I even ended up at GFA."

His white eyebrow shot up. "And how's that going so far?"

I bit my lip, wincing from the soreness. *He had a point.* The rabbit moved toward the picture frame, knocking it over. My eyes widened as I stared down at the picture of Miranda.

"She's my mentee," he said. "She's quite talented."

"Well, she made a mistake. She thinks I'm going to take Kai's side."

He adjusted the picture, placing it back upright. "Are you?"

"That's why I'm here."

"You want me to tell you how you feel?"

Well, it did sound stupid when he said it like that. "Of course not. I know it's not true."

He laced his fingers together. "Wonderful. Another satisfied customer."

As expected, this was a total waste of time. "Can I at least hold your rabbit?"

"No."

But his rabbit didn't seem to share his opinion and hopped over to my side of the desk. I reached, just in time to catch him and shoot the professor a victorious look.

I felt my anxiety lift. "He's so soft," I said, feeling the warmth of him in my hands. Suddenly having a rabbit around didn't seem so ridiculous. I eyed the cramped, mirror-riddled space. "So, what's with the mirrors?"

"What do you mean?"

I bit back a smile. "Nevermind. Professor… did you know about the attack on the school beforehand?"

He reached for the rabbit and I regretfully handed him off, my fingers brushing his.

He stared into the mirror and said, "No." The mirrors lit with reflections of my purple glow. *Liar*. I held my breath as I waited for an explanation. How could he do nothing knowing that Quan would die?

His expression grew somber. "Everyone always thinks they're one tragedy away from destruction. Our greatest fears never actualize until we're ready to face them—we just never seem to think we are."

"So you… you just let him die?"

"There's a bigger picture that most people are blind to. We're only able to see the current moment, our vision halted by negative events. But the darkness of tragedy gives way to the brightest light, the painful links in life's chain the strongest. Just as every good is necessary, so is every evil. Each a precious piece in the design too complex for mortal souls to comprehend."

I swallowed a lump in my throat. "So you let him die for the greater good."

My thoughts raced, straining to make sense of it. But it was senseless. "I… I think you did an awful thing."

His eyes glowed blue, the blue refracting like a webbed beam off every mirror. I squinted through it. A moment later, his light faded. "Miranda was correct. You're going to choose Kai."

I felt anger swell inside me, the day's events corrupting my sense of rational thought. "Then I'll take pleasure in proving you both wrong. I'm going to be the one to kill Kaito."

"Careful, that doesn't sound much like Fae."

I seethed. "Actually, I think it does."

Kaito

TWELVE

As I lowered DT gently to the ground and his face glowed with delight, he looked almost like a divine entity. Or an excited child.

"That was amazing," he said. "I mean, I heard your gift was levitation, but that was insane."

"I thought you might like that."

He shook his head. "I just... I never felt anyone's gift besides my own. It's so different from the feeling of mine."

"Oh yeah?"

Wendy, the little girl from the buffet table, tore through the crowd, Zane following closely behind.

"My turn!" she screamed. "I want to fly."

Zane grimaced. "Is it okay, Kai?"

I held my hands out and the little girl high-fived them, smearing my hands with frosting. I lifted her and the entire party stopped to watch. I'd never thought to make a kid levitate before and it was a shame. In the course of three minutes, she'd been an astronaut walking on the moon, a mermaid swimming in the ocean, and an angel jumping from cloud to cloud. It was impossible not to smile while watching her.

I realized that I was actually enjoying myself. It was almost unsettling how easily I fit in here. There was no fight, nothing to prove. For the first time, I felt like I was enough. My joy shattered as my attention was drawn to a muted TV screen behind Wendy's imaginary castle. I lowered her and turned my attention to it, where Oden stood speaking into a microphone. "Unmute this," I said to DT.

DT spun before standing on the balls of his feet, waving a hand to get someone's attention, and gesturing to the screen. Oden's voice shot into the room, and shortly after, the music died down.

"He was just the kind of person that you knew you couldn't trust. There was like… a darkness in him. I mean, the dude's first day he challenged me to a fight. What kind of person does that?"

"Oden," the reporter said, "I thought you welcomed him as one of GFA's Nobles."

"I always try to give people the benefit of the doubt. I mean… I knew he was bad news but I never could have guessed that he…" His voice caught. "…that Quan could…"

I swallowed a lump of guilt and washed it down with beer. *He wasn't wrong.* I did have darkness in me. Everyone did when pushed far enough. But I cared about Quan; I cared about all of them. That was the reason I was here, why I'd trashed my own reputation. Oden had been my friend once upon a time. And now… it hurt to see how quickly they all forgot I fought beside them that night. How easily they believed I had joined The Fallen.

I almost didn't notice that DT had turned back to me, reading my reaction. His cobalt eyes glistened as if wet. "You and I are not so different," he said with a sigh. "They say that same stuff about me. Glad we got you out of there."

I nodded. "Thanks, man." But all the air knocked from my lungs when, out of the corner of my eye, I saw Reina flash onto the screen. My body flooded with panic, but I kept my gaze fiercely locked on DT. I wanted nothing more than to see Reina's face, even just for a moment, even if she was only there to malign my character, but the smallest glance would be dangerous. She was the secret I'd die to keep. I clenched my jaw and raised my beer to DT to toast Oden's unforgiving speech as I hyper focused on the audio.

"Reina, can you tell us about your friendship with Kaito?"

"Leave me alone," she spat.

My heart stopped. *Reina.* DT glared. "I'm curious why you'd want to protect the school. They seem like rather nasty people."

Was he onto me? "They're just brainwashed and sad that their friend died. They'll eventually start thinking for themselves."

"Does that mean you've had a change of heart? You're glad to be on this side?"

"I'm honestly not sure." I took a deep breath. Across the room, I saw Carter saunter into the party. Now that the news had put a damper on my evening and Carter arrived, I knew the party was over for me.

"I'm going to head out," I said.

DT gestured to the screen once more and it muted; the music turned back on a moment later. "Thanks for coming. I'm a little surprised you made it."

I shrugged. "Thank *you*. I actually had a good time."

"I don't mean any offense by this, but you fit right in. Why are you so apprehensive to join The Fallen?"

I sucked in a sharp breath, my gaze dragging over to Carter who was quickly approaching.

"I don't like feeling manipulated. The whole time I was learning about what The Fallen stood for, I had Carter in my ear."

His mouth rose on one side. "Ah. Makes sense."

I shrugged. "Later." I managed to slip out of the room without speaking to Carter, but at the expense of not being able to thank Zane for forcing me to attend. I was sure he'd stop by later anyway. Maybe DT would too. I wasn't about to start offing Fae, but it was kind of nice to be around people who understood and appreciated me.

I was almost optimistic as I retreated to my apartment and sunk into my bed, blissfully unaware of my mistake. Someone was about to die, and it was entirely my fault.

Reina
THIRTEEN

After attempting to head back to Yemoja Roux's apartment and being bombarded by reporters, I decided to go back through the school's barrier and wait for her outside the office building. I wondered if Bri was faring any better than I was. I considered heading to our dorm to check on her, but I was terrified. It felt like I was teetering on the edge of my sanity. I'm sure Miranda already told her everything. What if Bri took the side of the Nobles? It would be just enough to push me over. *Fuck it.* I had to face her sometime.

I hurried to Pink House and raced to my room, hoping to get to her before Miranda did. I opened the door just in time for Miranda to strut out of my room with a malicious grin. I watched as she walked down the hallway with far too much enthusiasm. I spun. "Bri, I can explain."

Bri lifted her head, her purple hair loose at her shoulders and her makeup half on. She raised her hand to stop me. "Did that bitch put her *hands* on you?"

I exhaled a chest full of anxiety and inhaled relief as I took a seat beside her. "Yep. Apparently she had a vision."

"Doesn't she need to touch you first?"

I sighed, too exhausted to explain.

She rubbed my back. "I can't believe he's gone. We had this kind of flirtation, you know?" She sighed. "Now is not the time for us to turn on each other."

"Bri, I swear, it isn't even true. I'll make Kai pay for what he did to Quan."

We sat in silence on Bri's bed, our hands clasped together. Then I asked, "How are you holding up?"

She stared down at her hands. "I feel lost, you know? Would you hate me if I stayed here for a few days instead of at Yemoja's with you? I… I need a little time to myself."

"Of course I wouldn't hate you. But if you need anything, message me and I can be here in ten minutes."

"I can't believe Miranda's trying to start shit." She glanced around the room. "I wonder if I have the materials to make a voodoo doll."

I snorted and she looked at me, her eyebrows raised in surprise. She forced a smile. "Do you think she or anyone else really cares about Quan?"

"I do. Everyone does. That's why we're all at each other's throats. None of us are coping well."

"I just…" She choked. "I need some time."

I exhaled slowly and stood. "Alright then, I'll head out. You know how to reach me."

She nodded. "Thanks, Reina… you know, for understanding that I'm just like this."

I smiled softly and took her silence as my cue to leave. We were all fucked up, and it was starting to look like many of us might never recover. I was on my last legs when I reached the front office again, this time determined to stay put until Yemoja Roux came out. Luckily, a moment later, she emerged from the office building. She stopped short and I remembered that I was still bleeding, likely looking as rough as I felt.

"So," I said, reaching for a charm that was no longer around my neck, "are they closing the school?"

She sighed. "No, but they've cancelled the Varsity Games and most of the internships."

My stomach dropped. "Ours?"

"I fought for it, but they only agreed under the condition that you get permission from your… guardian."

My mind slung back to the torturous grip of my group home mother, Ms. Vivian. "Fuck…" I said without thinking. There was no way she'd do anything to help me, even if it was just a signature. As I remembered my former group home "mother," I could practically feel her gift pinching at my skin as I screamed. I could still see my bloodshot eyes in the mirror just after our last encounter.

"Oh boy," I said.

Yemoja Roux put a hand on my shoulder. "You're not the same person as you were last year. She's not going to be able to hurt you the same way."

I gulped. "That's not the point… It's…"

"The fact that she *wants* to hurt you."

I nodded. "But it doesn't matter. I can do this. Don't worry."

She bit her bottom lip. "There's one more thing…"

I put my hands on my hips. "Lay it on me."

"We're no longer allowed in the field with less than three, so I'm bringing Oden into our team."

I bit back a laugh. "Perfect." Things just kept getting better.

At least with Oden around, I'd have the chance to prove to him that I was capable of bringing Kai to justice, that was if I could even convince Vivian to sign for me.

I clapped my hands. "Alright, well, I have my work cut out for me."

"Where's Bri? Is she coming?"

"She's going to stay here, I think."

She raised an eyebrow. "Is everything okay?"

I pressed my lips together and nodded. *As okay as could be expected.*

"Do you want to head back to my apartment and rest for a few days, like we talked about?"

I shook my head. "No, I need to get back out there. I have to find Kai. I'm going to my group home to get the signature."

"Let me rephrase. You've had too much happen lately. Give yourself three days' rest and then go." She turned away. "Something in you is different. You're changing… I'm afraid you'll…"

I took a deep breath. If Yemoja Roux could see me unraveling, then I really knew I should heed her advice. "Three days' rest. Then I'll go."

The lines on her face softened. "You don't want me to come?"

"No, it's okay. I think I need to face this one alone."

kaito
FOURTEEN

I awoke feeling hungry and with a slightly less negative attitude toward The Fallen. I did not grow up the same way as most of the others, but they welcomed me just the same. All night my mind was locked on Wendy Blaque trying cake for the first time. Zane had mentioned that his family was poor, and that he used to sneak food to them from GFA's cafeteria, but it wasn't until I saw Wendy downing that cake that the reality sunk in. I knew things were not equal in Ancetol, but how bad was it?

I decided to head to the cafeteria for breakfast, instead of ordering in. I hoped to run into Zane to maybe pick his brain about The Fallen, and thank him for last night's party. I hadn't stepped into the cafeteria since my first night in the tower, and my head had been fogged from the whirlwind of the night's events—my appetite squelched by the fresh memory of Quan's skewered corpse. I remembered it as a dark and mostly empty hall with scattered strangers lurking in the shadows. But, this morning, during peak meal time, it seemed like a different place entirely.

It buzzed with energy as the ungifted ate together with smiles and an air of hope. There was a sense of community that I hadn't experienced anywhere else. Moments into watching them interact, I envied them. They hugged and brushed hands without a trace of fear. They may have been poor, but they had something the Gifted world did not—they could touch. They could comfort a friend or assist a stranger. Some time ago, my world had lost that. I grabbed a tray and got into line.

"Hi, Kaito," Ensley said from behind the counter. Her hair was wrapped up in some kind of net.

I smirked. "Good morning," I said, my voice groggy with sleep.

She scooped some beige-colored slop onto my tray, and I didn't bother asking what it was. Though the quality of the food wasn't a fraction of what I got when I ordered from my room, or even what they served at GFA, I couldn't overlook the grateful smiles of those around me. These were life sustaining meals.

I turned to take a seat as several people nodded to me in recognition. On the far side of the cafeteria, I spotted DT sitting alone. I took a seat across from him and he looked up. A bewildered expression flickered across his face before giving way to a smile. He took a mouthful of the slop.

"Is it any good?" I asked.

"Are you kidding? I love this stuff. I grew up on it."

I nodded and poked at it with my plastic spork.

"I know you grew up rich, Kai, but that doesn't mean your childhood wasn't total shit too."

"What makes you think my childhood was shit?" I said,

taking a bite. The texture of the mixture might've been off-putting, but it was nicely seasoned.

A touch of blush flashed across his cheeks. "I… uh… I saw the interview with your parents."

I sighed, dropping my gaze to my plate as I said, "That bad?"

"They had me nostalgic for my childhood."

I bit back a laugh. "I doubt that."

"They didn't come around when you got your gift?"

I shrugged. "Sort of. I mean… I got into trouble right away."

"What do you mean?"

I ran a hand through my hair. I didn't really want to talk about it, but I couldn't really remember the last time anyone really cared enough to ask me about my life. Though it was such a disaster, it was one of my favorite memories, and if anyone could understand, it would probably be DT. "I uh… kissed this girl and she floated away. I accidentally dropped her and she ended up in the hospital."

He snorted. "All I keep thinking is how much worse it would have been if I'd learned about my powers like that."

"I can imagine. I bet your childhood was rough."

He took a deep breath. "Yeah, well… yeah."

I narrowed my eyes at him, not about to let him get away with just "yeah". "I told you mine."

His stormy expression cut me. "I don't know if you'll understand."

I took a mouthful of mush. "Who could better than me?"

He shrugged. "What do you want to know? How I figured out my gift?"

"It's a good place to start."

"It's a long story."

"Well, get on with it," I pushed.

He clenched his jaw then released it in surrender. "I was only eleven when I killed my first Fae."

My heartbeat stuttered as the weight of what I was about to hear began to settle in, but, oddly enough, I already understood. I'd hurt someone with my gift when I unlocked it. It only made sense that with a gift much more dangerous, so too would be the consequences.

DT paused, as if waiting for me to stop him. When I didn't, he continued. "I'd grown up poor with parents who struggled to put food on the table. Like most kids in my district, I was hungry all the time, but my situation wasn't unique. Ancetol had always been a city of economic inequality, but ever since the Fae had become more than the protectors of the city, since they had moved to dominate everything from business to popular culture, the only places for its citizens to land seemed to be either the Elite or hungry. The Teal Street District was packed with protesters, hoping to catch the attention of the media, to shed light on the issue, and at one such protest, things got out of hand."

I thought I remembered something from my history class about the incident. A fire maybe? But it happened seven or eight years ago now.

"The news outlets were conveniently absent. Instead, the Fae sent Will Citrine to appease the crowd. After all, what could a group of coms and serfs do? Will was a young Fae at the time, rising in popularity because of his flashy gift of shooting fire from his feet and the way he used it to fly around. 'I'm here because I want to help, because I care,' he'd said, reading off his cue cards. 'Please, you must all go home for your own safety.'

"The crowd grew agitated and, in a manner of minutes, the peaceful protest turned violent. In a panic, Will Citrine cast a wall of fire between himself and the crowd and called for backup. At least," he sighed, "that was what we were fed on the subject through the internet. What I remember was the thick black smoke and how it burned my lungs as I cried out for help. I remember the doorway to my bedroom ablaze with orange flames and the crash of the surrounding buildings as they collapsed."

I leaned forward, searching his eyes for pain, but he seemed detached from the memory.

"Crouched in a corner in my room, I used the last of the air I had to scream one last time. It was a sound so blaring that sometimes I still hear it in my dreams. Just as I gave up hope, Ella Rosewood, a seasoned Fae at the time, smashed through my wall, holding her hand out to rescue me from the inferno.

"I reached out, and the second my fingers touched hers, the life drained from her body and she fell down, dead at my feet. Out of horror and confusion, I ran out through the hole she'd made in my wall. I collapsed on the street while people ran past me in the chaos. I sobbed until my head pounded, and finally a man reached for me. Afraid I'd kill him too, I screamed and told him what I'd done. 'I killed her,' I cried. 'Ella Rosewood! I didn't mean to. I think my gift... I think it was my gift.... She just... died.'"

My eyes pricked and my vision blurred from tears I held back as he continued.

"The man didn't know what to make of me or what I was saying, but a moment later, Yemoja Roux stepped out of the flames carrying the motionless Fae. The man raised a finger to his lips and tossed me his gloves. He... well, anyway, he renamed me DT... *Death Touch*."

I had a thousand questions, but before I could ask, he leaned back, sort of regained focus, and said, "Oh shit, man, sorry. I wasn't trying to bum you out. Let's talk about something else."

I shook my head, hoping to loosen the unsettled feeling in my stomach. Suddenly my sense of fairness felt confused. "Can I ask you one thing?"

He nodded, but his slightly raised eyebrows said he was a little irritated.

"Can I ask you what your real name is?"

He paused, as if trying to remember it. "C-Calvin." Then the corners of his mouth curved up. "But my friends call me Cal."

I smiled. "Cal it is."

Reina
FIFTEEN

Bri:
You're going over there today, right?

Me:
Yeah. Wish me luck.

Bri:
I'll light some candles for you.

Me:
You're the best.

I imagined confronting Ms. Vivian more times than I could count, and it always ended the same way—me once again breaking my promise to Yemoja Roux—wrenching the truth from Vivian with my gift. I wanted revenge: for Vivian to suffer. She wasn't my mother, but I spent a year in her care. I wanted to know how she really felt about me, but how could I use my gift that way? Especially after Kai's TV debut, where he called out practically all the Elites for their abuse of power... All I knew was that I didn't want him to be right. I'd find a way to convince her without my gift. I had to, or else what was the point of all this?

I pulled on the blazer of my school uniform, the finishing touch. She'd told me more than anyone that I'd never get into Gifted Fae Academy. I was certain that she knew already from the news, but if I wasn't going to be able to get actual revenge, I at least wanted to rub my uniform in her face.

"Now be strong," Yemoja said, "but not disrespectful. We need her to sign."

When I turned to face her, I was surprised that she looked considerably less confident than I'd ever seen her. She paced back and forth, picking at her fingernails and check-listing, half in her head and half aloud, always coming back to the same question. "Are you sure you don't want me to go with you?"

I smiled. Yemoja was a constant when I had no other. When I thought about it, she'd been there for me my whole life, even if I just came into hers. But what I really wanted from Vivian wasn't just a signature, so the only option was to go alone. "Thank you. Don't worry about me. I'm Yemoja Roux's apprentice after all. I'm tough."

She shook her head. "That's what I'm worried about." She spun and shook her finger at me. "Don't forget who you are."

I nodded, slinging my backpack over my shoulder and heading out of my temporary sanctuary to the cold mid-winter afternoon. The air bit at me through my jacket, the gray sky unsure whether to drop snow or rain. The wind seemed to push me from behind, urging me forward even as my apprehension grew and confidence drained with each step closer to my destination.

I walked up to the steps of the group home and froze. Suddenly, I regretted not allowing Yemoja Roux to come along. Even if Vivian's gift could no longer hurt me now that I could use mine to block it, it didn't mean she wouldn't find a way. I pulled the door open, only to draw the panicked stares of the other orphans who were huddled around a TV at the far end of the room. They let out a collective gasp. "Reina!" Jerome yelled as he sprinted toward me.

Alyssa grabbed him. "Don't," she said. "She has a gift now. You don't know what she'll do."

Jerome stopped, backing away.

"Hi, Jerome. Don't worry, guys, it's still me. I'm not going to hurt anyone."

Alyssa released Jerome, but he didn't return to my arms. A few of the others moved closer to me, but none closer than an arm's length or two. Alyssa shifted nervously. "Sorry, Reina, it's best to play it safe."

I understood, but it stung. I was no longer one of them, and that fact alone had raised a wall between us.

I walked into the crowded room, noting that not a single thing appeared to have changed since I left, except a few new faces among the orphans and a few missing ones. How could this place feel so familiar, yet I no longer belonged?

"What are you doing here?" Jerome asked. He was at least an inch taller but still oozed the sweet innocence he had when I left. "I'm looking for Ms. Vivian."

Alyssa scoffed. "Always looking for trouble."

Jerome beamed. "Are you going to beat her up with your gift?"

I smiled. "I just need a signature."

Alyssa rolled her eyes. "Just great. And when you're gone, she'll take it out on us."

"I promise I'm not here to cause trouble."

"Sure. I'm surprised you didn't bring your Fae friends to kill Ms. Vivian. I mean… unless you're going to do it yourself."

"What are you talking about? Do what? Kill Ms. Vivian? Relax, crazy." I didn't feel any different than when I lived here, but it was obvious they saw me differently. It was odd to hear Alyssa speak this way about the Fae, though. She was the one who'd woken me in the middle of the night to tell me one had been killed. What changed?

She shrugged. "All I'm saying is, what did the Fae ever do for any of us?"

I froze as I began to suspect the cause of her new philosophy. The last time I saw Alyssa, she'd been as much of a Fae admirer as anyone, and only one thing could have changed her mind. I hoped I was wrong when I asked, "Where is this coming from?" My gaze moved to the TV screen where a clip of Kai's speech was playing. I sighed. "Listen, what Kai said was—"

The door swung open behind me, crashing into the wall. I nearly leapt out of my skin as Vivian strolled in. The rest of the orphans shrank back. Her red lipstick was smudged, her auburn updo lined with flyaway hairs, but otherwise she looked more put together than I remembered.

"Crawling back, I see." She huffed. "Just as I said."

I felt my nerves give way and my body started to tremble. "I was actually wondering if you would sign something… as my guardian."

Kaito
SIXTEEN

I shoved one of Calvin's coconut cookies into my mouth. "You're kidding right? Ensley?"

Cal smirked. "Why is that hard to believe?"

"I don't know. She just… doesn't seem like a killer to me."

He shrugged. "She's a little sloppy, which is why we sometimes send Carter in to help her control them, but he's…"

"A dick?"

"I was going to say unpredictable."

I nodded, eying the half-eaten plate of cookies. "Why haven't you assigned me another speech?" I asked, grabbing a cookie and walking over to the window.

"The media is still buzzing about your first one. Why are you so eager?"

"I'm not. I'm just a little stir crazy."

Calvin grabbed his jacket. "Then let's go out for a bit."

I gaped. "They'll recognize me."

He shrugged. "So wear a hat or something. Come on."

I wasn't going to argue with that. I was dying to get out of the tower.

Cal said, "I'll meet you in the lobby."

I headed to my apartment to grab my jacket and to see if I had a hat in the closet The Fallen had provided. It was stuffed with clothes that suited me better than the goofy GFA uniforms, but I hadn't taken much time to look through it. I threw on my jacket and swiped a plain black hat from the shelf without browsing through my options. Calvin's entire organization hinged on me and he trusted me enough to let me leave the tower. It was a testament to how much time we'd spent together over the last few days. Since our heavy breakfast chat the other day, we stuck to simpler topics, but we shared a mutual respect, one I hadn't been able to garner with anyone else.

I stopped short when I opened my door to find Zane. "Ah. Sorry, man, I'm headed out," I said.

"Kai," he said, looking at his feet. "I... I just..."

"Spit it out."

"I think you should be careful with DT." His blue eyes looked blurred behind his smudged glasses, his hair vibrant cobalt in the tower lights.

"He's your boss, right? You're the whole reason I'm even here."

"I know, I know. It's just, he's dangerous. You've been spending time with him and I want to remind you not to tell him about... you know... anything he could use against you. At the end of the day, he's going to put his mission first."

I patted his shoulder. "I'll be alright."

This whole damn organization was a bunch of hypocrites. Where did Zane get off lecturing me about DT? I might've dropped my guard a little, but I wasn't about to start gushing about Reina. Her dream was to attend GFA and, even with all the chaos, I had the power to make sure she finished unharmed. Calvin had agreed not to attack the school. He'd put food on the tables of thousands of families, yet people only judged him for his gift. I understood that.

I almost stopped short when the elevator doors opened and Carter sheepishly stared back. I eyed his guitar before stepping into the elevator and pressing the button for the lobby. *Please don't say some dumb shit to me.*

"So uhm…" he started.

Fuck.

"I wanted to apologize. I shouldn't have used my gift on you. That wasn't cool."

I scoffed. "Whatever, man."

"What is it? Why do you hate me so much?"

"Quan is dead, man. And you helped kill him."

"And yet you're the leader of The Fallen. We all do things."

"Your gift is manipulation. I'm fucked up about everything we ever discussed. I never saw you without your damn guitar and I can't help but wonder what kind of shit you were tricking us all into. I mean... what about all the girls? Did you use your gift to—" I swallowed hard, desperate to shake the thought from my head. "That's rape."

"I… haven't done that in a long time." I turned away, pleading with the elevator to go faster. "Don't act like you're Mr. Perfect. I saw the video of what you did to Reina. You think that wasn't against her will? You think that wasn't fucked up? This isn't a contest, it's just what always happens when one person gets too much power."

"What about Yemoja Roux? She's the most powerful Fae in the world."

He smirked. "She has just as much blood on her hands as your new buddy, DT." Carter pulled a small box from his backpack. "I was headed to your apartment to give you this… but now I'm thinking you're not ready."

I hated him. He was everything I didn't want to become, but I couldn't deny that I agreed with some of what he said. It seemed no matter what side you were on, there was no way around getting blood on your hands. Curious, I took the shoe-sized box but was surprised by the weight. I lifted the lid, revealing five razor sharp daggers, already loaded into a belt.

"I'm not a killer, Carter."

"That's fine. But every Fae in the city wants you dead. I thought you might want something to defend yourself… you know… just in case."

I took a deep breath and stared at my former roommate. He looked sad, but I couldn't excuse any of his choices, not after all he'd done. He was lost, and part of me blamed him for dragging me to this side of the war. I missed the version of him that was just kind of an idiot. I missed the version of life that was just lunch boxes and recess. Life before power. I sighed. "Thank you for the gift."

The elevator doors opened and I stepped out and said, "I know we all sometimes do questionable things, but our reasons why matter. Who are you protecting, Carter?"

He nodded to the gift in my hands. "I thought it was obvious."

The doors closed between us. *This is shaping up to be a fucked up day.* Rather than carry Carter's gift around, I put on the belt and got rid of the box. I touched each dagger, feeling their sharpness move into my magical range. I'd never used my gift on a weapon before and felt guilty as I relished the possibilities. I told myself I'd only use them in self defense, but that wasn't the kind of world I lived in.

The lobby was crowded. I watched the sea of people part around Calvin, giving him a wide berth. He was unfazed, numb to the coldness of the very citizens he strove to protect. He wiggled his eyebrows when he saw the belt but didn't mention it as he ushered me into a car. He told the driver to take us to a familiar area on the outskirts of the city. There was a nice park there, one I visited often when I first moved to Ancetol due to its proximity to my closest friend's house.

I was pleased to learn that Calvin had planned to walk the park all along, and we did so mostly in silence. It wasn't long until my thoughts drifted to the last time I was there. It was summer then, and unlike today's bare trees that cut through the gray sky like cracked porcelain, back then they were full and green. My ankle was sprained from a scuffle I'd gotten into at school with the Elites, so my arm was slung around Reina's shoulders as I limped along. I could almost feel the brush of Reina's wild curls against my face, or feel the summer heat beat down on me while she gave me a break from my own life.

"Thinking of your parents?" Calvin asked as we moved into a more thickly wooded part of the park.

Zane's warning pushed into my head. "Yeah," I lied. "You?"

He shrugged. "I hardly ever think about them anymore."

The pine trees in this area were thick and pushed onto the walking path, scraping our jackets as we passed. I knew Zane was right about hiding my connection to Reina, but I resented the wall it cast between me and my new friend. He'd trusted me enough to let me out of the tower. He trusted me with his history, and I was nothing but a liar.

"I actually have a gift for you," Calvin said, pulling me back to our conversation.

I held out my hand. "Gimme," I said with a grin.

"We're not there yet. It's a little further ahead."

I scanned the path and, in the distance, I saw a figure I recognized from the night of the winter ball. He was the gemini who ported us from GFA to the tower. Like his twin, he was tall, red-haired, and freckled. Despite the comfort I'd developed around Calvin, apprehension seeped into my bones as we approached. "Are we going somewhere?" I asked.

Cal flashed his white teeth. "You'll see."

My pace slowed and I instinctively slipped my hands into my pockets. As I waited for Calvin to reveal his gift, my thoughts raced. Suddenly our isolated location didn't feel charming or refreshing. Danger hung over us, and Cal's calmness that I'd come to enjoy over the last several days now felt like a joke he never let me in on.

Calvin's red-headed companion waited for orders, but Cal turned to me instead. "I wanted to do something to show you my appreciation."

I looked into his cobalt eyes for a clue, but I saw no trace of the monster or my friend. Instead, I saw a twisted smile and a glint in his eyes that told me I wouldn't like what was coming next.

Reina
SEVENTEEN

Vivian glared at me, her brown eyes wide as if I'd slapped her. After a long pause, a smile stretched across her face. "Well, well, well, isn't this a treat? All that talk about when your gift came in and how you would go to GFA and never come back." She straightened her spine, peering down at me with a raised eyebrow. I handed her my tablet.

"All I need is your signature."

She pushed past me. "All I need's a million dollars."

"Ms. Vivian, please."

Before I got the words out, she spun, her hand clasping around my wrist. My gift rose to block her, but her malicious grin said she didn't know I couldn't feel it. Instead of freeing my arm, I yanked my gift back, allowing the electric pulse to burn me as I ground my teeth.

"You're nothing without me," she said, but a thrash of my gift told me she knew she was lying.

"Why?" I muttered through my teeth. I fought the urge to

counter her, to learn the truth. She was far weaker than anyone I'd encountered at GFA, and I could destroy her in a matter of seconds, but that wasn't why I was here.

"Please, I need you to sign for me," I said.

Her gaze shot up. "Get out of here, you little shits!" she spat, and I heard the footsteps of the other orphans retreating. She leaned in and nodded to my tablet. "I promise you, I'll never sign that."

The dull but relentless pain of her gift dropped me to my knees, and she leaned over me, her grip tightening.

"Why?" I asked.

"You're not worthy of a gift."

Lie.

"You'll never make anything of yourself."

Lie.

"You're going to get yourself killed out there."

Truth. My eyes widened. "You... you care about me?"

She ripped her hand away, as if she'd just remembered I had a gift.

I gaped. "You don't want me to get hurt. But why are you so..."

She turned away. "You wouldn't understand. It's not easy doing what I do."

"Explain it to me and I'll leave."

Her gaze swept the room and, when she was satisfied we were alone, she helped me to my feet. She took a deep breath. "You're all broken when you get here, every single one, damaged beyond repair."

I crossed my arms defensively, already unsure if I wanted her to continue. I'd already made up my mind about her. She was an evil person, but just a few words into her explanation, I felt my opinion of her waiver.

"I don't have pity for any of you."

Lie.

"That's just the way life is, and it only gets harder. Broken children come and go, all looking for some way to feel in control, all looking for someone to hurt."

My time at the orphanage ran through my head. The bickering, the anger. But when I thought about where my resentment settled, it was always Vivian. I couldn't recall a single argument between me and the other kids, because at the end of the day it was us against her.

I nodded. "You're mean to us on purpose so that we all hate you and not each other."

She turned her face away, but a quick brush of her hand across her cheek told me that her cold facade had broken.

"Get out," she barked. "I'm not going to sign."

I nodded, slipping the tablet back into my backpack.

She sniffed, but the softness was gone from her face. "You're the worst fuck up I've ever known."

Lie.

I reached for the door.

"I hope I never see you here again."

Lie.

I felt my heartbeat in my throat, and tears threatened to fall and choke my words. I looked back at her over my shoulder. "Thank you, Ms. Vivian," I said. "For getting me through the worst year of my life."

I thought about Vivian the whole way back to Yemoja Roux's apartment. I wasn't sure if I agreed with her tactics, and I was sure there were moments when she enjoyed hurting us, yet I could no longer place her easily into one box or another.

It seemed like the more I walked the path of the Fae, the less I understood the concept of right and wrong. Vivian, Kai, even me; we all seemed like we were one decision away from slipping from one side or the other. If Vivian had a reason, so did Kai, and I needed to find out what it was before Oden and the others got to him, or worse, before he got to someone else. It wasn't until I reached my destination and stood in front of Yemoja Roux that I even remembered that I'd failed to get the signature. My internship was over. With the school's curfew, I'd never be able to find Kai —unless I dropped out. I rubbed my face with my hands. He wasn't even in my life and I was still losing because of him.

"I take it it didn't go well," Yemoja said, plopping down beside me on the couch.

I shrugged. "Actually, I think it went really well."

Her posture relaxed as she started to braid my hair. "So you got the signature then."

"No. But I have a plan."

Her hands dropped from my hair as she waited.

A surge of uneasiness hit me before the words toppled out. "I'm going to drop out."

She stood quickly and started pacing, her body moving like she was holding back her words. "I… I don't think that's wise," she finally said.

"I need to find Kai."

Her voice came out sharper. "It's too dangerous. If I let you go, or even brought you along on my patrol without that internship, I could lose my position. And you could die out there without me."

I shook my head. "It's the only way."

"Actually…" She sat beside me. "I had a thought while you were gone." She wrung her hands. "What if… I adopted you?"

The air left my lungs.

"I could sign on your behalf. You could stay here if you want, or at GFA. You could be Reina Roux."

The name *Reina Roux* was like a slap to my face. "What? No."

"N-no?"

"I'm not available for adoption. My parents died, but it doesn't mean I'm just going to replace them." I stood, backing away toward the door.

"I'm sorry," Yemoja Roux said. "I didn't mean to spring that on you. I was just thinking—"

"No." I wasn't trying to be cruel, but the word kept falling out. "I'm sorry," I said before I pulled the door open and ran out.

kaito

EIGHTEEN

I held my breath as Cal nodded to the man with the red hair. A moment later, Carter stood in front of us. My stomach dropped. Carter's blonde curls were tossed freely as always, but he wasn't wearing a jacket, meaning he hadn't planned on being ported from the tower. Even more strange, he didn't have his guitar. His lips pressed into a hard line as he took in his new environment. I watched as the danger I'd felt a moment ago shifted to him. His eyes darkened with understanding and teared up as his gaze locked on me in a silent plea.

Oh fuck. I turned to DT, trying to keep my expression as neutral as I could. "Hey, man, send him back. You don't have to do this. I was thinking about working things out with him anyway. He gave me this belt and stuff, so we're good."

But DT had already begun to move toward Carter. Carter trembled. He winced as DT grabbed the back of his neck. "Wait!" I said too loud. "Don't. Just… just let him go."

DT grinned. "Kai, why don't you tell Carter how you feel about being manipulated by his gift."

"It-it's really no big deal."

"No, no. no!" DT said. "Tell him what you told me."

Carter broke into sobs. "Please, Kai," he said.

"DT!"

Carter's skin grayed, shredding into ashes. The death was instant but the decay of his body dragged out for several minutes. The disintegration of body quickly spread to his clothes until he was nothing but a gray smudge across the cobblestone path. Stunned, I stared down at it. A frightened scream lodged into my throat, choking the life from me. DT stood over him, his long fingers posed like a ballet dancer awaiting applause.

He was gone. *Dead.* Taken away by the death touch, and as a gift to me no less. My heart raced like I'd already begun to flee, but I was frozen. Terrified that I'd be next, I willed myself to run, but fear overtook me. DT watched me with curious eyes.

What the fuck? I wasn't sure what I thought a death touch would be like, but that wasn't it. It wasn't how DT had described. In his story, there was at least a body. What I had just witnessed was horrific. Did that mean that if I'd tossed my daggers at him they'd disintegrate when they touched his skin? Internally, I wanted to curl up into a ball and cry myself dry. Each nerve in my body screamed to distance myself from the most threatening presence on earth, and yet, as ever, he brimmed with serious concern. He was serious alright. Seriously dangerous, seriously calm, and seriously magnetic—and, above all, seriously insane. He was the devil, and I... Shit, I'm the devil's closest friend.

I felt vomit threaten to surge. It was at that moment that out of the corner of my eye I spotted a faint purple glow. Reina? *For fuck's sake.* I had no choice. Steeling my nerves, I smiled at DT. "Thanks, man," I said. "I know he was kind of important for your missions. You're a good friend," I added. My stomach lurched, but I suppressed the bile, this time by grinding my teeth. My eyes watered but I hoped I could sell it as gratitude.

He clapped his hands together. "I knew you'd get it," he said. He sighed dreamily. "I'm getting a little chilly. Wanna port back?" he asked, gesturing to his friend.

"Actually, I think I'm going to take the long way home."

He froze. *Oh shit. He's onto me.*

"Is… everything okay?"

I shoved him. "Yeah, Cal. Stop overthinking." It was the last thing on earth I wanted to do, but also my only chance of keeping him from discovering what was hidden a few yards away. I held out my hand.

He shook it, and I pulled him in for a hug. The contact immediately put him at ease, and his posture relaxed. "Text me when you're back."

I nodded. "Sure thing."

He touched hands with the gemini and, in an instant, they were both gone.

I was almost delirious as I trudged through the slushed leftover snow toward the purple glow. I wanted to run to her, to tell her everything, but knowing Reina she'd try to save me, and I knew that would end with a death touch for each of us. I couldn't be saved, but she could. My only option was to make sure she believed I was who I appeared to be and hope that the deaths of the Fae would stop the school from sending students off campus.

As I walked through the more densely wooded portion of

the park, the glow grew brighter. Reina stepped out from behind a tree. I stopped, my emotions reeling so intensely that they began to numb. Her eyes were bloodshot, her cheeks streaked with tears as some of her curls stuck to the side of her wet face. Even with the sadness in her eyes she looked strong, and just looking at her I felt barely capable of staying on my feet. *Holy shit, she's beautiful.* I was so distracted with making sure DT went back to the tower away from Reina that I hadn't considered her gift. *Truth.* I could probably still convince her to let me go, and give her enough of an explanation that she wouldn't go looking for answers, but if she asked the right question things could get complicated.

"Kai."

With one word, my resolve weakened, so I leaned against a tree as a crutch, hoping to pass it off as casual and unbothered.

"It's dangerous out here. Go back to your school," I said.

The wind pushed the coconut scent of her hair to me, and I took a deep breath to keep from walking closer.

"Did that guy *kill* Carter?"

Nausea clamored at me, but I stiffened my expression and nodded.

"And you… you thanked him," she said, her voice breaking.

"That's right. So you understand why you need to leave."

She stepped closer, her power swirling purple around her, her gaze lit with anger.

I sighed. "You're going to make yourself an easier target with that damn purple shit everywhere."

"What do they have on you, Kai? Did you know about Quan?"

I gulped, feeling the stray wisps of Reina's magic thrash

nearby. "There's so much more to this than you know. Stay out of it."

"It doesn't make sense. I knew you. I was with you last year. There was no way you were planning some kind of rebellion. If everything they say is true, then you really fucking fooled me." Tears cut down her cheeks.

I clenched my jaw tight to keep my eyes from watering and turned my gaze away so I wouldn't have to see her cry. The purple light licked at me, the truth coming forward before she even asked. "That night at the dance—"

"Don't be stupid, Reina," I barked, desperation screaming at me to shut down her questions. "I'm with The Fallen. You're in way over your head." I'd already pushed my luck with answering truthfully, so I turned to walk away when she slung her next words at me.

"Fight me."

I laughed and turned back. "What good would killing you do?"

"It would prove that I was wrong about you."

I'd tormented Reina on so many occasions, but things had changed. She was the only thing worth saving in the whole fucked up world. I didn't expect to have my bluff called. Maybe that she'd use her gift to purge the truth, but not this. I took a sharp breath in. "Reina." From a safe distance, I scanned her face, hoping to memorize it perfectly this time, because this would be the last. She froze, the glow of her magic dimming. Her lips tensed with fear, but her gaze softened. I knew exactly how she felt as I moved toward her because I felt the same— afraid. *I couldn't do it.* All I had in range were my daggers, and if I moved close enough to touch her, I wasn't certain I'd let go.

"You're not worth my time," I spat.

I turned away. A sharp blade sliced into my side before vanishing in a flash of purple. Stunned, I pressed on the wound as warm liquid slid over my fingers, my vision already blurring white.

Reina
NINETEEN

Enough was enough. My gift surged out of me, some slipping from my grasp and spiraling out of range. That speech he gave at the dance was all part of some sick game, and somehow I'd warped it into something redeemable. All the years that I'd endured his hot and cold bullshit fueled me, and I felt my gift break through a new barrier of potential. It was volatile yet intoxicating, so I held my hands at the ready, waiting for Kai to make the first move. His expression softened to a sad smile, and he stumbled back. A trick? I wasn't falling for that. I held my ground. "Whatever shit you're trying to pull, it's not going to work."

He dropped to one knee. A splash of red hit a patch of dirty snow. Every ounce of my gift vanished, like the flame of a candle blowing out, and without thinking I sprinted to him. I ripped open his jacket, and blood seeped through his shirt. "Shit. Oh my god, Kai. I'm so sorry."

"Sorry? You were the one that wanted to fight."

I pressed my hands over the wound to stop the bleeding, but the cut was deep. Kai's face was pale and clammy as I pulled him into my lap. Despite my panic, he looked perfectly calm.

"I'm taking you to a hospital. Don't worry. We'll get you fixed up."

He groaned, "I can't go there."

Kai's blood warmed my hands, tears springing to my eyes. "Then tell me what to do. Please! Tell me what to do."

I reeled as he closed his eyes.

"Kai!" I screamed. "Stay with me!"

"I'm with you, Reina." But his words slurred. I looked around for help, but we were alone. My old house wasn't far away. It was the whole reason I came to the park in the first place. I was walking in the park and working up the courage to check on the house, when I spotted Kai, Carter, and his horrifying friend. My old house was only two blocks away, if that. Maybe there was still something gift-infused there to clot it, but that was a *hard* maybe. Fuck. Fuck. I needed a Plan B, just in case. I pulled out Kai's cell phone and sent two quick messages, one blank one to myself and the other nothing but my former address to the only person I could think of who might help—Zane. Any of my people might kill Kai on the spot, and I at least got the impression that the two were friends. It was a gamble, but Kai's life was hanging in the balance and it was all my fault.

I stood and slung Kai's arm over my shoulder, and his hat toppled to the ground. "Please, Kai," I begged. "If you help a little, I can get you out of here." I felt the slightest lift of his body weight as his gift took over, but he couldn't do much. His breaths were even, and I suspected he was saving his energy by not talking. I began to pull him toward my old house, hoping that there was something left there that could save him. How the fuck did I do this? Why did I ever think that I could intentionally kill him? "Kai, I swear to god if you die, I'll never forgive you."

He snorted. "If I die, I'll never forgive *you*."

I exhaled a bit of relief; he was still joking. Maybe it looked worse than it was.

"Your hair smells nice."

Oh fuck, he's dying.

We made it to my now vacant neighborhood, and it seemed like the entire street had been shut down. Foreclosure and For Sale signs out front of every property, and not a single light was on despite the day giving way to early evening. The scrape of my shoes against the pavement and the heaving of my breath as I dragged Kai along were the only sounds to block out the thudding of my racing heart.

Kai leaned his head on my shoulder. "Did you miss me?"

My breaths grew labored, sweat beading on my forehead as we hobbled into my old driveway. "Yeah. Of course. How was your vacation?" I said, hoping to keep him talking.

"I joined a new club," Kai said.

"You mean a cult?"

The house looked just the same as I remembered, small but welcoming, set a touch back from the road. There was a Foreclosure sign on a patch of lawn out front that sent a pang of sadness through me. I knew my parents were dead, but something about being back at my childhood home made me feel like they were inside. The sign alone was enough to remind me just how vacant the house was. I wondered if it might've been better if someone had moved in. Perhaps we'd have better odds of finding something infused, but that would lead to questions which we couldn't answer. I pulled Kai up the driveway, my stomach tight with the memory of the last time I'd been here.

"Are you okay?" Kai asked.

I shook my head. "What? No. I just fucking murdered you."

"No, I mean like, how are things with Oden and stuff."

I moved the loose brick to the right of the door and pulled out my spare key. "Are you serious with this?" The moment I stepped inside, I bent down and put Kai on the floor. I sprinted to our medicine cabinets, past family photos and furniture laid out exactly as it had been, as if the day I left was frozen in time.

I tore through the cabinets. Gauze, ibuprofen, antibacterial wipes, but nothing gift-infused. *Dammit.* He was going to die. This wasn't going to cut it. I grabbed whatever I could carry and raced back to the doorway to grab Kai, but he wasn't there.

"In here," he called. I followed his voice to the living room where he lay on the couch with his feet up. "Any clotters?" I shook my head and dumped the contents of my medicine cabinet on the coffee table. I pulled off his jacket and picked up the scissors. Starting at the bottom, I cut off his shirt.

"This shirt belonged to The Fallen."

"Tell them to bill me," I said as I started to clean the wound. I wrapped my arms around him to reposition him enough to get to the wound, and felt something cold brush my lip. I lifted my head and my heart came to an abrupt stop. There, lying against his chest, was my missing owl charm necklace.

"Why do you have this?" I asked. "Kai?" I looked up and his eyes had closed again. "Kai!" I felt for his pulse, but my hands were shaking too hard for me to feel one. I leaned in to feel if he was breathing, but he wasn't. The door slammed open and I nearly leapt from my skin. "He's dying!" I screamed, tears rushing down my face as the blue-haired boy rushed toward me. There was an older man behind him. "Save him!" I yelled. The bearded man grabbed Kai and, in an instant, they both were gone.

Zane spun to me. "Who did this?"

I sobbed. "I'm so sorry. It was an accident," I said through tears. "Is he going to be okay?"

"You did this?" He pushed his glasses up his nose and paced. "This is so fucked, Reina. You don't even know. He's trying to protect you and you fucking kill him?"

"What?" I breathed, practically tripping over every word he said.

His phone buzzed and he looked at it then exhaled. "We got him in time." He looked up at me. "I won't have to kill you this time, but stay the fuck away from us. Go back to campus and don't leave. I mean it. If you care about him at all, let him go." He turned and headed back the way he came, my thoughts racing.

Panicked, I called out, "Take me with you."

He stopped in the doorway, head down and fingers to the bridge of his nose, just beneath where his glasses rested, but after a moment he shook his head. "He'd never forgive me," he said, then slammed the door behind him, leaving me alone. I looked around the ghost of my childhood home, my limbs still shaking and drenched in Kai's blood.

kaito
TWENTY

I awoke in a panic, my mind locked onto the memory of Carter's face as it crumbled away. *It was a horrible nightmare, that's all.* I sat up, tension easing as I looked around my apartment, but a sharp twinge in my side froze me with a torrent of fear. It was all real. Carter was *gone*. I pulled my blankets off to inspect my wound, but approaching footsteps drew my attention. Zane walked to my bedside, his face pale and his eyes rimmed with discoloration. The window next to my bed was open, but no light poured in.

I eyed him, stating, "You look like shit."

"So do you," he said, taking a seat at the edge of the bed. "You almost died."

"How did you know where I was?"

His brow furrowed. "You texted me the address."

"Reina," I breathed.

He leaned forward, his blue eyes dulled behind his glasses.

"What do you mean? No, never mind. Just tell me, what happened?"

"Carter..." I swallowed a lump in my throat. I could feel my heart start racing again.

"Carter did this to you?" he asked.

I shook my head. "I was at the park with DT—"

A knock sounded, and we both turned to see DT hurry in. I shot Zane a warning not to say anything. DT sat on the opposite side of the bed, and flipped his white hair out of his eyes before he turned to Zane. "Can I have a minute with him?"

Zane's jaw clenched, but he stood and left without a word.

"Kai," DT said, "I'm so sorry I wasn't there." His crystal eyes began to tear.

I wasn't sure how long I was out or how much Zane had reported. The last thing I needed was for DT to do me another "favor" and go after Reina. Her ability didn't require touch and it was obviously much harder to control. She might've wanted to fight me, but I doubt it would have come to something like this. Even if it did, didn't I deserve it? "What did Zane tell you?"

"He said you were attacked on your way back but managed to send him your location. We ported you back here and used our stock of infused clotters, but we were minutes away from losing you." He reached a sympathetic hand out to grab my arm. I shuddered, my mind instantly returning to Carter.

I pulled my arm away. "DT... really, it's okay."

His eyes widened. "You mean Cal?"

I paused.

His gaze shifted between my eyes like I was a book he was reading. "You're angry that I wasn't there. I'm so sorry."

"No, it's not that. We're fine, honest. I'm just tired, and a little disoriented from the shock, I guess. I meant Cal."

"I promise you I will find whoever did this to you, and I will kill them." He was practically snarling, his white canines gleaming like a rabid dog.

"No. I want to do it. Put me out in the field."

He sat back, his shoulders relaxing. "I'm glad to see this incident hasn't scared you off. Who am I to deny a man his revenge?" He looked out my window. "I'm sending Ensley in to administer your next treatment, so you can put in your food order with her."

"Thanks, Cal."

He flashed me a smile and stood. "Get some rest. We need you in good shape if you're going out in the field. Can't have our leader looking…" his gaze trailed up my body to my face, "battered."

After he left, my thoughts moved to Reina. My injury had made me drop my guard. I didn't fully remember what I said to her, but I doubt it was anything cruel enough to keep her away. She was going to come for me, and if I didn't go out there to fight with The Fallen, I wouldn't be able to protect her when their paths crossed. The door opened again and I expected to see Ensley, but Zane came instead.

"What did he want to talk about?" he asked, once again taking a seat at the end of my bed.

"Zane, I saw it. The death touch." The way he grimaced told me he'd seen it before too. "He killed Carter."

He stood as his mouth dropped open. "W-why?"

I looked down at my hands. "I think it's my fault. I told DT I didn't like Carter. It all happened so fast. I tried to stop him but—"

The door swung open, and Ensley pushed a cart with rattling bottles and a squeaky wheel across my apartment.

Zane's posture stiffened, and his already pale face turned pure white.

"Welcome back," Ensley said.

"Got anything for pain on there?" I asked.

As her fingers danced over the bottles, I nodded to get Zane's attention, but his gaze was glued to the energetic girl. She squealed with delight as she lifted a bottle and headed toward me. Her gaze moved to Zane, who was so frozen he could pass as a wax figure. "What's wrong with him?" she asked.

He laughed and opened his mouth to defend himself, but got tongue tied.

"Did you know that Zane saved my life? If he hadn't shown up, I'd be a goner."

She cut her eyes at him suspiciously for half a second, then moved to the bedside, bottle in hand. "Do you want me to do it or…"

Zane cleared his throat, and we both turned to look at him.

"I got it," I said. I pulled off my bandages to find that the wound wasn't as deep as it felt, but that might've been the work of the infused treatments they'd already used on it. I opened the bottle, and a sour wisp of light wafted out. I winced, anticipating from the smell that it was going to sting. Ensley handed me a cloth, and I poured a bit of the smoky liquid onto it before dabbing it on the cut. I gagged at the sour smell, but instead of pain, it soothed the ache within seconds.

Ensley grinned. "That's only going to last a couple hours. Should I get you some dinner?"

"How long was I out?"

She shrugged. "Just a few hours. It's eleven."

I nodded, taking a peek out my window.

"What are you in the mood for?"

I looked up at Zane, unsure whether I should give him another shot to redeem himself with Ensley, or just let him take the loss. I went with the former. "Why don't you go to the cafeteria with Zane and see what they have leftover from today. He knows what I like."

She pressed her lips together and turned to him. "Does that work for you?"

"Yeah. Food is… yeah."

She sighed, grabbing him by the arm. "Let's go."

My phone buzzed on my end table as the two left my apartment. No doubt Zane thanking me for the assist. The Fallen had provided me with a phone already programmed with a few of their numbers, including the two Gemini's, Zane, Carter, and DT, but Zane was the only one who had ventured to message me. I picked it up only to find a message from an unknown number.

UNKNOWN:
Kai, are you okay?

Reina

TWENTY-ONE

I hardly noticed the other passengers as I took my seat on the bus. My focus was on my hands and arms as I willed them not to glow. Even though I'd scrubbed them until my skin was sore, I couldn't wash away the memory of Kai's blood smeared across them. How could I let this happen? Kai was out there fighting for his life. No matter what he did, he didn't deserve to die. Who the hell did I think I was? The hand of justice coming to strike Kai down? Is this what it meant to be Fae?

All those years I wished for my gift to emerge, now it was growing more powerful, and I was no longer sure I could control it. At least when I was a serf, my hands were clean. What was wrong with me? One by one I was destroying every relationship. I wanted to call Bri, but I couldn't put this on her, not after she'd been through so much already. There wasn't a single person I could turn to anymore. Kai was dying somewhere, Oden and his Nobles hated me, and I'd refused Yemoja Roux's adoption...why, again? Because I didn't want to replace my parents? Ugh. That made no sense now. I was made up of their combined DNA; they couldn't be replaced. Maybe more than anything, the adoption caught me off guard. Yemoja Roux had been my real guardian for months. These days I talked to her more about personal stuff than training. Why then did it freak me out so much? It was just the paperwork at this point. Wasn't it?

I had my apology all worked out in my head as I knocked on her door. Hoping that my blood-stained clothing wouldn't make her change her mind about adopting me. I needed her. I'd done something terrible, and I was afraid of using my ability. The door swung open, and my heart leapt to my throat as Oden gaped at me. "She's here!" he called back over his shoulder. He yanked me into the room that was packed with people. A few of them were Fae I vaguely recognized, but most were police officers; I could tell by the turquoise uniforms with their gleaming badges—the same as my parents wore.

Yemoja Roux pushed through, her magenta hair tied into her ponytail. "Oh, thank god," she said, pulling me into her chest.

"What's going on?" I asked.

"Are you hurt?" she asked, looking at my shirt, then pulling my face into her hands. "Where did this blood come from?"

"It's not mine, it's—"

Her eyes bulged a warning for me to stop talking. "Officers, thank you for coming. She's safe."

An older gentleman with a salt and pepper mustache walked over. "We need to debrief her. She's obviously had a run in with

The Fallen." He turned to another woman. "Contact her guardian and have her come downtown to the station."

Yemoja Roux stepped forward. "Tomorrow. Can't you see she's injured?"

"Oh, well, yes of course," he said, looking slightly abashed, and with a nod, the officers followed him out. The Fae gave sympathetic looks to Yemoja Roux as they left. Oden moved toward the door behind them, but instead of leaving he shut the door and rushed back over to me.

"Whose blood is it, Rei?"

I gulped, my gaze moving past him to Yemoja Roux. "Kai's…"

Oden's face paled, but he pulled me into his chest while my arms remained limp at my sides. "Is he… dead?"

"I don't know." My lip began to tremble as my new reality settled in.

"Oden," Yemoja Roux said, "I'll take it from here. Why don't you get some rest and come back in the morning?"

Oden leaned in and whispered, "I'll text you."

The door closed behind him, and I turned to Yemoja Roux, ready to accept whatever punishment she would hand down to me. She rushed to me and pulled me in for a hug. "I'm so mad at you," she said. I smiled at the contradiction, but I hugged her back. "The Fallen is out there killing Fae. You can't go out there alone. If you had…" I pulled away and she covered her mouth with her hand before turning her back to me. Shit, she was crying. If I hadn't seen it, I would have heard it in her next words. "If anything happened to you, especially after how we left things, I would never forgive myself."

"I'm sorry. I went to my old house to, I don't know, feel close to my parents. And then, Kai…" It was as if the floodgates had opened. The purple glow filled the room, and I began to panic as the memory of Kai's wound raced forward. My hands shook. "Back away! I don't want to hurt you!" Yemoja's gaze softened as she gripped my hand, and I felt her gift snake through me, snuffing mine out.

I closed my eyes, my heartbeat double time.

"Breathe," she said. "You're safe. It's okay."

I took a steadying breath. Yemoja's voice was gentle and familiar, like I could hear my mother whispering to me through her.

She looked me in the eyes. "You're a mess," she said.

I nodded, biting back a laugh of surrender. "Do you still want to adopt me?"

She smiled, her head tilting to the left. "You're always welcome here, Reina." She lifted her hands off me, and waited a moment to see if they'd start glowing again. "I can show you how to control your gift. For now, I just need you to stay calm. How about you shower, then you can tell me what happened?"

A few minutes later, I stood motionless under the hot water, letting it beat down on me, watching the red swirls of blood from where it had soaked through my clothes circle the drain. My thoughts were empty, the whole terrible day washing with the blood, down the drain at my feet. I must have stayed in there for more than an hour. Yet when I emerged in the oversized t-shirt and sweatpants Yemoja Roux had given me, she sat patiently on the couch, with a cup of tea.

I took a seat beside her.

"Is he dead?"

I shook my head. "I don't know." I recounted the events, and she listened without any sign of emotion. Occasionally, she asked a question. I saw her objectivity slip when I got to the part about Carter, and how he'd been killed. She seemed most curious about the mysterious white-haired boy who'd turned him to dust with a touch. It felt good to let it out. I shared every detail with her except one. The text to Zane wasn't the only one I sent. The first sat unopened on my phone.

kaito
TWENTY-TWO

I stared down at the screen. *Reina*. Of course she'd messaged herself with my phone.

Me:
The number you've reached has been disconnected because the customer was savagely murdered.

UNKNOWN:
Thank God you're okay, Kai. That was the scariest moment of my life.

I snorted and saved the contact as R just to be safe.

Me:
The scariest moment of *your* life?

R:

I'm sorry.

I stared at the letter R, trying to picture her face.

R:
Are you mad?

I laughed. *She's so cute.*

Me:
Yes.

R:
What can I do?

My smile faded. What was I even doing? It was a mistake to message her back.

Me:
Stay on campus.

R:
So what Zane said is true then. You're trying to keep me safe.

Me:
I mean it Reina. Stay on campus. Forget about me.

R:
I can't forget about you. Believe me, I've tried.

My breath hitched, my chest heavy with sadness, as I rolled

over and stared at the message. When the light on my cell phone blinked out, and there was nothing in the dark of night but my thoughts, I felt the tears come.

∼

If Zane and Ensley returned with my food, they didn't wake me; it was morning when I opened my eyes again, the light of a new day streaming mercilessly through my window. My stomach ached with hunger, but I dragged myself to the shower before I set out for food. When I unwrapped my wound, I was surprised to see its progress. The Fallen must've had more expensive healing serums than my parents kept. I washed quickly, then wrapped my wound up again. I already knew I was going to DT's apartment, first thing. I knew if I changed my routine, he'd get suspicious, and after messaging with Reina last night, it was more important than ever for me to get out in the field. My phone buzzed, and I nearly jumped out of my skin. Was it Reina? I picked it up only to find a message from Zane.

Zane:
Bro, I had the most amazing night. Ensley and I kissed. I'll come by later to fill you in.

I smiled down at my phone. I definitely didn't think he had it in him. Good for him, though.

Me:
WTF? I can't wait to hear this one.

I pulled on a sweatshirt and jeans before leaving, my mouth already watering with thoughts of the baked goods that DT always had set out on his kitchen island. I hesitated before I knocked, reliving Carter's ashy death.

"Yes?" DT called from behind the door.

"Feed me," I groaned.

The door swung open, and DT stood in the doorway wearing nothing but a tightly wrapped towel and a smile.

"Oh, sorry, I didn't." He turned and looked over his shoulder. "Get out," he barked.

Ensley's pixie cut was all messed up. She squeezed past DT, most of her clothes scrunched in a ball against her chest, and scrambled past me.

"Sorry, I uh… I can come back later. You seem busy."

DT's face brightened. "Nonsense. We were finished. Come in."

I tentatively followed. I didn't turn to look if Ensley left, too afraid I'd see her bare ass.

I followed DT into his kitchen where he slid a plate of baked goods over to me. "Any of these coconut?"

"The round ones."

I took a bite, the buttery pastry tickling my taste buds. "So, you and Ensley? I gotta say, I'm a little surprised."

"Why?"

I shrugged. "I don't know. You're both really different."

He nodded. "It's just sex. We're not, like, a couple or anything."

"Got it," I said, but my phone buzzed again, and my thoughts moved immediately to Zane. What am I supposed to tell him? Of all the women he had to go for, he chose DT's? Shit.

Reina
TWENTY-THREE

I must've checked my phone a thousand times in the course of the morning, but Kai didn't message me again. The sun was barely up, but I slept as much as my anxiety would allow. I walked around Yemoja Roux's guestroom. The white canopy bed was lovelier than any bed I'd ever seen, and the vanity was fit for royalty, but like the rest of the house, it didn't feel like home. With her connections, she'd likely have the adoption paperwork ready to sign when she woke up, a few clicks, and it would be done. I wondered what my parents would say about it. I was sure they wouldn't protest, but guilt still bubbled at the pit of my stomach. I headed into the living room only to find Oden already seated on the couch, his hands pressed together. His body was tense, his dark hair covering his distinctive green eyes.

He smiled when he saw me. "You look better," he said.

I crossed my arms, suddenly aware that I was still wearing an oversized t-shirt with no bra. He patted the seat beside him, and I sat, the warmth of his leg pushing through my sweatpants.

"I'm sorry Reina," he said. "I'm so sorry. I was wrong about you. Miranda got in my head, and I'm upset about Quan. I just—" He cradled my face and rubbed my cheek with his thumb. "I will never doubt you again."

For the first time since the dance, I saw a spark in him. The same one that drew me to him to begin with. It reminded me of when we were happy—before the attack, when everything seemed simpler. I rested my head on his shoulder, and he rubbed my back. The morning sun drifted through the windows, and all was still except the steady beat of Oden's heart, and the comforting circles he drew on my back. My phone buzzed and my heart jumped to my throat. If Oden knew I'd messaged Kai, or that I'd even had his number, he would lose it. He looked into my eyes, reading my agitation. *Why am I like this?* Why was I thinking about Kai and my phone when Oden was here, apologizing? If I really liked him a few weeks ago, I could feel that way about him again, right?

I leaned in to kiss him, but the moment our lips touched he pulled away.

"Oh. You didn't mean…" I shook my head. "I thought—"

His contorted expression made him look like he was in pain. "It's not that. I want to be with you so much."

I tried to look into his yellow-green eyes, but he kept his gaze on the floor. "Oden? What is it?"

"I had sex with Miranda."

I stood, the wind knocked from my lungs. "What? We've been broken up for like twelve hours."

His eyes glossed. "I know. I know. I was angry at you, and Miranda, well, she was there, comforting me."

"Oh, I bet." My skin seared with heat, but I remembered Yemoja Roux's warning. I needed to stay calm, or else I might lose control. I certainly didn't want her to wake up to a bloody mess and a corpse. In the last 24 hours alone, I'd put her through so much; I couldn't add a murder to my rap sheet, even if I did kind of feel like it. I turned to walk back into my room, but Oden grabbed my arms.

He said, "It meant nothing. I'm in love with *you*."

I ground my teeth and said, "You don't get to say that to me." I felt my emotions swirl, and my hands began to glow.

"Please, Reina."

"Back away. Now!" Suddenly my vision was obstructed with the memory of Kai as he bled out. *No. Not again*. My gift snuffed out.

Taking it as a sign that I was calming down, Oden stepped closer.

"Stop. I… I just can't," I said before bolting back into Yemoja Roux's guestroom, locking the door behind me. I lay back in bed. *Maybe I just won't do today. I'll just stay here, and try again tomorrow.* What an asshole. Dating was a ridiculous thought. This wasn't a regular school year, it was war, and people were dying left and right. Still, my tears slipped from my eyes and rolled down to my pillow. I reached for my owl charm, only to remember that someone else wore it now. Perhaps I was just confused because I wasn't experienced with sex, but why did every guy suddenly love *me* after sleeping with Miranda?

Ugh. I waited until I heard Yemoja's voice in the living room before I dared leave the protection of my room. It might've been a guestroom and felt like a hotel, but it rescued me from Oden and gave me some comfort after Kai. I thought I might someday see that room as mine after all.

"Good morning!" Yemoja said. "You look like you've been crying."

My eyes bulged, my cheeks burning.

She started taking her hair out of her braid. "Not feeling any better?"

"I'm fine," I said, trying to keep my gaze from drifting to Oden.

"So, how do you want to play this? We can go to Vivian and I can pressure her to—"

"No. I want you to adopt me."

She lowered her voice. "Are you sure? You don't have to decide this now."

"I'm sure." I swallowed. "If you'll have me."

She smiled and hurried out of the room, no doubt to get her tablet.

Oden shifted his weight from one foot to the other. "Congratulations, Reina," he mumbled.

"Thanks."

She rushed back with a tablet, as I'd expected, and held it out for me. "You just sign here."

I froze. "Can I keep my last name the same?"

"Of course," she said. "I'm not trying to replace your parents, I'd just like to look out for you."

I nodded and signed, but the sad look in her eyes said that she could tell that part of me was apprehensive. She motioned for me to hit send, and I did. Either way, there was no going back now.

kaito
TWENTY-FOUR

Ensley unscrewed a second bottle from her cart. "This one's for the scar."

I thought of Reina... her worried expression as she tried to stop the bleeding. "Actually, I think I'll keep it."

"Why?"

"I don't know. I think it looks kinda cool."

She sighed. "Men."

I raised my eyebrows. "How interesting that you used the plural there."

Her gaze shot to me, a flush of pink across her cheeks. "What are you doing with Zane?"

"I-I don't owe you an explanation."

"I think you do. He's a good friend of mine, and what do you think is going to happen to him when DT finds out?"

The door swung open. "I have lunch!" Zane said, raising a lumpy plastic bag.

"Actually," Ensley said, "I have to go."

Zane stopped. "Is everything okay?"

"Yep," she said, but her usual pep was absent.

After she was gone, Zane shrugged and turned to me. "You ready for the story?"

"Zane, I have to tell you something."

"Me first," he said. "This story is so good."

I took a sharp breath in. "I saw Ensley leave DT's room this morning."

The way his smile dimmed was a punch to my gut. "Well, she could've just been—"

"No, she was half naked." His mouth moved, but he said nothing and moved over to have a seat on my couch. "I'm just...you know, worried. Because DT might—"

"I know," he said. "Thanks for telling me." He looked up at me. "So are we going to eat or what?"

I took a seat beside him, wanting to do more to ease his pain than pretend like nothing happened. "I have a bottle of gift-infused whiskey in the kitchen."

"It's like noon."

I smirked. "Where the fuck do you have to be today?"

An hour later we were practically screaming the lyrics to the openings of our favorite childhood cartoons.

Zane choked. "Drink! You totally fucked it up."

"No," I slurred. "That's how the song goes." But the shot was already on its way to my lips. It burned going down, but not as much as the first few. It was hot in my chest and heavy on my stomach before the infusion kicked in, and finally my worries were systematically stripped away.

"Why do you keep checking your phone?" Zane asked.

"I'm not."

He glared, his blue eyes resembling DT's as he did so.

"Please don't tell me you gave Reina your new number."

"Do you think I'm an idiot?"

He laughed, practically spraying me with liquor. "Yes, yes I do."

"Can I ask you something? How'd you go from tanking with Ensley to kissing her? I just can't see how you turned that shit around."

He leaned back, propping his feet up on the coffee table. "Kaito Nakamaru finally coming to me for dating advice." One of my throwing daggers floated between us before moving into the kitchen. I grinned as I poured him another shot. He downed it and held it out again for me to refill. "Just be, like, 'What's your gift? Hotness? The ability to give me an erection?'"

I buried my face in my hands as Zane laughed himself onto the floor.

"So that's what you said to Ensley? Because I'm pretty sure she'd slap you for saying that."

He stared at the ceiling. "No, man. We were talking, and there was this awkward silence, and she was looking at me for a minute, waiting for me to say something."

"Yeah, sounds like you."

"Then I said, 'I like you, too.'"

Whiskey practically shot out of my nose.

"I know, I know," he said. "And she looked, like, almost offended for a second, then she smiled and kissed me."

"That's the most fucked up story I've ever heard."

"I know, right? So, what's the deal with you and Reina?"

I wrung my hands. "There's no deal. I'm here now. She's there."

"You ever going to tell her how you feel?"

I glared at him. "Actually, I did tell her, but then you, Carter, and Ensley started killing everyone."

"My bad."

I tossed a pillow at him, and he jackhammered up. "Bro, make me fly."

"No way, you're going to throw up all over my apartment." I picked up my phone, turning it over in my hands. It was a bad idea, but who cares? One text couldn't hurt.

Me:
I miss you. Do you miss me too?

I poured myself a shot and pretended not to be waiting for my pocket to buzz. When it didn't, I poured myself a second one.

"Share!" Zane said, holding his shot glass out for me, upside down. I flipped it over with my gift. Just as I poured it, my pocket vibrated.

R:
Maybe. If you tell me where you are, I'll come get you.

Me:
You mean you'll come *for* me.

I threw my phone onto my couch and leaped away from it, hovering over the coffee table.

Zane shot up. "What happened?!"

"Risky text! Risky text!"

Zane reached for my phone. "You *are* texting Reina. Holy shit, dude! This is way worse than what I—SHE'S TYPING!"

I yanked Zane and the phone over to me, and we hovered over the coffee table waiting for the screen to light. Neither of us dared to breathe.

R:
It's a little early for whiskey, isn't it?

Zane turned to me. "Aw, she knows you."

R:
Maybe you should send me a picture of how your cut is healing.

Zane shook my shoulders. "She wants to sext, dude!"
"Get out."

Reina
TWENTY-FIVE

I had never been so glad I'd opted for a nap when we got home from the police station, because as I stared down at my phone, the image of Kai's bare chest and abs was enough to set my skin on fire. *He actually sent it.* This was wrong, I knew that, but that only made him sexier. Besides, trying to get over him never did me any good. Now that I'd been adopted, my internship was approved. I was going to find him, or die trying.

And that was the thing, wasn't it? Miranda was right. I was always going to pick him. He made me feel alive. I flew toward the flame without regard for what came next, and I didn't need a seer to tell me how this ended. The hot, dizzy feeling in my head moved to tickle every nerve in my body as I ran my fingers across the screen, wishing I could kiss the cut that ran just above his hip.

Kai:

I should probably check you for injuries. Just to be safe.

I pulled myself out of bed and rushed over to my vanity, having a seat in front of it. I slipped my shirt off and unhooked my bra. I knew the second my bra fell to the floor that I couldn't do this. I didn't even want to look at *myself* naked in the mirror. I put my face into my hands, then turned away. I sighed, exhaling the anxiety of what I had almost done. I reached for my shirt and covered my chest with it, turning to look for my bra. I caught a glimpse of myself in the vanity... peeking over my shoulder, my shirt pressed against my chest. Even though my back and shoulders were showing, I didn't look sexy. I wasn't sure that I even knew how, but I looked like me. I lifted my phone and took the picture, staring at it for a long time before I got the nerve to hit send. Mercifully, his reply came just a few seconds later.

Kai:
Reina...You're so beautiful it hurts.

Kai:
Fuck it. They can execute me. I'm coming over. Send your location.

Kai:
Better yet, join The Fallen.

I smiled at my phone.

Me:
Doubt my new guardian would approve of that.

Kai:
You got adopted?

Me:
I'm sure by tomorrow it'll be all over the news.

Incoming Call from Kai

Panic tore through my body, and I triple checked that my bedroom door was locked before leaping onto my bed and answering the call.

"Hello?"

"Rei?" Kai whispered. "You were adopted?"

"Mhmm," I answered simply, hoping I could mask the shake in my voice.

"By who?"

"Yemoja Roux," I said.

"Wow. That's huge, Rei. Are you okay? Do you want to talk about it?" he asked, but I could barely hear him.

"You sound far away."

"Oh, sorry, I was looking at your picture." His low voice sent a chill down the side of my jaw and neck. It was like I could practically feel his lips on my neck. "Is that better?"

"Mhmmm," I said in a stupor that felt like I was emotionally drunk.

"I... uh... like that sound."

My stomach fluttered.

He took a sharp breath in. "Oh no. Your name is going to be Reina Roux!" he laughed. "That's so cute."

"I opted not to change my name."

"You really think the media is going to pass up the opportunity to call you Reina Roux because of a little paperwork? Fuck,

I hope you're not thinking of going with Yemoja Roux on her missions now."

"I have to."

"Why? She's one of The Fallen's biggest targets. You're going to get killed."

"I have to save you."

"Then I'll have to fucking go with The Fallen to try and save you. You're not going to try and kill me, like last time?"

"I haven't decided."

He sighed. "Damnit, Reina. You're really not going to be happy unless we Romeo and Juliet this shit, are you?"

I laughed, rolling onto my stomach. "Do you mean fall in love or die tragically?"

"Both."

Butterflies tore apart my insides, my muscles tightening from the sensation. "I'm game if you are."

"Reina," he breathed. "I'm so game."

Kaito

TWENTY-SIX

By the time the evening news came on, the term Reina Roux was spiraling through the media. Reina's picture was everywhere, but none compared to the one I had saved to my phone. I couldn't stop looking at it. I knew it would be safer just to delete it, along with the rest of our messages, but I couldn't bring myself to do it. We were practically dead anyway, both stuck on different sides of a war. It wasn't like I could go to DT and say, "I changed my mind, I'm going back home to be with my girl." Knowing him, he'd probably kill her, then ask if I was grateful not to have to worry about her anymore. I shuddered.

I didn't know how Reina did this, kept believing in me after all the mistakes I'd made. I promised myself, in the next life, I wouldn't fuck it up. I'd be the kind of guy she could depend on. In this life, however, we were so fucked.

A knock sounded at my door and, before I could answer,

Zane burst in. "Have you seen the news?" he said, wide-eyed. Then he turned to the TV with the news blaring.

He rushed over and took a seat beside me. "I can't believe this. She's the daughter of the most powerful Fae and you're the face of The Fallen… you two are so fucked."

"Thank you for that evaluation."

"By the way, how did… the thing go?"

I turned away, and he leaped onto my back. "Why are you blushing like a little bitch?" He berated me with punches.

"I'm not," I said, trying to shake him off. I shoved him back onto the couch.

"Wipe that stupid smile off your face then," he sighed, leaning back into the couch. "See? That's what I wanted with Ensley."

I nodded, taking a seat beside him. "I might still be buzzed from earlier, but if she's worth the risk, go for it, man."

"Who even are you today? Let me see what she sent you."

"No way," I said, floating my phone across the room.

There was a knock at the door. I nodded to Zane, who was closer, and he hopped up to answer it. "Ensley," he said. I sat up as she pushed past him.

"We're going into the city tomorrow night. We're going to take down a Fae to bring the media attention back to The Fallen. Apparently some girl got adopted by Yemoja Roux. DT wanted to know if you're ready to head out there."

"Yeah. I'm ready."

Zane chimed in, "I'm ready too."

She bounced onto her toes. "*YES*! Okay, we'll train in the morning and then head out at dusk. DT wants to take Rolland with us."

"Rolland?"

"You know, red beard, gem gate guy?"

I nodded. "Ah."

"So we can port back if we get into trouble." She eyed my coffee table that had the half empty bottle of infused whiskey. "And maybe you two shouldn't drink anymore tonight."

Zane said, "Unless you'd like to join us for a drink."

"Really?" she said, her face brightening. Then it faded as she looked over at me. "Oh. I better not."

Zane jabbed a hard elbow into my side. "You totally should," I said through gritted teeth.

Ensley only stayed for one drink, but I enjoyed listening to her and Zane banter. He really did step up his game, and she seemed to find him as funny as I did. If life were fair at all, then Reina would be seated beside me, drinking with us. I missed her. All those precious years I wasted giving her a hard time... No, who am I kidding? All those years *humiliating her* were gone now, and all that was left was a world that wanted us to be apart. She was going to try to save me no matter what I did or said. That task was impossible. But I *had* seen her do impossible things before. It might have been selfish of me to want to see her again, and stupid of her to risk her life to find me, but no matter how much I fought the desire to be with her, I always failed. For once, I didn't mind being a failure. I found myself counting the minutes before I had my apartment to myself again so I could look at her picture.

I'd need the comforting image of her dark eyes, and her curls spilled across her bare shoulders if I had any hopes of falling asleep tonight. Tomorrow promised one of two horrors that were sure to keep me up. Either I didn't have a run-in with Reina, and would have murdered my first Fae, or worse, I'd find her and roll the dice that both of us could make it out alive.

Reina
TWENTY-SEVEN

I walked sleepily into the living room, relieved that Oden wasn't waiting there like yesterday. Yemoja Roux had put out a fresh vase of flowers on the end table and I moved immediately to smell them. It was a gorgeous mix of yellows and magentas that rivaled the beauty of Yemoja's hair. They looked happy in the morning light, and as I leaned in to smell them, I noticed a slip of paper.

I'm so sorry Reina. Please forgive me.
Love, Oden.

I cringed. I obviously owed him a conversation. How could my anger be justified when I'd practically done the same thing with Kai? Well... not *exactly*. I couldn't say that what he did was worse when I had no intention of stopping. There *was* no stopping anymore. I wondered if I'd be able to make amends with Oden long enough to work beside him in the field. Even if I could, I'm sure it would all go to shit if we actually found Kai. I needed a plan. I sat down and flipped on the TV only to have a heart attack after one look at the headline. *Yemoja Roux adopts GFA student who critically wounded The Fallen leader, Kaito Nakamaru.*

A second headline flashed across: *Meet Reina Roux.*

Panicked, I looked for my phone. What would Kai say about this? I ran back to my room and tore my bed apart, only to hear my phone hit the ground. I snatched it from under my bed. Five messages. One from Bri, three from Oden, and one from Kai. I opened Kai's first.

Kai:
Good morning, beautiful. Looks like I was right about the nickname. Don't worry, it's cute.

I exhaled my relief. I supposed the media had said worse things about the guy. I scrolled.

Bri:
Are you fucking serious? I saw the news. You got adopted? I can't believe you haven't texted me about any of this. You literally murder a guy and I have to hack the police database to read the report? I'm coming over there and when I get there I'm going to beat your bitch ass.

Oden:
I left a surprise for you.

Oden:
Are you awake yet?

Oden:
Message me when you wake up.

A clamor sounded from Yemoja's kitchen, and I shuffled over to investigate. The moment I walked into the kitchen, I was hit with the sweet and buttery aroma of every breakfast food I'd ever loved. Yemoja had a full spread laid out on the table, and she was scooping some eggs into a serving bowl when she noticed me.

"This looks so delicious!"

"Happy adoption," she said with a tentative smile.

"Thank you. This is… amazing."

She gestured to the table and chairs in the corner of the room. "Have a seat."

I sat, and my mouth immediately began to water.

"Dig in," she said, taking a seat in front of me.

She didn't have to tell me twice. I shoveled food into my mouth and loaded it onto my plate at the same time, as I had one delicious mouthful after the other. I hadn't had a home-cooked meal since my parents died, and I'd forgotten just how good one could be.

Yemoja smiled as she ate. "Here I was worried you might be a picky eater."

I tried to reply, but my mouth was too full of a bite perfectly balanced with biscuit, eggs, and grits. When I finally swallowed, I said, "This is the best food I've ever eaten."

"Good."

"So how long do you think it'll take me to be able to control my gift?"

She took a bite. "It's not as complicated as you might think.

At least, not as hard as some of the other aspects of using our kind of gift."

I nodded as I refilled my plate for the fourth time.

"As you probably realized, our gifts are tied to our emotions. Because of that, in times of extreme pressure, it's easy to lose control. But there's another, more reliable, way to use your ability, and that's through your will. Your will is steady and constant. You might be feeling angry or scared when you get out there, but if you put your will at the center, your desire to do the right thing, you'll be able to keep control. Does that make sense?"

"Kind of. I mean... I think I might've done it once when Oden said he... well, never mind. Have you ever lost control?"

Her gaze rose as if locked in memory before she said, "Oh yes, many times when I was younger. I've even had to resort to emotion on occasion to do my job, but I wouldn't recommend it. As you well know, that's how mistakes are made."

There was a loud slam at the front door. Yemoja looked at me with widened eyes, her eyebrows raised in mock fear.

I slumped. "That's probably for me. I... uhh... haven't been keeping up with Bri."

"Ah, well I was on my way out anyway. I'll let her in. Good luck."

"Yemoja," I said, halting her. "You know, I used to cook with my mom. Maybe you and I could cook together sometime?"

She smiled to herself. "I'd like that," she said, and she left the kitchen. I heard the front door open and close, and a half a minute later a deranged version of the angel of death stormed into the kitchen, purple pigtails and all. "Why the hell didn't you call me?" she said, plopping into Yemoja's seat and grabbing a piece of bacon.

"I'm sorry! Things got out of hand and I didn't know what to say."

Her face relaxed. "Congratulations on getting adopted."

"Oh. Uhm..."

"But I still hate you."

I'd never seen Bri so chatty. She had missed a whole lot in a short time, but a few months ago she was nowhere near as open with me as she was now. "So you actually murdered Kai? What's wrong with you? How does that make you any better than him?"

"It was an accident! I lost control over my gift and..." I wasn't sure if I should tell her, but I'd already hidden too much. "He's not dead."

She stared at me blankly for three seconds and said, "Spill, bitch."

It took a half hour of disclaimers before I even got to the meat of the story. I triple checked the lock to my door as I made my way through the last part of it, the part I felt most embarrassed to tell.

She gasped. "You ho! You've been sexting?"

"You don't understand, Bri, I can't help it. I cannot resist him."

She looked stunned. "I'm not judging you. We've all dated our share of murderers…"

"Putting a pin in that."

"But has he at least explained himself? The dance? That thing with Carter?"

I sighed and chewed on my bottom lip. "I'm… afraid to ask."

"Don't be a wuss. You have to ask. I'm serious, Reina. Ask him now."

"But what if he really did those things?"

She shrugged, "Then you have all the information and you decide for yourself… but FYI, if you still like him after that, *I'll murder him*… and you for that matter."

"Okay," I said. "Here goes."

Me:
Kai, there are a couple of things I need to ask you.

I glanced at Bri, but the reply came back right away.

Kai:
Fine, I'll answer two of yours if you answer two of mine.

Me:
Can I ask where you are?

Kai:
No. That's one of yours. Are you still dating Oden?

I bit back a smile, but Bri scolded me with her eyes.

Me:
No.

Kai:
Did you guys ever…

Me:
No… but seriously Kai? That's what you're worried about?

Kai:

;)

Bri nudged me.

"I'm shaking. Why is this so hard?"

"Because you don't want to know the answer," she said, snatching my phone away from me. She typed a message and handed the phone back to me.

Me:
Did you know about the attack on the school?

Kai:
I saw this one coming.

There was a delay before he started typing.

Kai:
No, I was just as in the dark as you were. When Quan got hit, I started looking for a way to get you out of there. That's when I saw Carter. He'd been using his gift to alter my mood all semester, but the joy in his face as he played, even as those monsters attacked, gave him away. I attacked him, but Zane stopped me and told me this was only the beginning. You were already unconscious. If things got worse, you weren't going to walk out of there, so I asked to meet whoever was in charge. He's terrifying, Rei. The guy probably would have killed me on the spot, but Zane was able to convince him that I'd be useful. He used my school ranking as leverage. I negotiated to have him delay the attack. As long as he wants me to do his bidding, you're safe at GFA. That's why I need you to stay there. Or else, this is all for nothing.

I looked over at Bri and her gaze was still jotting back and forth over the screen. Then she stopped and looked up at me. Her eyes drooped with sadness.

Kai:
Rei, you still with me?

"Respond!" Bri urged.

Me:
Yes. I'm here.

"Ask him about Carter."

Me:
What happened with Carter?

Kai:
That guy I was with? That was him, Rei, DT, and what you saw was his death touch.

I swallowed a lump in my throat.

Kai:
I couldn't stop him. Carter fucked up, but… he was trying to be better. You're not going to like me saying this, but The Fallen help a lot of people. They feed hundreds of hungry people every day. I've seen it.

Me:
What if we evacuate the school? You can come home.

Kai:

There is no coming home from this Rei. The Fae will execute me on sight. Especially since… I'm going into the field today. I might have to… kill a Fae.

Me:

Just come home we'll figure this out.

Kai:

Who would believe me besides you?

Me:

Hi, Bri here. I believe you too, but we need proof. Do what they say until me and Reina can figure out how to get you out of there.

Kai:

Bri, don't let her leave the campus. I don't know what's going to happen if our paths cross. I might not be able to protect her.

Me:

I heard she kicked your ass. So… maybe *you* should go hide on campus.

Kai:

Touche.

kaito
TWENTY-EIGHT

I hopped from the car and followed Ensley into the factory, smoke pouring from a vent at the top.

"Before we start," I said, "I wanted to apologize to you about… you know." I scratched the back of my neck. "I didn't know your situation and, like…we all have our shit."

She looked up at me with her light brown doe eyes. "Thanks for saying that." She shrugged, her dimmed gaze teeming with sincerity. "I don't know what I'm doing."

I simpered. "Join the club."

She forced a smile and spun quickly, not wanting to dwell on our shared failures, and led me into the belly of the factory.

The industrial building roared with life as I walked past dumpsters packed with shards of black glass. I slowed my pace while I picked up a handful from a pile that spilled over. It was enough to bring the memory of the glass demons back with a vengeance, and I shuddered to think how many Ensley, and whoever she'd previously been working with, could bring to life with the amount of glass they had gathered. The resting army could have wiped out the entire school, but they were not sentient as they seemed. They were only piles of discarded material. It was strange to think that in the hands of someone Gifted, even garbage could be dangerous. Ensley was only a com—her gift would be considered a party trick to anyone who mattered—yet she'd found a way to use her ability to slay the Fae. I wondered if that was the connection to GFA that I never understood. Why attack a school at all? Was it because the administration of Gifted Fae Academy ruthlessly decided whose gifts were worthy and whose weren't? I'd certainly been on the wrong end of that a few times. It was the institution that led all the others. The Fallen had a sound strategy. Wound the gatekeepers. If they'd been able to finish their attack on the school, they might even deter enough students from applying to bring the cycle to an abrupt halt. But then where would the Elite go to learn how to use their powers without losing control? I wondered if The Fallen had a plan for that. Probably.

Ensley waved me on. "We've been looking for more people who can puppet them, but it requires a unique set of skills. It's not like we can post the job opportunity online."

"Where's the rest of your team?"

She wiped a hand over her face. "Let's just say the position has a high turnover."

I wasn't sure if she meant people were dying or quitting, but I thought if I asked I might lose my nerve. She smiled at me, but all I could think about was how this small girl had taken the lives of the Fae. "You know, that's why you were selected to begin with."

Finding my voice, I said, "I can't promise I'll be any good at it." And by that I meant I couldn't promise I'd kill anyone.

She replied as if she'd caught my full meaning. "You better be, because we are dealing with Fae, and if you don't kill them, they will kill you."

I hadn't given opposing the Fae serious thought before that moment. My whole life I had idolized them. Now I faced the possibility that I'd either be forced to kill one of my idols or be killed by one.

"Can I ask you something?"

Ensley turned to me, her eyes already rolled, like she was annoyed with my question before I even asked it.

"How do you kill Fae?"

She shrugged. "I was just about to show you."

"That's not what I mean."

She exhaled through her nose, her voice flat as if the question was hardly worth the breath to answer. "I remember that the Fae are not innocent in all this." Her peppiness had vanished. The girl standing in front of me seemed *absolutely* capable of being romantically involved with DT.

I could tell from her obvious irritation that I should change the subject. "So what are you going to do, roll me in a pile of those things before we head out?"

"That's idiotic. We melt the glass into one sheet, you touch it, then we break it. Do you think it'll work?"

I didn't know, but the idea was both clever and terrifying. "I'm not sure. Worth a shot."

It was hard for me to imagine the vicious beings that attacked the dance as just piles of glass, manipulated by only a few people. I assumed that's why they oriented the glass in that way. If people believed them to be monsters, they wouldn't be peeking around the corner for the person who was moving them. Not to mention The Fallen stayed out of harm's way as their piloted demons took on the Fae.

That night at the dance, Yemoja Roux struck the dark shifting masses only to watch them rise relentlessly and continue until she'd used her gift to reduce them to dust.

"There's this place on the shore I go to practice," Ensley said. "By the shoreline. But, unfortunately, your face is a little too well known, so you'll have to make do here."

Another memory from my time at GFA rose: a dark claw jutting from the waves at the school's fort. Did Ensley know she was practicing so close to the cloaked hideaway? If she didn't, I wasn't going to be the one to clue her in.

She walked over, handing me a smooth slate of colored glass. "Please," she said quietly. "I know you don't want to be here. I know you're not the man we all thought you were, but you're my family's only hope. Zane's too, along with countless others. If you give it a real chance, you'll see it. The Fallen will earn your loyalty. I promise."

I nodded, taking the slate in my hands. *Sorry, Ensley. My loyalty is to Reina and no one else.*

Reina
TWENTY-NINE

I lay silently beside Bri in my bed as we stared at the ceiling, disappointed that our strategy session didn't yield any decent solutions. "Can I ask you something?" Bri said, finally filling the silence.

I nodded, taking a deep breath to steady myself for what was coming next.

"Why do you like Kai?"

I brought my palms to my stomach and pressed down, allowing myself a moment to brace myself for the memories, though I already had an answer. "The moment kids started getting their gifts, school became unbearable. In middle school, I remember being scared all the time. Then this new boy showed up, and he didn't seem scared at all. Despite being a serf, he always looked out for me. Broken bones, bloody noses... one beating after another to stop the Elites from hurting me." I turned to her. "Think about that. Protecting someone in a hopeless situation with no gift to lean on is just…"

She scoffed. "Stupid?"

I winced then took a moment to choose my words correctly. "It transcends the Fae. He was born with the instinct to protect, and I wanted to be just like him."

"And then he became an asshole."

I turned back to the ceiling, suppressing the burn behind my eyes. "Yeah. He changed." I wove my fingers together, the echoes of Kai's torment ricocheting in my mind. I gulped down a wave of emotion. "He got lost for a while. Lost in being a prodigy, his parent's expectations, his own hopes for the future."

She snorted. "He's still lost."

"I'm not so sure about that, Bri."

She jackhammered up. "You sure it's not just because you think he's hot?"

My cheeks burned. "That too, but, at first, when he was protecting me, he wasn't. He was awkward and he didn't have that whole Adonis thing going yet," I mumbled. "But think about it, after fighting his whole life to build his reputation, to accomplish his dream of attending GFA, he threw it all away in an instant to save us. Just like that. In a snap decision." My breath was shaky when I inhaled next. "Now that I think about it, he's even more of a hero than the boy I knew."

Bri nodded.

"We have to get him back."

Bri nudged me, a strand of purple hair falling into her face. "Do you *love* him?"

I covered my face with my hands.

"Oh my god, you totally do."

I bit down on my smile. "I never said that."

"You didn't deny it either."

A knock sounded at my door.

"Who is it?" I croaked.

Yemoja Roux peeked inside, her magenta hair already woven into a braid. She grinned. "Are we having girl talk in here?" she asked, her face beaming with excitement. She lay beside me and I shot Bri a warning glare not to say anything.

"So, what are we chatting about today?" she asked.

"Nothing really," I said.

The joy drained from her face so quickly it made my heart ache. She sat up, managing to fake a smile that somehow hurt worse. "Oh. No problem. I didn't mean to intrude, I was just popping in to say hi. I'll be in the kitchen if you need me."

"Wait," I said.

Bri's gaze met mine, but this time it was her eyes that held the warning. I patted the bed beside me and she sat down, her emotions bottled more cautiously this time.

I took a deep breath. "I need your help," I started, "but I'm afraid you won't understand."

"You can trust me," she said, but Bri didn't look convinced.

I turned to her, reading the lines around her eyes like they each belonged to a different chapter in her life. "I need you to trust *me*."

"Okay," she said, but I could tell from her shallow breaths she was nervous about what I'd say next.

"Kai's in trouble."

I could see the questions stirring behind her eyes. *Are you still in contact with him? Why don't his own people help him?* But instead of asking, she listened patiently.

"Kai joined The Fallen to stop the attack on the school. Zane confirmed it that day when I ran into Kai."

She nodded thoughtfully. "Are you sure he isn't just—"

"I'm sure. He's afraid of The Fallen's real leader. It's a boy with white hair, maybe a few years older than me. I saw him with Kai that day. It all happened so quickly that I couldn't really understand what I saw, when Carter just…" I shuddered at the memory. "But, now I know that he has a death touch."

"A death touch?" she asked, her body going rigid. "That's… impossible."

"Kai can't turn himself in because the Fae will kill him if they get the chance. Don't you see? He's a hostage."

Yemoja Roux stood quickly, thoughts racing behind her lined forehead. "How do you know all this?"

I wasn't sure yet what she thought of the news, and I wasn't willing to risk my phone contact with Kai.

"You don't believe me?"

She began to pace around my bedroom. "I-I do. It's just a lot."

Bri's gaze darted between us, her eyebrows raised like she was watching a TV special.

I needed Yemoja Roux more than ever, but even if she wasn't going to help me, I was going to save Kai. My next question would tell me everything I needed to know. "Can you convince the Fae to capture Kai without killing him?"

She looked up at me. "It won't be an easy sell, but we have to try."

I flew off my bed and tossed my arms around her, giving her a tight squeeze. "Thank you."

"We're family," she said. "I'll always be on your team."

Bri came up behind us and wrapped her arms around us both.

kaito
THIRTY

The glass shattered, and my gift's grasp of each tiny shard remained intact. I nodded to Ensley. "Okay," she said. "Now try moving them." I held out my hands and the black fragments rose like a wave from the pile.

"Good," Ensley said, her pep returning. "Can you make any other shapes?"

I didn't have enough glass in range to make a demon like I'd seen at the dance, and I didn't want to anyway. Instead, I pulled the shards into a larger version of Reina's owl charm. With the slightest shift of concentration, I made it flap its shiny wings, though it was my gift alone that held it afloat. It was awkward, but all the glass stayed within my grasp, and Ensley gaped at me, urging me to improve faster. The more that I thought of the glass pieces as one whole slab, the easier it was to make my design work cohesively.

"You really are Elite," Ensley said. She bounced onto her toes and grabbed another slab of glass. "Here. Let's add this one."

Slab by slab, we added to the pile, Ensley's admiring gaze filled with more awe each time.

"How did you learn to hold so much with your gift, and for so long?" she asked.

I thought for a moment and knew instantly; it hadn't been the result of the lessons my parents dragged me to each day but rather a game I invented for myself. Shortly after my gift unlocked, I started hovering over my bed before I fell asleep, curious if I could hold myself up while I slept. I never managed it, instead waking strewn across my blankets. But, as life became more complex, and sleep eluded me, the minutes I'd once spent hovering stretched to hours, and my gift flourished. "Born lucky, I guess," unwilling to share the rest.

We practiced for several hours before Zane showed up. His barrier gift could come in handy in a pinch, but he wasn't going to be able to help with the glass. His tossed hair and drooped eyes said he'd taken the opportunity to sleep in. I'd conjured three glass demons at once when he entered, and he seemed genuinely impressed, but shortly after, I lost control of the first slab of glass, its pieces dropping to the floor one by one.

"Well, well, well…" a voice said, drawing our attention. "Here they are."

My stomach dropped when DT entered the factory, his white grin sending a shiver down my spine. Then I saw the small arms and legs wrapped around him. My heartbeat raced, and my gaze slid over to Zane, whose ghostly expression mirrored the terror I felt. Gleefully enjoying a piggyback ride from DT was the cake-stuffed little girl I'd met at the party. It was Wendy, Zane's little sister—and it was apparent in her bright smile she was completely unaware of the danger she was in.

He walked over to me and grinned. "I'm glad to see the training is going well." He nudged me, and Wendy giggled. I allowed the glass to fall into piles in front of me.

I needed to do something before Zane did. "Hey! It's the cake monster!" I said, hoping my enthusiasm would draw Wendy to me and away from DT.

"We went to the park!" Wendy said as she wiggled off DT but remained at arm's length as he said, "Do you want to tell them the news?"

"I got my gift!" she squealed and ran to Zane.

We both shot each other a quick glance of relief that she was no longer in DT's range, then Zane turned his attention to his excited sister. "So soon? That's amazing, Wen. What is it?"

She hurried over to me with a smile and said, "I saw you at the park."

What? Her attention shifted, and she raced toward the glass with tiny outstretched hands. *She's going to get cut.* "Careful. This glass is sharp." She paused, only for a moment, before crouching down and patting the glass with her palms, and then the gray concrete beside it. A moment later, a smoky image filled the space. It was blurry at first but grew more defined until I could see it more clearly. I stared; it was *me*. One of my ghostly legs protruded through Wendy, and the other through the pile of glass in front of me. Wendy stepped back out of the image as he lifted his hands and conjured an owl from the translucent glass.

"Magnificent, isn't it?" DT said.

Zane and I stared, and after a few short seconds the smoky scene dissolved.

Zane's face brightened. "Wow, Wen! That was amazing!"

I'd never seen a gift even remotely similar. Not only did she channel my actions, but she was able to project the image back in the room for us to observe. It was beyond Elite.

"She's a prodigy," I said before remembering how that word had done me more harm than good.

Zane beamed. "Did you tell Mom and Dad yet?" She shook her head. Zane looked up at DT. "Can we go?"

"Of course," DT said.

Zane pulled his sister up and carried her on his hip halfway out the door before he turned back to me. "I'll be back before our mission. Don't go without me."

I nodded and he was gone, leaving me, DT, and Ensley alone. I wanted to ask DT how he ended up spending the day with Wendy, or how they came to discover her gift, but I didn't want him to know I'd grown distrustful. Zane would, no doubt, have a story for me tonight. I hoped like hell he'd pass along to Wendy how important it was to stay away from DT. Particularly for such a vulnerable little girl. After all, no good ever came from being nearby when the grim reaper called.

Reina

THIRTY-ONE

The Fae Agency Headquarters didn't seem like it belonged to Ancetol. Unlike the city, built with steel, glass and flashy neon lights, Headquarters was a white marble structure lined with columns and lit with two blazing torches. It was both a fortress and a monument to their importance—a pillar of wealth in the belly of Ancetol's crime-riddled streets. Even with Yemoja Roux at my side, it had taken us nearly twenty minutes to get through all the enchantments that surrounded the gates. But as I took a look around, I knew it was well worth the wait. There were fountains in the courtyard and hedges in a similar style to GFA, only on a smaller scale. I now understood that my school was paying homage to this very place. It was, after all, the agency the Academy was training us to serve. Still, even if GFA's courtyard was larger, the Agency's felt grander, most likely due to its location at the center of the city. It was a garden oasis in a concrete world, but I wasn't here for tourism. Yemoja and I needed to find a way to convince the chairman not to use lethal force on Kai at a time when that very topic was hotly debated and polarized. It was no secret what the chairman's opinion was.

When we reached the front steps, Yemoja Roux turned to me and nervously adjusted some of my curls. "Let me do the talking. They'll give me more latitude, and I don't want you to hurt your chances of being picked up by them in a few years."

I felt a lump in my throat, Yemoja's uneasiness intensifying mine. I doubt I could find my voice if I wanted to, so I nodded instead.

Being the greatest Fae on earth might've got Yemoja and me into the building, but it was an hour and a half before we were allowed to see the chairman. We pushed open the glass doors to find a room that appeared to be draped entirely in deep purple velvet. There were small gaps where the white marble peeked through the dusty fabric, and the room felt cramped and dark, despite being the opposite.

At the back of the room, the chairman glared down at us from what could only be considered a throne. There were torches on either side that matched those at the front of the building. The chairman's coral-colored hair was pinned to his head in loops, and he scratched at the back of his hand with long curved fingernails sharpened to a glittery point.

Yemoja Roux stepped forward, confidence evident in her sanguine movements but not in her eyes. The chairman flashed an unfriendly grin. "What brings you to my office today so… unexpectedly?"

"We have a lead on The Fallen. We'd like to ask the Fae not to use lethal force when capturing Kaito Nakamaru as we believe he can lead us to—"

The chairman's smile died. "I'll stop you right there. All Fae *will* use lethal force, if necessary. I won't risk the lives of our city's heroes."

I twitched, finding a touch of relief when Yemoja didn't waiver.

"We think he can lead us to the real leader of The Fallen."

He tapped his fingers, his agitation on full display. "It doesn't matter who the real leader is. The Fallen is nothing more than an image, and for the moment, it's the image of Kaito Nakamaru."

"He's innocent," I blurted. I could tell by Yemoja's contorted expression that it was a mistake, but there was no turning back.

His arched eyebrows rose. "Oh. I hardly noticed you, dear. Is this the famous Reina Roux?"

"It's Bennet. Reina Bennet," I spat. "Kai is being blackmailed by The Fallen. We have to get him out of there."

His smile made my skin crawl. "I just love when children burst into my office and tell me how to do my job."

"I didn't—"

"No." He shook his head. "You hush, now. The adults are talking."

My jaw locked, and I could see in the reflection of some exposed marble that I'd begun to glow, a fact that didn't seem to faze him in the least. The fire beside the throne began to thrash.

His gaze moved to Yemoja. "Of course the Agency appreciates all you do, Ms. Roux, but we can't change the policy with so little verification."

"I understand. I'm sorry to disturb—"

"This is so fucked up," I said, my hands balled into fists. "You can't just slaughter people just because you think they *might* be bad. Who are you to sit up there on that throne and decide who lives and who dies?"

I felt Yemoja's hand grip my arm. "That's enough, Reina."

The chairman gave a curt laugh, his face settling back into a mischievous cheshire grin. He sighed, his head tilted condescendingly.

"I'm sorry," Yemoja said, but he raised his hand to silence her.

His voice was so smooth it was as if he were reciting a poem. "I'm the law—the very bones of our society. Without me, Ancetol would be nothing but a pile of rubble in a chaotic wasteland. You can ask your new mommy what happens to a Fae who hesitates. I believe she was particularly close to Will Citrine and Raphael Mazarin."

Yemoja's gaze dropped to the velvet rug.

"But you want me to risk the lives of our city's protectors to save your broody, gothed-out boyfriend from his own poor judgment?"

Disbelief over his petty response showed in my half smile. "And I'm the child here? All I'm asking you to do is to capture him."

"And what if he attacks?"

"He won't."

"What if he does? What makes you so sure?"

I took a deep breath. "I've been in contact."

I wasn't sure who looked more surprised, the chairman or Yemoja Roux. I pulled my cell phone from my pocket and walked it over to him. Curiosity flared in his dark eyes as he reached for it, which gave me pause. But I opened my conversation with Kai, handed the chairman my phone, and held my breath as he scrolled through. His expression remained unreadable, except when he came to the picture I'd sent Kai when he briefly raised an eyebrow, and then scrolled back through the phone. My attention moved to Yemoja Roux, whose gaze was firmly on the ground in front of her. I knew she wasn't happy with me, but this was the only thing I could think of to save Kai. I had to try it.

Finally, the chairman spoke. "When you're young, it's difficult to see the bigger picture. Fae need to consider the greater good. They cannot worry about one individual with spurious claims of innocence."

"So, even with proof, you're not going to give the order."

"All this proves is that I was right about him being your boyfriend."

I gaped. "If you do this, and he dies, you're just proving that The Fallen are right," I said, reaching for my phone.

He pulled his hand back.

I froze.

"Careful. That sounds remarkably akin to treason." He stood, forcing me to step back to give him space.

"Give me my phone," I said, but his gaze was on Yemoja Roux.

"Take her out of here while I still permit it," he said.

"Give me my phone!" I demanded. Then, in a flash that I saw in one endless moment, he tossed my phone into the fire. Without giving it any thought at all, I threw my power at my phone and knocked it from the fire. It fell to the ground with a smack, but I snatched it before the chairman tried anything else. The phone was burning hot, so I threw it in my pocket before I risked getting burned. But, functional or not, I was glad I had it back. I didn't trust myself to look at the chairman or Yemoja without losing control, so I turned and ran from the building.

Kaito

THIRTY-TWO

Me:
Reina, training went better than expected. I'll be out in the field tonight.

Me:
I'm getting a little nervous. I don't think I could actually kill a Fae. What do you think the odds are that we won't run into anyone?

Me:
Are you going to be out there tonight? Is it too late to persuade you to stay safe on campus?

Me:
Rei?

Fuck. Something happened. No, she's just busy. If someone got ahold of her phone and found out we've been texting, she might be in a lot of trouble. They might also be able to track my phone and send the Fae to take me out. Was I jumping the gun? It had only been a few hours without a reply.

"Hey, man," Zane said, jogging me from my panicked thoughts. He had a tray of food and sat down in front of me.

I slid my phone into my pocket. "Hey, how's Wendy doing?"

He took a bite of a chicken burger and spoke through chewing. "She's excited."

"I bet. That's the most amazing gift I've ever seen. She'll have no trouble at all getting into GFA."

His blue eyes moved to me. "Oh. Uh. Yeah. Probably not. Sorry."

How quickly I'd forgotten. Wendy would never attend GFA. None of The Fallen would. In fact, it would be a miracle if it was still standing when Wendy was old enough to apply. I hung my head. "Right. Sorry. Old habits…So what was DT doing with her? What a weird way to find out."

He shook his head. "I don't know, man. Wendy told me she discovered her gift by accident. When she realized what it was, she ran to the tower to find me but ran into DT instead. He took her to some park so she could try it out in a larger space, then came here when she finally got tired." His gaze was loaded.

I frowned.

"I know," he said. "I don't like it either. It's hard for her to understand why she should be more careful. He's nice one minute and then…"

"And then Carter?"

He nodded. "A total wildcard."

Ensley dropped into the seat beside me, Rolland taking a seat beside Zane.

Ensley's cheeks flushed pink when she looked at Zane, but her voice came out in its normal, casual tone. "You guys having a strategy session without the rest of your team?"

"Did anyone bring me a burger?" I asked, eying their trays.

Rolland smirked. "It's like ten feet away."

I groaned.

"So, DT has given us specific instructions not to engage Yemoja Roux. If she's the one we run into first, we book it back to Rolland and he'll port us back to the tower. From there we'll head out to another area of the city."

Zane said, "You spoke to DT?"

This time Ensley's face turned a dark crimson.

"What if we run into another Fae?" I asked, hoping to rescue the conversation from the awkward bomb that seemed to be on a short countdown.

Ensley said, "We whistle once, to alert the group that we found someone. We'll follow the sound and try to corner whoever it is, with Zane playing defense for Rolland and Kai and me taking out the Fae. Whistle twice if you're in trouble and three times if it's Yemoja Roux, and we need to get the hell out of there."

"Maybe we should postpone," I said.

Rolland grimaced and I thought for a second he would speak, but he didn't. Ensley did instead. "Losing your nerve already?"

"Of course not," I spat. I looked down at my phone. "It's

just…" When my gaze rose to Zane, he shook his head slightly to stop me from saying more.

"DT wants the news coverage back on us. There's too much focus on that girl being adopted by Yemoja Roux. Plus some guy from the north side claimed his gift was 'stolen.'" She giggled. "But if you're not down for this, Kai, we'll go without you. I can handle the glass on my own, even without Carter."

Now that I knew how it all worked, I had no real reason to join… except one. If Reina happened to be out there, I needed to be out there too. At least she'd be with Yemoja Roux, meaning my team would retreat if they ran into her. But I couldn't risk it. If she strayed too far from her group, she might be the next victim of The Fallen. If I was there, I might be able to save her. I trusted Zane, but after watching Carter die, I knew Rolland was loyal to DT. Ensley's loyalty was impossible to gauge. The penalty for being wrong would be too great.

Reina
THIRTY-THREE

Yemoja Roux and I took a gemini gate home. Just a touch of someone's hand ported us across town. I concentrated on suppressing my emotions with all my will, but my purple glow didn't dim. Maybe it was because my last connection to Kai was broken and I had no way of recovering it. I'd failed to protect him, and now he'd be on his own. But it wasn't Kai on my mind as we made our way home, it was Yemoja Roux. She was so angry she could barely look at me, and when I'd tried to initiate a conversation, I was instantly silenced. It was barely noticeable in the bright afternoon sun, but I might have been subconsciously looking for it. Either way, I lost my words the moment I caught a glimpse of the faint magenta glow emanating from her hands.

This is bad.

I was arranging my apology when we reached Yemoja's apartment and found Oden waiting outside. *Perfect.* His alarmed expression suggested that we were glaringly distressed, but it didn't stop him from following us into the apartment. The moment the door shut behind us, Yemoja Roux whirled around and glared down at me. "How could you blatantly disobey me like that? I told you not to say anything and you went in there and threw a tantrum."

"Woah, woah, woah," Oden said, instinctively moving between us.

Frustration surged through me. "You gave up so quickly. You didn't fight at all. If you had pushed a little, he might've—"

"You have no idea what you've done, do you? If you think you were helping Kai, you're dead wrong."

Oden's face drained of color.

Yemoja paced. "And don't get me started on the texting. At least the chairman took care of that."

I gritted my teeth. "You knew he was wrong. You know what he's doing is wrong. Why do you just obey?"

"This is the system!" she yelled, her voice as sharp as shattered glass. "You play by their rules. If you don't like it, become the damn chairman, but nobody will take you seriously if you have a meltdown at the Agency."

I shook with anger.

"All you've done is put a bigger target on Kai. They don't care if he's innocent or not. He's the face of The Fallen, and killing him will crush their momentum. Why do you think the chairman was so quick to destroy the evidence? You're lucky he let you walk out of there alive."

I stepped back. "So it's true then. The Fae are just government dogs following orders. They're executing whoever threatens the system."

"I'm sorry this isn't all rainbows and unicorns, but this is how the real world works. I can't help anyone unless I remain a government Fae. I follow their rules, and make the best judgment calls I can in the moment. I don't have the luxury of falling apart because I disagree with a decision."

"How many innocent people have you murdered?"

She scoffed. "That's the question? Not how many I've saved? Everyone wants to be Fae until it actually comes time to do the job. Life isn't black and white. There's no clear right or wrong. You need to grow up."

"Everyone is so quick to tell me how I need to grow up, and that I don't understand," I spat. "I do understand. You're afraid that I'm right because you know this system that you fight to protect is broken. What you're doing..." I swallowed back tears, "what you're helping them do, is wrong."

I turned on my heel and headed for the door.

"Reina," Oden said.

I heard Yemoja say, "Let her go," before the door closed behind me.

I went straight to the school to find Bri. We were on our own now. I nearly knocked into Finn and Enzo as I darted through the office building and bounded down the stairs to the campus. I could also hear Oden chasing me down. I so didn't need this now. I burst through the doors of Pink House, my chest heaving with exhaustion as I stepped out onto my floor. I stopped short. Sitting in a ball outside my dorm room, with her legs clutched against her chest, was Miranda. My skin burned at the sight of her, my rage still hot from our last encounter. I was not in the mood for another battle, but she was in my way. And with Oden on my heels, I needed in my room.

"Move," I said, squaring up to her. She looked up, her eyes wet and heavy with exhaustion.

She shot to her feet. "Why haven't you been answering your phone?"

I shook my head. "What?" I pulled my phone from my pocket to look at it and realized it was burned pretty badly. Like, maybe beyond redemption. That's probably why I didn't realize she'd called. Perfect. I saved my phone just to find it wasn't saved at all.

Tendrils of her hair frizzed around her usually neat ponytail. "Has she contacted you? I had a vision Bri was taken."

"My phone is ruined. What do you mean 'taken'?"

I shoved her aside and opened the unlocked door. "Bri?" I called out, but the room felt empty.

There was nothing out of place, nothing to indicate a struggle, or even a forced entry. Just an unlocked door and an empty room.

I spun on Miranda. "I swear to God, Miranda, if this is another lie—" Standing right behind Miranda was Oden, his green eyes looking colder than I'd ever seen them. If he'd just waltzed into the girls' dorm without being stopped, that certainly didn't give the impression that this place was locked down.

"It's not." She sniffed. "I filed a report at the Agency, but they can't do anything until she's been missing for 24 hours. But, Reina, I saw her get taken in my vision. I came here, and when she wasn't here I waited a little while. I called her, called you, called Oden, called everyone, and when no one knew where she was, I filed the report. I've been waiting here ever since."

"I was waiting at Yemoja's to tell you about Bri. Seems I walked into something. Something, maybe, important? That I should know about, Reina?" Oden caught me off guard when he spoke. For just a moment, my heart went into my throat, worried about how much he heard and how much he understood about my conversation with Yemoja. But I didn't have time for this. I didn't have time for him and his hurt feelings.

"Not now, Oden. Bri is missing and I just don't have time for this shit now." He bristled. I could see it on his skin. But he'd have to wait.

I shook my head. "That's impossible. GFA is fully secure. They just increased security. She couldn't have been taken."

She spoke again, this time her voice filled with venom. "Why doesn't anyone believe me?" she hissed. Her eyes pooled with tears and desperation as she grabbed me by the shoulders. "I asked security to check the footage. Nobody came into this building, and Bri can only be seen entering, not leaving."

"Then what makes you think she was taken? Maybe she's on another floor."

Miranda looked around the empty hallway as if worried someone might overhear her. "My vision was blurred, but I heard her scream, I saw someone's hands grab her, and..." She took a deep but shaky breath, "red eyes."

My gift flared, *truth*. "This is so *fucked!*" Panic swelled, but now was the time for a level head. There was no one to turn to for help. Even the Fae wouldn't take Bri's disappearance seriously. I had the two people I cared most about with their lives on the line tonight and no time to worry about whether I was ready to save them or not. No graduation, no apprenticeship, no further training. It was too late for all that. All I had was what I was capable of now. I could either save them or I couldn't. No in-betweens. My body shook with fear. If I failed, I'd lose them. My thoughts moved to something Professor Tuberose had told me after Quan's funeral. *Our greatest fears never actualize until we're ready to face them—we just never seem to think we are.* Well, I couldn't think of a greater fear than losing Kai or Bri. Time to step up.

Turning back to Miranda, I said, "We have to go after her. If we wait 24 hours, she could be gone."

"What happened to your phone? We need to make sure she didn't try contacting you."

No time to go into all that. I nodded. "Right. Okay, so here's the plan. I'm going to get a new phone. Move my number onto it. We'll program Bri's number in, try contacting her, and if we don't hear back, we'll head out into the city to look for her... I was heading out there anyway."

"How do you expect to find her? The city's huge."

"I just need to get in her general vicinity. I'll be able to feel her. Also..." I turned and looked at Oden, who was still lurking behind us.

Oblivious to my apprehension, she wiped her face. "Got it. You're going after Kai too?"

I glared at her, trying to shut her up, to no avail.

"Look, I know you're not dumb enough to go after him because he's hot. You must have a reason."

Oden glared at me and growled, "I'd love to hear what that reason is too."

Dammit, why didn't I take the time to explain all this to Oden before? Now he'll just get in the way with his blind vendetta. I couldn't deal with him right now. I turned my back and ignored him, hoping he'd get the message that now wasn't the time.

"Who else but The Fallen would go after Bri? They're the only ones who have ever dared to target GFA. If we find Kai, he can help us get her back."

"And you trust him?" Miranda asked.

"Yes," I said, letting the silence hang between us. I saw Miranda's conflicted emotions start to cloud her eyes. She chewed on her bottom lip. The way she avoided eye contact with Oden made me feel it had something to do with him, but every minute we wasted Bri slipped further out of reach.

Miranda grabbed my hand and pulled me to the side, glaring at Oden to let him know to back off. We stepped far enough away that he couldn't hear us, and she whispered, "There's something you don't know… and I don't know how to explain it without upsetting you."

"Spit it the fuck out. We don't have time."

She started to cry. "It's Oden," she said so quietly I could barely hear her. "He's… so angry, all the time. I'm worried about what he might do if he finds Kai."

I shook my head. "He seemed fine just now, if a little pissed, but—"

"It's fake, Rei. He's not himself anymore. There's so much anger. I'm kinda… scared of him."

My gift sprouted to life. *Truth*. Why did the whole damn world have to fall apart at once?

"Thanks for the heads up, but I need you to pull it together. One problem at a time, okay?"

"Okay." She sniffed. "The phone first, right?"

"Yeah," I said, watching as she quickly smoothed out her ponytail, her aqua-colored eyes growing more determined. Oden walked up, once again asking, "Anything I should know about, Rei?"

"No. We need to go get a new phone. I need to find Bri, and that's all I can worry about right now. I'm sorry, Oden, but you'll have to wait. We'll be back soon, and we can talk then."

Oden looked at me, then, with as phony a smile as I've ever seen, said: "Sure, Rei, we can talk later."

After Miranda's warning and watching Oden's abrupt shift to casual, I had to admit she might've been onto something. I just didn't have time to work it all out. I nodded, dismissing Oden from my thoughts, and turned to Miranda.

"Follow me."

kaito

THIRTY-FOUR

Night fell with a howling wind outside the factory, cold enough to freeze, though the season so far had been uncharacteristically warm. I sat in silence as some workers toiled away, lining slabs of glass for Ensley and me. Rolland tapped away at the screen of his cell phone and Zane paced as he supervised the workers while Ensley picked at her nails—seemingly unbothered by the actions we were about to undertake. We waited for DT's signal, the moment when I'd truly take to the streets as one of The Fallen. My only mission was to find Reina and keep her safe if I could, but even that was a long shot now that we were no longer in contact. I might've had a better grip on the glass than Ensley, but she was still lethal. I'd seen it. I'd fought her, along with several students and Fae, and we still lost Quan.

Ensley had taught me more in one day than GFA did in an entire semester, and I hoped it would be enough. We planned to search alleyways separately, so I knew she'd always be three blocks away until one of us found a patrolling Fae. That meant my only chance at success was to find Reina first.

My skin pricked as DT walked in. I stood too quickly to seem casual.

"Is it time?" I asked.

His blue eyes were cold. "Can I... talk to you? I've had something on my mind all day."

"Sure, Cal," I said, hoping to loosen him up, but his posture remained rigid and his expression as stiff as a marble sculpture. I followed him as he led me away from the group to the far side of the factory.

"You lied to me," he said.

I swallowed hard. *Play it cool, Kaito*. "I-I... what do you mean?" *Fuck.*

"I was lucky enough to stumble upon Wendy today."

I nodded, remembering the pair's friendly entrance earlier.

"She was quite excited about her gift. *Touch memory*. It's always such a delight to get some promising gifts in The Fallen. I've been making due with finding creative ways for commons to assist, but having a new Elite is particularly alluring."

"What does that have to do with me?"

"The moment I understood what her gift could do, I brought her to the park where you were attacked."

My stomach dropped. *Fuck*. I knew something wasn't adding up. I'd totally forgotten that Wendy mentioned she saw me at the park. At the time, I had no clue what she was talking about and dismissed the comment. I wasn't sure how much DT saw, but at least Wendy's gift seemed to only be visual. He wouldn't have been able to hear what I'd said to Reina that day.

DT's clear blue eyes turned a deep navy. "I had planned to find your attacker using little Wendy's new gift, but once I saw the memory of the attack, I got the impression that you know who she is."

"Please, leave it alone. Please, Cal."

He looked sad. "Fine, I will, but you're going to have to face your fear sometime."

I supposed it was better to let him assume I was afraid of Reina. I patted his shoulder. "I promise I will."

He sighed, running his hand through his thick white hair. "It's just... there's something off about you lately. You seem..." His gaze softened, and I thought he looked a little dejected. "...distant."

"I'm sorry about that. It's just... it's been difficult. First my parents, then being down during recovery... I don't know... I'm just a little on edge, that's all. I promise."

He frowned, pouting a little. "I need you to kill a Fae tonight, for me. Prove to me you're still with me."

I nodded slightly, hoping to satisfy him.

"I've postponed my plans to attack the school for you, and if you're not on this team anymore, I need to know, so The Fallen can move forward."

Footsteps behind me made me whirl around. "I can vouch for him," Ensley said. "He'll have no problems taking down a Fae tonight."

DT's gaze moved between Ensley and me, but he took a long thoughtful pause before he said, "Good. See that he does."

His frosty gaze landed on me. "Don't let me down, Kai. You know I count on you. You guys should head out, it's already dark. Make sure you stay off the main roads. We don't want to lose anyone else."

I knew Ensley's team was once larger. I didn't want to ask what happened to them—especially now. It made sense that the media would hold back that the Fae were picking off members of The Fallen. With the speech DT had me read accusing the Fae of killing at will, it wouldn't be prudent for the press to bring up more Fae killings. Although they'd likely make an exception if I was killed in the field tonight. I tried not to think about it as our small team of rebels gathered around the forklifts stacked with glass slabs. Ensley and I touched the slabs, and I instantly felt their weight pressing down on my gift before they were shattered and stuffed into the back of a trash truck. One of the factory workers was to drive it around the district where we were headed, and once the truck pulled away, I knew there was no turning back.

Ancetol's neon lights bled into the alleyways as unwitting citizens failed to notice my team skulking through the shadows. I felt the truck's movements as it circled the block, its shattered cargo ebbing in and out of my range. Zane nodded to me, and the four of us went our separate ways, as planned, but I didn't feel the relief I'd expected. Instead, I wanted to reach out to them and tell them not to go. Anxiety weighed my limbs as I scanned the streets for Reina and watched my back for Fae. My body was on high alert, my hearing tuned in for the whistles of my team. One for finding a Fae. Two for being in trouble. And three for escaping Yemoja Roux.

I caught a glimpse of magenta hair and my body locked up. *Yemoja Roux.* My heart slammed against the owl charm on Reina's necklace. I leaned into the neon light to get a better look and exhaled my relief when it was only a teenage girl sporting a similar color. At this rate, I was going to give myself a heart attack. *Pull it together, Kai.*

I moved to the next alley, trying to stay in the bluer hues of neon instead of the brighter yellow or pink. My nerves began to settle, the strength returning as the truck scooted by loaded with the lethal glass shards. I should have known it was the calm before the storm—that it would all go to shit eventually. But I didn't. Not until the first whistle sounded.

Reina
THIRTY-FIVE

I fought my urge to ask Miranda to get Finn and Enzo to join me on my mission in the heart of the city. I was scared. I knew The Fallen were hunting Fae again, and now that Bri was missing, I was certain they were also targeting GFA students. I'd be exposed, but there wasn't anyone I could trust anymore. Finn and Enzo were probably just as messed up as Oden; they were all close to Quan. I'd been so busy avoiding Oden, and dodging questions about Kai, that I hadn't noticed the signs. I mean… he hadn't triggered my gift. Maybe Miranda was worried for nothing. My pocket buzzed, causing me to nearly jump out of my skin.

Miranda:
Did Bri reply yet?

Me:
No. Nothing yet. I'm almost at the city center.

Miranda:
Careful.

I was already on edge and didn't need the reminder, but it was nice to have an ally, even if it was Miranda. She'd done all she could with such a passive gift and would only be a liability if I brought her along. The rest was up to me. The neon lights flickered downtown. Scattered groups of bundled-up people hurried along the sidewalks on the main roads, passing by the shadowed alleyways where the Fae often did battle.

A few feet ahead, I saw two officers standing at the base of some stairs. I was struck by their jackets, the same aquamarine color that my parents wore when they were on the force. As I neared, I heard someone sobbing, no doubt whoever was seated in front of them, and I slowed my pace to listen in.

"Look!" he said. "My hands won't light. I swear I could do it yesterday."

"Sir, calm down," the officer said, her voice strong and nurturing, just as my mother's had been. "Maybe it's because you're all worked up."

I always admired my parents' profession. They weren't Elite, but they still looked after the city the best they could. If they encountered any real threat on their patrol, their orders were to call the Agency, but they weren't on duty when they died. They were still wearing the signature police blue-green, leaving me to wonder if that was the reason they were targeted.

The streets grew more crowded as I neared my destination, the cold already cutting through my jacket. I shivered and closed my eyes. A taxi beeped beside me, startling me, as a garbage truck cut into his lane. I turned into an alleyway, away from the main road.

My shoes scraped the pavement, the sound reverberating off the brick walls on either side, along with the dull buzz of decaying neon. *Where are you, Kai? Come on. Give me a sign.* My breath fogged in my face as I turned my thoughts to my parents. "Please, I need some help," I whispered.

A few seconds later, my ears pricked when I heard a whistle. In any other situation, I wouldn't have thought twice about it. It could have been anyone whistling for any reason, but to my ears, it was the sound of hope. I took off running toward the noise, cutting through the back alleys at my fastest sprint. I suppressed my heavy breathing, hoping desperately not to miss it if another whistle sounded. I came to a narrow alleyway and began to run through when something menacing moved in the shadows. I froze, adrenaline acting like a paralytic in my veins. The walls glowed purple around me, and I fought to suppress it. I inched backward. The sudden scrape of glass on the pavement brought me straight back to the night of the dance. The shadows rose out of the darkness like a wave. The fragments shuddered like hail, blocking out the last bit of light. My heart raced, my body on full alert. I backed against a wall and prepared to defend myself from the onslaught I knew was coming. I wasn't going down without a fight.

I was surrounded, shards of black closing in. I pulled my gift in to shield my body as best as I could. A blue light cut through the darkness, splitting the glass debris. The gap widened and my breath caught as a familiar figure stepped through. My body flooded with heat, and an electric pulse made of pure emotion zapped me from the inside out. I was unable to move closer, frozen like a mural against the wall. But if Kai's shock paralyzed him at all, it only lasted a heartbeat before he broke it. "It's you," he said breathlessly. Then he came for me—he came for me *hard.*

Kaito

THIRTY-SIX

I pulled Reina's body to mine, a glass waterfall plunging to the ground around us as my entire focus locked onto her. Her arms wrapped around my neck, her fingers swept over the back of it, yanking her into my gift's range. A chill slid through me as I lifted her and pressed her against the brick wall. Her face flushed as I watched the frenzy unfold behind her eyes. Her legs wrapped tightly around me, and before a groan of pleasure could escape my lips, they found hers. Her owl charm locked between us. I felt the heat of her body through her clothes and deepened the kiss as she rocked her hips against me. Her lips branded me, and I couldn't stop tasting them. She grabbed a handful of my hair, urging me on, so I yanked down the zipper on her jacket and gripped her waist, guiding her. She moved against me, the friction of her jeans driving me insane. I pinned one of her hands against the wall, using the leverage to bring us closer. Her fingers curled around mine. Whether from emotion or lack of air, my vision began to blur white.

Her head rolled back, exposing her neck. So I took a taste. "Kai...I—" Her chest heaved. "I might..."

But she didn't have to finish her thought. Her movements grew erratic, her body bucking under my hold as she moaned from deep in her chest. The sound alone was almost enough to push me over the edge. My heartbeat pounded almost loud enough to hear, her back arching off the wall. My eyes widened in awe as her legs tightened around me, and a tear slipped down her cheek. *Holy shit.*

She shook as her gaze lowered from the night sky back to me. Her mouth fell open. The surprise in her face must've mirrored mine. *Damn.* I hadn't even taken a shred of clothing off her. Our breaths synced for a moment, then she snapped out of her daze and threw a hand over her mouth in embarrassment. I felt my smile grow then break to a laugh. I pulled her hand to my lips and kissed it. It wasn't until she buried her face in my chest, and I wrapped my arms around her, that I suddenly realized I was shaking too.

Several silent heartbeats passed. "Rei," I whispered. "Are you okay?"

She pulled away and took a deep breath that skipped when she exhaled. "*Oh my God.* That felt so good," she said, biting back a laugh. I grinned, cupping her face in my hand and wiping away the line where that one tear fell.

"Who are you telling? You were... mesmerizing. I'm definitely going to revisit *that* memory later."

She chewed her bottom lip. "Was that... I don't know... typical?"

So cute. I pressed my lips together in amusement and shook my head. Shit, what was it going to be like when we actually *had* sex? "Rei, you're just so..." She looked at me expectantly and I lost my words.

A whistle sounded from a few blocks away, where Zane was posted. The sound shook me like an earthquake, dumping me back into reality. I looked up, hoping like hell there would be only one. But the second whistle followed. Two meant he was hurt, three meant we'd stumbled upon Yemoja Roux. I found myself wishing for the latter, practically willing the third whistle to blow. If Reina was here, Yemoja could be too, but the third whistle never came.

"What is it?"

I turned to her. "It's Zane. He's in trouble." I grabbed her shoulders. "Stay here. Stay hidden. I'll come back for you."

"No," she shouted. "I'm coming with you."

"I need you to stay safe."

"Fuck you. I'm coming, Kai."

I raised an eyebrow. "Again?"

A smile teased at her lips but didn't give way. "I'm not going to lose you again."

"You won't," I said and stole a kiss. "Let's go."

I threaded our fingers together and took off towards Zane. I'd gone off course when I saw the purple glow, disregarding that first whistle and straying away from my team. Fear clawed into me. *Please! Don't be dead*. As we neared the area where the sound originated, I peeked down the alleyways, a catalogue of Fae I might have to face tonight flipping through my muddled mind.

Reina gasped and my gaze shot up to see Zane crawling from an alleyway. He was covered in blood, one of his arms dangling unnaturally from his body. My body numbed as I raced toward him. A voice roared through the alley. "Where is he?"

I recognized the voice in an instant and bolted into the alley to cover Zane, pushing Reina behind me with my gift.

Oden's blood-spattered face darkened into a twisted smile when he saw me. "It's about time," he said. "Your buddy was running out of bones to break."

Reina

THIRTY-SEVEN

I gritted my teeth and shattered Kai's gift around me, landing hard. Darting between him and Oden, I felt my gift surge.

"Oden!" I yelled. "Back the fuck down."

His smile died, the hard lines of his face that were once handsome now threatening. His green eyes glowed in the darkness, cutting through the flicker of pink neon lights. He looked deranged, and I felt my anger morph into fear.

Oden shook his head. "Why am I not surprised to find you here with your little boyfriend."

I looked over my shoulder as Kai lifted Zane and started to float him out of the alley.

"Oden! Stop this! You don't have a clue what you're talking about! Listen to me!" But I was afraid he was too far gone already. I needed help.

"Miranda was right," Oden spat. "You are a fucking traitor, just like him."

I lowered my voice, hoping to deescalate the situation. "Miranda knows the truth now. And if you'd just calm down, you would too. Kai is innocent! He didn't kill Quan. He didn't kill anyone!" Despite my best efforts, my emotions had crept back into my voice.

"Don't bother trying to bullshit me, Reina. I was there, too! Kai fucking killed him. And nothing you say will convince me otherwise!"

I felt blood pumping through my body. Oden was out of control. He was dangerous, not just for Kai but for me too. There was no way he was going to stop. I really needed help.

"Is Yemoja Roux here?" I asked quietly.

"She's around. But I'll be finished with Kai by then."

"Oden, no! You have to stop! Please!"

I felt Kai's hand on my shoulder. He whispered, "Pull Zane east and whistle. Tell Ensley to take him and go. I'll handle Oden." I didn't see him take it off, but he slipped my necklace over my head, the familiar weight of it landing on my chest. I knew he'd had it ever since the day I nearly killed him but had no intentions of taking it back. I didn't like this. It felt too much like Kai was saying goodbye.

There was no time for questions. Based on the way he looked, Zane had minutes, if that. He was hovering above the ground, caught in Kai's levitation, so moving him would be easy as long as Kai kept Oden away.

I locked my hand around Zane's clammy wrist and began to pull.

I heard Kai's voice behind me echo through the narrow lane. "I wasn't the one who attacked Quan."

Oden gave him a sub zero look. "Save your fucking lies for getting into Reina's pants. I'm not buying it."

"Alright, then. Come get it, man," Kai said, his voice growing more distant as I turned the corner. A glass shard sliced across my cheek and I brought my hand to where it stung. Did *Kai* just cut me? The glass dragged clumsily across the ground and scraped into a pile. It shifted into a demon, one I'd seen before, only now I wasn't looking at the puppet but rather searching for the puppeteer. I whistled twice. "Ensley?" I called into the darkness.

"Who the fuck are you?" A small-framed girl with a pixie haircut stepped out of the shadows.

"Kai sent me; Zane is dying. Take him."

"Where is he?" she barked.

The brick building where I'd left Kai shook, a crash crackling through the labyrinth of darkness.

"It's a trick," Ensley seethed, and a spike of glass shot toward me.

"Stop!" I screamed, slicing her attack with a sharpened wave of truth. "Can't you see how much he's bleeding? Take Zane or he'll die."

A man with a red beard walked up next to her. I'd seen him before; he was a gemini gate.

I turned my gaze on him. "Please," I begged.

He nodded. "I'll take him."

"If you try anything," Ensley spat, "I'll kill you."

I pushed Zane over to her.

Ensley's face instantly drained of color when she saw Zane float into the dim red light. She turned to the man with the beard. "Go without us. I'll take care of her." In a flash, Ensley and I were alone. Relief filled me knowing I had done all I could for Zane. If The Fallen had been able to revive Kai, I was sure they could do the same for Zane.

I clutched the charm on my necklace for courage. "We don't have to fight."

She lowered her stance. "I think we do." She tilted her head and stepped closer. "I know you. You're all over the news. You're the infamous Reina Roux."

"We're not enemies. I swear to you, we aren't!"

She smiled. "That's where you're wrong. You're on the fast track to becoming Fae. That makes us enemies."

"I—" The glass monster surged forward, but the movements were clumsy. Its inhuman mobility was difficult to predict. But the glass shard I'd cut from the beast a few minutes ago remained motionless on the ground between us. I filed my gift into blades over each arm and saw the purple glow reflect off the spiked monster. I slashed at it with both arms, my hair standing on end at the screeching sound of our colliding forces.

Ensley was focused on her puppet, and she didn't notice me maneuvering around to get a shot at her. When I saw an opening, I went for it. My arm cocked back, the sheen of my ghostly blade reflecting in her widened irises as the sharp of it descended. At that moment, I thought of Yemoja Roux. My gift blinked out as I balled my hand into a fist and connected directly to her cheek bone. She slammed to the ground, knocked out cold. Her glass monster dropped to the ground in dispersed shards.

"Bitch," I muttered, and without wasting another second, I raced back toward Kai and Oden.

Kaito
THIRTY-EIGHT

The walls on each side of the alley were destroyed, the broken bricks adding to my ammunition. My ribs throbbed, and I suspected that Oden cracked more than one of them with his last attack. I scrambled around to touch as many bricks as I could before he rushed me again. "Stop holding back!" he shouted. He was crazed, but that didn't mean I wanted to kill him. I was afraid he was going to leave me no choice, though, if he continued.

I slipped his punch, and it connected with the corner of the wall where the alley branched off. The bricks exploded, and I blocked my face from the new debris. If I didn't do something fast, I was going to die here.

My daggers rose from my belt, my gift glowing blue as if aware of the danger it posed. Oden hesitated but shook it off as he cocked his arm back to strike. His fist glowed green, gaining brightness as he neared me. I sent all five of my daggers at him full force. But at that exact moment I saw Reina dart between us. I yanked them back, but it was too late. Their momentum was as unstoppable as Oden's fist as it sailed to Reina. The world froze. The neon light above us blinked out.

I heard the clash of my daggers hit the ground, and then everything went dark and still. A magenta light beamed in front of me, and I shielded my eyes, stumbling back. I gaped. Yemoja Roux stood between us, Reina standing safely at her side. *She'd done it*. Yemoja Roux saved us all.

Oden dropped to his knees and spit a mouthful of blood. For a second, I thought one of my daggers might've connected, but all five of them lay clean at Yemoja Roux's feet.

Yemoja lifted Oden and slung his arm over her shoulder to support his weight. He looked much the worse for wear, as if the momentum of his own punch had rebounded. Blood dripped from his nose and mouth, and the glow in his eyes was extinguished, and with it, his fight.

Yemoja Roux whispered something to Reina, but I didn't catch it.

"No," Reina said, then lowered her voice and whispered back to her. Yemoja Roux looked stunned, her mouth opened in an O, until she responded. She nodded, then Reina walked over to me, apprehension dripping from every movement.

Why do I feel like she's going to dump me?

"I'm so sorry, Reina. I didn't—"

"I'm fine. This is about something else." I turned her so my back faced Yemoja Roux and Oden, and she leaned into me.

I felt a lump in my throat the second I saw the cut across Reina's face. "You're cut."

"Really, I'm fine. This is about Bri. She's missing. Can you take us to where she is?"

"I don't know where she is."

She took a frustrated breath. "Look, Kai, I'm not going to go in there alone. Yemoja Roux is here. We have to get Bri out of there."

I shook my head, confused. "Out of where? You think The Fallen has her?"

"Yes."

"Reina, The Fallen is just a group of coms and serfs. It's just… us and DT now. And we were all here."

"What color are DT's eyes?" she asked, her voice much sharper than before.

I barely had to think about it; they were his most striking feature. "Blue. Why?"

"He's…" Oden said, his voice cut with a pained cough. "He's lying."

Reina turned to Yemoja Roux and said, "He's not." Reina's head dropped, and she careened to the side. I wrapped an arm around her to steady her. She spoke again, this time to herself. "If it wasn't The Fallen, who the hell took her?"

Yemoja moved closer to us. "We're going to find her, Reina."

Reina slipped out of my grasp and stepped between me and Yemoja Roux. She began to glow, her hair whipping in the energy of her gift as it surged forward.

I grabbed her arm. "Reina, what are you doing?"

"She wants to hand you over to the Agency. She'll have to kill me first."

The sadness in Yemoja Roux's eyes reminded me of how my mother used to look.

"Run, Kai!" Reina said.

I didn't immediately know why, but I felt the strongest sense of deja vu. How many times had I been in this situation? How many more times was I going to let Reina destroy her life for me? She'd been adopted by her childhood hero. It was obvious how much Yemoja Roux cared about her, and I would not be the reason she threw it all away. I didn't care if the Agency made an example out of me, whether that meant life behind bars or execution. I'd followed Zane and Carter out of GFA to protect Reina, and my job wasn't finished.

"Stop this." I pushed past her. "I'm going. Turn me in.... I'm ready."

I felt Reina's fingers dig into my arm. "No, you're fucking not." She started to tear up. "Please just…" She touched my face as a quick breath escaped, "let me save *you* this time."

I smiled. "Can't you see you already have?" I put my forehead to hers and whispered, "It's going to be okay."

She shook her head. "What do you expect me to do, let them take you? I… can't."

My chest warmed, and despite her tears, I knew I'd made the right decision. I took her hands in mine. "I want you to find Bri. I want you to go to GFA and become a great Fae like you always dreamed."

Yemoja Roux's gaze dropped to the ground. "Thank you, Kai," she said. "I'm sorry it has to be this way."

"I understand," I said, forcing my voice to remain steady for Reina's sake.

Reina
THIRTY-NINE

I lay awake, my heart throbbing as I replayed my last moments with Kai. I could still feel the touch of his fingertips, my mind haunted with the fear he tried to hide from me as the Agency dragged him into a cell. The chairman would decide Kai's fate in the morning, and I'd have no opportunity to prove he didn't deserve to be there.

I could hear Yemoja Roux pacing outside my door trying to think of the right words to say. But nothing she could say would make me forgive her for her cowardice. She knew Kai was innocent, yet she let him be dragged to a cell with no trial, no one allowed to prove his innocence. She allowed him to walk to his probable execution without more than a few words in aid. How could I ever forgive her?

I didn't know what I could do, but I knew I had to do something. I could practically feel Yemoja Roux lingering outside my door, cycling through the words she would never bring herself to say.

I wasn't just angry at her, I was angry at the whole goddamn world for its unfairness. But it wasn't the world or even the system that had broken my heart, it was Yemoja Roux. I didn't care if she tried to say she was just looking out for me. She wasn't. And it was wrong. Kai had no one. He could have run, but his chances probably would have been the same outside of Ancetol. And, worst of all, I think he stayed for me so I could be protected by the same system that wanted to kill him. I fought the urge to smash the room she'd given me as my body shook in frustration.

My phone buzzed, my heart leaping to my throat. *Was it Bri?* I scrambled for it, my trembling hands fumbling with the device. The screen lit and I squinted through the brightness.

UNKNOWN:

I'm downstairs. Come out.

Me:

Who is this?

UNKNOWN:

It's Kai.

Me:

What the fuck Kai? How did you get out?

UNKNOWN:

Are you coming or not?

Frantic, I leaped off my bed and raced out my bedroom

door. I caught a glimpse of Yemoja Roux sitting at the kitchen table in the dark. "Where are you going?"

"I just need some air."

"I don't think it's a good—"

I grabbed my jacket and slipped out of the apartment before she could stop me. Once I reached the bottom floor, I stepped out into the cold night. The air was icy. "Kai," I whispered, but there was no one there.

A lanky stranger stepped around the corner. His face was slender, his eyes as blue and crisp as the night air. His hair was a distinctive snowy white. He smiled at me like we were old friends, his gaze moving down my body in appraisal. I shuddered in the cold. Why hadn't I thought this through? I was so desperate for it to be true that I didn't even question it. Perhaps Yemoja Roux would follow me out. If this was who I thought, I was in big fucking trouble.

"Reina Roux," he said.

"It's Reina Bennet, actually."

He nodded, crossing his wrists behind his back as he paced in front of me. He looked like a vulture circling his prey, but his demeanor was superficially pleasant. He appeared to belong to the cold night, drawing in every last bit of crystal frost with his ghostly white skin.

"You don't know who I am, yet you don't look surprised to see me."

I took a slow breath. "I know who you are. You're DT."

His eyebrows rose. "You don't seem afraid."

"That's because I'm not." I balled my fist. "Are you?"

He bobbed his head, as if bored with the conversation. "I'm always afraid."

Truth.

I pulled my jacket closed. "What are you doing here?"

He stopped pacing and advanced on me. I felt the strength in the back of my knees falter, but I didn't flinch. I wouldn't give him the satisfaction. He spoke down to me. "I've been looking for you for some time. A while ago you hurt someone I care about. I had planned to turn you over to him as a gift. After all, is there anything sweeter than revenge?"

He was looking down at me, but his eyes were vacant as if entangled in his thoughts. I stuffed my hands in my pockets and began to sharpen truth into a blade around them, hoping I could mask the glow within my jacket. I saw what he'd done to Carter. If he touched me, I was finished. The only way to survive this situation was to fight my way out.

He continued, "When he didn't return home tonight, I thought you might be responsible."

My breath hitched. "I don't have Kai."

He lifted his deadly hands and reached for me. I had no choice; it was now or never. I yanked my hands from my pockets and sliced them both across this throat.

His smile was sweet, like an innocent child. Shards of sharpened truth shattering to dust in the wind against his perfectly uncut skin.

My chest heaved, fear and adrenaline flooding my blood. "Truth?" he said. "Can you think of anything more true than death?"

I stumbled back, but he only walked closer, reaching for me one more time. I froze as he reached into my coat and lifted the owl charm on my necklace. He held it up to the moonlight, his gaze soft and gentle as he rubbed his thumb across the charm. "I think you do have Kai."

His eyes moved to me, his face and voice sharpening. "I want him back."

Kaito

FORTY

My ribs screamed for medical attention, but the simple fact that they'd locked me in this dusty jail cell without it meant there was little hope of me not getting executed in the morning. The room was filled with cells, as if from a time long forgotten, but through the bars, there wasn't another person as far as I could see. The Fae didn't take prisoners, so I knew better than to hope for a life that extended past tomorrow. I thought of Reina, how we'd agreed on a Romeo and Juliet ending, and I couldn't help but feel like we were lucky. I thought of the picture she'd sent me. It sent an involuntary smile to my face. She was going to be okay. She was going to thrive, and for once, I wasn't standing in her way.

I slid down the cold concrete wall, letting my eyes droop closed in sadness and exhaustion. If I thought about it long enough, these captive moments were all I had left, but if they thought I had nothing but concrete walls and bars, they were wrong. I shut my eyes, pulling my legs to my chest and replaying everything I had left—Reina. Some memories returned like a storm of regret and others like a warm summer's afternoon. But my thoughts lingered on one moment in particular, one from today when I first saw her purple glow in the alleyway. She'd never once confessed how she felt directly, but she'd always shown it. My fingertips tingled with the thought of her quivering body beneath them, my jeans tightening with the memory of her spontaneous reaction to our closeness, and that one solitary tear. *She was worth it*. And even my most logical thoughts couldn't bring me to regret a second with her.

Reina had been proving to me how she felt since the day I met her. Before I even knew I loved her. I lamented the years I saw that as a weakness, as I now understood how strong she'd been all along. *Yes*. I was certain. Reina was worth dying for, and tomorrow I'd prove it.

Yet one regret lingered. Though she'd shown me, with every breath she took, how much she cared, I'd never heard her say it.

In fact, I couldn't recall a single person ever saying it to me. My chest rose and fell in the darkness, my pulse even and unaffected by the sudden bolt of sorrow that struck me—regardless of what had passed between us, how I was sure we both felt it. I would never hear her say that she loved me. Not in this life.

I remembered the night of the dance, how she'd purged the truth from my lips. I'd given her permission to pull my true feelings for her forward, but when they'd emerged they'd surprised us both. I could have loved her better if given a chance, and who knows, I probably could have been a better man too.

The ground beneath me shook, and for one doubtful

second, I thought I might've imagined it. The room shook this time, forcing me to retreat to the corner of my cell. I held my breath as I listened for clues, but it was several minutes until I heard the next howls of distress.

As a man practically condemned, I felt an odd indifference to the disturbance, able to observe with curiosity as I had nothing left to lose.

That's when I saw her burst through the door. Yemoja Roux lifted a guard up by the throat, her braided hair shooting out webs of stray strands in every direction. *What the fuck?* The guard wrangled in her grasp and sobbed beneath her furious grip, and in that fractured moment I felt the same detached fury that haunted me whenever I visited DT. She tossed the guard aside, and he collided with the bars on the far side of the room with a resounding clang. Finally, she stood with her hands on the bars of my cell.

A shadow filled the doorway and the disheveled chairman stepped to fill it. He spoke, "If you do this," he said, sleep evident in his weak voice, "you will be stripped of your title." She froze, which only served to encourage him. "You will never work as a Fae again, and your life's work will be tarnished by this act." He moved forward, close enough for me to see the age lines on his face matched hers in depth. "But if you walk away, I can guarantee—"

She spun on him, glaring at him with such intensity that he stopped mid-sentence. He stumbled as he scrambled back toward the door, retreating up the stairs to the main hall. A moment later the alarm sounded.

"What are you doing?!" I screamed over the blaring alarm, but seeing my childhood hero unravel drained all of my strength, and I fell to my knees. "I'm not worth this. Please just let me go."

"They got her. They got her." I could see she hadn't meant to say it twice, and that repetition and fear were sputtering from the inside out.

"Who?" Did she mean The Fallen got someone? The only person from our team that was still on their feet was Ensley, and I'd tracked some shards of glass to a trash truck, which meant she'd gone back to Fallen HQ and stayed there.

"Reina was taken by DT."

I shook my head. She couldn't have meant the actual DT. She must think it's my team. "That's impossible. We were all taken out at the fight."

"It was DT," she said. "I saw on the security footage. A boy with white hair."

I froze as a wave of desperation crashed down on me. All I could think of was DT's cold gaze on Reina's face. Why would he take her? Was it because I lied? What did he plan to do with her? The answers my mind conjured curdled my blood. I wanted nothing more than to flee from this prison and rescue Reina. Any punishment I'd receive would be worth it, and it was obvious, based on the current situation, that Yemoja Roux felt the same, but was this exact reaction what DT had planned? I needed to think logically. *It had to be a trap.*

Yemoja's knuckles paled as she clutched the bars of my holding cell. "He looked at her necklace and then she went with him. Why would she go with him?"

Struggling to breathe, I took a sharp breath in, my mind reeling. "He could kill her in an instant. She had no choice."

"So it's true then?"

I nodded. He must've been desperate, to leave the tower and

get his hands dirty. The only time I'd seen him do that was with Carter, and in his mind he'd done it for me. I could only assume this was the same. I thought I'd been so careful to keep my feelings for Reina hidden, for this exact reason. Either way, he knew now. We couldn't just run in there with no plan, and based on the look in Yemoja Roux's eyes, we were both too emotionally involved to do this rationally.

"Do you know where he is?" Yemoja Roux asked, her steely eyes penetrating.

"I.... I do, but—"

"But what?" she screamed. "You don't want to give up your buddy? If you don't help me get my daughter back—"

"That's not it." I walked up to the bars. I wanted Reina back as much as she did, but the look of horror in the chairman's face, and what he'd promised her, were fresh in my memory. "I put myself in here so you two could have a normal life together. Look, DT is always doing ten things at once. If he knows about our ties to Reina, he's probably banking that you'll do something reckless like this to get her back. Think about it..."

The muscles in her jaw tensed.

"He never goes in the field. He's banking that you'll let me out of here to help you find him. That way he can get to you... He wants me back and he wants you dead. If we run in there, gifts firing, we'll all die."

She clutched the bars between us and they began to glow pink. I backed away, and she bent the bars apart with little effort. I stepped through but stopped and remained motionless on the other side. I sighed. "He's trying to get you to destroy yourself."

Her eyes glistened. "What choice do we have?"

"I'm going after her alone."

"Like hell you are."

"I brought Reina into this. I'll handle DT. I'm a dead man walking, anyway," I said. "It's you alone who has something to lose here."

I closed my eyes as I felt the trash truck inch forward in the back alley of the Agency. It was packed full of glass shards, most of which were still in my gift's grasp. *So DT was expecting me.* If it was me he wanted, it was me he was going to get. Either way, I wasn't going to risk the life of Ancetol's last hope, my childhood hero, and Reina's only family.

"We need you. I know you're tired. I know you'd give it all up for her, but this city still needs Yemoja Roux," I said. "I'll save Reina on my own. I can't let you walk out of here with me. I can't let you throw it away."

"Let me? It's done. The choice is already made. The chairman already said—"

She was wrong. If I hurt Yemoja Roux a little, they'd believe she broke in here to talk, and that I'd jumped her. The Agency wasn't perfect, but they believed in Yemoja Roux as much as they needed her. I could still fix this. The only obstacle left was DT, but I might be able to bargain my life for Reina's. If I succeeded, she'd still have family to come home to, and Yemoja Roux could protect the city as Fae. I drew the glass shards toward me, and while I could feel them approaching, all appeared unmoving. Then there was a disturbance at the top of the stairs. Even with the wailing sirens, I could hear the yells of panicked Fae and the shift of the glass as it began interacting with whoever waited for us to emerge. I drew the glass together into a ball and released it in a massive explosion. I lost more glass from that attack than I'd wanted, but it was enough for what I planned next. I closed my eyes in concentration as I waited for the glass to move again, alerting me that the Fae called to stop my escape were still on their feet. Nothing moved. I yanked a wave of glass down the stairs and it finally crawled into view in a glittering black mass.

"Kaito, please," Yemoja said, but her voice lowered in resignation, as if she'd understood even with such a sparse explanation. I sharpened the mass into a spike and forced her into the cell, reconstructing it out of glass. "Save her," she whispered through tears. She lifted a glass shard and cut her face with it as white hot relief seared through my veins. With that single act, I knew I'd saved Yemoja Roux.

I thought I heard her mumble something else, but I couldn't hear it through the sound of the alarms.

I headed up the stairs and saw the piles of low-tier Fae that were supposedly supposed to stop me and Yemoja Roux. They began to stir weakly. But upon looking a little closer, many of them were pretending to be injured, probably to avoid facing her. I practically rolled my eyes at the charades and games we all played just to maintain the status quo. I performed my next line with the conviction of a drama student forced to recite a line in their school play to pass the class. "Remember, it was I, Kaito Nakamaru, who defeated Yemoja Roux."

I burst through the front door of the Agency and followed the leftover glass to the trash truck, instructing the driver to head to the tower.

I didn't want to admit that I was scared of DT. Or that I would have gladly taken the merciful execution of the Agency's water treatment over what I'd seen Carter endure. It was checkmate if DT had taken Reina, as she was the weakness that I, his closest friend, and Yemoja Roux, his greatest rival, shared. If I failed tonight, Yemoja Roux would follow, and if she fell, so would Ancetol—whether at the hands of The Fallen, or something else entirely.

I raced through the neon streets of Ancetol toward the tower like a man on borrowed time, fully prepared to die beside Reina, just as I'd promised. Or perhaps, for once in our lives, I could save her. My last hopes hung on the possibility that there was some force—some gift—greater than death, and that I possessed it.

Reina
FORTY-ONE

DT leaned in, a wisp of his snowy hair brushing my cheek. "Speak," he said, "and you will die right here."

Truth. My stomach churned, my gift's ability to detect truth a detriment to my deteriorating nerves.

He grabbed me by the arm and yanked me out of the car. "Act normal," he added.

He hooked his arm in mine, the coldness of his skin far more icy than the frigid air and just as unnerving. Despite his polished appearance, his presence was corpse-like, as if his gift had been draining his life bit by bit. We stepped into the light of the tower and his demeanor changed in an instant. The lobby was packed with families chatting and preparing to leave, as if we'd missed some kind of event. Everyone seemed happy and at ease. They didn't look like plotters or assassins, or even remotely like an evil organization. So when they smiled and waved to DT as he passed like they were one big family, it made no sense. Kai had told me The Fallen were helping people, but it was surreal to see these families interact with DT without fear, as if the only hostage here was me. How could they not see his evil?

An elderly woman approached. "Oh, how lovely your friend is," she beamed.

I smiled shyly, too terrified from DT's warning to risk any pleasantries.

"She certainly is," he replied with a smile.

She began to pull on her gloves, and just before she got them on, I saw the blisters between her thumb and finger that were always present on the ungifted who were laborers. My hands burned with sympathy pains from the brutal memories of the few shifts I'd worked last year to get by. I remember how, afterward, my hands had been bloody, but blisters like hers meant regular shifts over many years. *Was everyone here ungifted?* So The Fallen really did have only a few gifted people. And to think they had caused all this destruction.

"And how are you tonight, DT?" she asked.

"Excellent," he said, his ease and charm appealing. *Lie.* It was my first real peek into his head, and it gave me an idea. I hoped, once we arrived at his destination, he'd allow me to speak long enough to find out more about this enigma of a man—perhaps something that I could use against him.

He led me to the elevators and I dragged my feet a little, hoping to remain a few moments longer among other people, where DT relied on a mask of kindness. I shuddered to think of what kind of man he'd be when we were truly alone for the first time, and the mask came off. He squeezed my arm in warning, reminding me I had no choice but to go with him into the elevator.

"Good," he said as the doors closed. "Very good."

I stared at my reflection in the elevator doors. Beneath my winter jacket was nothing but a silky tank top and matching pants that were my pajamas. Yemoja Roux had lent me the top, and it didn't really fit, as she was much chestier than me, but at least I had my jacket to hide it. He was a murderer, I knew that for sure, but was he also a pervert?

He watched me carefully as the elevator rose. "You may speak now," he said. "I've been watching your face, and I find I'm curious about what you're thinking."

"Do you have my friend Bri?"

"Who?"

"Briara Phillips, she was taken from GFA."

He smiled. "No, the school has been off limits to me for some time." He tilted his head in curiosity, then said, "How interesting."

"What?" I asked, failing to keep emotions out of my voice as the elevator came to a stop. I needed to hold it together.

He gestured for me to move forward, and I was grateful that he didn't touch me this time.

"Well, you're in such a precarious situation, yet your first concern is for your friend."

I followed the hallway to the door at the end. "A normal person would understand," I mumbled.

"Hey, now, there's no need to get nasty." He opened the door.

My heart sank when I realized it was an apartment, my mind racing through worst-case scenarios. Being around him kept my nerves constantly on edge. "Actually, seeing that you kidnapped me, I think there is a need." Fuck, what was I doing? Antagonizing him was a terrible idea.

He nodded and turned on the lights before taking a seat on

his sleek couch. I stood frozen just beyond the threshold. The apartment was remarkably clean, to the point where it felt more like a hotel than someone's home. It was simply but expensively furnished, and out of the floor to ceiling windows, far below, I could see Ancetol's neon lights.

"Have a seat," he said in a companionable tone, patting the couch beside him. "I only want to talk… and we could be here a while."

Truth. The tension in my body relaxed. My situation wasn't much improved, but at least he didn't mean to kill me right away. I took a seat as far away as I could without falling off the couch, clutching my coat tightly.

"Take off your jacket and stay a while."

"I'd… rather not."

His eyes darkened, his jaw clenching with annoyance. Reluctantly, I peeled off my jacket, making sure to adjust my top to cover me. The fabric was too sheer for comfort, so I used my arms to block my chest, hoping he didn't notice. From the way he spoke about Kai earlier, though, I wondered if he preferred men; but that thought went out the window when I lay my jacket between us. He took one look at me and his eyebrows shot up, his lips forming an O. There was a distinct red blush that hit the top of his cheekbones before promptly extinguishing. He turned his face away toward the window, his gaze locked on the glowing neon lights of the city below.

After a silent moment, he stood quickly and hurried out of the room, making me feel even more exposed. I could practically hear my nervous heartbeat. DT returned with an oversized T-shirt and tossed it to me, without so much as a glance in my direction.

I immediately slipped it on. "Thank you," I whispered,

totally embarrassed. "That was kind of you." I'd hoped the second part would pull a reaction from him. I couldn't seem to get a read.

He sighed as if trying to discharge a feeling that I couldn't place based on his body language alone. He said, "Kai would kill me if he got here and you were dressed like that."

I watched him carefully. "Is that why I'm here? You think Kai is coming for me? News flash, ace. Kai was taken into custody at the Agency tonight. He's not coming back."

"Interesting choice of words," he said, tilting his head back. "'Taken into custody.' Not 'arrested by the Agency.'"

I didn't know where he was going with this, but I knew I needed to divulge less. However, maybe I could discover more.

He glared at me. "Why? Why would he turn himself in? What did you do to him?"

"Do to him? What are you talking about?" Ok, so he doesn't know as much about Kai and me as he let on. That's a good thing, at least.

"What are you not telling me? He's obviously still loyal to The Fallen, so there must be a reason he's doing this."

"What makes you think he was ever loyal to The Fallen? He told *me* you were blackmailing him. Using the school as a hostage against his good behavior."

He nodded casually, but there was a glimmer of knowledge in his eyes that gave him away. He was about to get cruel. "Let me ask you this, did he tell you where The Fallen's base is? Did he tell the Agency?" He put his hand behind his ear as if trying to hear something, but all was still. With a twisted smirk on his face, he shook his head. "I don't hear anything that sounds like an attack."

My thoughts raced, buying into DT's reasoning, and when

familiar doubts about Kai snuck in, my reaction surprised me. I smiled, and the more I did, the more I saw the dark humor in it. DT's face twitched, his expression slipping from smug, to agitated, to angry. I tried to hold back, but a laugh tore through me, and DT bared his teeth. He didn't like that at all.

I waved a hand to excuse myself. "I'm sorry. It's just, here I thought you knew Kai so well."

I saw a lump move in DT's throat. *Got him!*

"If you're hoping to know exactly where you stand, you chose the wrong guy." I laughed into my hand, relishing the irony that the almighty Death Touch was suffering through Kai's antics as much as I did.

"And you like not knowing?"

"I hate it."

His shoulders relaxed a little, and he rubbed his hands together in thought. Several minutes passed in silence, but I could see the wheels turning.

"Is Zane okay?"

He nodded my question away, his mind somewhere else. I had him wondering now. Just when I thought I wouldn't get a real answer he said, "I almost let him die when I saw an unreasonable amount of tears shed by *my* woman, but it's so hard to find good help these days."

I refrained from shuddering. Cold—this guy was an ice sculpture. "Let me go. Kai's not coming."

He leaned back. "He'll come. No matter his circumstances, he'll come if I have you."

I stood. "You're wrong. He's in prison. He's not coming."

DT's body twitched. "I sent him a little gift. He might already be on his way. I don't know what he sees in you, since you so vastly underestimate him," he said, his voice blade-sharp. "He's coming. *Tonight.*"

I sat, dropping my face into my hands, and exhaled a chest full of annoyance. It was time for a different approach. I needed to know what he thought he knew.

"What makes you think I underestimate him? What makes you think I *estimate* him at all? You say he's fully committed to The Fallen. What gave you the crazy idea that he'd come for me at all?"

"I'm not crazy," he said defensively, turning back to the window. "You're in love with him, obviously, which means he's most likely in love with you. He's going to come, and when he does, we'll find out which side he's really on."

"Does he have to be on one or the other? Is there no scenario where you can see him as your friend *and* my boyfriend? Why do you insist he choose between us, if there even is an *us* in this?"

"I just want to know where I fucking stand!"

Truth. I felt that. My thoughts raced to the memory of Kai's speech to me at the dance. That night he'd said, "I think I might be in love with you." My heart stuttered, my eyes closing so I could view the memory more clearly. I knew I had been furious with him back then, almost hated him, but still, I wished I had said those words back to him. I was starting to think I'd never get the chance. A question arose that froze my body: did Kai know where he stood with *me*? It was possible he didn't; I'd barely begun to understand how strong my feelings for him actually were. Things had been so turbulent that I never had time to truly consider my feelings. When did they begin to change? The shift between hate and love was but a whisper—a line in the sand that, with one gentle wave, was gone. Now the last thing I wanted was for him to risk his life by coming here. I needed to get out of this on my own, and then work on convincing the Agency of his innocence. If whatever DT sent him was enough to help him break out, my time was limited. I had to stop him from breaking out because he'd be on the run for the rest of his life. *And I might never see him again.*

My muddled feelings became crystal clear as I prepared my response to DT. Then I felt my gift splinter from the lie before I even said the words.

"He doesn't love me. And I don't love him."

My heartbeat quickened, my gift writhing in a potent mix of pain and pleasure as I fought my gift to be dishonest while the truth settled in for the first time. I was in love with Kaito Nakamaru, and I needed to survive long enough to tell him.

"Just let me go—"

"You fucking liar!" he shouted, pulling his hair.

My heart stopped, my bones rattled with fear, and my spine straightened. I'd misjudged, badly. He looked frantic. For some reason, my declaration that there was no love between Kai and me threw him. If I wasn't watching him unravel, I would have believed he saw through me, but he looked afraid as he chewed on his thumbnail. He needed to believe that Kai loved me so he could believe that Kai would come back. Was this his Achilles heel? Though I didn't know how I'd use it to my advantage, I'd discovered a weakness, but it was too early to tell if unhinging him in the process helped or hurt.

"I've told you the truth. There's no reason he'd come for me. If you've given Kai a way out of the Agency jail, and you're so sure he's loyal to you, what do you need me for?"

He gave me a sideways wink. "Insurance." I felt my stomach turn over.

He sat and leaned back on the couch, the tension in his body relaxing. Shit! My response had the opposite effect. I was losing him. I needed to make DT believe me. I needed to sell the lie, goddamnit! Squeezing the owl pendant to suppress my nerves, I pushed one more time.

"I don't love him," I said. "Kai might use whatever you sent him to escape, but he's not coming for me, and I highly doubt he'll come back to you either. You wanted the truth? Well, take my word for it. The truth hurts."

His eyes narrowed into blue lasers, scanning me for the truth. But the truth wasn't his gift. It was mine. "Where did you get that necklace?" he asked.

Dammit, he noticed. I shrugged. "Found it. Owls are cool, right?"

He looked nervously toward the window and then turned back to me. He grew even more agitated, his chest heaving as his breaths grew more strained. Finally, he exploded from the couch. "Prove it." He sneered. "Prove you don't love him, right now, and I'll let you go, and I won't go after you. I'll find another way to get him back here once he's free."

Letting DT finalize breaking Kai out was tempting, but even after the chairman so callously dismissed me before, I still believed in the basics of the system I was fighting to maintain. Otherwise I'd have to admit The Fallen had won, that Ancetol's downtrodden citizens had been swayed by this madman to believe the Fae were evil. DT had practically defeated us all single-handedly. I had no choice but to escape and put an end to this. But proving that I didn't love Kai was a test I was afraid I wouldn't be able to pass. If I had any positive karma built up, I needed to cash it in fast. "How can I prove it?"

I pleaded with my gift to allow me one last lie.

But DT's next words stole the breath from my lungs, and all hope from my heart.

"Kiss me," he said.

My time had run out. Death had called my bluff, and a pair of hearts was all I had left to play.

kaito
FORTY-TWO

I stood outside the door to DT's apartment. My pulse thumped in my ears like the deafening base of a concert speaker. The thought of Carter, as he turned to dust, weighed down my legs. The memory of Quan being impaled numbed my limbs. But Yemoja Roux had believed in me, more than my parents ever had. She trusted me to get Reina out of there alive. I had to end this now, no matter the cost. I'd considered trying to use my gift to sneak through a window, but the closer I got to the tower, the more certain I was that I should play this casually. If I charged in with emotions running high, DT might overreact. I needed everyone to stay calm. Then I heard DT's voice behind the door and I knew calm would not be an option.

"Kiss me," he said. I leaned into the door, waiting for Reina's angry reply, but I was met with only silence. Shaking, I reached for the door handle, my teeth gritted to brace myself for what I was about to see. DT moaned, and I heard the shuffle of movement. My heart stopped. I quietly opened the door so as not to startle DT and was paralyzed by the sight. On the far side of the room, Reina's hand was cocked back, her purple glow filed into a shiny blade aimed at DT. He clutched the side of his face with two hands, mewling in pain.

"I *am* in love with Kai," she said, "so I don't need to prove anything to you. And you should know I will take your life before I let you hurt him again."

Her words jolted my heart back to life. *She loved me.* Despite everything. "I knew it," I said, stepping into the familiar apartment. Her gaze moved to me and softened. My legs felt weak, and I was surprised by the burning sensation that flared behind my eyes.

"You came," she breathed. "He was right."

I turned my attention to DT. He slowly moved his hands away from his face, revealing a deep cut. His arms visibly shook as he stared at the blood on his fingertips. He looked like he was in shock.

His eyes widened, and an expression I'd never seen on his face completely overtook it. Reina must've caught him off guard, and from the crazed way he gaped at the red substance, it had been a very long time since he'd seen his own blood, if ever. In fact, it was starting to look like DT may have never been injured at all. This crumbled my plan of a casual approach. He was a time bomb, and I needed to get Reina out before detonation.

I sprinted across the room to put my body between him and Reina. I grabbed her wrist and pulled her behind me. A rush of emotion shot through me as her hand closed around my wrist. I had her now. I would keep her safe.

DT looked up at me. "Blood," he murmured.

I leaned forward slightly, unwilling to move much closer. "It doesn't look too bad. You'll live," I said, trying to calm him.

He nodded and stood, still looking shaky. "I knew you'd come."

My gaze was drawn to the couch where he'd just been sitting. Right where he'd last touched it, the white leather surface had turned dark gray. As I watched, the darkness crept across the fabric. I finally realized what was happening. I watched in awe as it slowly disintegrated into gray flakes. My stomach lurched, and my heart seemed to clench at the memory of Carter. I stepped back cautiously, easing Reina back as I moved. DT walked toward us, each step deteriorating the floor into floating gray pieces that spread, filling the air with dust. I nervously lifted us slightly off the floor, just in case. Reina squeezed my wrist like she was trying to tell me something, something she didn't want DT to hear, but since she was behind me I didn't have enough of a read on her to know what it was.

DT's usually confident demeanor had vanished, and in its place was a reckless man capable of anything. I grinned at him, hoping to rein him in as I moved Reina towards the door an inch at a time. "What's going on here, Cal?" I asked.

The nickname halted his gift's effect on the room, which unnerved me. Was he destroying this place unintentionally? He looked agitated, a fresh handprint made of blood across his cheek where he'd touch it, but this was an entirely new side to him. Even when he'd murdered Carter, he'd seemed in control. Now, the monster within was on full display.

"I need to know..." he said, his words low like a growl, "whose side are you on, hers or mine?"

I swallowed a lump in my throat. "I've seen all the good The Fallen is capable of doing, but killing the Fae won't—"

"WHOSE SIDE?" he screamed, quaking my bones. The windows cracked, alerting me that the room's deterioration had resumed.

I heard the faintest sniffle behind me, which was a kick to my gut. Anger tore through me. The moment DT dragged Reina into this, this fight was inevitable.

"Hers," I said.

DT's blue eyes widened, and he recoiled like I'd slapped him. I lifted my hands, preparing to defend myself, but the glass I'd been using all night was way out of range, my daggers had been confiscated by the Agency, and the objects in his apartment were rapidly being turned to dust.

He stepped toward us. "I should have known when you didn't return here after your mission. You don't have the nerve to do the right thing. You grew up too rich."

I listened, his gaze so fixated on me, I doubted he noticed the purple glow swelling behind me.

He continued. "You never learned what it was like to be hungry, yet somehow I fooled myself into thinking we were the same. I have news for you, Kaito…" My name sounded like an insult from the way he spat it out. "Once I kill you both, Yemoja Roux will come to me seeking revenge for Reina, showing all of Ancetol her true colors. I'll finish her once and for all, and the city will regard me as a hero." The dust snaked under us and I felt the floor give way, but I held us level.

"If she falls, the Fae Agency falls, and now that your precious academy is no longer protected, I'll have my pick of the lot for my new recruits."

I began a slow clap. "Excellent monologue, DT," I said, "Excellent. You had the whole plan in there. The 'threatening to kill me' bit without actually… killing me. I mean, a bit cliche, obviously, but spoken with conviction at least." Confusion swept over every one of his features. So I decided to help him out. "Are we going to fight, or…"

His eyes darkened, and faster than I anticipated, he lunged for me. I yanked the two of us down through the gaping hole in the floor, the air between a dusty gray mess. I flew through the room touching whatever objects I could that hadn't been affected by his gift. It was an office space with nothing but computers, chairs, and phones. Nothing that would really hurt DT. But there was no time to look for more.

DT jumped down to our level and instantly the purple waves shot out from Reina, one after the other, in his direction. They were sharp, each one as lethal as my daggers, flying toward her target. "It's obvious you're afraid, DT!" Reina shouted. Her waves bounced off his porcelain white skin without so much as a scratch, but she bought me a few seconds to pull more objects into range. The lights flickered and all went dark.

I couldn't see DT. I couldn't see anything except Reina, glowing brightly, making herself the perfect target. I began to throw objects at where I'd last seen DT, but the way they crashed uselessly on the floor said I missed. My breath stopped. Either they had no effect or DT was somewhere else in the darkness. We were one touch away from death, and I needed to make sure that when he attacked, it was me he came after. I willed my emotions, fear, pain, and love into my gift and thought of that specific tropical sky shade of blue. I glowed, and so did every object I'd touched. It was enough light to see DT charging for Reina.

I pulled her toward me, the blue of my gift straining away from Reina's purple. She crashed hard into my chest, my arms around her so tight that it knocked the wind out of me. "I know your truth!" she shouted. DT froze, the anger slightly easing from his features.

She continued. "You're afraid you'll never find anyone else who understands you. You were born a monster, and you're afraid you'll die a monster. But, most of all, you're afraid you'll die alone."

I shook as I watched him, knowing that I'd felt all of those things, too, before I had gotten close to Reina. If she hadn't believed in me, could I have been standing beside DT?

"You don't even *want* to do this."

DT lifted his hand to prepare his final attack. "See, now, that's where you're wrong. Because, yes, I definitely do."

With our backs against the wall, and nowhere else to go, I felt the tension in Reina's body ease. It was the same sense of resignation that washed over me. "Kai," she whispered as DT walked towards us. "I'm sorry I couldn't save you."

I held her body to mine, unwilling to let her go, not even for death. "Don't give up, love. Let's buy another minute."

My left arm pulled back, to send everything I had left toward DT, while I held tight to Reina with my right. I felt her right hand cock back, the purple glow so bright that even DT's bloodthirsty eyes squinted as he reached for us. Our heartbeats fell into sync as we released our power.

The blue and purple gifts locked together, releasing a bright white light that tore through the room, shooting straight through DT.

The light dimmed but never quite went out. An eerie glow, with no obvious origin point, settled around us.

DT stood in front of us, hand outstretched but his gaze firmly on the floor. His chin lifted, and he set a molten glare on me. No matter how much I wanted to hide my fear from Reina, my body shook as the truth of what transpired became clear. He was completely unharmed by our attack, and we were out of time.

A cruel smile stretched across his face, and he reached for Reina. *No.* I won't live without her. Desperate to block his touch, I threw my hand at his, but Reina gripped my wrist to stop me, just as his hand lay flat on her collarbone.

A horrifying scream ripped through the room.

Reina
FORTY-THREE

DT stumbled back, his voice cracking through his hysterical screaming. He stared at his hands, then shook them, then brought them back to his tear-filled gaze.

Kai spun me, checking me for signs of DT's deadly touch, but there were none.

He shouted, "What the fuck just happened? Did you d—"

My gift sliced through DT like warm butter. His mouth dropped open, his gaze passing over me and jumping right to Kai. His breaths were shallow and punctuated with coughed blood. He looked down at the blood on the floor, complete disbelief covering his features. "What... how...?" Watching him try to come to terms with his own defeat was a little satisfying but mostly frightening.

"I don't understand," he coughed out. "How is this even possible?"

I looked at Kai, the sadness and shock in his eyes pushed away by relief. It was all worth it just to see that. I looked down at my hands and shook my head, unable to find an answer. What *was* that white light? If I didn't already know it to be impossible, from one of my lessons at GFA, I might've thought our powers combined. Another deep, wet cough drew my attention. I looked at DT, but he wasn't looking at me. He was watching his life bleed away with such a look of despair I was almost inclined to pity him.

His gaze lifted to Kai. "Was any of it real? Were you ever really my friend? Could you have..." He choked, his gurgled voice a raspy whisper. He was fading, almost gone. I stared at Kai, unable to pin down how he felt.

Kai's jaw clamped down and I felt certain he wouldn't answer, but he surprised me. "In another world, one without gifts to twist us all up, I think maybe we could have been friends."

My breath caught. It was a mercy, granting DT's dying wish. It was a kinder gesture than I thought myself capable of. Gone was the bully, and with him the anger. In its place, there was a glowing empathy that he extended to the darkness in DT, well beyond anything I was even willing to feel.

A faint smile brushed the corners of DT's mouth as his eyes grew vacant. But my rage was still raw.

Even as DT's body sank into a pile on the floor, his life blinking out in front of me, I considered striking him again. He had destroyed my life, and my city. Though his plan wasn't complete, there was no telling how much damage he'd done to the Fae, to Ancetol, or if the Fae even had any control. Kai would spend his life in prison, if he wasn't immediately executed. As DT's body convulsed, I felt death was too easy.

Kai pulled me into his chest to block me from witnessing DT's horrific final moments. My emotions swirled inside me, the most prominent being a cocktail of guilt, fear, and relief. I was a murderer, just like I'd accused the Fae of being. DT had killed the piece of me that believed in the separation of good and evil. My body numbed as I finally let the last bit of my idyllic view of the world die.

I'd almost forgotten that Kai was there when he took my face in his hands. "Reina," he said, so harshly that I realized he must've said it more than once. "He kidnapped you. He was going to kill us both. You *saved* us. You saved *me*."

Those words echoed in my head as Kai led me down the twenty plus flights of stairs and out into the frosty air. It was so cold that it jogged me from my cloudy mind and propelled me back to the moment. "Bri wasn't in there," I said. "I checked for her gift as we came down the stairs."

Kai nodded. "Okay. We're going to find her. Well…" he said, remembering the jail that awaited him, "you will."

"What are we going to do?"

He took a deep breath, but based on his neutral expression, quick movements, and confident gait, he was more relieved than anything else. "I'm going to the Agency in the morning to tell them the whole story. Yemoja Roux is already there, but based on how I left things, I'm sure they're not letting anyone in or out tonight."

My emotions choked me, crashing over me like a riptide drawing me deeper into despair. He took out his phone and began texting. "I'm letting Yemoja Roux know we made it out of there." He slipped the phone back into his pocket.

As the first tears slipped down my face, Kai hugged me and said, "Don't cry. You were so brave. I was so proud of you."

The thought of him being ripped away from me again infuriated me. "It just feels like it was all for nothing," I said, my voice skipping as the emotions poured out.

He smiled gently then leaned in, holding my face close to his. He bit his bottom lip and my blood burned hot, the rush overpowering everything else. His mouth tickled mine as he whispered, "You saved me. That's not nothing."

I looked up into his dark eyes, sadness fighting to reclaim my heart. "Maybe only for another night."

The smallest hint of a smile touched his lips. "We better make the most of tonight, then." I pushed his shoulder and laughed half-heartedly as he put his hands up in surrender. "I was kidding. Sort of." A huge smile took over that beautiful face.

As Kai walked me back to Yemoja Roux's empty apartment, we avoided any topics related to what had just happened. I needed time to process, and I had a feeling Kai felt more about DT's death than what he showed. There was so much I wanted to say before I lost him. I could have spent the whole night talking, and still wouldn't have gotten to everything, which is why, in my head, that joke he made became more of a wish with each step toward my home.

"Stay here tonight," I said as I pulled him into the apartment. He followed, but his lack of response was a clear indication of his apprehension.

He laid his cell phone on the end table beside mine and took a seat on the couch. His posture was too stiff to hide his discomfort. "You can take off your coat," I said as I hurried out of the room. I pulled off the T-shirt DT had given me, revealing the sheer pajamas underneath. I turned to my vanity, my heart racing as I looked at myself. If we only had one night left, I wanted to remember every second of it.

A knock sounded at my door, startling me.

"Look, Reina," Kai said from the other side of the door. "You've had a very hard night. I think you should get some rest."

He had a point, I knew that, but my mind was already made up. I eased the door open and, looking at him as he leaned against the frame, his hair still tousled from our battle, made me certain that I did not want to rest. He stood up straight, a red blush splashed across his neck as his gaze traveled down my body.

His exhale shuddered, and I fought myself not to laugh at his waning willpower. *Maybe it was time I bullied Kai a little.* "You're right," I said. "We won't do anything, but will you lie with me awhile?"

He gulped. "Uh. Yeah. That should be fine."

I began to crawl slowly onto my bed, fully aware of the show I was putting on. I felt Kai's gift lift me as he pushed me back onto the bed to end it quickly. The blue glow jerked the blanket up to cover me past my chest. He was determined to be good. *How sweet.* I bit back a laugh and he smirked as he lay beside me. I rolled over to him, inching closer.

"I know what you're doing," he said.

I wiggled my body closer to his. "Oh? And what is it I'm doing?"

"It's not going to work." His gaze didn't leave my face for a second. Despite his words, I caught a glimpse of something hot and hungry behind his eyes.

I leaned in and kissed him softly, and when I slowly pulled away, his head bobbed forward to chase it. The sight sent a victorious shiver through me.

"Oh yeah?" I whispered. "It seems to me like it's working."

Kai's body went rigid. He rubbed his hands over his face.

"Don't get me wrong, I *really* fucking want to, but I'll never forgive myself if we do this before you're ready."

I didn't question the impulse as I pulled his hands away, placing them around my waist. His eyes reflected a purple glow as I whispered, "I'm ready."

Truth.

A tingling sensation rose as the next truth reached my lips. "I love you."

Those three small words cracked whatever willpower he'd been exercising. He caught my jaw and tugged my mouth to his. My heart hummed inside my chest. *Man, the guy knew how to kiss*. The thrill radiated down to my toes, and I felt my body work itself into a frenzy the way it had in the alleyway, each kiss calling forward my need to get closer. My breath caught, my heart beat in overdrive as I slid my hands under his shirt, only separating long enough to pull it over his head. I pulled him back to me for another taste, feeling the flex of his muscles as he ran his hands over my body. He flashed a smile against my lips between kisses. I wasn't surprised that he liked seeing me this way. I liked it too. I'd gotten a preview in the alley, and now I wanted everything. I liked the feeling of his jeans as I rubbed against them, but I wanted them gone.

An alarm rang out in the living room, halting us mid-kiss. Based on the volume and tone, it was a city-wide emergency alert that came through our cell phones, no doubt telling people to avoid the tower and the Agency until they had everything settled. Had it been an ordinary message, we would have ignored it but, unfortunately, it was the kind that would ring until we stopped it. I forced my body to separate from Kai's, taking a moment to fully appreciate the view. Kai let out a wordless sound of irritation, and I couldn't help but smile at the reaction. I wanted to assure him that one more minute wouldn't kill us, but the need between my thighs said otherwise. I hopped off the bed, my weakened knees far wobblier than I was prepared for. I bounded into the living room as Kai's phone zipped past me, and I followed the remaining alarm to the end table where my phone blinked red. Wracked with an overabundance of energy, I did a silent "Omg, I'm going to have sex with Kai" dance before picking up my cell.

"It's a weird alert from an unknown number," Kai said. "It says—"

But I already knew. I gaped at the message, my heartbeat stopped dead in my chest. On my phone, the message wasn't from someone *unknown*. It was from someone who was *missing*. My blood ran ice cold as I read her message aloud.

Bri:
Get out of Ancetol!

∽

Pre-order The Strong & The Stolen

BRITTNI CHENELLE

THE strong AND THE stolen

THE FALL OF GIFTED FAE ACADEMY
BOOK THREE

BRITTNI CHENELLE

the strong AND THE stolen

THE FALL OF GIFTED FAE ACADEMY
∽BOOK THREE∽

THE strong AND THE stolen

BRITTNI CHENELLE

For my sister, Kisha.
(The last hopeless romantic in the world.)

Also Available in Audio

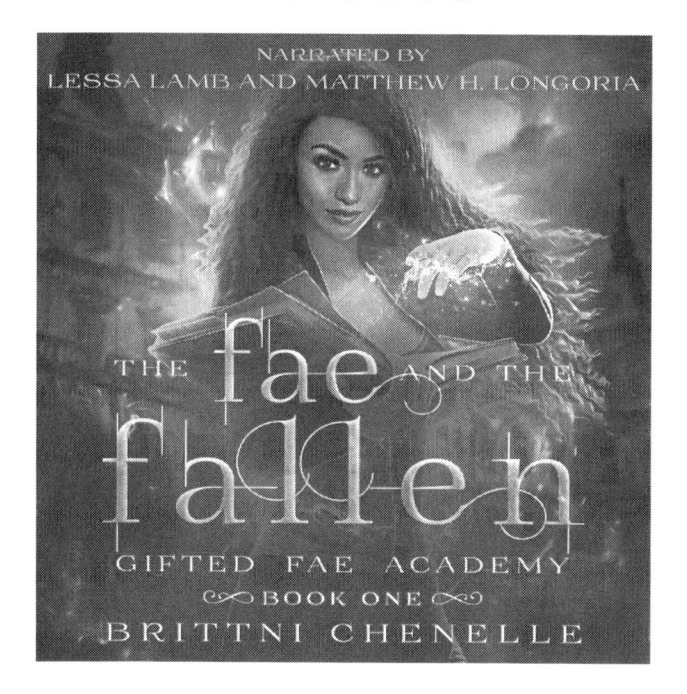

Take advantage of the discounted price.

kaito
ONE

Some nights, even two years later, I swear I could still feel the warmth of Reina's tears on my fingertips—her quivering body as I held her to my chest. "Stay strong," I'd whispered as the guard stepped forward to take me. "You have to find Bri." There was so much to say, but our time was at its end. I wanted to ask her not to forget me, but I knew what she would say and, though I desperately wanted to hear those words one last time, I wasn't sure I could bear them. Her lips trembled against mine as I stole a final kiss.

I smiled at her, grateful to know those tears were for me. Despite it all, she loved me. I wish I could say I was a man with no regrets, but I found many to dwell on even in the short walk away from Reina to the cell I'd spend the remainder of my life. But not all was lost. I liked to think that I'd managed a bit of redemption toward the end. The Fallen's leader was no more, Yemoja Roux was cleared and back in the field, and I hoped I'd done enough to ensure Reina a happy life.

Someone had to be made an example of for The Fallen's assault on the Fae and, while I hadn't taken their lives, I was far from innocent. I'd been the face of the Fae-Killing movement. I'd questioned the chairman, broken out of the Agency prison, and I'd helped Reina take DT's life despite not being licensed as Fae. I'd gone so far into the darkness, not even the great Yemoja Roux could clear my name. I'd done it all for Reina and for the safety of the other GFA students. If I had to do it all again, I wouldn't change a thing. Still, the Agency judged me much harsher than I felt I deserved. A teenager with somewhat good intentions given life in prison hardly felt just. It was a testament to how far the Agency was willing to go to keep the power in their hands. Life in the Agency prison without a trial, in exchange for Reina's love, was hardly a sacrifice. I only wish I could have been there when she needed me most.

The walls seemed to do nothing but scream my life's shortcomings in a constant loop. My parents had abandoned me, and I'd become exactly what they feared. Despite missing it with my whole being, I sometimes blamed my gift for how I ended up. If I had been a Serf, I never would have been targeted by The Fallen. I wouldn't have to spend my life alone and wonder what happened to my best friend, Zane. I never would have turned on Reina and I might've even become the kind of guy who deserved her.

The isolation was maddening. There was nothing to do but think about how I'd ruined my life. I must've cried the entire first year. I couldn't stop thinking about what I lost, or rather *who I lost.*

Even on nights when I could hold back tears, there was always another inmate to fill our cold cells with sounds of sadness. The others, from what I heard, weren't hardened criminals but a group of strongly gifted guys who the Agency didn't feel they could control. I was permitted outside with the other Elite criminals for an hour each day, but the entire prison was sealed off from gifts, with a barrier system much like the one they used at GFA. Instead of an infused barrier designed to keep unwanted gifts from breaking through, the prison barrier neutralized the abilities of the inmates inside without affecting the guards. There were certainly a lot of conspiracy theories about how the Fae set up the barrier, but as a secure facility, there was no concrete information about it online and very few of its kind. It was almost flattering that I'd been sent here as a teenager. Only the Fae Guards could manifest abilities inside and I couldn't help but glower at them every time they did. I missed tapping into my ability—the feeling of total weightlessness—and dreamed of it often.

Because of the severity of my crime, I couldn't have visitors or make phone calls, but there was no one I wanted to see. My only comfort was believing Reina's life was better without me, and I didn't want to see that contradicted. But there was one basic need that the Agency fiercely denied: news. For three years I was left to wonder what had become of Ancetol, the Gifted Fae Academy, and Reina. For three years I speculated worst and best-case scenarios.

In that third year, when Walter Gamboge—the Fae Guard I was least fond of—escorted someone down the stairs, my blood ran cold. Routine was everything in prison that breaking it after so long felt deeply unsettling, but when I recognized the figure I was certain I was minutes from death.

Fear pricked my body, my adrenaline the only force keeping me on my feet. DT strolled cooly down the hall. *Impossible. He's dead.* I was sure of it. I blinked hard as if I could break the hallucination. I saw his corpse, I watched him bleed out. Yet now he stood, only a few feet outside my cell.

Since my cell was closest to the stairs, I saw everyone who came and went. The only time I'd ever seen someone new arrive was when a new prisoner was brought in, and that was extremely rare. Judging by DT's lack of restraints and his new weatherman-like demeanor, he was no prisoner.

Breath left my lungs as the fate of everyone I loved suddenly seemed uncertain. He wore a neatly tailored suit, his snowy hair was slicked back, and his smile suggested he didn't realize or care that he was in a prison. He sucked in a deep breath like the dingy underground was a field of daisies. I looked away, wishing I could disappear into my cell, but I knew he'd undoubtedly come to take my life. His energy and cheerfulness unnerved me. I ventured another look, my mind still unable to accept this new reality when his gaze met mine. His crystal blue eyes sent a shiver down my spine, and his gaze lingered over my face just like it used to.

He turned his focus to the other inmates. "Can I have your attention?" he asked, his voice a lance of familiarity. "My name is Calvin Hall."

"What of it?" shouted one of the more aggressive inmates, Wolfe.

You fucking idiot. He'll kill you.

DT turned to Walter, his voice almost a whisper, "They know nothing about it, right?"

Walter nodded.

My ears pricked. If DT wanted to tell us something, it wasn't going to be good.

"Ancetol is experiencing a… restructuring of sorts. One of

the issues near and dear to my heart is to ensure Ancetol's criminals a fair trial."

Shit. What the hell is happening out there?

"It's a new world, gentlemen. I'm ungifted and, just this morning, I've been named the Interim Chairman of Ancetol. Of course there will be an election in a few weeks, but I'm hoping to drum up enough support to keep my position."

His mouth twisted into a smile and I dreaded whatever he had planned next. "I'd like to offer you all a deal." He paused for dramatic effect. "I'll offer you your freedom in exchange for your support in the upcoming campaign."

No fucking way. He's... going to let us out? No. I knew better. We were all going to die there.

The cheers of excitement as the other inmates processed the promise of their freedom filled my cell.

DT's gaze moved to me, his eyebrow raised as he basked in the joy of the other inmates. *This sick bastard is toying with us.*

"We'll start at the back, and then we can save the best for last." His gaze moved to me... and I swallowed hard.

The other inmates didn't seem to share my horror, but what was scary about a Serf politician? I knew DT had money, he'd also made a lot of connections during his time with The Fallen, but I was so caught up in my arrest, I didn't realize that he'd never gotten media coverage for his role. I watched him die, the snake's head cut off from the rest of The Fallen, but now that I knew he'd somehow survived, it disturbed me to know there were only a small handful of us who knew him for what he really was. And what was with the Serf act?

Dread pooled in my stomach as DT began speaking to the other inmates, letting them out one by one. I remained frozen, leaned against the back wall like a trapped rat. There was nothing I could do. Whatever he came to do to me was a done deal.

I cautiously watched the inmates walk free, listening for a commotion at the top of the stairs, but none came.

DT moved closer, one cell at a time. He spoke to each inmate, shook their hand, and let them out. I kept waiting for the monster to show his face. I kept waiting for his death touch to drain the life out of someone, but perhaps he was saving that honor for me.

My body went rigid. Yanis, my only friend from the inside, stepped up to the bars outside my cell. Yanis was twenty-one, just a year older than me. He had dark brown skin, kind eyes, and a smile that scored him extra pudding from the cafeteria ladies. He'd used the extra pudding as a way to become somewhat unanimously liked, though most of the inmates still kept to themselves. Seeing him free felt surreal.

Yanis flashed his white teeth, his gaze moving toward the staircase every second or two as if he was afraid he'd miss his chance to run. He fought the impulse just long enough to shake his head and say, "This is fucking crazy, man. He's letting us all out." He gave an impatient shrug and hustled toward the stairs.

I inched toward the bars, eying the unguarded staircase. This was obviously a trap.

I watched still as several cells down Wolfe shook DT's hand and stepped out to the free hallway beyond. Not wasting a second, he ran by me. He smirked and waved before bolting up the stairs.

I had more questions than answers as my mind raced to make sense of what was happening. *Okay, he's pretending to be a Serf... no one would elect someone with a death touch. As long as there are witnesses around, he can't touch me.* My hope drained as one by one the prison cleared. Finally he stopped outside my cell. I stepped up to the bars, knowing that resisting was futile.

Walter leaned in. "Kaito Nakamaru."

DT's face lit, as if my name brought him joy. "Oh? The leader of The Fallen?"

I snorted. *The fucking irony.*

DT turned to Walter. "If you don't mind, I'd like to handle this one on my own."

Walter nodded, handing him the key to my cell. "Yes, sir. I'll be at the top of the stairs. Shout if you need me."

DT watched Walter leave then faced me. We glared at each other as my heart beat so hard I could practically hear it. His icy stare stirred my fear—the waking nightmare paralyzing my body.

"I saw you die," I said.

He grinned. "I am death, remember? I should actually thank you for taking the fall..." He peeked around at my cell. "This place looks miserable."

I clenched my jaw.

"I learned two things from you. First, the only way to get power and hold it is to do it legally. And second..." his eyes darkened, "you can't trust anyone."

"So you're going to kill me then?"

He smirked. "Not today." He sighed, drinking me in like a long-lost friend before he caught himself and cleared his throat. "I'd just like to say that I know your mistakes don't define who you are. Everyone deserves a second chance." He grinned and slipped a hand through the bars for me to shake. "Can I count on your vote?"

I swallowed a mouthful of fear and shook it. "You can count on me to do what's best for Ancetol."

He bit his bottom lip, his eyes glittering, no doubt tickled by the vague threat. He whispered, "Oh, how I've missed this."

I tried to drop my hand, but he held it a second too long. He unlocked my cell and I considered attacking him. My gift was locked away, but I could still punch him. My body didn't move though. Instead, I waited until I could no longer hear his footsteps on the stairs, before I felt brave enough to walk out.

My mouth dried as I started up the stairs. How was he getting away with this? Letting out convicted criminals to score votes hardly seemed like the work of a sane man.

Unwilling to push my luck any further, I climbed the four flights to freedom. There was no ceremony, no battle, and no fuss. Just an open gate and my freedom returned to me on a Tuesday in mid-March.

My apprehension dissolved the instant I stepped out into the sun, even if there was another gate and a barrier between me and freedom. I'd accepted a life behind bars. I never gave any thought to what I might do if I was free. I'd failed to protect Ancetol from DT, but it seemed he was game for a rematch. I had a second chance and I wasn't going to waste it.

Reina

TWO

I was on full alert as I crept through the darkened alley, but the night was unforgivably quiet. Each time a member of my team moved, the scrape of shoes on concrete echoed up the walls like a siren. I could feel Oden on my heels, as ever, eager to be in the field, but the rest of my team had grown wary from years of dead ends and cold trails. *This time for sure.*

I came to a gray door with a thick chain and padlock. Lifting the padlock as soundlessly as possible I turned it over in my hands. I wasn't sure if my gift was strong enough to cut it, but if I tried, the noise might spook whoever the hell had Bri locked in there. Before I could look back, Oden stepped around me, taking the padlock as his broad shoulders blocked my view. His body flexed and a slight click ricocheted up the alley.

This is it. I was sure this time. We'd tracked Bri's signal to this exact location. Sensing my fear, Camilla squeezed my wrist from behind in silent support, but I wasn't afraid of a battle inside. I wanted nothing more than to unleash my fury on whoever stole my best friend—but that didn't mean I wasn't afraid. What frightened me was the thought that kept me up most nights—the possibility that I'd keep opening doors and not finding her there. My team was on its last legs. I needed this to be it.

I turned back, signaling the four others with a glance, then I stepped in front of Oden. My heartbeat drowned out my thoughts as I pushed open the door. I sharpened my free hand into a blade, and despite my best efforts it glowed a little. Adrenaline surged as I soundlessly slipped inside.

I stopped short as the rest of my team filed in and stood beside me, their battle-ready stances released as they had a look around. *This can't be real.* In an instant, my hopes were stolen from me. The entire building was gutted. I could see clear across the room even as the moonlight was obstructed by dirty windows. Exposed pipe and insulation but no Bri. My body numbed.

"Reina," Oden said.

I walked toward the center of the room. "Spread out. We need to check for a hidden door or—"

"Reina."

I wanted so badly not to take out my frustrations on him, or any of the others for that matter, but my anger was potent, ready to spill out like a shaken soda.

"She's not here."

I glared at him as my thoughts filed into a point, ready to impale him. *Don't you think I fucking know that? I don't need someone to follow me around stating the obvious.* But of the five team members along for this mission, Oden was the only one who could even make eye contact with me.

"We'll reset, look back at the data, and try again tomorrow."

I pushed past him, bumping his shoulder and forcing myself to use anger to block out my disappointment.

∽

The next morning, I tapped my fingers on the desk as the morning light spilled through the dusty window and warmed the side of my face. I gazed outside at the once perfectly manicured lawn that was now overgrown with weeds. As usual, the classroom was empty. Gifted Fae Academy was no more—just a shell and I just a hermit crab trying to make a home of it.

The school was on thin ice after our winter formal was attacked by The Fallen. The royal Warsham family had nearly succeeded in closing the school after their son Finn was wounded in the attack, but it wasn't until Bri was kidnapped from the newly fortified campus without a trace that GFA closed for good. It was two years ago and still I couldn't bring myself to move out of the decaying campus. Yemoja Roux had purchased the property with hopes of someday resurrecting it, but no one could have predicted how broken Ancetol would become almost overnight. The cobwebbed corners and padlocked rooms were a constant reminder of that.

The memories of my time at the school lingered in its neglected halls and classrooms, and I unmindfully sat in the same seat I had when I was a student, back when being admitted was everything. But losing GFA was nothing compared to losing Bri. My heart tightened and I willed his name out of my head before it slipped in. *He* was gone forever and the open-hearted girl I was along with him. Now my sole purpose was to recover the one thing I could: Bri. I didn't care about my chances of finding her, I'd never give up until I found out who took her. How could I call myself a defender of this city if I did? I saw movement outside, out of the corner of my eye, and knew I didn't have long before one of my team members found me. Normally, I'd be overjoyed to see them. All twelve had joined my investigation two years ago and, in my mind at least, they were the most admirable Fae I'd ever known. They'd risked their abilities far longer than the seasoned Fae, all to find my lost friend, but on that particular day I knew they came to give the bad news—they came to say goodbye.

They were justified. I failed. All of my leads went cold and now the city was no longer a safe place for Elites. Too many were losing their gifts, and the ungifted didn't want us here. Even the chairman had been evacuated, and I was eagerly waiting for the announcement to see who would replace him. Whoever it was would likely be ungifted, which meant the protection for Elites would no longer be adequate. Still, I couldn't bear to lose another friend. I'd said enough goodbyes for a lifetime. Above all, I wasn't ready to face the fact that I may never solve the mystery. If my team was throwing in the towel after all this time, they were probably right in doing so.

Though I'd been expecting it, I flinched when the knock sounded at the door.

"I'm here," I croaked, my throat constricting in anticipation.

Oden peeked in, his yellow-green eyes catching the golden sunlight as he walked over and pulled up a chair in front of me.

I was relieved he was alone, but the solicitous look in his eyes said that my fears had been valid.

He took my hands and rubbed them between his. We sat there without speaking. I was afraid if I let any emotion slip out, it would open the floodgates, but the tension never eased.

Anything spoken would have only twisted the knife. If I'd been told three years ago that Oden would become one of my closest friends, I wouldn't have believed it. Perhaps more so than even with Miranda, who had her own complicated history with me. Oden had been my first boyfriend back when I attended GFA, turned enemy when I defended Kai after the winter ball attack, and Kai and I had to hospitalize him to get to DT. But once he started to heal from losing Quan Levout, and understood Kai's motivation for joining The Fallen, he'd become one of my closest allies. Oden knew me well, and life felt a little easier when he was around. Out of my entire team, he and Miranda were the only two who personally knew Bri.

Oden watched me closely, as if trying to read my thoughts. He could read me well enough to know when to step in or when I needed space. He seemed to come to terms with my decision not to date, though that first year the topic came up quite a bit. We'd settled on a mutual appreciation and helped each other accomplish our goals. I drank in the allure of his bronzed skin and long eyelashes for a few more seconds, then I stood and he followed. I leaned in and planted a kiss on his cheek before heading for the door. I felt him fall in step behind me, the way he had two years ago and never stopped.

When I reached the Fishbowl, GFA's former cafeteria, the rest of my team was already gathered. They were spread out across several tables, bags piled on them. Suitcases cluttered the space between the benches and the nervous energy in the room said they expected a battle.

My gaze ran across each of their faces as I waited for the right words to find me, but I halted when I got to Miranda. Her hair was pulled up in her usual ponytail and she picked at her fingernails with disinterest, but what struck me was her absence of luggage. From where she sat, she didn't appear to have any bags. If she did, they'd likely take up half the cafeteria.

Camilla must've drawn the short straw because she stood, her jet black hair glossy and straight. "The chairman evacuated."

I slipped my hands into my pockets. "Yes, I heard."

"Nobody wants to lose their gifts, and the ungifted don't even want our help anymore," she said. "Without protection, it's too much of a risk. It's time, Reina."

"Of course." I said, willing my voice not to crack. I felt Oden touch the small of my back. I turned and quietly offered him my thanks. "I completely understand. I won't ask any of you to risk your abilities any more than you already have."

Asher huffed from the table at the left, his fiery red hair falling over his eyes. "Where was this speech before I lost *my* gift?" He had freckles that suited his face and was usually the shortest one in a room and also the most charismatic.

Camilla teased, "Shut up, Ash, you were barely a Com to begin with."

The group did a poor job muffling their laughter.

I was grateful for Asher's attempt to lighten the mood. He had taken losing his ability in stride, and I wasn't sure that the rest of us would have done so with the same level of grace.

"We might not have found her, but you've given me hope. I just... I don't know how to thank you all for your efforts these past few years. I wish I had something to give."

Camilla's eyes darkened. "Come with us, Reina. Please. It's too dangerous in Ancetol... Bri knew that before any of us."

"I'm staying," I said automatically, but I couldn't ignore the longing I felt to agree. What would it be like to leave with them and start over? How would it feel to finally let go of GFA and everyone I met there? But those thoughts were fleeting and empty, drowned out by the unbreakable need to find out what happened to my friend. Even if all the other Elites abandoned the city, even if the city thought they were better off without Elites... I couldn't leave.

It might've been just a last ditch effort for the old chairman to keep the Elites in power, but my heart echoed the vow I made last year—to protect Ancetol with my dying breath—when I was finally sworn in as Fae.

Kaito

THREE

I waited for the sound of freedom, my heartbeat kicking up a notch as a few more inmates joined the rest of us where we gathered behind the gate in the Agency courtyard. I was stunned by the silence. It was as if each of us held our breath, waiting for our luck to turn sour. *Any second now all hell will break loose.* Most of the other thirty or so prisoners watched the gate suspiciously, but I scanned the crowd for DT. My eyes were drawn instead to Wolfe as he paced in front of the gate like a predator stalking his next kill. Though I wouldn't consider us closer than acquaintances, I liked that Wolfe was easy to read. He had spent a ridiculous amount of his imprisonment doing pushups but never outwardly seemed to put on any muscle. He was a beanpole of a guy with a permanent greedy glower in his eye. I lamented never asking what he'd done to be imprisoned because he looked like he'd be the first to rush through the gate when it opened, and I'd miss my chance.

The buzzer sounded and the steel gate released—the magical barrier tearing open in its wake. A sudden rush pulsed through my blood as my gift flowed back to me. The intense wave of magical energy was so powerful I had to clamp my jaw shut to avoid yelling. When it passed, the silence around me and the absence of reaction from the other prisoners threw me. I cleared my throat, the extra second buying me enough time for the rush to die down. Did no one else feel their gift rush back?

I scanned the courtyard and, to my surprise, there were no other guards around. What kind of game was DT running? The place was deserted.

I followed the other prisoners in a daze, as if in a lucid dream. When I reached the outside of the Agency gates, I was surprised to find at least half of the inmates still standing there, looking as aimless as I felt. Before I could do a search for Yanis, he came up beside me. "What now?" he asked, fear evident in the rough timber of his voice.

It was a valid question—one I couldn't answer. "Let's go," I mumbled, and I only paused for a second as I stood on the property line between the prison and the sidewalk. I realized none of us knew what we were about to walk into. All we had were two deeply unsettling pieces of the puzzle. Something had gone horribly wrong in Ancetol and a madman was vying for the chairman position.

As we scattered, the inmates with families or loved ones vanished quickly into the streets. The rest of us lingered a little to come up with a strategy. "I… uh… need a minute," I said over my shoulder, unwilling to stop putting distance between me and DT. What could I even do here? I was as lost and alone as they were, not to mention a rush of thoughts clouded my reasoning. Things that, a few minutes ago, didn't matter. Things like where my friends were or even how three Serfs were going to survive in Ancetol.

Yanis followed quietly, leaving me to my thoughts. The only place I could think of going to was my childhood home. There was a good chance they'd sold it off—even when I'd lived there they hardly ever visited—but even *that* was more than a lot of these guys had, based on the way they loitered.

Wolfe hurried sheepishly over, his gaze darting between me and Yanis. "Can I tag along with you guys?" he asked. Wolfe choosing me and Yanis to tag along with was only slightly less random than a dice roll. We were a little closer to his age, or perhaps he was a little more familiar with us than with the rest of the guys. The most likely reason was that we just happened to be standing closest to him when he started to panic. He didn't wait for my answer but instead asked, "How much further do we have to go for our gifts to be reactivated?"

I felt a lump rise in my throat. *So I was right.* His gift was gone.

"I don't know, man," I said. I turned to address them both. "But I might know a place where we can lay low." Yanis and Wolfe exchanged glances, but despite whatever apprehensions they might've had, they followed just the same.

My thoughts raced, still muddled with the fact that the world's most dangerous criminal had Ancetol in the palm of his hand. The more I filled in the gaps of what I'd missed, the more appealing evacuation seemed.

I doubted many people knew the truth about DT, but at least his face was finally on a public forum which meant his little disappearing act wouldn't work again. One thing I'd learned years ago was that the moment evil had a face, it could be stopped.

Reina

FOUR

The cafeteria was so quiet you could hear a pin drop. I scanned the faces of my former teammates and could see them processing my decision with their tortured expressions as they started to preemptively mourn me. I understood their concern, but I wasn't ready to give up on Ancetol just yet. I felt the words lock in my throat, and my conviction held strong as they stared at me.

Oden cleared his throat. "I'm staying too, Reina. I started this with you and I want to finish it."

I exhaled. I couldn't say I was surprised. Oden had been by my side every step of the way. We'd had our problems, but he never gave up. Still, he'd risked enough. "Look, I appreciate you being here to help me find Bri, but I really can't ask you to risk your ability for me. You should go."

"Luckily you didn't ask me to, I volunteered. You weren't the only one who took that oath."

Oden was Fae through and through. We'd been sworn in

together and were the last to become Fae before the system collapsed. Before I could protest any further, Miranda interjected, "I'm staying too."

Miranda's decision hit me like a truck. Where I could have predicted Oden's decision, Miranda was always a wildcard. She raised an eyebrow, as if my bewildered expression had been the exact reaction she'd hoped for. "Someone has to keep this operation on track."

Then Asher spoke, "I'm not saying I'm a hero or anything, but I'm also going to stay."

Oden smirked. "Bruh."

Warmth filled my chest. They'd stuck by me all this time and, even without the protection of the Agency and most of the Fae already evacuated, they stood by this mission. There was no way I'd ever be able to pay them back for this, and a new burden lowered onto my shoulders. The worst of it was knowing that Asher and Oden had given up on both Bri and Ancetol long ago and were staying solely based on our friendship. I was responsible for them. Asher had already sacrificed his ability for this cause, but Oden had way too much to lose. If he lost his ability, it would be entirely my fault. Miranda was different. Since she had the original vision of Bri's abduction, she'd been single-mindedly searching for her. As much as I didn't want to admit it, I needed her. She was the only other person who hadn't given up on Bri and, without her, I wasn't sure I would have hung onto hope this long. Still, I'd expected her to leave with the others when the time came, or I hoped she would for her sake.

I'd meant my goodbye to be brief, but I needed each of the teammates I'd grown to love to understand that I held no ill will against them and that I'd appreciated every second I spent with them. There was so much to say, so I took the time to pull each person aside to explain what their partnership had meant. I was relieved they would no longer be in danger and felt comforted to know they'd be safe together.

By the time they actually collected their belongings and made their way off the GFA campus, the shadows grew larger around me on the cafeteria floor, the day's intense light fading from the windows. I was so emotionally drained that I could barely stay on my feet. The four of us sat in silence, the emptiness of the room deafening. None of us dared to speak. We'd all agreed to go down with Ancetol's ship. Normally, we would have been going through the day's reports. Logging who had lost their gifts that day and marking their location to see if we could find a pattern, but goodbyes were all I could emotionally manage that day. Even Asher, who normally had a joke for every occasion, couldn't manage to lift the blanket of despair that covered us, so after a long while, I pulled myself up and left the cafeteria.

Later that night, the moonlight poured through the old GFA battle dome, refracting into bright colors as it filtered through the magical barrier. It had become my favorite spot on campus, but the barrier had dimmed without the school's teachers reinforcing it, and I thought I could almost see the stars through it on clear nights like this. I sliced a sharpened katana made from my gift into the practice dummy on the far side of the arena, heaving for breath as I lunged for another attack. I pushed through fatigue as sweat trickled down the back of my neck. Training until my body gave out was the only way to trick myself into sleeping and, even then, I wasn't guaranteed a good night's sleep.

It always started the same. The boy with the crystal blue

eyes and frosty white hair laying on the ground, his crimson blood on my hands. I knew it was part of the memory I'd struggled to suppress in my waking hours, but the dream wasn't exactly the same as how it had happened. For one, in the dream, I was alone. I fought only for my own safety and something about that unsettled me. Secondly, the boy with the death touch did not attack or defend himself. Instead, he looked regretful and scared. I knew that these differences mattered and that, in the moment, I'd done my best to protect the guy I loved, but based on the frequency of the image, I never really got over it.

I was hung up on one moment in particular. There was a split second where DT paused his assault. I'd taken it as a moment to attack, but that second often lingered in my thoughts. Perhaps there was another way to defeat him. Even all these years later I hadn't made my peace with it and I worried that I never would. I knew the world was safer without him, but the state of Ancetol still seemed to diminish after he died, and I couldn't help but feel it was my fault somehow.

The arena was far more open than the battle dome I'd used as an underclassman. When Bri first went missing, Ancetol rallied all their efforts to find her, but it was in vain. After a few short weeks without results, the world gave up on her. The Warshams had enough concern and ammunition to finally shut down the school. I don't think Finn wanted to leave or say goodbye to Oden or the rest of the school's remaining Nobles, but he was the first to depart. After that, we all kind of went our separate ways.

I thought that was the end of my dreams to become Fae and to protect Ancetol. For many students, that was the last of their professional training. Too many of the top schools closed thinking that they'd likely be targeted next. But I was one of the lucky ones. I had Yemoja Roux, or Mo as I now called her.

I felt a presence behind me and whirled around, snuffing my gift out instantly to be sure I didn't hurt someone.

Oden strode in. I lowered my hands, grateful for a reason to take a short break. "How's the training going?" he asked.

Through heaving breaths, I said, "Well, you know... it's training."

"I know you had a tough day, but I want you to know that Miranda, Ash, and I are here because we want to be. It was our choice to make." He broke eye contact and shifted his weight.

My throat threatened to fill with tears. "I—"

"And just because we have a smaller team doesn't mean we're not going to find her. Don't give up."

I took a step towards him, wanting to hug him, but I stopped short when I realized how sweaty I was.

Reading me, he smirked. "Bring it in, Rei." He walked over and started to pull me toward him.

"I'm sweaty," I muttered, but he pulled me tightly into his chest.

"Like I care."

kaito

FIVE

"I swear to god, Yanis," Wolfe barked, "if you touch me one more time I'll wrap a vine around your throat."

Yanis grinned and threw his hands up in surrender. "Sorry, man, I'm just nervous because my gift still hasn't returned... I mean, we have to be far enough away from the prison by now, right? I mean... *can* you still use your gift? Or were you going to steal a tomato plant from someone's kitchen garden?"

Wolfe responded with no more than a disinterested grumble.

I'd prepared myself to see a changed Ancetol on our walk home, but it wasn't at all how I pictured a city run by DT. I didn't see empty streets and scattered citizens. I saw the opposite. The seemingly ungifted walked around in droves without gloves. They held hands, unafraid of touch. Was this part of the restructuring DT mentioned? I used to enjoy sorting the Serfs from the Elite with a glance. I prided myself on my accuracy, only now I didn't see a single one. Where were they? I supposed that without them, the Serfs were free to live a more peaceful existence. But to see people actually holding hands was surreal. At least on the surface, things seemed better. I'd always been interested in life before gifts and to have a peek at it was like stepping through time. The sight of it was practically a fucking DT campaign poster and I was beginning to understand how he'd snaked his way into power.

We rounded the corner to the block where my childhood home was situated, but I felt no comfort from the sight of it—just the sting of buried memories as they sprouted.

I told myself that I didn't care how things went down with my parents. Were they bad parents for giving up on me or had I just been an unbearably disappointing son? Returning only served to stir feelings I'd long thought settled. I realized I had stories I was unwilling to share with my new crew, but when we reached the door I froze, giving myself away.

"We in the wrong place or something?" Yanis asked. Wolfe silenced him with a jab of his elbow.

I swallowed and stared at the front door, remembering all the times I returned home after school, hoping my parents would be there, only to find an empty townhouse and a loaded debit card. I knew they wouldn't be inside, but even after everything the hope that they would be lingered. Remembering myself, I hustled to enter the code, hoping it hadn't changed.

The door swung open and I stepped into the empty foyer. I slid off my shoes and noticed Wolfe and Yanis follow my lead. I flipped a switch and was surprised to see the space fill with light. I started exploring the rooms and was astounded to find them all in excellent condition. It was like no time had passed. I wondered if the electricity and continued use of the cleaning staff meant that my parents still spent time there or if they'd forgotten to cancel those things in their haste to disappear.

"You didn't tell us you were rich, man. Nice place."

I smirked. "Uh... make yourselves at home," I said, suddenly aware that I'd let two convicted strangers into my home. I'd hardly gotten the words out before Yanis threw himself onto the couch and put his feet up on a dusty ottoman. I turned to Wolfe to see what he'd do first. His whole demeanor shifted, the harshness of his expression slipping into excitement. It was as if he thought our release was a dream and he'd only just realized it was real. His eyes widened. "Can I take a hot shower?"

"Yeah, man, let me show you the way."

I pulled out some fresh towels and sent him into one of the guest bathrooms to get situated but nearly sprinted back to the living room when I heard the TV echoing around the vaulted ceilings. There was no need to think about what I wanted to do first with my freedom; Yanis beat me to it.

I took a seat beside him on the couch and watched a somber reporter address the public. "Last year's mass evacuation of Elites and Commons has led to a staggering drop in our city's crime rate."

"What's the deal with this evacuation, man?" I asked, hoping he'd gotten a little more information when I was sorting Wolfe out.

He shook his head. I popped up and headed for my bedroom. I snatched my laptop from the desk along with the charger and returned to the living room. This time I took a seat on the armchair to keep my search out of Yanis' view. I flipped open my laptop, my pulse rising as I anticipated my first search. The password bar popped up and I smiled as I typed in R-E-I-N-A.

"Let me know if you find something," Yanis said. "They're not really saying what happened."

But I could hardly hear him as this time I typed Reina's full name into a search engine. My screen flooded with images of her. It felt like the first snow of the year, or pulling my favorite book off the shelf for a reread. My heart warmed as I scanned her face. Two years and she still knocked the wind out of me. She looked just as I remembered only more refined, grown into her features and bloomed into the woman she'd wanted to be. It took everything in me not to burst into tears when I read the headline. *Reina Roux, Ancetol Division: Gold Tier Fae.* She did it.

I looked up to see Yanis' crinkled brow, wide eyes, and clenched jaw. "What is it?"

Shit. I was supposed to be looking up the evacuation. Unwilling to close my search on Reina, I opened a new tab, this time searching for news. "Apparently there was some kind of epidemic." My gaze darted across the screen. "Some Elites started losing their gifts… permanently."

I gulped. Those gifts were the pillars of our society. It didn't surprise me that an opportunist like DT used whatever this was to gain power. I feared there would be no comfort to offer Yanis or Wolfe. Once a gift was gone, it was gone for good. I needed more information.

The forums were loaded with theories, and they all seemed to agree that gifted citizens who lived in Ancetol were losing their abilities and they weren't returning. The rest was an array of theories that got more bizarre as I read.

The most popular was the one the media adopted, that this was some kind of virus. The only evidence they seemed to have of this was that it was spreading in high density areas, but after I'd been passed over, I had a hard time believing it.

I wasn't alone either. There were thousands of theories—everything from God purging the earth of abnormalities to chemical warfare and my personal favorite: alien parasites using Elites as hosts.

I had no more answers than when I started, but I did find it interesting that there was a large group of people who saw the epidemic as a good thing. I thought about the carefree families that I saw on my way here and how different their lives must've been without fear of touch.

The city was proud that their interim chairman was ungifted, as were most of the candidates in the election. The fact that all of this epidemic stuff seemed to be benefitting DT more than anyone was impossible to overlook. If this was his doing, it was even more elaborate than The Fallen scheme, and the effects were more widespread. *How could he possibly pull something like this off?*

As much as I could see the appeal in the changes for some citizens, Ancetol without Fae would be easily targeted and controlled. Plus, I didn't like the idea of losing my gift, especially as it had only recently been returned to me. I trembled to think of how lucky I was not to have lost it already.

Guilt tore through me as I realized I was the last of us to possess a gift, a fact I would hide until I found a way to break it to them.

I searched Calvin Hall next. The news he'd been nominated as interim chairman until the elections concluded had only been up for a few hours. I searched his opposition. The only one who seemed to have much support was a woman named Rachel. I searched conspiracies on DT but came up short. No one had made the connection. I pulled up a picture and glared at it. Something about his eyes freaked me out. There was once a time that we were almost friendly. We bonded over things that most people couldn't understand; now those similarities haunted me. It was true that we were both capable of cruelty, but I hated that he considered us the same.

After an exhaustive search, I was convinced that I'd been right to doubt the epidemic was natural. I couldn't prove it yet, but the epidemic was not something that happened to Ancetol. It was someone.

Reina

SIX

I walked across the campus to Pink House, a hard breeze whipping my hair that was still wet from my recent shower. It chilled me but felt good after a hard workout. No matter how many times I saw Pink House with light pouring out of only Miranda's room, I could never quite get used to the unsettling look of it. I understood Miranda's need to hold onto routine. She could have chosen anywhere on campus to make a home. Asher had chosen a classroom to convert to an apartment, and Oden one of the conference rooms in the front building. But Miranda stayed in her tiny dorm room as if she wasn't ready to let go of her time as a student.

I could hear the music playing through the door and heard her scramble to shut it off before swinging open the door.

"I've been expecting you," she said as she spun and led me into the room.

"You have?"

She sat on her bed and I took a seat at her desk. "You're here to pick my brain about me staying. I assure you, I'm a big girl and I can make my own decisions."

"Look, Miranda, I just want to make sure that you're doing what's best for you and not just staying because you think you're responsible for what happened to her."

She rolled her eyes and swept her blush-pink ponytail off her shoulder. "I know you're scared. The council is gone, but there are still people here fighting. Your mom is still here fighting."

I nodded. "They need us more than ever, you know? They're vulnerable."

She eyed me, her ocean blue eyes glinting in the warm light. "I think maybe you need them too. What is a Fae without people to protect?"

My gaze dropped to my hands. She wasn't wrong. I'd fought so hard to become Fae, to try and fix the system, and just after I was sworn in that system collapsed. Did that mean my job was done?

Miranda picked up a magazine from the corner of her desk, leaned back into a pile of pillows, and flipped through. "How are you holding up, you know, with everyone leaving and stuff?"

"I... uh..." I swallowed hard. "I'm glad that they'll be out of harm's way. I appreciate all they've done to help us."

I looked up to see Miranda's lips pursed and one eyebrow raised. "The cameras aren't rolling. You can say how you feel."

I swallowed a lump in my throat. "I'm sad."

"Mmmmm." Miranda's expression was notably displeased, so I continued.

"I'm frustrated." I stood and started to pace. "All of our leads on Bri were dead ends and honestly? I'm stunned by how quickly everyone just... gave up. And I'm not just talking about the team..."

"Uh huh."

"I mean, I know nobody wants to lose their gifts. I get that. I know that statistically our odds of finding Bri are pretty fucking bleak, but how can the council just up and abandon the city? How can the Fae actually leave the people unprotected? Where are the heroes I looked up to all my life? Why isn't anyone still fighting?"

"I heard they made some Serf the interim councilman." She sighed. "Like that's going to do anyone any good."

I hadn't heard, but I'd expected them to choose someone ungifted. Everyone was so ready to live in a city without gifts. Everyone but me.

"Is there anything else?" Miranda pushed.

My thoughts tangled with all the ways the situation was fucked. The council had evacuated last year and the chairman was the last real hold out. Without him, the Elite were screwed. An ungifted chairman would have absolute power; he could outlaw gifts if he wanted. Based on the way the city turned on the Fae, it wasn't out of the realm of possibility. I struggled to remember why I still fought for them, but the reason rang through my thoughts like a bell cutting through the rest of the noise. "No, it's not. My parents died protecting Ancetol. Kai—"

Miranda's back straightened and she set her magazine aside.

I shook my head. "Never mind."

"No, Reina. Let it out. It's time."

I felt my throat constrict. "I don't know what to say about it.

It's all fucking unfair... Wait." A prickle ran across my skin. "Holy shit."

Miranda leaned forward. "What? What is it?"

"If the chairman is gone, what did they do with Kai?" Most of the Fae-related programs were shutting down. *They weren't heartless enough to execute all the prisoners... right?*

She stood. "Oh, my god. Should we—"

But I was already headed for the door, my mind racing, my veins loaded with adrenaline and fear. What if I was setting myself up for another heartbreak? But that fear drowned in the promise of what could be.

"Wait, Reina! You don't want to put on a little makeup or try to wrangle your fro a little?"

I could barely hear her over my thoughts. "What?"

"I mean... you might see Kai."

I grinned. "You coming, crazy?"

"I wouldn't fucking miss this for the world."

As we hurried out into the night, I felt Miranda's fingers brush across my wrist. Out of the corner of my eye, I saw her excitement dim, but she didn't stop me, nor did she share the vision that she stole from our future. Ever since Bri's case went cold, she'd been more reluctant to share her visions and preferred instead to let things play out.

But the sudden change in her temperament, even with her best efforts to hide it, had told me everything I needed to know. I would not see Kaito tonight. It was more likely that I would never see him again—a fact I'd fought to come to terms with. I was grateful for the clouds that blocked the moonlight and the fog that dimmed Ancetol's neon lights. The darkness hid the silent tears that fell as I realized I'd made a horrible mistake. For a few minutes, I'd allowed a parasite back into my body, one that had nearly destroyed me years ago. A parasite called hope.

kaito
SEVEN

"You're fucking kidding me," Wolfe said, shuffling into the living room with a towel wrapped around his waist. His wet hair dripped onto his face, making his menacing gaze look unhinged. "So that's it? We were infected and now we're all just fucking Serfs?"

Yanis glared down at me as I shuffled through articles on my laptop. "I mean... I think our gifts should have returned after we left the prison." I shook my head. "They might be gone."

Wolfe stormed over. "Do you think those council fucks did this on purpose?"

My thoughts moved to Walter. "No, I mean... they evacuated too. They must've been afraid it would happen to them. I guess that's why everyone's evacuating."

The crash of shattering glass made me and Yanis jump. Wolfe turned back to the shelf, pulling a second vase from it. He slammed it down, scattering its shards across the hardwood floors.

"Calm down!" Yanis shouted. It was a sentiment I echoed but I didn't have the right to speak it, not while I still possessed my gift.

I took a deep breath. "This sucks, but at least we don't have to worry about the epidemic."

Wolfe gaped at me. "What the fuck do you mean by that? We're fucking broken!"

"I mean, we won't have to evacuate. Without a gift, the epidemic can't really hurt us."

His voice broke. "What are we going to do now?"

My words caught in my throat, but Yanis filled the silence, giving his best attempt to lighten the mood. "We can do a hell of a lot more than we could in prison. I'm not happy about this either Wolfe, but... I mean... we got girls out here."

Wolfe's shoulders sagged a little and relief washed through the room. Yanis exhaled loudly, eyeing the shattered glass. "Where can I get a broom?"

I gestured to the closet tucked away in the corner and he hurried over to sort out Wolfe's mess. Wolfe took a couple deep breaths, each relieving the bright color from his face, until he said, "Speaking of girls, these total babes came to the door a few minutes ago. I invited them in but they were bitches or whatever. It's like they were mad I was naked... like... whatever, you came here to my house at booty call hour."

"Your house?" Yanis said with a smirk.

I smiled, bringing my attention back to my laptop.

"Bruh," Yanis said as he swept, "what are you even talking about? Is this a real story or something that happened in your head?"

I chuckled, firmly on the side of it all happening in his head.

If someone knocked I probably would have heard it, even with the TV blaring.

"I'm serious. They were the hottest girls I've ever seen."

Yanis grimaced. "Are you going to help me clean this?"

Wolfe shrugged.

"How long were you in?" Yanis asked.

Wolfe's gaze dropped to the floor. "Eight long years."

I tried to focus on my search but Yanis said, "I'm sure any girl would seem hot to you at this point."

"No man, really. One had these, like, curves in the right places. Her hair was all wild and shit, you know like she likes to get down. My type, you know? And the other was a pinkish blonde, with legs for days."

I looked up from my laptop. "Was there really someone here?"

Wolfe turned to me as if he'd forgotten I was in the room. "Yeah, they knocked when I was walking by."

"What did they want?" I asked.

"Nothing. I was showing them my abs and shit, told them I'd drop the towel if they wanted. Then I invited them in. They looked confused and left."

I leapt up, my laptop toppling to the floor. "That's because you don't fucking live here." I snatched my laptop from the floor and turned it to show him the screen where I'd been searching Reina.

"Was this her?"

He nodded sheepishly.

"Fuck!" I tossed my laptop onto the couch and sprinted towards the front door. "How long ago was that?"

"I don't know... ten or twenty minutes maybe."

I bolted out the door, calling back, "Which way did they go?"

"Uh… I don't know."

I tore down the street, desperation choking every labored breath. *Where are you?* I pleaded to the universe, called in every favor, every karma point I could have possibly stored in my lifetime, but apparently it didn't amount to much, because three hours later my shaking legs brought me back to my house empty-handed.

Yanis sat on the couch watching the news while Wolfe scrolled through my laptop.

I slumped onto the couch beside them.

"She's gone."

"Bro, you owe us a story on this one."

I nodded, my body heavy from both my search and the disappointment that accompanied it.

Wolfe said, "So, obviously that was your girl before you went in."

I bobbed my head in agreement.

Yanis grinned. "I see you. Dating celebrities and shit."

"Not to be a dick…" Wolfe said, "but you're a Serf now and a felon. She's a Gold Tier Fae."

I leaned forward and sunk my face into my hands.

"Plus there's this guy," Wolfe said, pointing at the screen.

I didn't need to look to know what picture he was referring to. I'd seen it in my search, and it seared into me. It was one taken on the day Reina was sworn in. She stood in the courtyard of the Agency building smiling brightly, Oden Gates beside her.

Reina

EIGHT

My limbs were heavy as I plopped into my bed for the night. It seemed like in one short day, everything I'd built over the last three years had fallen apart. My team was disbanded. The council, chairman, and Fae had officially evacuated, leaving Ancetol unprotected and in the hands of some Serf. The worst, though, was that, for the first time in years, I'd allowed myself to backslide into sadness over Kai. I didn't know what I was expecting to find when Miranda and I arrived at the Agency. It was eerily vacant, the prison abandoned and any trace of Kai or anyone else wiped away. As if that wasn't enough to kill my hope, I'd insisted on checking his childhood home. Who even was the naked guy who answered the door? Somehow knowing Kai was gone was worse. I was not ready or willing to take on another case. It had been a while since I'd felt so defeated, and when it all seemed too much, I knew it was time to visit Mo.

Things between me and my former hero turned adopted

mother, Yemoja Roux, had been a little tense as of late. She had to take herself off of Bri's case to focus on the rest of the city as it self-destructed. She would have preferred if I spent less time on Bri and more on helping her slow the city's collapse, but regardless of our differing views, we were family.

My eyelids drooped, my thoughts mixing with my subconscious as I slipped in and out of sleep. My attention orbited Kai, and I tried in vain to draw him into my dreams for a visit. But, after years of trying to move on, I could hardly picture his face. Bri's face, however, was clear in my mind. I often dreamed about her off-beat personality and the memories we shared during our time at GFA. I missed the feeling of those days. I missed the possibilities and the hopes I had for my future, which all seemed to be replaced with fear. The vibrant moments that used to make up my life dwindled down to nothing more than tiny wisps of light, like stars that flickered through the wide expanse of darkness.

More often than anything else, I dreamed of Miranda's vision. I made her describe it so often and with so much detail, I sometimes forgot that I wasn't in the room when Bri was taken. She'd even shown me it once or twice. Those red eyes haunted me the moment I drifted off.

My thoughts cycled through the only words that could ease me: *tomorrow will be better*. I knew it.

I awoke feeling refreshed. Even if I couldn't remember, it was as if my dreams had brought me back a piece of myself. The day teemed with potential, and if things hadn't been going well, I was due for a win. Bri was waiting for me to find her and I'd never give up until I did.

I slipped on my boots and had a look in the mirror before I bolted out the door toward the Fishbowl. I felt strong, like the universe was pushing towards something. The morning splashed a golden glow across the campus. The air was filled with the chirps and whistles of spring, and I knew that despite everything it would be okay.

Oden waved from inside the empty cafeteria. A weight landed on my shoulders, nearly knocking me off balance, as Asher grabbed me from behind. "Mornin' boss," he said. "You ready to find the girl today?"

I shoved him back playfully. "Sure am."

He raised an eyebrow, gesturing to the vibrant pattern on his shirt. "You think she'll like this look on me?"

I shrugged. "You'll have to ask her about it when we get there."

We reached the cafeteria and joined Oden. Miranda didn't usually join us this early, so I went right for the table with my maps. It was weird to have such a smaller team, but it also meant there were fewer people at risk and that weight seemed like the greater one.

Oden straightened. "You look better," he said, his green eyes a golden yellow in the sun's rays.

"I feel better." I spread the city map across the table, the colored zones covered in notes from previous shifts.

Asher moved to the corner of the room and turned on the TV, flipping through the channels. He paused a little longer on a cartoon before Oden urged him to change it to the news.

I steeled my nerves as we watched, conditioned for bad news. The woman on screen had sandy brown hair with strands of silver running through. Her eyes were focused and serious behind her glasses while her gentle smile made her seem approachable.

"What Ancetol really needs is an experienced leader." She

addressed the cameras directly, folding her hands on the podium in front of her.

Asher snorted. "Oh boy."

Oden shushed him.

The woman continued. "Since the remaining population is ungifted, we should have someone ungifted to represent our interests. I, like most of the people left in Ancetol, was not born lucky. I've been poor, so I understand what this city needs. The epidemic has hit the reset button. This is a chance for a fresh start. A chance to level the playing field. I've been in leadership roles for many ungifted organizations and have more experience than some of my younger opponents. That's why you should vote Rachel Blaque for your new chairman."

My gaze moved to Oden. "And what do you make of her?"

He sucked in a breath through his nose. "She seems okay. I kind of like the idea of not having a gifted chairman. What do you think?"

Before I could answer, my phone buzzed in my pocket. The number was unfamiliar, but I answered it anyway, my nerves churned. What if it was Bri?

"Hello?" an unfamiliar voice said. "Is this Reina Roux?"

I tried to hide my disappointment. "Yes. May I ask who's calling?"

"This is Doctor Patel from Willow East Hospital. Yemoja Roux had an incident. We need you to come down here immediately."

kaito

NINE

I spent half the night searching online for clues to where I might find Reina, but she'd gone off grid. The media was concerned with nothing but the epidemic and the election for the new chairman. It seemed like some cruel trick of the universe that Reina was right here and I missed her. The fact that she came to my house at all had me reeling. Did it mean that after all this time she still thought of me? Had she gone to the prison first? Would she stop by again? Of course she wouldn't, not after Wolfe threatened to flash her. Why did I let him stay again?

Wolfe took every opportunity to remind me how different things were now. I wasn't sure why it was so important to him, but as I scoured the internet for clues, he never went more than a few minutes without reminding me that I was no longer a prodigy with the world at my fingertips.

He relished the chance to point out that I was now ungifted. I didn't correct him, but it was true that in the three years I'd spent away I hadn't trained my gift while people like Reina and Oden went on to become Fae. But none of that mattered if Reina came to my house looking for me. I needed to find her.

I awoke with a crash as my laptop hit the floor beside my bed. I rubbed the sleep from my eyes and retrieved it, before checking it for damage.

A knock sounded at my door. Yanis poked his head into my room. "You okay in here?"

"Yeah, sorry. My laptop..." I yawned.

He nodded. "Did you find her?"

I shook my head. "Not yet. I will."

He walked into the room, pretending to browse the bookshelf near the door. Hoping to avoid any further conversation, I opened my laptop and began my search where I left off, but Yanis didn't seem to take the hint.

"You know, I think Wolfe has been too harsh about the girl and stuff."

I sucked in air through my nose, feeling the tension of whatever was coming. "I don't need a pep talk. I just need to find her."

He picked a book off the shelf and pretended to thumb through it, and even though I was focused on my search, I could feel his gaze on my face.

"Yeah, I know, man. It's just... I don't want you to get your hopes up. She's a Gold Tier Fae and you're..." When I didn't interject, he closed the book and slid it back in its place. "I just don't want to see you get hurt."

I glared at him but softened when I realized that I had also viewed everything through that lens once upon a time. I'd made a sport out of reminding Reina of her place. I clung to the comfort of knowing exactly where my place was in society. I knew what I deserved and never strived for anything out of bounds—except Reina. Oddly enough, it was my fall from Elite status that showed me what kind of man I wanted to be and, unlike my parents, Reina thought that was the kind of man worth loving.

"Sit," I said, gesturing to the chair next to my desk with a sigh. "She wasn't like an ex-girlfriend or whatever you and Wolfe think. It was..." I rubbed my hands over my face. "Different. I know things change. This whole goddamn city has gone to shit. I have no delusions that Reina still feels the same way about me. What I do know is that she came here. She needs me. In whatever capacity, I'm going to be there for her."

He blinked at me, his face deadly serious. "We ate lunch together for two years and I never knew you were such a softie." He stood and let out a long exhale. "You aim high, man... I'll give you that."

I looked down at my hands, heat rushing to my face. "You have no idea."

He stopped when he got to the door. "Can I ask why you never mentioned her?"

"I...." I swallowed hard as a thousand reasons collided, leaving me with one. Because it hurt too much to know I'd never see her again.

But I couldn't give my answer before he said, "I get it."

"Yanis! Kai!" Wolfe called from downstairs.

Yanis shook his head. "He's an idiot."

"I'm serious, get down here."

Was Reina back? Yanis' wide smile said he might've had the same thought. I leaped out of bed and we sprinted downstairs, tripping over each other as we raced to Wolfe. My hopes dimmed as we turned the corner to find Wolfe stretched out half-naked on the couch.

"I'm serious," he said, offended by our obvious disappointment. He pointed to the screen. I walked over, fully intending to smack him on my way by, when the screen came into view. *Yemoja Roux hospitalized. No word if she's been affected by epidemic.*

I sucked in a sharp breath. "How long ago was this?"

Wolfe paused to delight in our full attention, a pleased smile plastered to his face. "You guys should take me more seriously. I called you right when I saw. Do you think she'll be there?"

"Definitely." My pulse felt deadly fast as I sprinted up the stairs for the quickest shower of my life, threw on a collared shirt, and pleaded with myself to calm down to no avail. I took the stairs back down too quickly and stumbled. My gift activated for a fraction of a second, and I got my feet under me, but clumsily enough that neither Yanis or Wolfe seemed suspicious.

Wolfe grinned. "Awe. He got pretty."

Yanis asked, "You want us to stay here?"

Wolfe scoffed. "Like hell I'm staying here. No fucking way I miss this train wreck."

"Bro," I said, "keep it up and you'll be paying rent."

It took thirty minutes to reach the hospital and my legs were jelly by the time we made it. I was shaking so badly that I leaned on my gift with each step, risking discovery. There was a large crowd gathered out front, and this time the sight was strange enough for Yanis to mention the change. Once again, the citizens were no longer wearing long sleeves and gloves. The bulk of them were obvious Yemoja Roux fans, carrying posters and flowers. But the rest seemed to be members of the press. Several reporters spoke into cameras, including the one Wolfe had us watching on the news at home. Most of the press, however, concentrated on two people, both I recognized as chairman candidates. Dread filled me when I saw DT giving an interview —a mask of sincerity slipping with every forced gesture.

It was disgusting how politicians always used tragedies to win votes. I'd barely given the election any real thought as I sorted through the articles, looking for conspiracies about DT, but now that the campaign was in my face, I was certain. Despite new circumstances, the spirit of this election would be like all the others.

With so many people outside, security was tight. Police officers in their distinctive aqua-colored jackets roped off areas for both press and fans, and it didn't look like they were letting anyone in that wasn't coming directly from an emergency vehicle.

"What's the plan?" Yanis asked.

A familiar face caught my eye. It was a girl with sandy brown hair and blue eyes standing at the front of a crowd just off-camera. She looked about nine or ten, and I didn't immediately know where I'd seen her before, but when her gaze met mine her eyes widened. She smiled and began to push through the crowd until she stood in front of me. "You're out," she said.

My brain was empty until recognition hit me like a tidal wave. She was not the cake-loving seven-year-old I remembered; she looked more like Zane. My chest was heavy with the reminder of my friend. There were so many things prison had taken away from me that I dared not dwell on, but now it was time to face them. "You're almost a real human now," I said, looking around. "Is Zane here?"

The glint in her eye darkened. "No."

Something was off. "Do you know how I can find him?"

She shook her head. "We're not in touch."

An awkward silence passed as Zane's sister appraised my friends.

Wolfe noticed. "Who's your friend?"

"Fuck no," I said, sending him a gaze full of daggers. "She's like nine."

"Ten," she corrected.

"Same difference."

"It wasn't even like that, I swear," Wolfe said, stepping back, but his guilty smirk gave him away. "You can never tell these days," he mumbled.

Yanis cringed but sympathetically patted Wolfe on the back.

I turned my attention back to her. Zane seemed like a sore spot, so I tried a roundabout way to get more information. "Who are you here with?"

She pointed a thumb back over her shoulder toward the crowd. "My mom's running for councilman."

"That's amazing," I said. "Tell her congratulations from me." From all Zane had told me of his parents, I never could have imagined them running for a position like this. I supposed they had some money from the payout they received from The Fallen, but it was hard to get used to the idea of ungifted people in power. To think she had no idea she was running against the man responsible for helping her. No wonder Zane bailed... His family was everything to him before I went away.

"Calvin's running for councilman too. Did you see?" she said, pointing to DT.

I moved my head in affirmation. We'd shielded her from a lot of what DT did, but she had to pick up on some of the connections between him and The Fallen. Either she couldn't remember the details or she was playing dumb. Either way, she was safer if she stayed in the dark.

"I have to get going."

"Wait," she said. "How can I call you?"

I shrugged. "I don't really have a phone or anything."

She dug through her purse and a crumpled receipt fell to the ground before she pulled out a marker. She grabbed my wrist and I was stunned by the brazen gesture. She'd already gotten used to this new world. I remembered her amazing gift and wondered if she'd lost it in this so-called epidemic. It didn't seem like the kind of question you could ask. She wrote her phone number on my arm and smiled before pushing back through the crowd and taking her place beside the woman who must've been her mother.

I turned to Yanis. "I'm going to do a perimeter sweep, to see if there's another way in." My real plan was to find an open window and fly in, but I wasn't ready to have a conversation about my gift and this epidemic just yet. "Both of you stay here so I can find you. If I'm not back in half an hour, I'll meet you at home."

Wolfe threw his hands up. "What? We don't get to see anything?"

"Plus utilities, Wolfe. I swear."

He rolled his eyes. "We need the code."

"Yanis has it."

Wolfe scowled."Why does he get to know it?"

Yanis interrupted, "Good luck, man."

I nodded my thanks and turned toward the hospital. I'd find Reina this time and, after I did, I wasn't losing her again.

Getting into the hospital was as easy as I'd anticipated. Just a quick float through a patient's window and an awkward scurry out of the room into the hallway, but now that I was inside I wasn't sure where to start looking for Yemoja's room. If I asked someone, I'd be mistaken for an obsessed fan and dragged out before I got anywhere near it.

I was wandering the halls trying not to look as suspicious as I felt when a hand grabbed my shoulder and spun me around.

Oden's green eyes bore into me. From his stone-like expression, I could tell I was unwelcome, but he was a familiar face. I couldn't help but grin. His shoulders were broader and he was an inch or two taller than I remembered, but his face was for the most part unchanged. "Wow," I said. "You're here." I took it as a good sign when he didn't immediately try to kill me like the last time we'd met. I was sure by now he understood why I left GFA for The Fallen.

"I need you to leave," he said coldly.

Apparently not.

"It's cool you got out and everything, but she won't want to see you."

My smile dimmed. "I don't know what you think I'm trying to do but—"

"This is about what's best for her. Do you really want to put this emotional burden on her right now? Do you know how long it took her to accept the fact that you went to prison forever?" He nodded to a door on the right. "Now you're just going to waltz in there, the same old asshole you always were," he glanced down, "and with some other girl's number on your arm no less." He scoffed. "What's your goal here, to hurt her worse than she already is? If you care about her at all, you'll leave right now."

"So..." I said with a shaky exhale, "she's in there?"

"Did you not fucking hear what I said?"

But I had already pushed passed him. I was drawn to the door, ready to accept whatever reception I found on the other side.

I heard him mutter, "You're just as selfish as always. She'll see right through you."

Good. Reina's ability to see through me was the only reason she'd given me a shot in the first place. I didn't care if Oden, Wolfe, or even Yanis believed that it would be a mistake to see Reina after all this time. I didn't need their approval. My breath caught as I reached for the doorknob. All I needed were the guts to push open the door and face her.

Reina
TEN

The cold hospital lights made a faint buzzing sound that chipped away at my nerves. *Don't be dead.* I'd lost my parents seven years ago, but the wound felt fresh as I prepared myself for the worst once again. *Please. I'm not ready to say goodbye. I still need you.* Yemoja Roux had stepped into my life as a mentor but grown into a parent when I needed her most. Part of me knew this was my fault. It was my job to make sure she was safe. She had gotten older. I knew she was slowing down and said nothing. Why hadn't I made her stop? Was it because I needed her to look after the city while I looked for Bri? Due to her status as a celebrity and Gold Tier Fae, the hospital was not releasing information quickly enough, leaving ample time for my mind to race through every worst-case scenario. Had she lost her gift in the epidemic? Was she injured in combat? All I knew was she was in danger and I could only hope it wasn't too late to make things right.

My body shook as the doctor pulled me aside just outside of

her room. "I'm fine," I whispered to Oden, squeezing his hand only so I could release it without offending him. I appreciated his support, but the way he fawned over me made me more nervous.

"Ms. Roux," Doctor Patel said, tapping his clipboard with his pen. "It's not the epidemic. Her abilities are still intact."

I exhaled the flicker of relief that passed through me before my fear shifted.

Oden asked the question that seemed lodged in the back of my throat. "What happened?"

Doctor Patel's gaze bounced between us. "She had a heart attack, but we operated and she's stable."

I felt Oden's body relax a little. He'd been so calm all morning that I almost forgot he was as invested in Yemoja's welfare as I was. His relief was obvious, but I didn't share it. A heart attack was so much worse than losing her gift—even if it was the greatest in the world. If she'd lost it to the epidemic, at least I'd be sure she'd stop fighting. She was killing herself and it was because she knew I wasn't ready to take her place.

The doctor's neutral expression waned and his gaze avoided mine. "It's no longer in her best interest to continue Fae work."

I shook my head, finding my voice. "Of course she's going to stop."

His eyes grew somber. "I'm not sure she'll agree to that. She's resting now, but she made it clear she had no intention of slowing down, nor does she have plans for retirement."

Like hell I was going to let her continue. I wasn't going to lose her. My parents had been taken from me so suddenly, I couldn't bear to lose Mo the same way. "I... I'll talk to her."

I felt Oden's hand rub across my back.

Doctor Patel scratched his thick beard. "She should be out for a few more hours."

I nodded. "Can I see her anyway?"

"Of course."

I turned to Oden, but I didn't need to tell him I needed time alone with her. He had already stepped away from the door. I appreciated his company, his support in all this, but I couldn't fall apart in front of him and I was already exhausted from putting on a brave face.

"I'll be around. Call me if you need anything," Oden said.

I offered a small smile then pushed open the door, closing it behind me.

Yemoja Roux lay still, her magenta hair spread out in a halo around her head. The monitor beside the bed beeped rhythmically, like a ticking clock. Despite her stable condition, each beep sent a nervous pulse through me, as if it threatened to be her last. My emotions overtook me when I saw the tubes and wires connected to her. She was the strongest person in the world and she looked helpless. I pulled a chair from the corner to the side of her bed but, instead of sitting, I took her cold hand in mine. I knew she couldn't hear me, but perhaps I could gather my words and have a practice run at telling her it was time for her to retire.

"It's me. I'm here," I said, the tears spilling over my cheeks. "You scared me."

She remained motionless.

"The doctor said you have to slow down. I need you to stop. You've given this city enough."

My breath hitched and I slumped into the seat beside her. "I can do this. You can leave the city to me. I promise not to let you down."

My throat tightened with guilt. If I had just listened to her. If I had helped her more and let go of my obsessive search for Bri that never got me any closer, I might've been able to take some of the burden off her. She might've even retired by now.

"I'm sorry I'm a bad daughter," I whispered, running my thumb over her soft hand.

It was hard to see her this way, so weak and broken. It was official, the time of the Great Fae had ended. Despite my promise, I didn't know if she could trust me to take it from here. I was no Yemoja Roux.

My head split with pain as I cried into my hands. It had been some time since I called out to my parents for help. I wasn't sure if it was because it hurt to reach out with no response or if things just felt beyond saving. But I needed all the help I could get. I wasn't ready to lose Yemoja. I wasn't ready to lose the only family I had left. I sniffed and I whispered, "Please. Mom, Dad, if you're out there, I need a win. Please... If there's anything you can do." I swallowed a lump as soft sobs rose to the surface. "I need a little help, just a small win... anything and I'll take it as a sign to keep going." I sniffled. "Please..."

I heard the door creek open and I wiped my face, hoping that the doctor hadn't heard me.

"Rei?"

The familiar voice sent a jolt tearing through my body. I turned to the door to see Kai. My heart raced as I stood, trying to understand how this had come to be. Was I imagining him? Had I fallen asleep in my chair? Kai's gaze swept over my face as he closed the gap between us, stopping a few feet away.

"Kai," I breathed. His hair was longer than I'd ever seen it, partially covering his charcoal-colored eyes as they read me.

His features were more defined and traces of boyhood gone. "She's okay?" he asked.

I nodded.

"Are you okay?"

I was frozen—stunned by his arrival. My heartbeat deafened me as everything I'd fought to keep at bay threatened to unleash at once.

Kai shifted nervously and put his hands into his pockets. "I uhm... I'm sorry to show up like this. I didn't know how to find you and when I heard..."

Heat rushed to my face and I wanted nothing more than to rescue him from the limb he'd climbed out on, but I was paralyzed.

His gaze bore into me, but neither of us looked away. "Do you want me to go?"

Say something. His vulnerability only made it harder to speak. *Come on, say something.* "I went to your house," I managed.

He pressed his lips together to push back a smile that broke through anyway, lifting the corners of his mouth. "Thought so. I'm sorry for my friend. He didn't know who you were."

Silence drowned out the beeping of Yemoja's heart monitor until I blurted, "She had a heart attack, but she's stable."

Kai took a deep breath. "You don't..." He shook his head. "You don't have to be strong right now."

My heartbeat skipped, recognizing its broken counterpart. "You either."

He stepped closer, his gaze intense and serious. "I don't?"

The space between us narrowed, sending a prickling sensation down the back of my neck. I mouthed the word, "No."

Kai's hands slid around my waist and I threw my arms

around him, burying my face in his neck. I could feel the intensity of his heartbeat even as my emotions spilled out. I cried so hard that I almost didn't notice his tears as they slid down to my shoulder. He moved a hand into my hair, pulling me closer for a second before his gift pushed into me. My body rose and settled into his arms, then he carried me across the room and took a seat beside the bed. From his lap, I nuzzled closer, unable to stop my tears from falling as he held me tight to his chest. I couldn't help but think that my parents had something to do with Kai's arrival, which could only mean one thing—they'd been with me all along.

kaito
ELEVEN

Reina cried herself to sleep in my arms. The warmth in my chest never eased even as an hour slipped by. I felt intoxicated by the coconut scent of her hair. I was so afraid that three years away had been enough to break whatever bond we'd formed. Even as I stood in front of her and looked into her eyes, I worried that coming had been a horrible mistake. Oden's words flashed through my head. *Was it selfish to be here?* But as her even breaths pushed against my chest and her body warmed mine, my doubts melted away. I shuddered to think of the hard times she must've been forced to endure without me.

The memory of her was all that kept me going most days, but especially today. I wished I could hold her forever. But the beeping of Yemoja Roux's heart monitor was a constant reminder that time was passing and that moment would also slip away.

The door opened and Oden poked his head in. His gaze met mine and he glared at me before rushing into the room.

"What did you do to her?" he asked, his tone hard and threatening.

Before I could shush him, Reina stirred, her eyes blinking open. She looked at me, her eyes widening like she was seeing me for the first time. Her face was swollen and her eyes were still pink from crying.

I smiled at her but Oden cleared his throat, drawing her attention.

"Oh," she said, hopping off my lap. I eased her landing, and she shot me a thankful glance before turning her attention to Oden. "Kai's here."

His expression was neutral but his fists were balled. "Yes, I see."

"I was crying and stuff and I must've fallen asleep."

His gaze shifted to me for a second but he spoke to her. "You don't need to explain. I just wish you told me you needed me. I would have come right—"

"I know," she said.

Oden moved to the foot of Yemoja's bed. "She's still not awake?"

"Not yet," I said, but Oden didn't seem eager to acknowledge me. When he did, I regretted speaking up.

"How was prison?"

I felt the back of my neck flush. Reina stepped between us. "Nice, Oden. Really? This is how you're going to handle this? Not even going to wait until my mom is out of the hospital?"

His gaze dropped to the floor. "I... I'll wait outside."

He left and Reina turned to me. "You should..."

"Yeah," I said, heading for the door.

"But." I spun. "Stay close, okay? I want to... We should..." She reached up and touched the owl charm on her necklace and my pulse stuttered as I tripped on memories.

I clenched my jaw, drinking in this new version of her. She had grown into a beautiful woman, one I didn't know well anymore. But I could still see the magnetic force that drew us together had remained unbroken. We would once again get a chance to face-off against a world determined to keep us apart. She may have had her doubts, but I was sure this time we'd win. I didn't want to leave her for a second, but she needed time and support. Her life had changed and I didn't know if she had room for me in it.

But I knew I had to try.

I could see the rise and fall of her uneven breaths as I closed the distance between us. I slid my hands to the back of her neck and unhooked the chain. I held her gaze as I put it on, bringing the owl charm to rest against my chest. I had stolen Reina's necklace once before and, in doing so, she'd uncovered how I felt about her. I had a feeling this time she already knew—I wasn't going anywhere. I paused for a moment, giving her a chance to protest, but she stayed silent. *So, you're still with me.*

I nodded my understanding, a smile teasing my lips as I turned away.

As I stepped out into the hallway, Oden shot me a victorious smirk. "She kicked you out too?"

I softened and simply waved at him. Oden had been there for Reina all this time. Regardless of our turbulent history, I owed him a lot. He was loyal to a fault and I wondered if, however unlikely, there was a future for us as friends.

Reina

TWELVE

My body was wracked with nervous energy as I paced at the foot of Yemoja's bed. Kai was back and that complicated things. My heart and head struggled over what to do about him. Mo would need help with her recovery, not to mention I needed to find her something to do that would satisfy her need to serve others without compromising her health. It was time to push my search for Bri to the sidelines and focus on helping Ancetol transition. Where did Kai fit in with all that?

I hoped he didn't think I'd be able to drop everything and pick up where we left off. I rubbed my face with my hands. Who was I kidding? My stomach was full of butterflies and even the thought of him filled me with electricity that I found both excruciating and fervid. I'd made my peace with him being gone years ago and closed myself off to romance. It was the sacrifice that most Fae had to make, to devote their lives not to a person but to the city itself. When I took that oath, I accepted a life following the footsteps of my mentor. The other Fae could flee and the council along with them, but my job wasn't finished. The city's fate rested in my hands and saving it was no longer some far-off goal—it was the culmination of my life's work. Why did I feel afraid?

I put my hand on my chest as if the gesture could steady my heartbeat. *Kai was back.* And I knew what came next—the greatest love I'd ever known, shortly followed by the greatest sorrow. If there was one thing I'd learned, it was that with him one always accompanied the other. I wasn't sure I could bear it —not again.

"That's a lot of fear, honey."

I spun to see Yemoja smiling softly. I rushed to her side and took her hand in mine, my relief surging. "Hi, Mo. How are you feeling?"

"That's a little better, but not much." A bit of color returned to her face, but the light didn't reach her eyes. I wondered if my fear was strong enough to wake her. It seemed too soon for her to be using her gift, even in a small way.

"You should be resting," I urged. "I'm fine, I promise."

"I'm sorry I worried you."

I brought her hand to my cheek. "Worried? Nah, I knew you'd pull through."

She snorted. "The only person with more fear than you right now is that boy in the hallway." Her eyebrows rose.

I turned away, hoping to hide my burning cheeks. "Yeah, uh... Kai's out."

"Oh?"

"It's... not like that."

She flashed a bright smile that almost made her look well again, then she looked up at the ceiling. "Nobody's buying that one, Reina. Not even you. Isn't that why you gave him your necklace?"

My hand rose to where the owl used to rest. "How'd you know about that?"

"You just told me."

I smirked. "That's it, I'm telling the doctor that you faked the whole heart attack thing."

"Please do. I have to get back out there."

My smile faded, but I wasn't about to lecture her after she'd just woken up. "Let's focus on getting you better."

The door squeaked and I nearly jumped out of my skin. Oden stepped in. "Do I hear voices in here?" His green eyes widened and he rushed over to Yemoja's side. "Hey, boss. You gave us quite a scare."

"No need to worry. I'll be back on my feet before you know it."

Oden looked at me, his gaze loaded with the same thoughts that passed through my head, but like me, he didn't say any of them to Yemoja. At least he'd be an ally in my attempts to slow her down.

I took a seat in the chair on the far side of the room while Yemoja and Oden chatted. Despite my best efforts, my gaze kept moving to the door, wondering if Kai would walk in.

My nerves only held me there for a half-hour, and when Kai still didn't join us, I excused myself to find him. I needed to find out what his plans were.

I scanned the crowded hallways as doctors and patients rushed about until I saw Kai across the hall. His face lit when he saw me, his posture straightening.

I was so fucked.

Kaito
THIRTEEN

I bit back a smile as I ran back to my townhouse, but I stopped to catch my breath before I went inside. The sound of the closing door brought Yanis and Wolfe to meet me. The glint of sadness in their worried expressions spoke volumes about what they thought my chances were.

I planned to push past them and milk their curiosity for every second I could, but Wolfe's gaze moved right to Reina's necklace. "No fucking way."

"What?" Yanis asked, his gaze darting between us. Catching on, Yanis' eyes bulged and, out of pure excited impulse, he leapt onto me. The bulk of his weight crashed down on my shoulders. Forgetting myself, I used my gift to slow his descent. *Shit.* Realizing my mistake, I dropped him. It had only been a split second. Did he notice? His excitement died and he stumbled back.

"Y-you still have your gift? How is that possible?"

Wolfe's neutral expression darkened. "Seriously?"

I dropped my head. "I'm sorry I didn't say anything. It just… didn't seem fair."

"That's because it isn't." Wolfe stalked out of the room and my gaze moved to Yanis.

"I'm sorry, man."

He patted me on the back. "Maybe give Wolfe a little time."

"Yeah. Alright."

His face brightened. "So what happened with Reina Roux?" I put my hands into my pockets and let out a slow exhale. "I'm not going to lie, I didn't think you had a shot."

I shrugged. "I'm not even sure I do."

"What are you talking about? She gave you her necklace. I've only been searching her online for like twenty minutes and even I know that's her thing."

We wandered into the living room. Wolfe was sitting at the piano in the corner, pretending not to listen.

"Well…" I tousled my hair, "she didn't really give it to me… I kinda took it."

Yanis laughed. "Annnnd we're back to jail."

I sunk into the couch, my brain replaying the afternoon. Yanis sat beside me as if he expected me to continue with the story, but there wasn't much to tell. When he got tired of waiting, he asked, "So, what's the next move?"

"She wants us to join her team."

"Us?"

Wolfe cut in, "He means him. We're useless now."

So he had been listening. "Actually, all of us. Apparently some of her other teammates don't have gifts anymore either. It's not as rare as it used to be."

Wolfe stood. "That's rich coming from you."

"Look, man, I shouldn't have lied. But I wasn't the one who took your gift away."

He returned to the piano, but some of the tension in his shoulders eased.

This time I spoke deliberately, punctuating every word to try to pique Wolfe's interest. "Reina said if we want we can move in with her team at Gifted Fae Academy."

From my spot on the couch, I could only see the back of Wolfe's head as he sat motionless at the piano, but I could feel his excitement from across the room.

"Are you fucking serious? The actual Gifted Fae Academy?" Yanis asked as he began to pace.

Wolfe said, "I heard on the news it's closed."

"And Yemoja Roux bought it. We can have our run of the place."

Yanis was spinning, but Wolfe's attentive posture made me think I had him if I only pushed a little more. "Haven't you ever wondered what the legendary campus looks like?"

His shoulders slouched as he let out a sigh. "Fine. Whatever." He hopped up, his face filled with repressed excitement as he headed for the stairs.

"Where are you going?" I asked.

"To pack my stuff."

"What stuff?" But he was already bounding up the staircase.

I turned to Yanis. "He's going to steal my shit, isn't he?"

"Afraid so. Actually, I'm a little thin on supplies too," he said with raised eyebrows.

"Go."

Without a moment's hesitation, he sprinted after Wolfe.

I sighed. "We're going to look like a fucking boy band."

I sat in the silence of my living room with the same excitement I'd felt the night before I first attended GFA. Only this time I wasn't thinking about my rank or my status. I no longer cared about winning the approval of my parents. Gifted Fae Academy had only one dream left for me—Reina.

Reina
FOURTEEN

I closed the door to Mo's room and stepped into the hallway. It was far less crowded at the hospital than it had been during the day. As was typical with my mentor, I'd watched her energy and strength return much quicker than the doctors thought possible. It was comforting to know she was okay, but I worried it might make retirement a harder sell.

Doctor Patel waved me over and, even though I'd just seen Yemoja resting, I prepared myself for bad news. It must've shown on my face because the first thing he said was, "She's fine." I exhaled my nerves. "I just want to ask you to make sure she stays put for the next few days."

"Of course."

"She just seems eager to get home and we don't want to rush these things."

I admired her spunk, it was one of many reasons she was my favorite Fae, but it was obvious she still needed time to recover, especially since she would most likely try and jump back into crime-fighting mode. "I'll make sure she stays."

He nodded, but I wasn't sure I convinced him.

I headed into the waiting room to meet up with Oden, but before I even turned the corner, I heard the click of high heels on the linoleum.

Miranda stood next to a magazine rack at the back of the room, flipping through them before making her selection. As usual, she looked like she had walked off a runway, a stark contrast to the doctors and nurses in scrubs, and the rest of us who all seemed to be in emotional survival mode. There were a few scattered people seated in the waiting room, but I didn't see Oden. I figured Miranda must've sent him home for a good night's rest and took his place. It was strange to think Miranda and I had been at odds when we were students when the version of her I knew now was packed with qualities I admired. Her brutal honesty for one. Her persistence and sense of justice. And, above all, her unbreakable loyalty. She didn't have to be here, especially since hospitals were a sensitive place for her.

Miranda was many things—opinionated, confident, and glamorous, not to mention, she'd become extremely powerful—but it wasn't until we found ourselves on the same side, both searching for Bri, that she shared with me her past. She'd spent her childhood in hospitals and was a cancer survivor. I'd always known she was strong, but the clues to what made her that way eluded me for my entire first year at GFA. I was lucky to finally be on the same side as someone so formidable.

"Oh, god. You look like hell," Miranda said when she noticed me.

I smiled. "Feel like it too." It had been a long day, and I felt more than a little sticky.

She took an empty seat and waved me over. "How's Mo?" she asked casually.

"Well... she's doing a little better. She seemed to—"

"Not to be a bitch, but I really don't care. Tell me what happened with Kai."

I rolled my eyes. "Ah. Yeah, he came here."

She nudged me. "And?"

"And what?"

Miranda's soft features dripped with irritation.

I played with the upholstered seat beneath me before saying, "It's bad timing. You know? Mo needs us to take over, we're not even going to have time for Bri."

She looked down at her perfectly manicured hands. I decided in that moment that was what I loved about her most. For the last three years, she was the only person who truly felt how I did about finding Bri. I felt the battle raging inside her, but she straightened and flashed an easy smile.

"We'll still find her," she said. I looked into her eyes. *Truth.* Miranda had never admitted having a vision of us finding Bri, but I'd suspected for some time that she had at one point. Each time she said we'd find her, I felt the truth in her words.

We sat in silence, my exhaustion getting the better of me.

The drowsiness almost got the best of me, when Miranda spoke again. "Can you at least tell me how he looked?"

I closed my eyes and leaned my head against the wall. "He's fucking hotter than I remember."

She laughed. "Dibs."

I lurched forward, glaring at her.

She grinned. "You know... since you'll be too busy and all."

"You're the worst."

She tossed her silky ponytail over her shoulder. "You love me... the question is, do you still love Kai?"

My chest warmed and I leaned my head back against the wall. Miranda studied me for a second before she apparently saw what she was looking for. Her voice was barely audible as she muttered, "Thought so." She sighed. "Let's get you out of here. We'll come back and check on Mo in the morning."

"But I—"

"There's no reason to be here while she's asleep."

Before I could protest, she stood and held out her hand. I sighed in resignation and took it. For a day that had started so horribly, I made my way home feeling as if my parents had been looking out for me after all. Yemoja Roux was in recovery and maybe I was too.

kaito

FIFTEEN

For the time being, my debit card was still working. I'd tested it out on ordering food for the guys before we left my house, but in the back of my mind, I worried it might alert my parents that I was out. I didn't expect them to rush home, but they might cut off my account. Still, until then, I figured it couldn't hurt to make life a little easier. On our way to GFA, we stopped at an electronics store to pick up some cell phones. It was the perfect alarm system. When the service dropped, it meant my parents were onto me. Until then, I could come and go as I pleased from my childhood home and use my card until I found another way to get by.

I felt responsible for Yanis and Wolfe. They'd chosen to follow me and I didn't want to let them down. I didn't have a plan beyond the day and hoped by some miracle we all got along with Reina's team. Yanis was sure to make friends quickly, but Wolfe took a little longer to warm up.

I never considered that it might be me who struggled to

belong until the gate to GFA opened and Miranda stood on the other side.

"Oh. Miranda..." I said, trying to morph my wince into a smile.

Surprisingly, it was Wolfe who rescued me. "Remember me? Or do you need me to take my shirt off?"

Miranda's judgmental gaze swept over us, landing on Wolfe. "Firstly, ew."

I spit out a laugh. Wolfe dropped his shirt back over his stomach and crossed his arms as Miranda shifted her attention to Yanis.

"Please tell me you're not a weirdo too."

Yanis shrugged. "Hi, I'm Yanis."

She paused and then nodded approvingly. "One for three. "

I scoffed. "What did I do?" But she ignored me. "Alrighty guys, follow me and I'll give you the tour."

Wolfe was a little dejected as we walked the empty campus, but he couldn't mask his excited glow as we explored. I was certain by the end that GFA had also been a dream for him. Yanis hardly seemed to notice the campus as he chatted with Miranda. He was an excellent conversationalist and I appreciated having him around as a buffer for awkward pauses that would have been the bulk of any conversation between me and Miranda. When our tour concluded and we headed toward the Fishbowl, where I had eaten lunch as a student before everything went to shit, it dawned on me that I might've been judging Miranda based on a version of her that was long gone. She looked like the old Miranda, but the way she made an effort to include all of us in her conversation, and to puff up Wolfe's bruised ego after she'd adequately crushed it, showed how much she had changed.

A guy with red hair waited for us in the cafeteria. I hadn't seen anyone else during our tour, so either the rest of Reina's team was out in the field, at the hospital with Oden and Reina, or that guy was the final member of Reina's team. If this was all Reina had left, and the rest of the Fae had been driven out of Ancetol, it seemed likely that DT would get his way.

Miranda took the lead. The tables weren't spread out like they had been at school. They were pushed together into large islands, each littered with maps and charts. I wasn't sure if they were tracking the epidemic or if they were still looking for Bri, but since I hadn't seen her during my tour, I figured it was the latter. I knew better than to ask, so I nearly choked when Yanis did.

"It looks like you guys have been busy. What are you looking for?"

Miranda turned to me, her stilted expression confirming my theory. Of course Reina hadn't given up. If this team hadn't found her yet, the odds weren't good. After someone went missing, the odds of finding them were next to nothing after a week. By now the trail had to be completely cold.

"I'm Asher," the red-headed guy said. "I'm a Serf now."

Miranda spun. "Way to just blurt that out. What do you expect them to say?"

Yanis jumped right in. "I'm Yanis, lost my gift too. So did my buddy Wolfe here."

The whole room turned to me. "Uh... I still have mine."

Miranda sighed. "Okay, now that we have this awkwardness out of the way... do you guys want to choose a dorm room or something?"

Wolfe ran his fingers over a map that was almost completely covered in scribbles. He shifted his attention to the rest of the cafeteria, taking in the remnants of the legendary campus. "Can I ask why Yemoja Roux bought this place?"

"I guess she hoped that the epidemic would pass and things would go back to the way they were, but..." She shrugged off the rest. "So... Blue House?"

We nodded.

She offered a Cheshire grin. "Kai, are you going to be staying with Reina because her room is—"

"What?" I asked as heat crawled up my neck to my cheeks. "No."

Asher's head snapped from me to Miranda. "Wait, what's going on?"

Miranda seemed a little too delighted by my discomfort. So much for the new her.

She tilted her head. "This is Rei's old boyfriend."

I exhaled loudly and headed for the door, but I could still hear Asher when he said, "Oh man, Oden's going to be so pissed."

Reina

SIXTEEN

There was a gift-infused entrance to the hospital that allowed me to sneak in and out while avoiding the media circus. It was just a door that the staff programmed to allow certain high profile patients and their family to have special access. I stepped out to get a few minutes of sunlight when my phone buzzed.

Miranda:
The guys are all settled in. What should I do with them?

Me:
I'm coming back for dinner tonight. Maybe we can eat as a team, you know, get to know each other. Can you throw something together?

Miranda:
Hellz yeah! Like a party?

Me:
Like a dinner.

My gaze shot up as a white-haired man stepped into my personal space. My stomach dropped as I recognized the impossible. *No fucking way.* DT? I stared into his cold predator eyes, my power flaring to life in my defense.

"You're alive," I breathed. My body shook as I looked into the eyes of a corpse, my thoughts slingshotting to the moment I saw him bleed out.

He smiled as if I'd complimented him. "No thanks to you." He ran a hand through his white hair and I flinched. "How?"

"You're not the only one with Elite colleagues."

Kai never mentioned DT having a team member with that ability, but maybe he had more cards to play than he'd shown.

I could tell by the way his face brightened that I wasn't going to like what came next. "I thought I'd introduce myself since I'm the Interim Chairman and you're the last of the Fae vermin to exterminate from Ancetol."

My mind superimposed the memory over him like a filter, and I could practically see the blood spilling from his neck. "You're lying. They would never—"

"I'm very well connected." He let out a cheery breath. "Look, we were bound to run into each other… all I'm asking is that you do me a favor and stay out of my affairs."

"Why should I?"

"Because I hear you're still having trouble locating your friend. It would be a shame if she turned to dust."

My body shook, half in fear and half in rage. "You took her."

He shrugged and I lunged forward, cocking my fist back. I halted midair as a pair of wide arms slipped around me.

"What the fuck, Reina?"

"Oden, let me go," I spat. "You don't understand, this is DT. He's still alive."

DT watched with an amused grin. "Calvin Hall actually."

Oden's grip didn't loosen, and I struggled to break free. "Let me fucking go. He has Bri!"

I looked up as an officer jogged toward us. "Is there a problem here?" he called.

Our confrontation lured some of the bolder reporters, their cameras already pointed at us as they rushed over.

Oden's voice was close enough for me to feel his breath on my ear as he whispered, "If what you're saying is true, this can only go two ways." DT's eyebrow rose with interest. "Either he kills you with a death touch or he takes the beating and you go to jail for assault or... even assasination."

"We're fine, officer," Oden said.

I struggled to free myself.

He whispered, "Fight another day, once we have Bri back safe."

DT began to walk away, back toward the media circus. Over his shoulder he said, "You should listen to your puppy, Reina. Stay out of my campaign."

When he was just a few strides away, Oden released me and I spun on him. "He's pretending to be a Serf. He'd expose himself if he used it in public, and I'd gladly go to jail forever to know Ancetol is safe from him."

"We need a plan. A strategy. What would Mo say about charging in out of anger?"

I shook my head. "This is so fucked up. I watched him die, Oden. I saw him bleed out."

"We'll figure it out, I promise."

But this time I wouldn't swallow my hatred. DT's gaze met mine and he smiled like he knew exactly what was coming. I didn't remember the run over to him, just the pop my fist made as it collided with his cheek and he dropped to the ground.

"Fight back, you coward!" I yelled, but the police had already pulled me back. Oden jumped to my aid as cameras flashed over DT who took a moment to flounder helplessly before getting to his feet.

Everyone paused, their attention split between me and DT.

DT smiled. "It was just a misunderstanding. Everything's fine."

"You're not pressing charges?" the officer asked.

With lips pursed, and a shiner starting to drip blood, DT shook his head.

Oden pulled me away.

A reporter's voice cut through the air. "Mr. Hall, is Reina Roux lashing out at you because of the Pro-Ungifted movement? Do you think the Fae should be removed from Ancetol?"

I looked back and DT winked at me.

Oden's grip tightened until it hurt, and he practically dragged me back into the hospital. My head was spinning. He was a monster and now he had the public in the palm of his hand. I just made that so much worse, but fuck it felt good to punch him. He had Bri and I hoped she'd see the mark I'd made and know I was still coming for her.

Oden was so angry he couldn't speak, but I had too much on my mind to worry about him.

In truth, I should have been paying closer attention to the election. Whichever candidate was chosen would be in charge of the police force and the Fae, but I'd checked out a while back when I heard that all the candidates were ungifted. I never thought that DT could possibly be alive, let alone the Agency's first choice for Interim Chairman. There were hardly any Fae left and it seemed like the management of Fae wasn't considered an aspect of the chairman's role. That explained why he was faking being ungifted.

I paced in the hallway and finally Oden spoke. "That was pretty fucking stupid."

"I'm sorry... but he took Bri."

"You're lucky you're not in jail or that he didn't kill you. There will be consequences for what you just did."

"Right. This is going to be a battle, so you should really think about whether or not you still want to be here. Because that passive let-him-walk-all-over-us nonsense isn't going to get it done."

He turned his face away, but his gaze was firmly locked on me. "That's not even what I meant—but maybe I do need to think about things."

I stared at the floor, my eyes moving to a discolored square of linoleum.

"I'm going back to campus." The ice in his tone wasn't lost on me.

I nodded.

I deserved his indignation, but things had shifted a lot in just a few hours and it felt like the time to have the conversation I'd been avoiding. It used to feel like all of our conversations led there, a place where he'd force me to reject his feelings and remind him that all I had to offer was friendship. We'd talked about it so many times that I couldn't stomach it again, but I never explicitly let him go. I thought we were getting past it, as it had been almost a year since our last go-round, but with Kai back, I sensed Oden was going to force my hand.

I detached myself from the events of the afternoon for the sake of my sanity and, luckily, Mo was uncharacteristically chatty. Before I knew it, my phone was blowing up with threats from Miranda telling me that if I was late for the team dinner she'd make sure I wouldn't leave the hospital again. I kissed Mo goodbye and hurried on my way, just as the sky turned a dusty blue.

Even across the campus I could tell that Miranda had outdone herself. I could see the flicker of candles as they turned the Fishbowl into a lavish banquet hall that glowed like it was draped with Christmas lights. Before I could reach it, I saw Miranda standing outside Pink House, dressed for a red carpet event.

"Wow, you look amazing."

"I know," she said, ushering me into the dorm.

"We're not going to eat?"

Her eyebrows rose. "Oh, we decided on more of a black-tie theme, and your grungy, ten-years-at-the-hospital look is... throwing off the aesthetic."

"I can just head to my apartment and—"

"And deny me the joys of making you over?"

I turned on her. "Miranda Rose Callix, what are you up to?"

She feigned offense. "What? You asked me to do dinner. I did it and now you're complaining." She headed to her room. "I don't work for you. I just thought it would be nice to—"

"Okay okay. I'm sorry. Beautify me."

She grimaced. "Shower first. You have five minutes."

By the time Miranda pinned my last curl, I was certain she was up to something. She'd put me into a stunning teal dress with a layered skirt and a bodice that pushed my boobs up practically to my throat. She'd done my makeup for me, pulled my hair into an updo, and completed the look with a choker and a pair of heels. I enjoyed the process. I hadn't gotten a chance to see Miranda so in her element. I even thought she did a great job picking a look for me that felt more like my style than hers. I hadn't seen myself that dressed up since the winter ball, which brought forward memories of Quan's blood smeared across the floor and a glass shard scraping my forehead. It wasn't a particularly pleasant memory, nor an easy one to forget, but even with the twinge of sadness that came from it, I had to admit I cleaned up pretty well.

"You don't think this is a little much?"

She beamed at me in the mirror. "Are you kidding? You're my masterpiece. It's perfect for the occasion."

I would have protested had she not been equally dolled up, but I at least wanted to know what she was up to. "And this isn't about Kai?" I pushed.

"We're late," she said, looking at her bare wrist.

She knew better than to lie, but if that wasn't the most obvious question dodge I'd ever seen, I didn't know what was.

I felt a little silly in my dress and a little wobbly in my heels, but Miranda held my hand the whole way to the Fishbowl. I wondered if I would have felt less nervous if she'd chosen a more relaxed look, but perhaps she was doing what she could to ease a stressful few days.

The bulk of the tables were pushed against the side walls, but a few were gathered together near the windows and covered with a velvety tablecloth that shone in the candlelight. I walked over to inspect the spread.

"Shit."

I spun and Miranda looked frazzled. "I forgot my phone. I'll grab it and round up the guys."

She hurried out and I turned back to the table, smiling at the box of pizza among the rose petals and candles.

This is cute. I picked up the bottle of wine and started reading the label when I noticed something awry—there were only two wine glasses. I riddled out Miranda's plan a second too late because, as I turned to run and find her, Kai stepped into the doorway.

kaito
SEVENTEEN

I looked into Reina's befuddled expression, her eyes blinking far too quickly, and knew that we'd been set up. Miranda just couldn't let things happen on their own, huh? Did she really think it would work in my favor to ambush Reina like this? My body refused to move any closer than the doorway, but my gaze traveled all over Reina. *Holy shit.* I didn't mind in the least that I'd been forced into this suit, not if this was going to be my view for the night. *Keep it together, Kai.*

"She set us up?"

I nodded. "Looks like it." I tried not to smile, but I wasn't exactly mad about it.

"Are you going to come in?"

"I haven't decided yet."

Jazz music burst from the speakers then dimmed as someone adjusted the volume from the front office.

Reina laughed. "They're not subtle but... there's wine."

I ventured a step into the room to get a better look at the

setup. How did Miranda get Oden to agree to this? I had to at least give her props for that. A dinner date with Reina seemed a little too normal for us, when we usually spent time together when the fate of the city was on the line. But every part of me wanted it, even if Miranda's taste was cheesy. But this was going to be too much too fast for Reina, and I wasn't sure how to get out of it without making her feel rejected. "Wine *is* good. Are you sure this is okay? I mean, those assholes are still on campus. We can hunt them down and kick their asses instead."

"We could, but then this pizza and wine would just go to waste. We can kick their asses later." Her smile teased me.

A matching grin stretched across my face. I could never resist her. "Good point."

I headed for the table and poured wine into both glasses. I handed one to her, but I was having trouble keeping eye contact, especially with her all dressed up.

She eyed me suspiciously. "Kaito, are you nervous about dating me?"

Fuck. She'd know if I lied, but I didn't want to admit to that. No problem, I could just say something true. "You look beautiful..." *Good. Be done with it.* "Of course I'm nervous." *Shit... I was so close.*

She smirked. "You don't look terrible."

"You can say sexy. It's written all over your face."

Her eyes flickered a devious glint that sent a pulse of desire through my extremities before she turned away shyly. "Shut up. No it isn't."

I moved closer. "Tell the truth, Reina."

Her gaze moved to my lips before she looked away and took a sip of wine. Who was this goddamn temptress? So much of her had been what I remembered that I hadn't counted on seeing facets of her personality I didn't know yet.

Take it slow. She needs a friend right now. I took a sip of wine and the bitterness filled my mouth. It slid down my throat and warmed my chest. I looked down at the glass. Why hadn't I thought to drink after I got out?

"Not bad, right?" Reina asked as she took a seat at the table.

I responded with another mouthful.

She laughed. "You missed drinking?"

I took a seat beside her. "I missed a lot of things."

"Me too."

I felt her gaze on my face, but I couldn't muster the courage to look at her. "Yeah, I… uh… I'm sorry about that. Really. Maybe if I had done some things differently—" I felt a weight on my glass as Reina refilled my wine. "Annnd she's trying to get me drunk."

"Is it working?"

"Yeah, one more glass and you could probably have your way with me."

I took a sip but nearly choked as she tipped the bottom of my glass up. I swallowed a huge mouthful. "Oh, it's like that?" I stood and pretended to push the contents of the table to the floor. The jazz song dragged to its natural end and a soft piano followed, mixing with Reina's laugh. The sound made me want to touch her. I knew she was messing with me, relishing in the power of knowing I wanted her. I'd put all my cards on the table and I was still waiting to see hers.

I shook my head as if I could shake off her attractiveness before I moved to sit across from her. "Say it."

"Hmm?"

I leaned forward. "Why did you agree to go along with this?"

Her eyelashes fluttered as she took another sip of wine. I could see the words forming. "It's okay... I can take it."

"I mean... obviously this thing between us is still here."

"But."

"But I..." She shook her head. "DT's alive."

"I know… I saw him. Do you have a plan yet?"

She shook her head. "No, but I have a responsibility to this city. It's my job to protect everyone."

"You're afraid I'll get in the way."

She finished her wine. I reached for the glass to refill it, but I froze when her hand came to rest on mine.

Fumbling to keep my composure, I said, "I read that most of the Fae left. Maybe it's time to just—"

Her tone landed hard. "I'm not giving up on Ancetol." Her hand lifted and she traced the tip of her fingers over the top of my hand, sending goosebumps up my arm.

My mouth went dry so I wet it with another gulp of wine. "And you don't think we can be together while you save the world? You don't think I can help?"

"I don't know, Kai. I can't get distracted by relationship stuff… There's too much on the line."

"Well, I'm not going to try and convince you to be with me, but I need you to know I won't stand in the way of your goals. I'll be around as a teammate or a friend."

Though my words were meant to comfort, the way her mouth tensed said they'd done the opposite. I didn't want to give up, but if all she wanted was a friend, that's what I had to be.

Don't be sad, Reina. I knew this wasn't going to be easy. She put her hand to her forehead and wouldn't meet my gaze. *Don't be sad, Reina.* I needed to do something. "The future will handle tomorrow. We still have tonight."

She lifted her face and smiled, but I noticed a teardrop caught in her eyelash. "You better make the most of it then."

She was right. If tonight was all we had left romantically. I refilled our wine glasses. "I plan to."

"Do tell." She leaned forward and put her chin on her curled hands.

"First, we're going to eat this pizza. Then I'm going to ask you to dance."

Her eyes widened. "You dance?"

I winked. "Then I'll walk you to your dorm and kiss you goodbye."

She smirked. "Oh. There's going to be a kiss? You seem pretty sure of that."

"Definitely."

Reina

EIGHTEEN

By the time we finished eating, the wine had begun to kick in for us both. We laughed so hard that I thought it would shoot out of my nose. True to his word, Kai walked around the table and held out his hand. "Would you like to dance?"

I took it. "I have to see this."

Something about knowing his expectations for the night took the pressure off, and the wine did its work to hold me in the moment. Kai led me away from the table and, with a measured pull of his hand, he spun me.

I gasped. "No fucking way."

His grin said it all. He pulled me to him, but when our bodies came together, my breath caught. Our smiles vanished. An inferno of intensity burned through me as his gaze landed heavily on my face. The rise and fall of his chest against mine beckoned me to pull him closer. We held each other, swaying softly, too afraid to let go. I slipped my fingers up into his hair as he rubbed his hands down my back.

My thoughts moved to the night in the alleyway when Kai had pushed me to orgasm, and the need arose like an ache between my legs. I could practically see the same memory playing behind Kai's dark eyes and then, in a flash, it was gone.

His arms fell to his side and he stepped back as he blew out his breath like a silent whistle. "I think I'd better walk you back."

No, I don't want this night to end. Take me right here. "Yeah. Okay."

He took my hand and we walked slowly back toward my apartment. Even dragging our feet, it wasn't more than a few minutes, and even though it was a little chilly outside, it did nothing to cool me down nor slow my racing heart.

As we stepped up to the door, my thoughts tripped over the words *goodbye kiss*. It was so final. A goodnight kiss would have been different, but we'd already agreed that this was the end of our romantic relationship.

Friends is fine. But I felt my gift combat the unspoken lie. The pained look on Kai's face told me he was more than a little reluctant to kiss me—no doubt struggling with the *goodbye* part.

"I can't..." he started.

If this was goodbye, I was not going to miss my last chance to kiss him. "You promised."

He pleaded with his eyes not to hold him to it, but when I said nothing, he sighed and leaned in. His lips skimmed mine for a fraction of a second before he pulled away, leaving me to lean after it. He nodded a goodbye and turned to go.

"Wa-wait, I wasn't ready," I stammered.

He froze and turned on his heels.

His smirk destroyed me and so did the velvety voice that he used next. "Are you ready now?"

I waited for him to walk back over, then I adjusted my dress to emphasize my cleavage. He turned an agonized face away and sucked in a sharp breath through his nose. "You're killing me, woman. Killing. Me."

"I'm ready."

He reached for me, but I put a hand up to stop him.

"Wait!" I reached up and pulled my hair out of the elastic, spilling my curls over my shoulders.

He shook his head. "Really, Reina? Two can play at that game." He put a hand through his hair and tossed it, then loosened his tie. I gulped. My stomach fluttered, and he moved forward so suddenly that I stepped back into my door. He pushed me back against it. My knees buckled as his hungry gaze bore into me. He leaned in. "I want you to remember," he whispered, his voice tickling my lips, "that you asked for this."

This time, he moved in slowly. He snaked an arm around my waist and branded me with a kiss that deepened instantly. His mouth scorched mine as I pulled on his collar, drawing him closer. He ran his hands over my body and I could taste his need. A metal click sounded and Kai's lips slowly parted from mine. His gaze was locked on me as I traced the sound down. His hand was frozen on the doorknob to my apartment.

I slid my hand down his arm and threaded my fingers through his to grip the handle. Together we turned it and the door pushed open. We slipped in and he turned me as I kicked the door closed.

I unbuttoned his shirt, leaning up to kiss his neck between buttons. His breath hitched, but he took my chin and looked me in the eye. "Rei, are you sure about this? We had wine and..."

I shushed him with a kiss. "I'm sure. I promise."

The zipper on my dress slid down as Kai pulled me and kissed me hard. Button by button, I made my way down his shirt as Kai's mouth scrambled my focus. In the darkness of my apartment, I fumbled to unbuckle his belt. I'd never taken one off someone before. Kai's gift took over and the belt slipped loose. He pulled me back up and kissed me sweetly as my unfastened dress slipped down to my waist. He kissed along my jawline, back to my neck as he began to work his way down. His tongue sent chills to my toes. "Kai," I breathed. "It's not a big deal but..." He straightened and cradled my face in his hands as he listened intently. "It's nothing. Nevermind."

He shook his head and smiled lovingly. "It's okay, Rei. What is it?"

"It's just... I still haven't had sex. Like, with anyone."

His mouth fell open.

"It's not a big deal. I still want to."

He scanned my face, put his forehead to mine, and exhaled slowly. "You're still a virgin?" he asked, his eyes brimming with sincerity and warmth.

I felt more exposed than when he tore off my clothes. I scrambled to pull my dress up to cover my chest. "It's okay, Kai. It's really not a big deal."

"It is." He stepped back.

My body went numb. "You're not seriously about to leave?"

"I'm sorry, Reina. I never thought that you'd still be a virgin. If that's the case, I don't think we should do this now."

I was frozen, but my eyes pricked. "Wh-why? The wine?"

"Yeah, but also..."

"Also what, Kai? Finish your goddamn sentence."

"Because as far as you're concerned this is goodbye!" His voice cracked, his emotions spilling out.

I swallowed a lump in my throat.

"You want me to take your virginity and then what? Be just your buddy after?"

My body shook. "You were just okay with it. Why does me being a virgin change that?"

He buttoned his shirt. "It just does," he said, heading for the door.

The tears slipped down my cheeks, but I wasn't sure he could see them in the dark. "Kai, it's our last night to be together like this. Please, I want this."

"That's the fucking problem." He put his hand against the door.

My voice was barely a whisper. "What do you want?"

He spun on me. "I want you to be with me. Not just tonight. I want to make love to you, slowly, every night. I want a million mornings of waking up next to you. I want us." He shifted a fraction and a sliver of light peeked through my curtains, highlighting a tear as it slid off his clenched jaw.

Something inside me shattered. "I don't want our last night to—"

"Then maybe you should rethink whether or not this is our last night." He walked back into the hallway as the door closed between us.

kaito
NINETEEN

I marched through the hallway, heat filling my face. I heard footsteps behind me and prepared myself for another battle with Reina. I nearly leapt out of my skin when I turned to see Wolfe with a cheesy grin.

"Bruh, I wasn't trying to eavesdrop or anything, but did you just get that girl to beg you for sex?"

"Not the time."

"You're a legend, man. I'm serious."

I headed straight for my dorm, but just before I reached Blue House, I heard the unmistakable sound of crying. I peered through the darkness and saw Miranda seated outside Pink House.

"Nope."

I pushed open the door but heard my name. "Kai, is that you?"

I sighed and poked my head back out. She waved me over, wiping her tears and feigning a smile.

"How was your date"? she asked, false enthusiasm straining.

"I don't know," I said flatly.

She patted the bench beside her, but I didn't have the slightest interest in taking it.

Shit, I was going to regret this. "Why are you crying?"

She sniffed. "I didn't think you could see in the dark." She looked out to the hedge mazes for a moment before she brought back her attention. "I had a vision, a bad one."

"I'm sorry," I said half-heartedly.

Her head dropped and she sobbed.

It wasn't that I didn't feel for her, I did. I was even a little curious about the vision. It would be nice to know beforehand if a meteor was about to crash into Earth, but I was in no shape to comfort anyone. Reina had broken me and I wanted to be alone.

"Well, goodnight. I hope you feel better." Before she could stop me, I made a beeline to Blue House, locking myself in my dorm. I pulled off Reina's chain and threw it against the wall.

I turned on the light and sat on my bed, rubbing my face with my hands. What was wrong with me? I'd gone into that dinner specifically so I could find out where Reina stood and offer my friendship if it came to it. How did I go from that to demanding to be in a relationship? I lay back, crossing my arms over my eyes. My eyes stung as fresh tears coated my cheeks with salt. *She doesn't love me.* If she did, she would be trying to make a relationship work, like I was. But Reina would rather give up on it before it started. *Fuck, I was still in love with her.* It wasn't that she was a virgin that triggered me, it wasn't even the extra emotional weight that comes with that. It was that she was ready to say goodbye. A weight pressed in on my chest, heavier as I willed my tears to stop.

There was nothing left to do, or say. I wiped my face and sat up. I wasn't as strong as Oden. I couldn't stay here and pine after Reina while she sunk with the *S.S. Ancetol*. That only left me with one option—leave and know that life will always be a little worse moving forward.

A knock at my door turned my blood to fire, and I stood. Was that her? Had she changed her mind? I swung the door open, a lance piercing through my hopes as Miranda stood in my doorway.

She pushed her way in and sat down on my bed.

Having her in my room after our history set me on edge. As innocuous as it might've been, the last thing I needed was for Reina to find Miranda in here. "Look, I know you're going through something, but if Reina—"

"Shut up, shut up. I set up the date, remember?"

I held my tongue, but I knew with one hundred percent certainty that when the wrong woman was in your bed, the right one always found out about it. It was Mother Nature's way of setting things right.

"I know you're in love with her. It's written all over your face even worse than when we were in school."

I exhaled. "So what do you want?"

She swallowed. "It's about my vision. I have a theory about you and Reina. Can I show you?"

"Show me your vision? You can do that now?"

She flipped her ponytail. "The world didn't stop just because you got yourself locked up."

"Get on with it," I said, growing agitated.

"Right, so you can get back to crying."

I had half a mind to drag her out of here by her hair, but if her vision had flustered her this much and it was about me and Reina, I needed to see it.

She got off my bed and onto her knees at the center of the room. She gestured for me to do the same in front of her. The severity of her expression compelled me to comply, and I waited anxiously for further instruction.

She took a deep breath. "This is going to be intense. It's also a little jumbled because these visions aren't set yet."

I slouched. "Then why do we care?"

"It's a matter of life and death. But Kai, no matter how painful this is to see, don't let go until I say."

The hardness of her eyes was an injection of nervous energy straight to my veins. My worst fear came into my head first. *Reina's death.* Even if the vision could be changed, I didn't think I could take—

"Clear your head," Miranda said, lifting her hands.

I mirrored her, too afraid to find my voice.

"This is very important. Reach inside yourself and think about the part of you that doesn't want to be with Reina."

I shook my head. "There's not. I do want to be with her."

She searched my eyes. "The part of you that wants to leave so you won't get hurt." She watched me carefully. I didn't want to admit it, but the thought had crossed my mind. Every road I walked with Reina led to the same dead end, with us hurting. I'd be doing us both a favor if I never let it get that far.

I could almost feel Miranda inside my head. "Good. Hold onto that feeling. Stay focused on it."

My heart ached, but I held myself in the emotion. I barely felt Miranda's hands press against mine. A blue glow flashed through the room but was swallowed by a flood of images. I saw myself leaving GFA. The vision flipped. My breath caught as Reina cried on the floor so hard that she choked. "Kai," she whispered through sobs. Horror flooded my body, and I tried to snatch my hands away, only to feel Miranda's nails dig into my flesh.

"Don't let go," I heard her say, but she sounded distant.

"Please," I begged as pain shot through me. I couldn't watch Reina for another second. "No!" I screamed, but Miranda held tight.

Before I could pry my hands loose, the image of Reina blurred. Color clashed, like fireworks. The next image pushed through. A flash of purple, blue, and piercing white. Reina whipped her gift into a sea of swirling colors, her body locked in a frozen attack. A dagger cut across her leg, but she gritted her teeth and attacked again, her target off the edge of my vision.

My blood pressure rose as panic choked me. The image flipped again. This time to Zane, standing with his arms crossed and a smile. He had his signature neon blue hair and his gaze was locked on two figures too distorted to see.

Miranda's voice swept through my head. "Let go of Zane and focus on *them*."

I obeyed and the figures drew near. I recognized Reina first. She was panting—and bleeding—wrapped in an embrace with a second figure.

"Look closer," Miranda urged. "Away from Reina."

My body screamed for release, my gift threatening to pull the vision away, but I held it back long enough to see her—Bri.

"If you can see her, let go."

I yanked my hands away and plunged back into my dorm room. I was sobbing and shaking, my throat raw from screams I never heard.

Miranda pulled me to her. "It's okay. You did fine. It's over. Breathe. It's over."

I cried as she ran circles over my back with her hand, and each breath swept the vision further away. Miranda seemed no more shaken than when she'd come to my dorm. Was this always what her visions felt like? How could she take it? Even as my body adjusted and my breathing eased, I could do nothing but lay limp in her arms as she cradled me.

"You're okay. Deep breaths. It's almost gone."

The vision of Reina crying on the floor was the one that lingered under my skin. It had an endless echo that pushed fresh waves of pain through my body that took effort to swallow. I wiped my face only to find smudges of Miranda's black makeup on my hands. It was probably all over me. Finally, my voice found me. "How can you endure that?"

She giggled but her heart wasn't in it, which suggested she was also feeling her gift's effects. "You're not such a tough guy after all."

I sat up and wiped my nose on my sleeve. "Yes, I am."

She raised her eyebrows in pity. "Good, because we have to do it one more time."

I stood too quickly and nearly toppled to the floor.

"Whoa, take it slow." She leapt up to steady me.

I shook my head. "No offense, but I'm never fucking doing that again. I understand what you're trying to show me, but it's irrelevant."

I took a moment to gather my words and Miranda waited.

"Reina hurt me tonight... so badly that I did consider leaving for a second, but even before that shitty fucking vision, I'd already decided that I'd never give up on her."

She swallowed. "You were *always* going to give up on her."

Her words sliced me into ribbons and Earth felt as if it tilted on its axis. "What?"

Miranda grabbed my arm and helped me take a seat on my bed. Her eyes welled as she sat beside me. "The vision I showed you first came to me a year ago."

I reeled, my head packed with questions.

"I knew you'd come back into Reina's life only to leave for good."

I wanted to scream, but it all hurt too much so it came out like a whisper. "That's a goddamn lie."

When she broke eye contact, I knew the worst was still to come. She stared at the floor for several agonizing minutes before she said, "Something changed tonight."

I desperately strung things together. "The second vision? That's good, right? It can't be worse than..."

She stood, causing me to trail off as she moved to the center of the room and knelt.

"No. I won't."

She dropped her hands to her thighs. "Fine. You don't have to see it. You can just trust me."

"Okay. Let's do that."

She nodded. "Leave Reina and never come back."

"Are you fucking insane?"

She gestured to the floor in front of her.

I seethed but still knelt, my body involuntarily pulling away. I held my fists to my chest, too afraid to touch her. "This is going to be worse than the last one?"

"This time, focus on how much you love Reina."

Fear had full control of me. "How bad is it, Miranda?"

She held my gaze but her silence spoke volumes.

My head screamed at me not to ask, but my voice rang out, "Is she going to die?"

"Worse."

I shook, unable to muster the courage to touch Miranda's hands. My voice broke, "There's nothing worse."

"Yes, there is." She held her hands up and I felt the tears begin to fall before I even reached for them.

Reina
TWENTY

As I slipped into a hoodie and pajama bottoms and headed back onto campus, I told myself I just needed air. I wasn't going anywhere in particular.

My gift wrestled the lie the whole way to Blue House. That *asshole*. Wasn't it my choice how or when I lost my virginity? He knew how I felt about him... But I couldn't just derail my life, my calling, to be somebody's girlfriend. *And fuck virginity*. I should have had sex with Kai years ago. Every year I didn't lose it, it turned into a bigger deal.

I wasn't fooling anyone, least of all myself. I had loved Kaito since I met him, and when he went away to prison… Ugh. What was with that guy? I gave up relationships altogether because I couldn't be with him. Was it so wrong for me to want to express my love for him in that way one time before I had to fulfill my oath to this city? He'd had sex with Miranda and god knows who else and he couldn't find it in him to make love to me once?

I wasn't sure what my plan was. Barge in and... demand sex? Yell at him? Seriously, where was I going with this? I ran through some potential opening lines that crossed the spectrum all the way from "Get naked" to "You asshole."

I was too in my head to notice that his door was ajar. Too worried I'd lose my nerve to do anything but thoughtlessly push the door open without warning, I froze.

Miranda sat on Kaito's bed, her face buried in her hands as she cried. Kaito was on the floor at the center of the room, sitting with his back to Miranda.

They were both sweaty and panting. Even from the doorway, I could see Miranda's makeup smudged all over Kai's face and hands. The immediate thought should have been that I'd just missed a romantic interlude, but several things prevented that theory from growing legs. I trusted both Miranda and Kai, and the energy in the room was too morbid for a funeral.

Miranda looked up but couldn't catch her breath to explain. She nodded towards Kai. I walked around him to get a view of his face. His eyes were wide but vacant.

"What happened?" I asked, reaching for his face, but he pulled away.

I turned to Miranda. Her hand shook as she covered her mouth.

Unable to bear the suspense of it, I pushed my gift recklessly into Kai.

He spoke but didn't look at me. "I saw what happens."

My eyes flicked up to Miranda. A vision? Fear filled me. "What was it?"

"Rei," he breathed. "You looked so beautiful in your wedding dress that I swear my heart stopped."

I tore my gift back, but Kai kept on of his own volition.

"In front of all our friends, we became husband and wife." Kai started to shake, tears brimming his eyes. "Our life together was full—" He choked, shaking his head, his tears falling. He turned to me. "It was so much more than I dreamed."

Pain pulsed from his body and filled the room. "What happened?" I asked.

"You hid your pain from me. Resentment poisoned our marriage, and one night, out of the blue, you left."

How? Part of me was overjoyed at the idea of us having a future together, especially after the way our date ended. "I don't understand."

"You loved me, I could see it. You just couldn't forgive me for being the reason Bri died."

I stood. "What happened, Miranda?" My voice was sharp, a dagger of emotion aimed at my friend out of grief for a future potentially years away as it was ripped away like it was never mine. "What did you show him?"

She dragged herself off the bed and knelt beside us, raising her glowing hands. "No matter how painful this is to see, don't let go until I say."

∼

The next morning I lay awake as the sun rose, drenching my makeshift classroom-apartment with morning light. My thoughts were tangled and my heart broken. I understood why Miranda hadn't allowed me to see her visions before then. It was unbearable. Not only was there no future for me and Kai, but I'd also gotten a good look at everything I was giving up.

I'd been committed to fulfilling my duty as Fae and to finding Bri, but maybe deep down I thought Kai and me would find our place together somewhere down the line. I knew it would be a challenge to say goodbye to him, but I'd survived it before. Even during our date, I'd managed to keep up one last wall to protect myself from the inevitable heartbreak that marked every round with him. But watching Miranda's vision had crumbled it. I was no longer sure about my choice. Since he'd been back, Kai hadn't been shy about his feelings for me—but that wasn't the same as watching him *marry me*, or seeing his devastation. There was no longer a way to pretend that Kai was just my first love or that somehow I'd built up our connection in my head. We loved each other.

If it was just Ancetol, I could have let it go for Kai, but Miranda's visions had dropped a second bomb. Bri was out there, so all of the searching hadn't been in vain. I could still save her.

The cost was steep and, this time, there was no way around it. The only thing left for me and Kaito was a goodbye. Now or after years, it all ended in heartbreak.

kaito

TWENTY-ONE

After a long restless night, I knew exactly where I stood. There was no way in hell I could accept that I had no future with Reina—I just didn't know how to change it.

The decision part was easy. I had to leave her.

Letting her love for me die slowly wasn't an option. I finally understood what Reina was trying to tell me. She had to find Bri, she needed to settle things with Yemoja Roux and Ancetol. I would be in the way and she'd resent me for it.

But I wasn't a quitter. Reina was my dream and, now that I'd seen our life together, I knew more than ever what I wanted. Protecting Reina's dream was the most important thing, and that meant I'd have to ask a little more of Miranda.

I picked up Reina's owl charm from the corner of the room where I had tossed it and strung it over my head before I jutted out of my dorm, straight for Miranda's.

I knocked with no regard for the fact that the sun was barely rising and we'd all retreated to our rooms only three hours before. Every second I hung around was a risk to Bri's life. I listened at the door for signs of life but heard nothing. I knocked again, this time letting adrenaline seep into it.

I heard a thump and shortly after Miranda pulled the door open. Her eyes were barely open, her hair on end like she'd been struck with electricity. She didn't seem surprised to see me, she merely turned and shuffled back into her dorm room. I followed, not bothering with the pleasantries I desperately owed. "What does me leaving have to do with Reina finding Bri? Why can't I stay and help her?"

She collapsed onto her bed. "I don't know, Kai... maybe you leaving hurt her so much that Bri was all she had left to believe in."

"So... no matter what I have to hurt her?"

She sat up. "I know it sucks, but if you love her, you'll do this."

"I have another plan. But I need to know it won't affect Bri."

Miranda groaned but moved to the center of her dorm room. She knelt on the pink rug and held out her hands. "It's better if I don't know the details. Focus on your plan."

The last thing I wanted was to suffer another one of Miranda's visions, but I needed to be sure. I knelt in front of her and put my hands against hers.

This time I knew what to expect so the emotional onslaught didn't land as heavily. The images flashed forward, identical to the first round that Miranda showed me, with one exception. This time when Reina cried on the floor of her apartment I didn't try to pull my hands away. I focused on her necklace. As expected, the charm had changed. I held my breath waiting to see if the end of the vision had been altered, but it wasn't. *Bri was still alive.* I kept my hands on Miranda's, hoping this time the vision would show what came next, but it didn't.

After several stale minutes, Miranda pulled her hands away and the vision blinked out of my eyes.

"I'm sorry, Kai," she said. "It didn't change anything."

You're wrong. Miranda must not have noticed the change in Reina's necklace and I needed to keep it that way. Reina needed to believe I was leaving forever and, for that, Miranda did too.

Hope flooded me as my plan came together, but I didn't show a shred of it on my face.

"Thank you, Miranda," I said, standing and helping her to her feet. "I have to let her go."

She nodded but surprised me when tears welled in her eyes. Tears for me? For Reina? Miranda was so exhausted she was barely on her feet. Just from looking at her uncharacteristically lethargic movements, I could tell it was more than lack of sleep. She was drained from overusing her gift and she hadn't even complained. All this time she'd looked after Rei, keeping her on the path that led to Bri. She'd even set up that date for me and Reina, knowing that a brutal goodbye was the only way to stay the course. How many burdens did she carry alone?

"You know, I was wrong about you," I said with a smile.

"And I you." She sniffed. "Goodbye, Kai. Have a happy life."

"Take care of Rei and give Bri a big hug when you see her."

I left, knowing Reina would be in good hands. I had work to do before I said goodbye, but I figured she'd be gone for most of the morning with Yemoja Roux. If I hurried, I might have time to get it all done before she returned. This afternoon, I would leave her and trust that we were both strong enough to change our fate. But first, goodbye. And if it had to happen, it should be the way she wanted.

Reina
TWENTY-TWO

I was eager to get to Yemoja's apartment—like a child who skinned their knee running to their mother for comfort—but I was determined not to allow my problems to spoil a perfectly good morning with Mo, especially since she was supposed to be taking it easy.

An older woman with short bleached hair and dark roots loitered by the security booth, so it took me a moment to get the guard's attention so he could buzz me in. "Give me a minute," I heard her say as she strutted over to me. My confusion bounced between the locked apartment door, the security guard, and the woman as she charged at me like I was committing a crime.

"Hi. Can I help you?"

She crossed her arms. "Do you live here?"

"No, I was just visiting someone... but he knows me," I said, gesturing to the security guard. He pretended not to see me.

She stuck her chest out. "You're Reina Roux, right?"

"I'm afraid to say yes."

"You're a disgrace and a criminal. This city doesn't want you anymore."

It was so sudden, so out of the blue, that I almost laughed. I was about to ask her who made her a spokesperson for the city when she stepped closer.

"What?" she poked. "You going to hit me like you did our chairman?"

I swallowed a lump in my throat. *So this was about what happened with DT.* With everything going on with Kai, I hadn't exactly had time to switch on the news. Didn't Oden mention something about repercussions? Ugh. I had no doubt that that incident was a gold mine for DT's agenda, but I didn't think it would spread so quickly.

The security guard must've taken pity on me because the door slid open. I didn't waste a second before walking through, determined not to let her rudeness affect me. If she knew the truth about DT, she would have punched him too. I didn't feel it hit me, but the sound was enough—she spit. I held my head high and ventured into the lobby without so much as a glance back.

I texted Yemoja that I was running a few minutes late as I cried it out in the lobby bathroom. Why was I still here? Did they know what I was giving up for them? Did they know how vulnerable they'd be once there was no one left in Ancetol to protect them? Eventually all the DTs of the world would make their way here. All I wanted was to save them and they *hated* me. I heard the water run, so I swallowed my anger and walked out of the stall. A little girl no older than seven stood on her tiptoes and washed her hands.

I swiped at my cheeks, hoping she hadn't heard me crying.

The little girl stared at me in the mirror, then she turned off the faucet and pulled two paper towels from the dispenser.

She handed me one and said, "It's okay." Without another word, she went on her way. A simple and kind gesture that was too kind to be anything other than my parents lending a helping hand. I thought of the orphans from my old home. They were the most vulnerable, the most in need, and it was they who would suffer most from DT's plan once other cities moved to exploit Ancetol's weakness. Yemoja once told me that the Fae stepped up when everything fell apart—and even if my title was given in desperation and from merit, I still had time to turn things around. I needed to be strong because that's what the city needed from me and, I was willing to bet, that's what Yemoja Roux needed too.

~

"I'm getting the feeling there are two broken hearts in this apartment," Yemoja said as I handed her a cup of tea. Now that she'd been discharged and settled back into her home, she was more at ease but also more observant. I'd consciously made an effort not to show any of my unease, but either she knew me too well or was on her guard since Kai was in town, because one way or another she was onto me. I loved that my gift allowed me to detect the truth, but Yemoja Roux had picked up a thing or two since we started training together. She always made me feel like an open book, a trait I both loved and hated.

"What? No, I'm fine," I said with a forced grin. I sat beside her on the couch.

She took a sip, her eyebrows raising above the cup. "Mhmm."

"I'm just happy you're home. I was thinking that maybe I'd move back in for a little while."

Her expression hardened. "I'm not helpless."

"I know. I just miss you."

"That might be true, but something's wrong. You don't have to tell me everything, but maybe it'll help to get it off your chest."

I was glad to get away from the academy, to focus on anything other than saying goodbye to Kai. The last thing I wanted was to rehash it with Mo. Between the city and her health, she had enough to worry about.

"Please," she said, "I just want to be a part of your life."

I touched her hands. "I know, I know. I just don't want to worry you."

"This is about Kai, isn't it? Spill. He's always been so hot and cold. If that boy doesn't just make up his—"

"That's not it."

Her magenta eyebrows knitted together.

"He's... just hot now." Tea nearly shot out of my nose when I looked up at her. Her lips were pursed, her eyes loaded with sass as if to ask, *How hot are we talking?*

"So what's stopping you?"

Was there any way to spin this so it wouldn't sound as horrible as it was? "Miranda had a vision that I found Bri."

Her smile waned. "You mean she's still alive?"

"Only if me and Kai end things."

Without a moment's hesitation, Yemoja scrambled for her phone.

"Wh-what are you doing?"

She ignored me, holding the phone far too close to her face and typing into it. A minute or two later, she looked up. "Done."

"What did you do?"

"Only you can make a decision like that, but either way we're going to need ice cream."

"You really think there's a choice?"

Her gentle gaze was a blanket in an otherwise frigid world. "Honey, I've been making those choices my whole life. That's the job, really. I always saved the day at the expense of my own happiness, and sometimes I wonder if that was the right way to live." She set her tea down on the coffee table and sighed, staring out the window. "Especially now. The city moved on so quickly, away from Fae, away from me." Her gaze swept the room. "And all I have left is this empty apartment."

"You have me," I said.

The warmth in her demeanor returned. "Well, I'm never going to have grandkids at this rate."

I sighed. "Trust me, there's no chance of that."

"Well, I'll just have to live forever then."

"Deal." The conversation came to a natural pause and it felt like the perfect time to bring up some of my concerns. "Mo, I think it's best if you take things easy for a while. Let me handle things."

She sat up straight. "You mean like... retire?" The word held the threat of a blade's edge. I winced. "You know I can't. I made an oath. Even if the city won't acknowledge it, they still need me."

"I need you too. I need you to be healthy."

She shook her head. "What do you expect me to do? Stay here and do nothing?"

"I don't know, Mo, maybe you can pursue some of your other interests. Maybe it's time to put yourself back out there and date. It's not too late for—"

"Stop this. I'm fine. I'll be good as new in a few days."

I looked down into my tea and sighed.

"What? Say it."

I shook my head.

"Say it," she urged.

I mustered my courage. I didn't want to hurt her, only protect her. I didn't even want her to retire, if I was honest. I wasn't sure I could do her proud, but she wasn't the only one who had picked up a trick or two from training. Where she learned to detect truth, I'd learned to detect fear. "You're afraid. That's understandable, but I don't think that's a good enough reason not to try it."

She turned her face away and it hurt to look at her. I was grasping at straws, but there was one other alternative that I hadn't tried. "What about running for chairman? You still help the city, but it wouldn't be as strenuous on your body." Her ears pricked up but she didn't look at me. "You could rally whatever Fae are left in Ancetol and do some good."

She eyed me, but I saw a bit of interest flicker on the edge of her irises. She leaned back, adjusting a couch cushion. "Now I need ice cream too."

I wasn't sure if it was her vision starting to go south or if she was struggling with the delivery app, but instead of two ice cream cartons, the delivery man brought twenty-one. We had a good laugh and gave the mountain of creamy goodness our best try. When we were stuffed and sticky, we both felt a little better. There was a safety in Yemoja's presence that I felt nowhere else. Perhaps it was selfish to deny the rest of Ancetol that feeling, but if it was finally time for me to choose the city, maybe it was time for Yemoja Roux to choose herself.

Kaito
TWENTY-THREE

"Of course I'm going with you," Yanis said.

Wolfe exhaled. "Me too. We missed all the fucking action last night and that Miranda chick thinks she's too good for me."

Yanis smirked. "She is."

"Whatever."

If I still had any reservations about my new friends, they died on the spot. I hadn't expected them to want to join me. They had a nice setup at GFA. They didn't owe me anything, least of all their loyalty, especially after I lied to them about my gift and only started to fill them in on everything with Reina. Yanis, to my surprise, turned out to be a hopeless romantic, eager to offer suggestions. I liked his optimism and was happy he'd be around for what would most likely be the most difficult months of my life.

Wolfe just seemed suited for trouble. I hadn't worked up the nerve to ask him what landed him in prison, but it was the danger in my plan that appealed to him. He had a restless soul and a penchant for acting impulsively, but his bravery, however stupid, was contagious and I needed it more than ever.

After a long day in the city, I paced at the front of a store—the last step before we returned to campus for our goodbyes. Wolfe groaned. "They said it was ready. Why is it taking so long?" Yanis silenced him with a backhand to the chest.

Finally an older woman emerged from the back room. I hustled over and she handed me the finished product to inspect.

Wolfe and Yanis hovered over my shoulder to get a closer look.

"Seriously, how rich are you?" Wolfe asked.

I turned to Yanis for his opinion. "It came out great. Are you ready?"

My heartbeat pushed a simmering heat to my cheeks and neck. I would never be ready to hurt Reina. Miranda's vision leapt forward. Reina crying on the floor of her apartment. Whispering my name as she choked on her grief. There was no way around it. It was an essential part of my plan's success—but that didn't make it any easier.

I took a deep breath.

Yanis looked as nervous as I was. "Why don't you get a new chain for you, so you can give her back hers?"

I nodded. "Yeah, let's do that."

∽

My stomach dropped when we pulled up to campus and Miranda waited for us outside. Did something get thrown off? She rushed to me. "Reina's back. She's in her apartment."

I searched her eyes. "Did anything change? Are we still okay?"

A bright red flashed across her cheeks like sunset peeking through a cloudy day. I looked over my shoulder at Wolfe and Yanis then pulled Miranda out of earshot.

"What is it?"

She looked more nervous to speak to me than when she'd come to my dorm room. "You're scaring me."

"Your plan hasn't changed, but I saw..."

"What, Miranda?"

"Look, this is super awkward so I'm just going to say it and you and I will never speak of this again, okay?"

I gulped.

"It's romantic and stuff that you're going to take her virginity and everything before you go, but just so you know there won't be any lifelong consequences if you guys aren't... safe or whatever."

I froze. *What the fuck?* Did Miranda have a vision of me and Reina having sex?

As if she could read my expression, she said, "Relax, I skipped over it, but I mean... you could have warned me. I had to see if you were going to mess up the timeline. Luckily, it's still the same. With you leaving and Bri saved."

"Firstly, you're a huge creep," I said. "You know that?"

She rolled her eyes.

"Secondly..." It was a complete invasion of privacy, way over my boundaries. It was fucked up and I needed her to know it... but also as a bro, she'd kinda done me a solid by giving me the heads up. She'd even risked the embarrassment of the confession to do it. "Thanks." I did not want to dwell on the implications of what I'd seen of her gift just in the last few hours alone.

Shit, levitation was lame by comparison. "Wait..." I said, turning back to her. "Can I see?"

She scoffed. "No, you perv, because then I'll have to see."

"Right, right."

Wolfe popped his head over Miranda's shoulder. "I couldn't help but overhear... Do you have any dirty visions of me and you?"

Miranda's gaze flicked to Yanis for a fraction of a second before she replied, "Not a one."

Interesting. I wondered if there was something going on there. I sighed. "Well, this is... so weird now."

Wolfe grinned. "Yep. You better get to it. If you don't perform well, we'll all know."

"For fuck's sake. I appreciate you all, but I'm serious everyone here needs to butt out. Besides, at this point, it's more likely that some natural disaster will strike before anything goes down anyway."

Miranda snorted. "Not this time."

Nerves weighed my limbs. W*as this actually happening?*

We all spun as the scuff of footprints behind us drew our attention. Oden walked over. "What's going on?"

We all spoke at once, a jumbled mess of excuses that lit Oden's eyes with suspicion.

"I'm leaving, for good," I said finally. "Yanis and Wolfe are coming with me."

His intense glare softened. "Well, I can't say I'm surprised. You lasted longer than I thought you would."

My immediate instinct was to punch him, but there was some truth to what he said. I had left Reina twice before, all while he remained loyally by her side. It wasn't fair to ask, but I needed him to step in once again.

Holding his gaze, I hoped he understood those things. "Take care" was the most I could offer, and I hurried away from the group before things got more tense.

The sun grew stale as I walked in silence across the GFA campus with Reina's owl charm, hitting my chest as it swung on my new chain. I couldn't bear to part with it, knowing that we might never see each other again. I was taking it with me, but I didn't intend on leaving her with nothing.

Reina
TWENTY-FOUR

Knowing Kai was waiting for my decision only made it worse. I'd rehearsed a hundred ways to tell him, but none felt right. How could I possibly explain to him how much I wanted to choose him? No matter what excuse I gave, he was going to walk out of here thinking I didn't love him, but delaying the decision only risked Bri's life.

A knock sounded at my door, causing my skin to prick as if I'd been stabbed with a million needles. I rushed over and opened it.

Kai stood in the frame, his black eyes lighting as his gaze met mine. I drank him in one feature at a time. The way his top lip bowed and the bottom one was swollen and alluring, his dark hair as it fell over his eyes, and the pointed way his dark eyes pierced my will to leave him.

It had been us against the world since we'd met. Why wouldn't the universe cooperate?

He watched me carefully. Was this it? The end of love? The

end of the wild and boundless energy that bolted through my veins? I exhaled but my breath skipped.

"Are you okay?" he asked.

I motioned him in and he shut the door behind him. He walked around the room, this time with the lights on. He took a look around. *Stay with me* echoed in my mind, as much a part of me as my own heartbeat.

"I'm just about ready to go," he said. "I got my stuff packed. Yanis and Wolfe are coming along."

I should have known he'd choose to go. Of course he wouldn't let me make that kind of sacrifice for him. It should have filled me with relief because I wouldn't have to be the one to say no, but it didn't. With him standing in front of me, it was all too real. Suddenly, those few happy years we'd get if he stayed seemed worth every sacrifice.

"So you've made a decision, just like that?"

To my dismay, he smiled.

Frustrated tears pricked the corners of my eyes. "Why are you smiling? This isn't funny, Kai. I'm... dying."

He swallowed. "I'm dying too. I just... think it's sweet that you even considered it."

"Of course I did. Didn't you?"

"No, not for a second. It's like trading your dream for mine."

His dream? Us being together? Did he think this was making it easier to say goodbye?

His teeth scraped over his bottom lip, drawing my attention to it. What I wouldn't give for one last kiss. A shine shot through the room and I noticed my owl charm hanging from his neck on a new chain.

I walked over and picked it up to take a final look. "I suppose you're keeping this, then?"

"Is that okay? I don't think I can make it without it."

"I just always thought you wearing it meant... I don't know."

He smiled, sending a flush of heat through my body. "It means that my heart belongs to you, even if this is goodbye."

He sat down on my bed as my thoughts tried to break the surface only to be tossed under by each new emotional wave.

The word *goodbye* triggered me, the same way it had for him the night before. "I never expected you to give up." The second I said it, I knew it was unfair. Shit, what was wrong with me? I could see in his tortured expression that I'd hurt him. Then I felt the smallest hint of a lie on his tongue, but he never spoke it.

Desperate to ease the hurt, I sat down on his lap, wrapping my arms around him. "I'm sorry. I'm sorry," I whispered as I peppered his solemn face with gentle kisses. "I just don't want to say goodbye. I know we have to, but Kai, that vision of our life together didn't make me want to stop being with you. I'm so in love with you—"

He caught my jaw and drew my mouth to his, stopping just before we touched—so close I could almost taste him.

He whispered against my lips, "Then we better make the most of it."

I froze when his meaning sunk in, butterflies and nerves doing the tango inside my chest and stomach. It was strange to think I'd proposed the same thing the night before. Only now that I knew this would be goodbye forever, I understood how Kai must've felt. Sex as a goodbye was a surefire way to maximize the pain of separation. I could feel it even as he held me, waiting for me to gather my thoughts. I knew this offer was for me, that he'd thought carefully about our argument. He was determined to give me what I wanted—one last memory between now and goodbye.

It was my virginity to give and I wanted him to have it, to carry it with him through life like my owl charm. My heart raced and his eyes lit like he could feel it. "Is that what you want?" he asked.

It was harder to be bold without wine, so he'd have to settle for a less confident reply. "Yes."

He squinted at me suspiciously. "If you change your mind, tell me and we'll stop. Okay?"

I lost my voice so I nodded, the small spaces on my wrist and lower back where our skin touched stinging like a sunburn. Worry, sadness, and guilt all took a backseat to fear. Kai leaned in and kissed me slow and deep. It didn't taste like a goodbye, fervent and full of desperation, but rather like he savored it like a fine wine or a decadent cheesecake. His tongue sent a pulsing, tingling sensation through my body, sending an ache shooting between my legs.

He cradled me back onto my bed, where he stole another kiss, each one more potent than the last. My head fogged, my body shaking with adrenaline. He crawled over me as his gift slid me up the bed to my pillows. The restlessness in his eyes made me wild. My hoodie rose up, slipping over my head and flying onto the floor. He must've assumed I had something underneath because his breathing quickened, his chest heaving stronger with each breath.

It was a challenge to stay in the moment and not to watch him. A war raged behind his eyes, between his desire and his resolve to move slowly and take it easy on me. I didn't know why, but the more I watched him struggle, the more I hoped the former would win. I wanted everything.

His shirt rose over his head and my hands moved immediately down his chest to his abs. Shit, did he spend the entire jail sentence working out? My hands stopped when they got to a scar—one I'd been responsible for—and it brought a smile to my lips.

Kai's mouth descended, this time on my neck, his tongue sweeping over nerves that sparked to life. The heat of his bare chest on mine pulled my attention to my hardened nipples as they pressed against him. Losing myself, I struggled out of my pants.

Kai let out a soft laugh. "Do you have somewhere to be?"

"You're making me crazy. I'm so ready for this." Damn, it was like his kisses made me drunker than the wine. My panties slid down my legs, sending my heartbeat into overdrive. As they moved, I could feel the sticky wetness that clung to the fabric against one of my legs. Kai's gift tossed them off the bed with the rest of my clothes. I pressed my knees together as the fear of being totally naked in front of someone assaulted me. Kai at least still had his sweatpants on... although, now that I was looking, they did little to conceal what was bulging underneath.

I held my breath as I took it all in. I already felt so vulnerable, emotionally speaking.

"Don't be afraid, love. I have you."

His certainty eased me, so I let my body relax.

"I just want to make you feel good." He lay beside me, putting his weight on his elbow and cradling me in his hand. He traced over my body with a free hand. A chill tore through me, covering my skin with goosebumps.

"Mmm." Kai breathed as he watched. His fingers ran over my collarbone. He moved to my chest and teased my nipples, sending an involuntary moan up my throat. The sound must've rattled his restraint because he leaned forward, bringing his mouth to the base of my neck, then lower to sample my chest with smooth flicks of his tongue. Tendrils of desire caressed my every nerve. I pawed at his back to urge him on, my mind sliding toward the white-hot sensation between my legs. He lifted his head to study me as his hand moved lower. Curiosity and desire were a cocktail in my blood, hazing out my fear. Kai's finger brushed my slit as he whispered, "Are you ready?" I was an even mix of relieved and disappointed to learn he'd start with a finger. Begging my shaking body to relax, I nodded.

A gasp escaped my lips as Kai slid his finger in.

"Is this okay?" he whispered. I pulled him in for a kiss, tasting his tongue as desire boiled over. His fingers moved and another moan broke our kiss. He drank the sound in with a ragged breath. He began to work magic with his hands, his thumb sliding onto my clit. Pleasure slivered up, each time his thumb moved, or the pulse of his middle finger each time it shifted, but his gentle touch grated on my patience.

I reached for his hand and pushed it harder against my body, working his thumb in a way that caused my back to arch.

"That's right, Rei, show me what you like."

"More," I muttered, barely keeping my tone from begging.

A second finger filled me and the pleasure moved from my tailbone up my spine.

"Is that okay?"

I wiggled to test the feeling, but his fingers were locked between my thighs, so I squeezed the muscle there. Kai's eyes rolled. I could tell he was struggling to keep his composure—his cheeks hot. I rocked my hips against his hand and he started to work me. I started to bead with sweat as Kai's thrusts grew more intense... the waves of bliss overlapping.

"Kai," I moaned. "Please." My body shook, my primal instincts grabbing hold.

"Tell me what you need."

"All of you. Now."

He froze then slid out his fingers. I panted, hoping to cool down a little before we started up again, but Kai tossed his pants off the bed. I told myself not to look, but I couldn't help but peek. Kai moved back over to me. Oh god. It was way wider than two fingers, and far longer. *Now I see why he wanted to take it slow.* I was going to die. He was literally going to kill me with that thing. Should I have watched porn or something? Should I have tried shoving something up there to prepare? Girls talked. They all seemed to agree this would hurt. What did I get myself into? My thoughts raced. *I'm too scared.* But as he crawled on top of me, my urge to flee faltered, and I widened my legs, angling my hips to receive him.

Instead of rushing in, he paused against me. I braced myself, but he didn't move. My heart raced so hard that I felt my body vibrate with each beat—then I realized that the racing I felt was *his* heart. I searched his eyes. It was the same neutral expression that he always had when he looked at me, only I saw more in it. His thoughts rang crystal clear in my head. *This is goodbye.*

His lips devoured mine as we poured a lifetime of love into one scorching kiss. He pulled me closer, holding me tight by the waist. I grabbed a fistful of his hair as I clasped my arms around him, as if trying to absorb him into myself. *Love me, Kaito. Don't forget me. Don't ever let go.* His hardness leapt before coming to rest against me once again. My body screamed for more. I bit his bottom lip as a distraction, and while he watched me—the devious glint in his eyes fraught with wanting—I wrapped my legs around his body and pulled him into me.

A grunt passed through his lips that mixed with my breathy moan. My legs exploded with a mixture of physical pleasure and emotional pain.

"Are you—"

Impatient, I rotated my hips. Pleasure tore through me, and Kai and I cried out in unison, his eyes clenching shut. I couldn't stop watching him. His arms shook as he began to lose the battle of restraint. Before I could adjust to the sensation, the emotional weight of it crawled up the back of my neck. *Don't cry. He'll think you're hurt.* But I was hurt. *Broken even.* This was goodbye. *Remember me.* I rocked my hips, the pain and fullness drowned out by a fresh wave of white bliss.

Kai's jaw tightened, his face tinged with sadness.

I wasn't sure if I was ready yet, but I could see in his dark eyes how he felt, and I wanted to *feel* it. "It's okay," I whispered. "Show me."

He thrust into me hard and my bed frame smacked into the wall. *Holy shit.* Before I could recover, he drew out and pushed in again. "Yes," I breathed. I reached up and pressed my palm to my headboard to give myself leverage. This time, I timed my own thrust to meet his. My vision blurred as my eyes rolled back, my senses locked to the radiating bliss. We fell into a rhythm, marked by the slam of my bed frame against the wall as the pace quickened. I felt a delicious pleasure build up as Kai began to lose control. With each drive into me, I felt his body say, *I love you. Don't forget me. Don't let go.* Kai moved back onto his knees, pulling me up against him. My breath caught as he reached a depth that almost immediately pushed me over. The new position hurt more, but desire had taken hold. We moved together, slowly at first. Then Kai pushed my body into a bounce.

My bedroom filled with my voice, my back arching as an orgasm burst between my legs. Kai held tight, keeping the rhythm, punctuating the pleasure—then his body jolted, a breathy shout slipping out that made me want to start again. He pulled me tightly to him, and through the waves of spasms, I could feel him release. Our breaths heaved as we stayed meshed together. He slowly released me, sliding out of my body and easing me back onto the bed. I couldn't tell if he was using his gift or his strength, but his gaze never left me as he lay beside me, his arm draped over my waist. My body shook so badly, and I could no longer tell if it was due to the physical or emotional impact of the ordeal.

Concern settled into his features as if he'd realized that he'd been swept up and forgotten to go easy. As my body relaxed, I could feel the soreness settle into place. *Stay calm.* But the tears began to fall against my will. *Stop it, Reina. You'll ruin it.* But it was no use. I covered my face with my hands.

"Did I hurt you?" Kai asked, his arms wrapping around me.

My body felt euphoric, but tears still fell. I didn't want him to worry. "It was so amazing," I said through sobs. Laughter broke through my tears, the mixture spilling out. *Why am I crying?* Kai rubbed my back as the heaviness settled into my chest. *This is so embarrassing. Why can't I get a grip?* I shook, trying to rally enough to check Kai's reaction, but it was no use. With my guard completely lowered, my gift pushed the truth out.

"You're leaving," I cried. "You were right, that changed everything." I buried my face in his chest. *Why was he so quiet? Did I freak him out? Was he going to make a break for it?*

But the words kept coming. "I... I'm not going to survive losing you. I'm going to regret my choice. Please, Kai... I don't care. Don't leave. *Please.*" I sniffed. "Don't leave... I can't—"

I froze as a sound broke through my sadness, paralyzing me. Pressed against his trembling chest, I finally realized that Kai was crying too, each word I spoke an ocean of salt on his wounded heart. Regret broiled my every nerve. *How could I say such selfish things?*

Love was a sunset, slipping away so quickly that I could watch it surrender to the horizon in a few relentless minutes. The night that followed was sure to be a starless one—not the smallest sliver of moonlight to see me through. In those last moments, my gift would not allow me to ease Kai's pain with a lie. I wished for the first time that I'd never unlocked it, or that the epidemic could sweep it away.

But since I could not comfort him, we cried together, letting our emotions steal our consciousness as we fell to sleep in each other's arms. I blamed myself and those frantic words I'd inadvertently cut him with.

When I woke in the darkest part of the night, he was already gone, the bed cold beside me.

I sat up quickly, Kai's absence shattering the last fragment of my heart. Forgetting he'd taken it, I reached for my owl charm. My stomach dropped when I felt it. *He hadn't taken it?* Did that mean I no longer had his heart?

Stunned, my thoughts were interrupted as my finger slipped through the dainty, metallic object. It was not the familiar owl shape that I knew so well. I swallowed as I slowly looked down, squinting through the darkness. My blood ran ice cold as I held it between my fingers and angled it to my eyes. I scrambled for the phone on my nightstand and fumbled for the light, beaming it on the ring. The band was made up of two studded white-gold owls that framed a pear-cut diamond that glittered.

What did it mean? Was it a proposal? Some kind of promise for the future? But that hope drained away when I got to the third probability. He'd left it as a reminder of the life we gave up—the choice we didn't make. I needed to know for sure, so I stood with every intention of tracking him down. I'd throw on my oversized hoodie, some sneakers maybe, and track his ass down. It would not end like this. I could not live with this choice—not without knowing.

I threw on my hoodie and adjusted the necklace to hang on the outside. I slipped on my shoes and creased in the heels with no time to put them on right. I reached for the door but froze when I remembered Bri. Her chilling screams as her life blinked out in Miranda's vision. My hand dropped from the doorknob and I stumbled back. I collapsed into a pile on my floor. *I had to let him go.*

I choked on my pain, his name barely a whisper on my lips as the rest of my hope surrendered. "Kai," I whispered again through tears. *Love may be over, but it's not dead.*

Even though I'd never see him again, each memory was vividly etched into me. I could still feel him on my body and taste him on my lips. I clutched the ring against my chest. He'd taken my charm with him but left me with a lifetime of love to dream about.

My strength broke. I didn't have enough time with him. No amount would have been enough, but at least I know that it was real. Otherwise, it wouldn't hurt this badly.

I couldn't move beyond the rise and fall of my chest as I gasped for air. *Goodbye.*

Kaito

TWENTY-FIVE

She'll forgive me, I promised myself again and again as Wolfe, Yanis, and I hopped a bus back to my old home. Yanis leaned over. "So... what's the plan?" Yanis asked, pulling my attention back to our group. Across the aisle, Wolfe slumped against the window with disinterest.

"We're going to hunt down Zane. He's involved in this somehow. If we find him, he'll lead us to Bri."

Yanis bobbed his head. "And is this Zane person a friend or foe?"

I leaned back in my seat. "We'll see."

Wolfe let out a groan. "Ugh, why are we not talking about you getting it on with that Fae girl?"

Yanis chuckled. "Getting it on? Seriously? How old are you?"

Wolfe leaned across the aisle. "You could at least not blush like that when I bring it up." I turned my face to the window. "And now you're smiling. Look, I can see it. She was totally great, wasn't she?"

I bit back my smile and tried to shake it off. "I'm smiling because you're an idiot."

"Actually, man," Yanis said, "I think he might have you on this one."

I crossed my arms over my chest and leaned my head back, determined not to let my mind drift back to my most recent memories. The bus slowed and out the window I could see a crowd of people gathered outside a stadium. At first I thought it odd that an athletic event would be held when the government had just collapsed, but then the bus pulled close enough for me to read some of the posters. This was no game; it was a political rally for Calvin Hall. I remembered running into Zane's sister the other day, but Rachel Blaque wouldn't be brazen enough to attend a rally for her opposition. Still, it wouldn't be hard to find someone public. Wendy may not have known where Zane was, but her gift could be useful in tracking people down.

At least we had somewhere to start.

It was odd how easily the three of us settled back into my parents' old place—like GFA had been some kind of holiday. I headed straight to my room to be alone. I wasn't feeling particularly chatty, and I had a ton of research to do before morning. I researched Zane first, hoping I could bypass the campaign trail altogether and leave his sister out of it, but as expected, all trace of an online presence vanished around the time I went in.

An hour after I'd settled in, I heard a knock at my door. Yanis poked his head in. "Bruh, you have a lot of books. Is that your thing?"

"Kind of."

He took the response as an invitation in and sat down at the edge of my bed. "Can I ask you something?"

His tone made me uncomfortable enough to shift in my seat. *Where was this going?* "Yeah, sure."

"What would you do if you didn't have a gift?"

The question struck me. Yanis hadn't seemed too bothered by losing his gift. Wolfe complained constantly about it, but not Yanis. I felt for him. Since puberty, I'd drawn the bulk of my self-worth from my gift and I shuddered to think who I'd be without it.

I took a deep breath as I flipped through my memory. "You know, I was really late getting my gift and, for a while, I didn't think I'd ever get one. Part of me wished I wouldn't, that way I could disappoint my parents one last time and be done with it."

He smiled that pudding-winning smile. "I used to be able to melt things with a touch," he said, shaking his head. "Got mixed up with some bad people, you know? Melted a bank vault and wound up underground at the Agency. I just think, though, how long do you plan on letting us be here? And what happens to Serfs like me and Wolfe when this is over?"

"Look, man, I'm glad you and Wolfe are here. I consider you friends." I took a pen off my desk and threw it at him. "No matter what happens, we'll figure it out."

His head bobbed. "Alright, alright. You know, you never did answer my question. What would you do if you lost your gift?"

I leaned back in my chair, looked up at the ceiling, and sighed. "I'd be a librarian."

"Bullshit."

I smirked. "I'm serious. I could read all day every day."

"I mean, the massive bookshelf should have been a giveaway but... it still feels a little random."

I nodded. "Just think about what you like to spend your day doing and the rest will sort itself out." It dawned on me as I said it that Yanis might've been trying to prepare me for what might come next—the loss of *my* gift. The urge to flee with the rest of the Elite amplified, but the gifted giving into those fears was what caused this mess to begin with, leaving no one to fight for it but Reina and her friends. No, this time I had a chance to be on the right side—Reina's side.

It seemed like everything I had to lose was what I might finally earn if we somehow succeeded—my friends, my gift, my life, and even my love.

It was worth the gamble.

Reina
TWENTY-SIX

The next few hours ran together. I could practically feel Kai getting further away with each painful tick of the clock. I let myself melt to nothing as I took a long hot shower, determined to let it out all at once. Once I joined the others, I would not allow myself to be weak again. I dreaded the look on Miranda's face the next time she saw me, the pity in Asher's eyes, and god I hoped that I wouldn't see something smug in Oden's.

Instead of sulking, I spent a little extra time on my makeup. I put on my favorite workout leggings and tank combo, tied my hair up in a high ponytail, and smiled at myself in the mirror until it felt real. When I headed to the cafeteria, I was grateful that the remnants of our little event had been wiped away, and the tables returned to where we usually kept them.

Asher and Oden sat up straight when I walked in.

"Hey, guys. How are you?"

Ash stood. "We're good. Are you okay?"

Oden's attention was on his phone and I had no doubt Miranda would shortly follow whatever message he just sent her.

"I'm good," I said, unnerved by his concern. Asher always made light of everything, and this new dynamic said that everyone knew what was going on. The last thing I wanted was to talk about it. "We should get back to work."

"Yes, boss... Wait."

I cocked an eyebrow.

His eyes narrowed. "Something is different."

Oden looked up from his phone, his eyes scanning me in appraisal.

"Oh," I said, "I'm wearing a little makeup."

He walked closer. "No... that's not it."

My concern only rose as he tilted his head in observation. Oden joined in, trying to find the source of Asher's worry.

"I'm really fine, Ash, I swear. Just... leave it alone."

He beamed. "That's it! You're not a virgin anymore."

My cheeks burned hot but I couldn't help but snort a laugh before I shoved him. "Shut up, Ash. You're such a dick."

His gaze softened and I saw the pleased glint of a mission accomplished in his eyes. Of course he'd meant to cheer me up, a task he knew would take drastic measures. Out of the corner of my eye, I felt Oden turn toward the window to sulk. Asher must've weighed that into his little scheme and determined that Oden was a minor casualty, but I felt for him.

"I need to talk to you," he said, his eyes a mossy green and, just in case I didn't catch the urgency from his practically hostile tone, he added, "now."

He led me out of the cafeteria and Asher shot me a concerned look before I followed Oden out. Since we were out of earshot, I expected him to stop and tell me what was on his mind, but he took the extra effort to pull me into an empty classroom and shut the door. *Whatever this is, it's going to suck.*

"Have you seen the news?"

"I—"

"I told you this would happen. Calvin Hall or DT or whatever is getting support from other cities to forcibly remove the Elite from Ancetol. He's calling it a free city and it's all because you gave him exactly what he wanted."

There was nothing quite like having my shortcomings served to me by my closest friend. "I know. I'm so sorry, but I can fix this."

He shook his head and it almost seemed like the worst of it was over.

"I'm sorry," I repeated, touching his arm.

His gaze snapped to my hand, and the tension in his body intensified. The desks around us shifted as his eyes glowed green. "Don't say that, because you don't actually give a shit."

"Of course I do."

He made no effort to hide his tears. "You're too goddamn busy fucking Kaito. Your friend is missing and your city is going up in flames. It's one hundred percent your fault." He shrugged. "Well, I guess you're trash in bed because he still left you."

The words should have made me mad. They normally would have been enough to bring my temper to a boil. But my heart was already broken and it recognised its equivalent in him. My strength broke, spilling out as I realized just how badly I'd hurt him and, in the moment, that was my greatest failure.

"He doesn't want you. No matter what you do, she'll never want you again."

There it was, *she*. It seemed to catch him off guard and he slumped down onto a desk, dropping his head. "I'm sorry, Reina," he whispered through sobs.

I was frozen—disgusted with myself for my part in breaking him. Gone was the vibrant and sweet Fae apprentice who charmed the whole world. His light had gone out and I understood because mine was barely aglow.

"I'm so sorry," he whispered again. He slid down to the floor and wrapped his arms around my shins, crying into my knees. "I didn't mean it."

I moved away just enough to have a seat on the floor across from him. I wiped my face. "I'm sorry I hurt you. It was selfish of me to keep you here, knowing how you felt." He nodded and swallowed like his words slipped back down. "So you're leaving then?"

He studied my face then took my hand. "Please come with me. Kai left, but you and I could still have a good life together, away from here. If you give me a chance, I know I can make you happy. You don't have to be alone."

It would have been so easy to go with him. To grab Mo, pack up my things, and have a normal life with Oden somewhere else. What hurt the most was knowing with absolute certainty that he *could* make me happy.

"I can see in your eyes that you want to."

Instinctively, I closed them as if it would erase all the time he spent learning me. "Oden, I'm grateful to have known you."

He turned his face away like I slapped it.

"I believe that I could be happy with you, but I've hurt you enough."

"So, it's Kai or nothing?"

"It is..." I said, pulling my necklace to rest outside my shirt.

Oden's gaze crept down the chain of my necklace to the ring. He tilted his chin up and his Adam's apple moved against his throat. "But my decision to stay isn't about Kai. It's about the kind of person I want to be. I've vowed to help and protect the people of this city, not some other city but the place I've lived all my life. I can't go because I think about the people like the kids from my orphanage who depend on the system for survival. The city might be angry, but the people don't know how much danger they're in, and everyone else has given up on them. I became Fae so I could protect those who needed it most—regardless of whether they have powers or not."

"You're really going to die for these ungrateful people?"

"If that's what it takes."

Oden took a slow breath in and stood, so I did too as I prepared myself for yet another loss.

He leaned in and kissed me, and it happened so fast that there was nothing to do but remember what we'd once been. He pulled away, his green eyes searching mine, and without another word he left.

I don't know how long I stood in the empty classroom, but when I was ready, I returned to the Fishbowl to join the others.

"Reina!" Miranda said.

"Oden left," I blurted.

Her lips pressed into a hard line. "We know. He said goodbye. Wanna talk about it?"

I shook my head.

It was so quiet that we could hear the rustle of the trees outside.

Then Miranda took control of the room. "What are we all standing around for? We have a lost girl to find."

"Right," I said as I headed for my laptop and I thought of the little kid from the bathroom who had said, "It's okay." That was my new mantra—as much as I could manage. Oden would be better off and that was what mattered.

The three of us poured every ounce of our energy into the task, mapping out our next search location and researching internet chatter for leads. The distraction was welcomed by all of us. It felt good to focus on something other than how I felt.

Still, thoughts of Kai slipped into my head, tearing my nerves and reopening the wounds, no doubt leaving scars I'd never heal from. Kai was such a force of nature, a tornado that tore through me every time I drifted. *How could one person do so much damage?* I swallowed a lump in my throat then gasped as the question flipped a switch on a tangent train of thought. *How could one person do so much damage?*

Miranda looked up from her laptop. "What is it?"

I shot up and my chair tumbled backwards, the crash drawing Asher's attention.

"I fucking knew it. There is no epidemic. DT is doing this."

Miranda tilted her head, pursing her lips as if she was unconvinced. "I know he's evil as shit or whatever, but maybe you're reaching a little here... I mean, there have been cases where huge groups of people lose their abilities at once."

"But always in Ancetol. Why? People travel in and out of the city all the time. If this was some kind of virus, it would be spread across the whole world, not just here. Think about it. We know he has a death touch..." I lifted my hand and sharpened my gift into a blade around my wrist. "We know we can manipulate our gifts to target in very specific ways."

Miranda said, "But he'd have to be able to target someone's gift specifically. It's not possible."

I shook my head. "Not for us, but we didn't even finish at GFA and DT was a prodigy."

Miranda shifted in her seat. "That doesn't explain how he's targeting large areas at once."

Silence filled the air as the answers to our questions fluttered around the room just out of reach.

A very specific memory floated into my head. "I fought DT once... Miranda knows, but I don't think I've told you guys the story. It's been hard for me because all these years I thought I'd taken his life. I literally watched him bleed out and fade away. Everything he touched turned to ash in seconds. He had me and Kai beat... backed into a wall. He charged across the room like the grim reaper—hand outstretched to take everything away."

Asher's face drained of color.

"I knew we were both dead, so I panicked and projected my gift's energy straight out." I searched their eyes for signs of judgment but saw only their attention. "Kai must've had the same thought because I felt the sudden rush of his gift too. There was a bright white light that shot out when the two collided and DT just sort of stopped."

Asher's gaze dropped. "So you think they combined somehow?"

I shrugged. "I don't know. It seemed like it."

Miranda said, "Maybe DT thought so too."

"Exactly. Now this could sound crazy, but what if he's using someone else's gift to project his."

"You mean Bri?" Asher asked.

We all turned to look at him.

His eyebrows rose. "You didn't think I was paying attention. If her gift is manipulating radio waves, and he'd somehow figured out how to combine gifts, he could probably use her to target large areas."

Miranda stood and began to pace. "But... but, if that's true, he's unbeatable. He has taken thousands of people's gifts. There's no way to stop him. You said that you watched him die and he's stronger than ever."

I swallowed hard. "But... maybe I shouldn't have been attacking his body. Maybe I should have been aiming for his gift."

Asher's shoulders slumped. "But that was a fluke. We don't know how that happened, much less how to repeat it."

I shook my head. "Right, but there are Fae out there who might. If they knew this was just one person, they might return and fight. Surely someone would know how to stop him."

Miranda picked at her nails. "Personally, I think you're all crazy. If the Fae left because they were afraid to lose their gifts, what makes you think they'll come back now?"

"We have to try, right?" I scanned their faces. "If you think Ancetol is in bad shape now, you're not going to want to see what happens when DT wins this election. I guarantee there's a whole lot more to whatever he's planning. He's sick, and I really think we're right about this."

Asher tossed his red hair. "Okay, but if what you're saying is true, why hasn't he targeted us?"

More than a bit of the room's enthusiasm waned. A few silent moments passed.

"Maybe the school's barrier is too strong. I say we go to the media. We expose him, send a distress call to the Fae, and lure him to campus. We can hold tight inside the barrier until the Fae arrive."

"And what if..." Asher started, "what if they don't come?"

A flare of anger moved through me. "I have to believe they will." But the concern on Asher's face was echoed on Miranda's.

I could hear the anguish in Miranda's voice when it came out as almost a whisper. "Do you maybe want to bring this to Yemoja Roux?"

My gut twisted, remembering how washed out she still seemed. "I'm afraid she'll try to help. Most of the Fae abandoned Ancetol too early... but not her."

Miranda said, "Then maybe go to her as a daughter asking for advice... because you're not exactly a media darling right now."

Asher put his hands up. "Don't look at me. I already signed up to die."

I exhaled slowly. "I'll ask what she thinks of us taking what we know about DT to the media. I need both of you to shift your efforts from finding Bri to any proof you can dig up against DT. We don't need the city to believe us, we just need the public to doubt him. If they do, I'm sure the Fae will come back to stop him. Let's get on it."

In my gut, I knew this was the break we'd been waiting for. The connection. All roads led to DT. We'd wasted years blindly believing what the media said about the epidemic when the truth was there all along. A person did this—a person I should have stopped three years ago. Once I exposed him, this would inevitably turn ugly, and I was putting a lot of faith in Fae who had already given up. All I could really do was hope the Fae answered our distress call and that the barrier would hold.

I wasted no time and rushed to see Yemoja Roux at the apartment.

"It's me!" I called as I propped open the door, but I didn't see her. "Mo?" I called. I trembled as I looked around the empty apartment.

I heard a muffled voice yell, "Reina?"

I followed it into Yemoja's bedroom and then to her closet where she sat slumped on the floor.

I rushed to her side. "Mo, oh my god, are you okay? What happened?"

She wiped her tear-stained face with the back of her hand.

"I'm fine," she said, wiping her tears with a balled garment.

I helped her to her feet. "What happened?"

"I've been following the doctor's orders… staying away from the news. But since I've been feeling better, I figured it wouldn't hurt to watch for a few minutes." She lanced me with a look. "Why didn't you tell me? Calvin Hall… That's him, isn't it?"

I broke eye contact.

"Why didn't you tell me?" she repeated, her voice as hard and cold as a glacier.

"I didn't want you to worry."

"You thought punching him was going to solve the problem?"

"Admittedly not my best move. Mo, why are we in the closet?"

She sniffed. "I came in here to put on my battlesuit and I realized… I don't want to fight anymore. I'm so tired, but if I don't stop him then all my years of service will be for nothing."

"I'm going to handle this, Mo. Put your faith in me and I'll finish what you started."

She smiled, but it didn't reach her eyes.

"How about we grab some tea so I can tell you my plan." I was pretty sure Mo would agree to anything if tea was involved, so my suggestion was a safe bet.

A few minutes later, we sat down in our usual spots on the couch with the type of tea we typically reserved for holidays or special occasions. I hadn't noticed that my necklace slipped to the outside of my shirt when I helped Mo up, but her gaze moved to it and stayed. My stomach clenched. I'd almost forgotten about that ring and I hoped she wouldn't ask me about it.

"Tell me what's going on with you," I said.

"I guess I just... I've been so programmed to jump in to defend Ancetol that I thought that was what I wanted, but it's not. Now that I've had some time off, I realize how many things I've never gotten the chance to do and now I'm running out of time."

"You don't owe this city another second, and you have plenty of life left to live."

She looked thoughtfully out the window. "I never thought this day would come, but I think I'm done. Just..." she shook her head, "done with being Yemoja Roux." Her breath hitched. "I don't want to let you down."

I put down my teacup and took her free hand in mine. "You've given me everything." My tears started to well. "You've protected and guided me for my whole life, before we even met." She squeezed my hand. "I love you, and you will always and forever be my hero." Her gaze dropped away and she choked out a sob. "I am the daughter of Yemoja Roux and I will save this city because you taught me how."

She pulled me in for a hug and cried against my shoulder. "I'm so—" She sniffed. "I'm so proud of you."

I sat beside her and she laughed as we wiped our tears. She reached for a box of tissues and put it between us before blowing her nose, but even through her tears she looked more at ease than I'd seen her in a long while. She hopped off the couch and hurried out of the room, only to return a second later with her uniform.

She practically bounced on her toes as she handed me the iconic garment. I traced over it with my fingers and relived every moment I saw her wear it, from the time I was a kid dreaming of becoming Fae to the last time we fought side by side. We both dove for the box of tissues.

After we settled and my new role sunk in, I felt the weight of Ancetol transfer from Yemoja to me. No matter the outcome, I was ready to give it every ounce of my being. I reached up and squeezed the diamond ring, but my new charm didn't soothe me the way my old one had. I felt a pang of sadness each time I touched it. But what was on the line was bigger than my broken heart.

Mo sipped her tea, but her gaze made repeated trips to the ring on my necklace. "You're sure you want this life?"

I looked up, a little started by the broken silence. "Of course."

"And I suppose something else someday too?" she asked, gesturing at the chain.

My gaze dropped to my cup. "I'm afraid not." She knew better than anyone that being a Fae almost always meant family came second. The necklace was merely a reminder of what I was giving up. "I've given it a lot of thought and my mind is made up."

"I want some grandkids."

I laughed. "Sorry, Mo. I might have to disappoint you there."

"Do you want to talk about it?"

"Actually, I wanted to talk to you about something else. DT." She nodded, lowering her teacup. "We think that the epidemic was really just DT taking away people's gifts. And he has Bri. I plan to make the announcement, at the debate tomorrow, and ask the Fae to return and fight."

"He'll come for you."

"Yes… yes he will."

"What makes you think you can stop him this time? What happens if the Fae don't return?"

"If anything happens to me, Ancetol will know the truth. Protecting this city was never going to be an easy job and, to me, being Fae means putting myself in harm's way to protect others, no matter the cost. You taught me that. Have faith in me. I can do this."

I ran a finger around the rim of my cup while I waited for her response.

She took a moment to think about it then said, "Be ready, just in case... In case they don't come. Remember, as long as there is one great Fae left in Ancetol, the city has a chance."

Kaito

TWENTY-SEVEN

I felt Reina's presence before I saw her. Just a feeling that hit me like a punch to the gut in a sea of strangers. My body moved to full alert as I scanned the crowd. Then I saw her, curls bouncing as she made her way to the stage at the front. I'd half expected to see Yemoja Roux here instead, endorsing one candidate or the other. With elections just a few weeks away and Yemoja being so well-known, it seemed natural for her to make an appearance at some point, unless she'd already asked Reina to step in. If Reina saw me here, it could put Bri at risk.

I spun. "Wolfe, we have a slight complication. Reina's here."

He turned. "No shit? Where?"

"The left side of the stage near the front. We have to get to Wendy without Reina seeing us."

Yanis pushed through the crowd. "Kai, I think I just saw Reina," he said.

"Did she see you?"

He shook his head. "How are we going to get the girl out of here?"

Wolfe perked up. "Didn't she write her number on your arm? Did you add it into your phone?"

"Yes! I mean, I didn't add it but I remember."

"You remember her number? How?"

"It was only one number different than Zane's."

I pulled out my phone.

Me:
It's Kai, meet me outside by the vending machines to the left of the entrance. It's important.

We walked out of the crowded auditorium and waited by the vending machines while Wolfe tried in vain to knock a snack loose. I stared at my phone for some confirmation that Wendy was coming, but nothing came through. A minute later, the door swung open and she hurried out, half out of breath. "Sorry," she said, steadying herself. "I just got your message."

"We need to find Zane," I said.

She frowned. "I... told you already I don't know where he is."

I shook my head. "He must've left you a clue or something."

Her expression grew colder. "You think I haven't been searching for my brother? Believe me, if I knew where he was I would go after him."

Oh crap. I upset her. I softened my voice. "Wendy, we are going to help you find him. Think about him. Did you have some kind of secret code or a special place you liked to go?"

She grew quiet then looked back at the stadium doors, her arms crossed over her chest. "There's this place at the beach."

"Will you take us there?"

She nodded, biting her lip. "My mom is going to kill me... but I guess... if we find Zane, she'll understand."

"Yes! You're awesome."

An hour later, my shoes sunk into the sand. The wide-open space seemed to benefit all of our spirits, but none more so than Wolfe, who ran around like an unleashed puppy. He was so excited that I wondered if he'd seen the beach before or if he'd just spent a lot of time there before he got thrown into prison. The chirp of the seagulls sounded a little like a siren as they rode the wind with outstretched wings. The crash of the waves against the shoreline seemed foreboding against the overcast sky.

Wendy stopped. "Here. This is the spot."

I looked around. There was nothing here. A few hundred yards away I could see the pier where I used to come with Reina. Was I wrong? What was I expecting, for him to be sitting right here?

"Can you use your gift?"

"My mom doesn't want me using it in public... You know, because of the epidemic."

I shrugged. "I don't see anyone around."

She smiled and I thought she looked a lot like Zane for a second. "I need a general timeframe to target. Can you go back to February fifteenth, three years ago? That's when he last made a post."

She knelt and touched the sand. I waited for the image to take shape like I'd seen before—for a shadow of the memory to burst from her hands and imprint on the sand. The fact that her gift could bring forward a memory so long past was incredible progress from what I'd seen her do three years ago. It was a shame that the time of the Fae had ended because she'd definitely make a good one.

"I can't," she said. "The sand... it's too many pieces. They're scattered."

I squatted in front of her and could see tears welling in her eyes. I wanted to comfort her, but finding Zane was the best chance at that. She needed confidence and encouragement.

"It's okay, Wendy," I said, "Sometimes we have to do something that we think we can't. That's the best way to grow. Try thinking about the sand as one big rock."

She buried her hands deeper. This time the grains of sand shifted as if a strong breeze pushed across them. Then I started to see the faintest shadow form. A dark and translucent Zane crouched over the sand. He smoothed it out with his hand then with his fingers began to draw something in the sand. *I knew it.* I moved out of the way, crouching over to get a look at what he was drawing. I held my breath, for fear of breaking Wendy's concentration. I could tell this was more difficult than usual because, instead of watching Zane's shadow form, Wendy's eyes were squeezed shut. I felt Wolfe's presence as he rushed over and I held out my hand to stop him from interrupting as Zane completed a map in the sand, marking an X before standing. I knew the location the instant I saw it. It was the old factory where Zane and I prepared for DT's missions. I was lucky to recognize it because a second later Zane swept away the image with his foot. He walked away, the image of him fading with each step away from Wendy's hands.

Wendy's eyes blinked open. "Did it work? Did you see it?"

I grinned. "Great job, Wendy, you found him. I know exactly where he is."

She brightened, and I wasn't sure it was for finding her

brother or the amazing leap forward she made with her gift. Probably a combination of the two.

Yanis walked up behind me, his voice startling me. "You know, if that librarian thing doesn't work out, you might want to take a look at teaching."

I smiled but kept the thoughts to myself. As Wendy jumped up and down in celebration, I felt a warmth inside me. It was a rush to see her succeed. It was odd to suddenly consider what I wanted to do. I'd always been on the path my parents set, and by the time they gave up on me, I was in prison for life. Gifted or not, I wasn't sure that becoming Fae was what I wanted anymore. I'm not sure it ever really was.

"That shit was crazy!" Wolfe said as he joined us. "You made ghost people and shit."

Wendy tossed her sand-colored hair over her shoulder. "Thanks! I'm kind of a big deal."

I dusted the sand off my jeans. "Let's go find your brother."

∽

We arrived at the factory within the hour. The concrete building looked so still, it was hard to imagine anyone inside. But as I slid the door open and saw how much of it had been rearranged, I knew we were in the right place. The leftover glass had been swept to the left. A mattress lay on the floor in the opposite corner with some blankets draped clumsily across it. There was a table between them with a glass of water that still had ice floating in it. *He's here somewhere.* Zane had been loyal to DT once upon a time. It was risky dragging him in without knowing which side he was on, but I did know what kind of person he was. He would help me, if he could.

A voice shot out and echoed around the high ceilings and exposed pipes. "Who's there?"

"Zanieeee!"

Zane stepped into view, his gift's shield blinking out as he lowered his guard. "Wend? Is that you?"

Wendy threw herself into Zane's arms and I felt a little awkward, turning to Wolfe and Yanis who seemed mostly interested in exploring the factory. "Why is there so much glass here?" Yanis asked.

I smirked. "It used to be a glass factory."

"Ouch!" Wolfe yelled, throwing his finger into his mouth and glaring at me like it was somehow my fault he'd decided to poke at the glass barehanded.

I sighed.

"Kai?" Zane said, his eyes wide.

I waved sheepishly.

"You found the map."

Wendy whined, "Zanieeee, how could you just leave me behind?"

"Hey Wend-bear. I'm sorry. I just wanted to keep you safe. Why are you hanging around with this criminal?"

I smirked, but before I could think of a witty retort he pulled me in for a hug.

Wolfe stepped in. "Don't tell me this is another old flame."

Yanis elbowed him. "Hey, man, I'm Yanis. This is Wolfe."

"Old flame? Let me guess, you guys found Reina."

I felt my face go hot, and I turned away so Wolfe wouldn't call me out on it.

Zane exhaled, "Look, man, your girl is driving me crazy. You asked me to look out for her but... shit. She hasn't made it easy."

I shook my head. "What do you mean?"

"I mean I've been sabotaging her little mission for the last three years. Sending her team around in circles by messing with their data. Bri, the epidemic... all roads lead to the same place."

I stepped back. "Wh-why would you do that?"

"I'm sure now that he's taken his campaign public, you know that DT is back."

"Yeah. Are you saying he has Bri?"

"Yep. He's the one taking away people's powers too."

"How? That's not his gift."

"I don't know, amigo, but can't you understand why Reina needs to stay the hell out of his way? I mean… you told me he was dead." He took my silence as his cue to continue. "I think that's a good reason to believe he's unkillable. Think about all the Gold Tier Fae who lost their powers... We can't win. He's a one-man army, capable of taking down the whole world. It's only a matter of time."

"Why didn't you just tell Reina? She spent years looking for Bri."

"Well, first I tried to go to the media, but I was written off as a conspiracy nut. Then I thought of going to Reina, but I knew as soon as she found out DT was behind all this, she'd just go right for him, instead of fleeing. Shortly after I came forward with all this, I started feeling like I was being watched, so I fell off the grid. But if I hadn't intervened and sent Reina in circles for the last few years, she'd be dead."

"She used to have a big team. How did you manage to do this for so long?"

Zane waved a hand. "Follow me."

He led me around the corner, where he had several desks pushed together, a wall full of computer monitors, and a wheeled office chair.

"And you... uh... built a spaceship?" I asked, eying his setup.

Wendy clung to his arm like she was afraid to lose him again.

He laughed. "That's the thing, I had help. Someone has been virtually assisting me in scrambling her data all this time. I noticed it shortly after I started. I wasn't nearly as tech savvy, but I picked up a lot as I started to track the patterns."

I shook my head. "Who?"

His blue eyes glistened. "That's the thing, based on how the transmissions are coming through, I think it's Bri. We know she was taken. She'd already used her gift to warn us to flee. Obviously DT would have prevented her from doing something like that again, but she'd probably try to help her friends in some way. I mean, who else would sabotage Reina?"

I exhaled a mountain of pressure on my chest. "So you think Bri is helping you protect Reina... which means she doesn't think Reina will win a fight against him?"

"I mean, there's no way. How can you beat someone powerful enough to literally kill you with a touch?"

His question stopped me. My memories pulled forward the image of that white light pulsing through the room, stopping DT in his tracks. He'd looked down at his hands and screamed. Before he could say another word, Reina had cut him down, but I wondered what had actually happened.

"I... I always wondered. The reports were so vague, but how did you take him down before?"

Why didn't he kill us? What was that light? And more importantly, was it possible to repeat the process? "I... don't know."

"Zane! Look, Reina's on TV," Wendy said. "She's wearing Yemoja Roux's uniform!"

Reina stood at the debate podium. Zane snatched the

remote off his desk and raised the volume so the sound cut in mid-sentence.

"...the epidemic. There is a person behind it—Calvin Hall. He goes by DT, *death touch,* and we think he's found a way to use it to take away gifts from Ancetol's citizens. If the Fae don't return to put a stop to this, the world will never be safe again. We can band toge—"

The program cut out and a rainbow screen accompanied a stale tone. I turned to Zane. "What happened?"

He shook his head. "It's citywide. DT must've blocked the broadcast." He looked at me. "This is complete shit. I can't protect her anymore. She's made herself a target."

I shook my head. "You don't think the Fae will help?"

"No. I don't. I think you should grab her, change your names, leave the city, and never look back."

"She won't go," I said, but Zane had a point. DT was practically a zombie, unkillable and bloodthirsty. He had the public and the police force on his side. Reina was never going to back down from a fight, so my only option was to rush back to the school and die with her. We had no chance...

My thoughts shifted and Zane studied my face as if he could see it. *We did have a chance.* My eyes widened as a tidal wave of realization crashed into me. Miranda had a vision where we defeated him. All we had to do was play our part and have faith that it would all go as she saw it. The pieces of Miranda's vision came together and I understood. I couldn't be with Reina... not yet.

"Could you get me DT's location?"

Zane hung his head." I don't think this is a battle you should be running toward, my dude."

"Could you?"

He sighed. "Yeah, probably."

I put my hand on his shoulder. "Look, man, I really appreciate everything you did for me while I was gone with taking care of Reina and stuff. If you give me the location, I'll get out of your hair and finish this." I said the words and I meant them, but I knew what his response would be because I saw in Miranda's vision that Zane was present at the end of this thing.

"I doubt you'll need his location. It's more likely that he'll come after Reina at the school."

"I know," I said, waving Yanis and Wolfe over. "I need you two to go straight to GFA. Stay outside the barrier and out of sight, and alert me if anything happens. Do not engage, no matter what. Understand?"

"You got it, man," Yanis said, heading for the door.

Turning back to Zane, I said, "I'm not going to help Reina. I'm going to get Bri." I finally understood. If I had stayed with Reina, I never would have gone after Bri, especially knowing DT was coming for her. It wasn't Reina's heart that needed to break, it was mine. I needed to learn that saving Bri was essential to keeping Reina. This was my opening.

Zane's eyes narrowed. "What is it? What aren't you telling me?"

"Miranda thinks we have a chance."

"Miranda Callix, the seer? She's still around?"

I nodded.

"Wait... so you already knew that I was going to come along?"

I shrugged.

He thought it over for a second, and I could see the wheels turning as he tried to decide if Miranda's vision meant I'd tricked him into this. He exhaled deeply. "We better get moving."

I felt a little relieved that our friendship wasn't the only reason he decided to tag along. I turned to Wendy. "You're going to have to sit this one out, Wend."

She scoffed. "You're joking, right? There's no way I'm sitting this out."

Zane walked over and pulled her to his chest. She hugged him as he patted her head and I could hear her muffled voice as she said, "You have to let me come."

"Next time, I promise."

Reina
TWENTY-EIGHT

The crowd spun into a flurry of questions. My name had been slandered—DT had made sure of that—but even if there were people out there who suspected Calvin Hall was hiding something, I was sure I could at least damage his campaign enough to buy Ancetol some time… even if my plan failed. I could practically see the headlines: *Reina Roux has Second Nervous Breakdown*. I wasn't anywhere close to knowing all of the answers, nor did I have much evidence to support what I knew, but I had to try and convince the Fae to return. I didn't get far in my message before a man I didn't know leaned in to tell me the broadcast had been cut. But, even with it gone, the crowd wanted answers.

My thoughts clouded with a hundred voices shouting my name, then I felt a firm grip on my arm. Miranda stepped up to the mic and began answering questions, the crowd hushing to hear her better. She perked up a little more than was appropriate, relishing in the attention, but I was more than grateful that she came along.

I'd delivered the message and there was no telling if or when the Fae would return, but one thing I knew was DT was coming for me. Many of GFA's defenses were still in place, the barrier infused with the gifts of Fae that taught there. That was likely why he couldn't blanket sweep our base to steal our gifts. Knowing the campus well would also be an advantage, as would having a few people on our side. The barrier wouldn't hold forever, I'd seen it penetrated before by Zane. All it took was the right gift, and I didn't know how big DT's team would be. I'd grown strong in the last few years and I hoped my ability could stand up against his. As long as he didn't touch me, I should be able to hold my ground. One thing I knew from Miranda's vision was that this confrontation would somehow bring me to Bri. It felt like a lifetime since I'd lost her. Years of failed attempts, even letting Kai go, all led to this last battle.

I refused to lose.

Miranda's voice echoed through the gym, finally registering in my head. "That's all the information we have. We're going to try and stop this, but we can use all the help we can get."

Asher nudged me. "You with us, Rei?"

"Yeah, sorry. We should get back. DT could be on his way already."

When we got to campus, I spent a few minutes checking the barrier and consequently lost track of Miranda. When I was satisfied that it was functioning normally, I headed straight for her room, but it was empty. I texted her but was too impatient for a response. I figured she must be in the classroom she sometimes camped out in. I turned the handle and pushed open the door only to have it slammed back in my face. "What the hell, Miranda? We have to get ready for the—"

The door swung open and Asher emerged, closing the door behind him and holding it shut. If his raised eyebrows didn't give him away, the deer-in-the-headlights look certainly did. "What's going on? What's in there?"

"I need a few minutes," he said.

Now that the campus was on red alert, I was more than a little on edge—my body teemed with nervous energy. "You need to tell me what's going on, right now," I said, but my voice came out harsher than I'd expected.

Asher nodded and pushed open the classroom door. Miranda grinned at me, but I could see in her bloodshot eyes how rattled she was. Her ponytail was lopsided, her makeup smeared, her face blotchy.

"Are you okay?" I asked, rushing in. "What happened?"

Her fake smile waned. "My vision split again… and…" She swallowed the words. I knew in an instant what she meant. My worst fear unfolded before my eyes. The announcement, challenging DT, it had all been a mistake.

She sniffed. "We, uh… still have a chance. The future where we save Bri is still possible, only now…" Her gaze dropped to the floor.

"Tell me, Miranda."

"If it goes the other way, we'll all die." She choked. "I can't see the difference in the two. I don't know how to make sure we win."

I turned to the window. "Okay, here's what we're going to do. I need the two of you to evacuate."

"You're not serious," Asher said. "You'll die."

"Hear me out. Turn on all of the school's security cameras. If he uses his death touch, we'll have the proof we need."

"I don't know, Reina," Asher said. "We just leave you here to fight him alone?"

"You can. We're not going to risk everyone's life when we only need to draw out one death touch to finish this. Make sure the footage gets uploaded and he'll become a target, not just in Ancetol but worldwide."

Miranda exhaled loudly. "It's a suicide mission, Rei."

"Only if you think I can't win."

There was a pause, so I looked them each in the eye before I said, "You've done everything you can. Neither of you have combat gifts. Get going before it's too late."

"Wait!" Asher said, turning to Miranda. "Did the future change?"

Miranda shook her head.

He shrugged. "Worth a shot." He put his hand on my shoulder and headed out. With a pleading gaze, I urged Miranda to follow.

I took a walk around the empty GFA courtyard, my body numb to the task at hand. All the training I'd done, all the dreams I had of becoming Fae, boiled down to this—my eminent death.

If it saved the people I cared about, it would be enough.

Kaito

TWENTY-NINE

I dropped Wendy back at the debate and got a text from her a few minutes later that her mother hadn't even realized she was gone. Zane stayed behind to see if he could figure out Bri's location, and I checked my phone every few seconds waiting for it to come through.

Time was precious. Every second, DT got closer to Reina. In the back of my mind, I wished things were different. I was sure Reina would've loved to be the one to find Bri, and I still had a score to settle with DT.

I returned to the warehouse, but I knew if Zane didn't have the location when I got there, I might have to leave to back up Reina. My hand froze outside the back door as I recognized a familiar sound coming from inside—the scrape of shifting glass that marked my time with The Fallen. There was only one person I knew who might still be using the glass this way. I pushed open the door and Zane was backed up against his desk, his arm ablaze with this gift, a glimmering orange shield. A wall of glass shards hovered in front of him, each piece tied to a yellow thread that ran to the end of Ensley's fingers.

She'd grown her hair out to her shoulders but otherwise looked the same as I remembered. I could see in the precision of the glass that she'd greatly improved her abilities since we last fought. The last I'd seen of her, she was knocked out, but out of everyone in The Fallen, Ensley was probably the most likely to still follow DT, as they had some kind of romantic relationship. She'd also dated Zane, and now I regretted that I didn't know how their story concluded because suddenly it felt like dire information.

"Ensley..." I said, casually slipping myself between them.

"If it isn't the other traitor," she said, but her gaze never left Zane.

"So I take it you two broke up." I kept my tone as casual as possible while I strolled around, running my fingers over various objects and pulling them into my range. I needed more ammo, and it was obvious that seeing Zane again had thrown her.

"You didn't just defect from The Fallen, you fought against us." Her attention was fully on Zane, so I pretended to tie my shoe so I could touch some sharpened glass that was swept into the corner.

That's when I noticed a mass of black shards on the far side of the room. It reminded me a little of the beings we'd formed to attack the Fae.

Ensley continued, "And now I find out you've been tracking us."

My hair stood on end as a piece of glass stung the back of my neck.

"DT is going to be so disappointed that you're not at the

school, Kaito," Ensley said. "He really wanted to bury you in the place you tried to save."

I straightened, the cut on the back of my neck stinging as I turned to see several more shards pointed at me. I gritted my teeth. "I don't really care what DT wants. Unlike you, I can think for myself."

Her eyes darkened. "Don't you get it? He's already won. He thinks ten steps ahead and he always has an insurance policy." With the last word, her gaze moved to the mass in the corner.

"Is Bri in there?"

She smiled. "Yes, and unless you want her skewered, you'll die with dignity."

I backed away from the glass, returning to Zane's side. We'd have to take her down, but I needed to know if he'd have my back or if their past relationship was going to complicate this. My gaze moved to Zane, and the intensity I saw in them gave me what I needed—permission to beat her ass to a pulp.

Zane's gift flared, forming a barrier to protect us. With a twitch of Ensley's fingers, glass fragments launched at us like an avalanche.

I threw everything in my range at Ensley, but waves of glass deflected it all easily. Zane's arm began to shake, and I searched the desk for anything I could hit Ensley with.

The computer monitors lit and words appeared on the screen. *Touch the barrier.* My gaze snapped to the dark mass across the room, but with Ensley's focus on breaking Zane's barrier, half of the form had toppled to the floor. Bri stood with her hands clasped around the computer wires, her determined expression marked by the focus in her eyes.

I threw my hand against Zane's barrier and could feel the

energy pulse with each of Ensley's attacks. The barrier was malleable but strong. I fought the urge to pull my hand away from Ensley's onslaught, as the thin barrier was all that separated us from certain death. I closed my eyes to focus.

"I can't hold her much longer," Zane said, his voice strained and husky.

Focus. Breathe. Then I felt it—each glass shard slamming into the barrier. I felt them drop to the floor and Ensley yank them back to slash at us again. I pushed my gift into the barrier and the color changed from orange to blue.

Zane's eyes widened. "What is this?"

"Hold it as long as you can," I said, but his arms were shaking.

Ensley's gaze shifted at the color change and her attacks slowed, but it was too late. Every fragment that collided with the barrier fell into my range. The weight was unbearable as more shards pierced it. Levitating them all already wore on me. I was way out of practice and, after three years of being blocked from my gift, I was a fraction as strong as I was during my GFA days, and Ensley had practically mastered hers.

Before I could make a move, I noticed a tiny break in Zane's shield no longer than a hair pin. It cracked like fresh ice dropped in water, and a wicked smile stretched across Ensley's face.

With all my might, I thrust every piece of glass in range back at Ensley. The shrill scrape of colliding glass filled the factory.

I sagged in exhaustion, gasping for breath. Everything was still.

Zane ran to the pile of glass in front of us. "Ensley..." he whispered.

His gaze shot to me, so I lifted the glass as carefully as I could. I turned my gaze away. Ensley was covered in blood, probably bleeding out. There was so much blood, it was impossible to know how many shards had penetrated her.

Zane pulled her into his lap. "Ensley," he whispered again. I backed away to give them space but could feel some of the glass that was lodged in her body. If I pulled it out, I might kill her faster. I hesitated, looking away.

"Zane! Look out!" Bri screamed.

I spun to see a shard hovering in the air between Zane and Ensley.

I yelled, but it was too late. Ensley drove it straight into her own chest, the light in her eyes blinking out instantly.

We stood frozen until Bri pulled Zane away from Ensley's body.

I shook, wanting nothing more than to run and get those fragments still lodged in Ensley's body out of my range. *I don't want to be this anymore. I don't want to fight.*

"I know it's hard," Bri said, "but you guys saved me."

I nodded, unable to meet anyone's gaze. Bri grabbed me by my wrists. "We need to get to Reina. If she faces DT, she'll die."

The words trapped me. For a moment, all I could picture was Reina, as covered in blood as Ensley. The image sent my head spinning. "Hey," she said, lifting my chin. "Let's save your girl."

My limbs felt weighted, both from the emotional burden of what I'd done and the strain of overusing my gift. Zane walked over and held his hand out. His eyes were wet.

I took a deep breath and shook his hand. He nodded. I felt too weak to go on—too broken to do anything but disappear—

but the battle wasn't over. Across town, Reina and the others were up against DT.

I swiped at my cheeks and headed for the door, my mind focusing in on Miranda's vision. I had a reason to go on. Reina needed me and, this time, I wouldn't let her down.

Reina
THIRTY

I stood in the courtyard behind GFA's barrier and gate, my nerve wilting like a flower with every passing moment. I could hear my heartbeat in my ears. The garden lights blinked on as the setting sun was lost to the horizon, and I hoped that the people I loved had gotten far enough away.

My spirit was resolute as the barrier buzzed with the energy of the Fae. In a way, they were all with me—their collective defense wrapped around the school and the last GFA student.

All I needed was to make DT show his power, even if that meant using his death touch on me—but in the back of my mind I couldn't help but wish I could see Kai one last time.

Then, between blinks, DT's form slid into view through the glowing wall. He glared at me, his usual easiness replaced with an icy stare that dripped with malice.

Calm down, calm down. I focused on how many Fae had infused the barrier. It wouldn't hold forever, but it could at least buy me a few more minutes. DT's pale hand rose and, with a gesture akin to wiping dirt off someone's face, he brushed the barrier.

Without a second of resistance, the barrier turned to dust, soundlessly floating out of place like flower petals in the wind. Fear paralyzed me like poison in my blood as the protection I'd counted on fell away in chunks of charred gray ash.

The air surrounding the school darkened as it mixed with the dust—the remains of decades of Fae abilities snuffed out in an instant by DT's corrupted touch.

I didn't hear any indication that the gate had also been breached, but I assumed it would be. It was only iron, no match against his power. DT emerged from the dust, the stone-like inhuman quality of his skin and neatness of his collared shirt a contrast to the turbulent storm in his frosty eyes.

"I told you not to interfere," he said, stepping onto the campus. "All you had to do was keep to yourself, but you're just desperate to die playing the hero."

I walked backward, keeping a measured distance between us. "If that's my role, yours is the villain, which means it's time for you to tell me if you have my friend or not."

His eyes widened and my limbs trembled beneath his gaze. He scoffed. "Even after everything, you've learned nothing. Oh, the blissful ignorance…" He sighed. "How I envy it."

"Enlighten me."

His voice softened and he looked away. "There is no good or evil, just those in power and those against it."

I shook my head. "You take people's gifts. You take their lives…"

"And you purge the truth, not just from your enemies but

from loved ones. The only difference between us is which gift we were born with."

His words stung, but I knew who I was. I wasn't convinced he was as certain about himself. "The difference between us is that I'm fighting on the behalf of the city and you're fighting for yourself. So, tell me, did you take Bri or not?"

He clenched his jaw then breathed out slowly. "Yes," he hissed.

My question got lodged in my throat. "Is she—" I swallowed. "Is she still alive?"

He watched me, his head tilting in curiosity. "It's your fault I took her."

I'd known it was, but his words still cut. I wondered if this was his way of torturing me before he put me out of my misery. "Is she still alive?"

"She is."

I knew it. She was still out there, which meant I couldn't die here. I had to find a way to beat him. "Why did you take her?"

He put his hands in his pockets and I felt my body ease a little. "Initially, I'd taken her as a sort of insurance plan in case I couldn't get you back to the tower without killing you. When you came easily, I knew I had no use for her, so I planned to let her go."

"Why didn't you? What changed?"

He reached down and thoughtlessly turned a shrub to ash, then he smiled, his gaze distant as if caught in the memory. "I was hopeful then. I still thought Kai cared and I remember you laughed." His gaze swept across the courtyard. "Where is he, by the way?"

"Gone. We're not together anymore."

DT grinned a smile so dazzlingly beautiful and destructive

that it drew in my morbid attention like a trainwreck. He let out a laugh that made me stumble back. "That's perfect," he said, calming down. "Here I thought killing you would be great revenge on him, plus a neat little invitation to Kai, but he doesn't even want you?"

I balled my hands into fists. We'd only spoken for a few minutes and I felt myself already losing this battle, but I hadn't lost Kai for nothing. "Tell me why you kept Bri."

He pinched his nose in frustration as if my question disappointed him. "I had an epiphany. That night we were fighting, I was overcome with rage at Kai's betrayal. You'd both put up more of a fight than I'd expected, but you never had a chance. In your final moments, you both attacked, your gifts merging together and creating this pure white light." His eyes glistened. "Do you remember? Did you… see it too?"

I nodded.

"The light shot through me, into my gift, and I could feel it… your intent to end me." He searched my eyes. "But death itself can't die. I'm no more capable of it than you are of lying."

I listened, fascinated by his strange perspective. That night had always baffled me. Part of me felt relieved that he stood in front of me now because I'd suffered over his death and my hand in it. He was wrong about me, though; each time I lied, I felt the strain of my gift, but I was still capable of it. Either the truth was less absolute than death or DT was capable of dying and didn't know it.

"I learned something that I'd previously thought impossible. Gifts could be combined. The Fallen was losing momentum, and it looked like the Agency was going to pin the whole thing on Kai anyway, so it was time to fall back and gather my resources for a more direct approach—one I'd already begun cultivating long before I took your friend, back when I first began killing gifts without harming the hosts. Of course, no one believed the first victims and wrote them off as crazy. Oh, how I love this twisted city. I had no reason to keep Bri and went to release her. Her gift was intriguing but not useful for my purposes. And then I remembered that white light and I saw this image of broadcasting my death touch across different sectors."

He ran a hand through his moon-white hair. "What might've taken me a decade to set up took only three short years with your friend's assistance, so really I should thank you."

"So she realized you couldn't die and sent everyone a message to leave the city."

He began to pace, but he seemed more in control than the night Kai and I faced him. Even with his explanation, I couldn't fully understand why he was doing all this. He didn't really care about the people of the city. He didn't even seem to care about his own life. I'd known broken people like him... I'd been broken until GFA saved me. Would he have turned out differently if given the same opportunity, or was he locked on the path of destruction the second he unlocked his gift? These were extraordinary lengths for acceptance.

He straightened. "Why are you looking at me that way?"

I held his gaze. He moved forward and my gift flared to life.

"You pity me?" His voice was so soft that I almost thought I imagined it.

"You don't have to be this."

"Don't. Don't try and get in my head. What are you suggesting, we become friends and skip off into the sunset? Once you're on a path, you can't change it."

"Kai did."

He rushed me, wrapping his lethal hands tightly around my arms. His chest rose and fell as he glared down at me. *Please be quick. Please don't hurt.* "You don't know shit about me."

Forgetting myself, I slapped his hands away. "Maybe not. But I can see how unhappy you are. This path that you think you're stuck on is taking you further away from what you want."

"And what is that?"

"Connection. Friendship."

"And you think if I turned it all around, you could be my friend, Reina?"

I swallowed a mouthful of fear and pushed the purple glow of my gift forward to prove my answer. I let out a relieved breath when I felt my gift still intact after DT's touch. "Yes."

He walked closer and I worried he might touch me again. His nostrils flared before he spoke. "It's a shame how people drop dead these days. I mean, you're alive one second and then one touch later you're dead."

It was a strange tangent that I struggled to connect.

"Five years ago, when The Fallen was still new, I used to enjoy taking shots at the establishment by testing out all the different ways my gift could kill. That is how you become an expert, you know… Of course, nobody really cared until I targeted Fae specifically…"

It clicked. It was only a few heartbeats of understanding, but just like that he'd broken me. Darkness settled in, extinguishing every bit of me and leaving nothing but unchecked hatred. Rage sent a cyclone of purple energy whipping around me. The force so strong I could hardly hear the question as it tore out of me, "You killed my parents?"

Kaito

THIRTY-ONE

Yanis' text confirmed my worst fear. The barrier was broken. With the Gem gates closed due to lack of Elites, Bri, Zane and I had no choice but to take the bus across town. I could barely sit still. From the way Zane's leg bounced, he seemed unnerved to be moving towards the danger. Bri's eyes were closed and I could hear her chanting something under her breath.

Finally, the bus came to a stop, so we bolted off the bus and tore up the hill towards the campus. I stopped short when I recognized the group blocking my path. Miranda, Asher, Yanis, and Wolfe stood together. They were so engrossed in conversation they didn't see me approach.

"What's wrong? Where's Reina?" I asked, drawing their attention. Miranda's mouth dropped open and she ran to Bri, hugging her tightly.

Bri chuckled. "I… didn't know you cared."

The ground shook as a crackle filled the air. We all scrambled to keep our balance and turned to the school to try and get a look at the commotion.

"Is Oden with her?"

Miranda shook her head.

"She's fighting him *alone*?" My anger was misplaced; there wasn't much any of them could do without a combat gift.

Miranda grabbed my wrist. "Kai," she said, "things have changed… There's a good chance that we're all going to die today."

This time when I looked into the faces of each person, I saw the choice weighing behind their eyes.

The sound of shattering glass in the distance set my nerves on edge. "Look, no one has to go in there. No one would fault you for staying out of harm's way, and I certainly wouldn't think any less of you, but Reina saved me from DT once so I figure I owe her one."

Zane shifted. "She saved me too."

Asher grinned. "Dammit… she saved me too and, Miranda, I *know* she saved your ass."

I could feel their spirits rising.

"She didn't fucking save me," Wolfe said with a smirk. "But I'm not going to miss this shit." Yanis patted him on the back. We paused for a moment, a silent goodbye passing between us with each gaze we met.

I turned my attention to the commotion, but the campus was shrouded in the black ash that had once been the school's proudest feature. I ran into the darkness, knowing that either way this would be the last time.

I sprinted up the hill, my heartbeat forceful not from the run but from fear as I made my way in. "Stay hidden," I whispered over my shoulder, and most of the footsteps behind me grew fainter. My pace slowed as I peered through the smoke. A purple blast shot through the darkness and DT's voice rang out—the malevolent laugh of a madman.

I ran toward his voice and stopped short as a sudden gust of Reina's magic cleared the air.

My eyes moved toward the threat. I could feel the bloodlust in the air as I gazed into dark, murderous eyes—Reina's eyes.

DT's laughter echoed through the shattered courtyard. It looked like it had been devastated by an earthquake. The garden lights spit sparks and a shrub was on fire. The ground was torn to shreds as Reina's gift spiraled off her body in sharp waves that cut like daggers.

DT grinned despite the deep cuts on his body. His shirt was shredded and covered in his dark blood. Whatever she was doing, he was the cause somehow. I had to stop her before her power consumed her.

"Reina!" I yelled. "Stop this!"

Ribbons of power flashed past me. I was far enough away to dodge her shots, but any closer and she could've sliced me to ribbons.

DT's gaze met mine. "Kaito, so glad you could make it."

"What is she doing?" I asked through my teeth. "What did you do to her?"

"Everyone thinks they're a hero until they're pushed. Some of us just got pushed earlier in life." He smiled, gesturing to Reina's crazed expression. "This is Ancetol's last Fae. Go ahead, Reina!" he yelled. "Be free! Let it out!"

"NO!" I screamed, but it was too late.

Two purple blades shot out at DT, meeting their mark. The ground where he stood shattered, filling the air with dust. I held my breath, certain DT was gone. I heard a giggle and saw him stand again, spitting a mouthful of blood.

DT smiled with blood red teeth.

So it's true, he can't die.

"Reina!" I yelled, but she couldn't hear me. I picked up a rock and threw it at her, guiding with my gift, but her magic sliced it.

DT clapped his hands in mock applause. "By all means, attack your own people. Humanity never disappoints."

"Reina!" I yelled again, but her gaze was fixed on DT. *I need to get over there now.*

I need Zane, but calling him would put him in danger.

The ground was broken enough for me to start pulling ammunition, but I wasn't sure having any would help the situation. I drove myself crazy during the bus ride here imagining horrors, but never this. The biggest threat here was Reina and it wasn't like we could attack her. "What did you do to her?" I asked again.

"I finally had the time to do a little research. Turns out Reina and I have some shared history."

"You took everything from me!" Reina shouted. "They did not deserve to die."

DT bore his teeth. "And who deserves to die, Reina, me? Well, I say it's you!" He charged and my blood ran cold. I was certain it was over until a flash of magenta knocked me off balance and I looked up to see Yemoja Roux, cut between DT and Reina. I gaped; she shouldn't have come while she was still in recovery.

I watched as Reina's magic ricocheted off Yemoja. She was strong enough to block most of Reina's attacks.

Reina stumbled back. "Get out of here, Mo. This is personal."

"What luck. I can kill another parent," DT said with a snicker.

Yemoja held out her hand and DT flashed his teeth as his dark magic collided with hers. Yemoja pushed him back, and for the first time I saw the black glow of DT's magic outside of his body.

My body shook as the two titans faced off—all the while Reina's power surged like a storm, growing in size and danger. Her gift sliced into the ground, stirring the wind into a cyclone around her—one filled with blades of truth. I moved further back as I watched helplessly, unsure if Yemoja wanted us to fight alongside her or get out of her way.

Her gaze was cold as it met mine, her magic never ceasing its clash against DT's. She whispered, "I don't think I can beat him."

Dread seeped into me. "We need to get to Reina."

For the moment, she had him distracted, so I turned and took off away from the battle. "Zane! Where are you?"

"I'm here!"

I followed the sound through the dust and ash and found the rest of our group huddled together, trying to get a glimpse of the battle. "What's going on over there?" Bri asked. "It's shaking the ground. I thought I saw Yemoja Roux."

"Yeah," I said. "She's fighting DT, but we have a problem. It's Reina. DT's the one who killed her parents. She's lost control and I need to get to her."

Miranda gaped. "Reina's doing this? Then I'm going too."

"Me too," Bri added.

I turned to Zane. "We're going to need your shield, buddy. Are you up for it?"

He nodded, but his wordless answer told me how afraid he was.

The ground shook, nearly knocking us all off our feet. *Fuck. Something happened.*

We huddled around Zane who had a glowing shield around us in seconds. The four of us moved as quickly as we could while staying inside the barrier.

The dust cleared and my attention snapped up to Yemoja Roux. She knelt in front of DT as she stared down at her hands. *No.* Without a trace of magenta in the air, I knew he'd taken away her gift and with it our last hope of winning.

I could see cuts against Yemoja's back as Reina's gift spun out of control, and Yemoja could no longer defend herself. Sandwiched between Reina and DT, I wasn't sure who would kill her first, but she was going to die.

Our group sprinted towards Reina, into the maelstrom of her power. Zane's shield held, and together we pushed until we could only move an inch at a time, buffeted by her magic. Zane clenched his jaw, his blue eyes blazing with determination, and I pressed my hands against his shield, willing my gift to reinforce it. Miranda and Bri followed and we started moving closer again.

"Reina!" DT shouted. "Watch me kill your new mother!"

Reina moved into our reach, but to get to her we'd have to drop Zane's shield and take the brunt of her deadly gift. Zane's frantic gaze met mine. Pure energy ricocheted off Zane's barrier—his nose bled as his shaking hands held it in place.

I gazed through the barrier. Reina was so close I could almost touch her hand. I pressed against it. "Reina, you're not alone. We're all here for you," I yelled. Her dark eyes moved to me.

"He killed..." she said and her voice hitched. "He killed my parents. He's going to kill Yemoja."

"Not if we stop him now."

"I hate him. I want him to die."

"I know, Rei. But he's broken and you're strong. I love you, Rei, and I believe in you. You're Fae, you can stop him. You can *save* him."

Reina's magic halted, specks of glowing purple orbs suspended like stars across the courtyard.

Zane dropped the barrier. Reina's gaze snapped to Yemoja Roux. "DT!" she called. "Stop this."

DT's eyes narrowed. "The homicidal maniac speaks. Welcome back."

She smiled, but there was kindness in it now. Pride. "I'm going to save you."

DT kicked Yemoja Roux to the side and walked toward us.

Reina turned her gaze back to us and came to rest on Bri. "Thank god you're alive," she breathed. "I'm so sorry, guys... But don't give up. We still have a chance."

Adrenaline raced through me as DT closed the gap, his hands raised and his dark magic pulsing to turn us to dust.

"Everyone, give me your power—all of it."

I didn't hesitate, feeling the power rising as we grabbed hold of her arms and willed our power into her. I felt weak as my gift drained away through my hands, the full force of gravity weighing on my body. I didn't know if she was planning to kill him. I didn't know what would happen if we combined all our gifts, but I trusted her, as did the rest of the group. Tears streamed down Miranda's face and Zane closed his eyes, feeling DT's hatred inches away.

The ground beneath us exploded as the full effects of DT's

ability rained down on us. Blackness filled my senses and drowned out a scream that sounded like Yemoja Roux.

Then there was nothing. No pain or sound or fear.

A piercing white light began to glow above me like a beam of sun cutting through the darkness. It flared and all my senses rushed back, but the light remained. The smoke lifted and my hand still gripped Reina's tightly. Bri and Zane held on as we stared up at her. Her head was tilted back, her mouth stretched open as if caught in a scream. White light beamed from her mouth and eyes. It poured from her fingertips and off the ends of her hair as the five of us hovered. We were all caught in my levitation gift, only it wasn't mine. I felt the hug of Zane's shield wrapped around me like a second skin and Bri's gift spread as the staticky air crackled. The world blurred at the edges as if we were watching one of Miranda's visions. Reina's head tilted down, her gaze meeting DT's blood red eyes. His death touch struck us, but all his desperate and violent attempts were in vain. Our encased group was protected by Fae.

Reina lifted her hand, turning it over as the glowing white light blossomed into a flower in her palm. She lifted it up to her lips and blew.

The flower floated through the air, arresting all of our attention as it floated down straight for DT. The moment the ethereal petals collided with his darkness, a blast of energy exploded through everything. The five of us dropped from the air, Reina's body taking the brunt of the blast. I slammed to the ground too quickly to slow with my gift and Reina landed hard on my ribs. Nothing moved in the wake of the blast. It was as if my heart was too shaken to beat.

My consciousness drifted away.

Reina

THIRTY-TWO

I stared down at my hands, too afraid to look up—too afraid to find out who survived and who didn't. I lifted my chin to see cold blue eyes wet with tears. DT shook, his posture mirroring mine as he looked up from his hands.

"How did you do this?" he whispered. "Last time you tried to kill me... and this time, after everything, you—" His voice broke as he began to sob.

"I healed you. I took away your gift," I said. "You can't hurt anyone anymore." *And neither can I.* I'd felt my gift slip away in the blast. There were no more monsters here. "You're just Calvin now."

"I'm free of it," he choked out.

Mo bolted over and wrapped her arms around me. "How did you—"

"Are you okay? I'm sorry I—"

"You saved us." She took my face in her hands, her voice lowering as she repeated herself. "You saved us."

I nodded, but I was shaking. I'd gone so far into darkness that I lost myself, and Yemoja paid the price with her gift. I understood DT and how blurred the line was between us. Anyone was capable of terrible things, and the only difference between me and him was the people who fought to save me. That's why, in the moment, when I felt the energy of my closest friends, I used it to save him.

I turned to see Kai, Zane, Miranda, and Bri helping each other up.

I blinked hard, certain I was imagining Bri, but she hugged me so hard that she practically tackled me to the ground.

"How are you here?!"

"Kai and Zane rescued me."

It was really over.

Approaching footsteps drew our attention as Wolfe and Yanis emerged from the dust. Miranda looked ragged, like she had when I'd previously made her overwork her gift. She panted. "Holy shit. We were not supposed to win this. We should all be dead."

Zane said, "Still the comforting presence you always were."

Kai lifted me off the ground into a hug and I felt the wrap of his gift as I hovered in his arms. He put me down and looked into my eyes. "I never doubted you."

"Me either!" Bri said, yanking me back from Kai. I held her and my joy spilled from my eyes. We both cried until it turned into a laugh. My long-lost friend finally returned to me, and I had no idea how Kai had pulled it off.

I was so consumed by our reunion that I didn't notice the white-haired boy who watched us with a longing gaze. Mo stood. "I'm going to call this in." She grabbed Calvin by the arm. "You're coming with me."

When the shock started to wear off, our group exchanged theories and listened to each other's versions of what happened. We all experienced it a little differently.

They sat in awe of my version, but it was cut short as Asher joined us with a huge smile. "So... I just checked GFA's old security network...We got it!" His words were rushed as if he could barely contain what he had to say next. "I got that whole freaking thing on video."

We watched it immediately—at least ten times in a row. Even through the dust, darkness, and the occasional broken lens, we all felt the video accurately captured the essence of what happened. I felt a whole lot better about losing my gift after I saw it. I was equal parts ashamed of losing control and proud of overcoming it. I'd somehow shielded the rest of the group from the blast that took away my gift.

We knew that we'd done something that had previously been thought of as impossible but we didn't know the impact those twenty minutes of footage would have on Ancetol.

~

A few weeks later, my phone buzzed in my pocket. I slipped it out and glanced at the screen, but my eyes rolled back as Kai trailed kisses down my neck, his tongue blurring my senses.

I dropped it and it landed beside the couch with a thud as Kai's skillful fingers deftly unbuttoned my top. Heat radiated down my body as I hyper-focused on Kai's lips. They moved over my skin and I squirmed under the pleasure. "You promised me we could try zero-g this time," I teased.

His gift slid me down the couch until my lips brushed his.

"You sure you're ready?" he said against them, making quick work of my belt buckle.

His phone buzzed and he tossed it to the side but eased its landing across the room. I pushed up to my elbows as I glanced at his phone. "You don't think there's somethi—" He claimed my mouth with his, sending me into a daze. It seemed like ever since I'd lost my gift, everything had gone into hyperdrive, except this. Every second I spent with Kai, we savored. It silenced the noise like nothing else could—an escape from all the chaos.

In fact, if our team didn't check in on us from time to time, I doubted we would come up for air at all. Maybe I was avoiding it because unsurprisingly Ancetol's problems didn't get solved with Calvin's arrest. The Fae started to return, but Ancetol no longer wanted a Fae in charge of the Agency. The election campaign sent a constant flood of reporters harassing us every time we stepped out of our new apartment. Releasing the video had told the world that gifts could be taken away, and the Agency was eager to figure out how to utilize the technique to police the city. It was hard to live with being a Serf again. My dream of becoming Fae was every bit as spectacular as I'd hoped, but far too brief. I didn't care much for the fame and praise the world showered me with since the video was released. When it came down to it, I could never help Ancetol again—not in the way I wanted.

I tilted my head back as Kai ran his hand up my body and stopped at my chest. I looked down, flummoxed by his delay. Between his fingers, he held the ring he'd put on my necklace. My breath caught. *Do it, please.* Ask me. My stomach fluttered and Kai's eyebrows rose slightly like he could feel it.

I will kill you if you don't ask already. Kai's eyes were cold and his smirk teasing. He was every bit the bully that he ever was. After we'd all recovered from our injuries, Miranda had shared with me and Kai one last vision, *our wedding*, without the cloud of Bri's death hanging over it this time. We both knew it would happen eventually. I knew Kai would ask. He knew I'd say yes, we just didn't know when. He used the *when* to torment me and loved to fluster me by making me think he was going to propose.

"Reina," Kai whispered, his voice a little husky. I gulped. *Oh my god, this is it.*

A knock at the door sent me scrambling to button my shirt. I held up my finger. "We will continue this conversation later."

"What conversation?"

I shoved him back on the couch. "Kaito, stop teasing me. I know what you're going to ask me."

I hopped up and headed for the door. "Coming!"

Kai zipped his pants and mumbled, "Who's teasing who?"

I pulled open the door and our old team stood in the doorway. Zane shifted uncomfortably as he surveyed me. "Oh, I hope we weren't interrupting..."

"Just tell her already," Bri said.

"What's going on?"

"You haven't been watching the news, have you?" Asher asked, pushing past me.

"Come in, come in."

Miranda poked her head in. "Kai's not naked, is he?"

"Probably not... We were just—"

"Your shirt is misbuttoned."

I felt my face warm. "Whoops," I said as I fixed it.

Wolfe watched me pointedly and Yanis suppressed a smile as they all moved into our apartment.

"What's all this?" Kai asked, greeting everyone in their own unique ways—a nod to Miranda, a smile to Bri, a hug to Zane, and two distinctly different handshakes for Yanis and Wolfe.

The group exchanged glances.

It must've been big if they all showed up together. Everyone had been laying low since the fight and they usually only showed up unannounced in groups of one or two.

Miranda sighed. "You pussies, I'll tell her. Reina, you were just elected as the Chairman of Ancetol."

I blinked. "What? What are you talking about?"

"Mo had you put on the ballot. They voted you in."

The words hardly made any sense. I had just started to come to terms with not being able to help the city. Mo must've hidden it from me, knowing it would be a long shot. "Wh-why did they vote for me?"

Asher grinned. "You really should watch the news, Reina."

Bri chuckled.

Ash brushed her off. "I'm serious. Ever since the video, you're all anyone can talk about, and since you're a Serf now... no offense, you're sort of the best of both worlds."

Wolfe smirked at Zane. "Bruh, doesn't that mean she beat your mom?"

Zane shoved him. "It's whatever, man. I voted for Reina."

Wolfe nodded. "That's... kind of messed up."

Bri glared at Wolfe. "You're ruining the moment."

I spun to Kai, but he looked less surprised than he should have. "You were in on this."

"I knew you wanted to get back out there. There's still so much good you can do, Rei."

My heart stuttered in my chest as he peered down at me. I felt the weight of the undertaking before I'd even fully decided to take the job. Maybe I could be the bridge between those with gifts and those without. As I looked around my apartment at all the people I had in my life, I knew that all the struggles I'd faced led me here.

"Everyone out!" Miranda said. "I need to make Reina presentable enough for the public... I doubt this sex hair is going to go over well."

Bri's eyes lit up. "I call dibs on doing her makeup."

Miranda sighed, her voice dripping with annoyance, but her face was a monument of unmasked joy. "Fine, but either way boys out!"

As Miranda and Bri made me over, my thoughts were consumed with what I might say to Ancetol. I supposed more than anything I wanted them to know that the gifts we were given didn't define us. A person's worth comes not from their superhuman abilities but from their human ones. Our will to help and protect others is what makes us strong. It's true that some people are born with extraordinary gifts, but we're all capable of heroic deeds. I know that things won't sort themselves out overnight, but one act of kindness at a time is all it will take to heal Ancetol.

∼

Three weeks later, after I was inaugurated, and on Kai's first day as a professor at GFA, he suggested we take a walk, just the two of us. I'd expected he'd want to have a quiet night in, but I jumped at his suggestion. The sun was setting as we reached the beach, but we walked hand in hand towards the pier.

His emotions swirled behind his dark eyes like the crash of waves against the rocks below us. I knew that this time for sure he would ask me to marry him, and I narrowly fought the urge to throw my arms around him and say yes all so I could hear what he would say.

He took a sharp breath in that skipped and I felt myself begin to tear up.

"Reina," he said as he lowered to his knee. "Will you help me with my lesson plans?"

I snapped into attack mode, leaping onto him and trying to pull him down to the rickety pier, laughing. *I'll kill him. That's it. He's dead.* He laughed and fought me off, relying heavily on his gift to keep us upright. I was still scrambling around taking shots at him when the sun kissed the horizon, and I'd noticed that I was no longer wearing my necklace. A second of panic slammed me before Kai lifted my hand, and I saw that during our little brawl he'd slid the ring on my finger. My mouth dropped open, my breath shallow.

"Reina, marry me," he said.

Words tangled with joy and got stuck in my chest.

"Marry me because I will always do what's best for you. Marry me because it'll take a lifetime to make up for what I put you through. There will always be darkness in me and I need your light to keep it at bay. You saved my life and every good thing in it has been brought to me by you. Reina, be my wife and you will be loved for every second of the rest of your life."

I wiped my eyes, my racing heart beating his name. It was strange to think that I used to sit with my future husband and watch the sunset when I was twelve and stranger still to see how much he'd changed since then. Considering the tough guy he pretended to be in high school, he turned out to be more of a romantic than I'd predicted, and it was his love that held us together through our darkest days. I think I always knew that our bond was unbreakable, but we still tested it and, in the end, he had every part of me except the rest of my life. I couldn't wait to promise it to him.

I managed a smile, composing myself before I said, "I'll think about it." I spun on my heel and headed back down the pier on my own.

"Reina," Kai whined. "Reina! Don't bully me."

AUTHOR'S NOTE

Thank you for reading The Gifted Fae Academy series.

If you enjoyed this story, don't forget to leave a review and let me know what you thought. Reviews are an author's best friend. A simple, "I liked it." makes a huge impact and it's a key factor in deciding whether or not I'll continue writing a series.

Thank you for your support.
Happy reading,
Brittni Chenelle

LOVE TRIANGLE

Did you know I have another trilogy out? It's a YA Fantasy/**guilty pleasure** with a **love triangle**. A princess tries to murder her betrothed.
Free with Kindle Unlimited
Click Here to Learn More

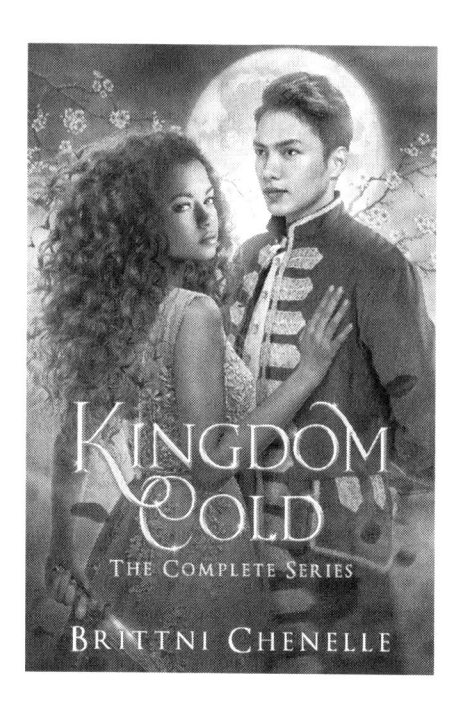

MORTAL GIRL + GOD

This is the Hunger Games meets Percy Jackson. It's a NA Romance where a girl tries to win back her soul which her mother bartered away to Hades.

Free with Kindle Unlimited

Click Here to Learn More

PORTAL FANTASY

This CLEAN YA Romance, is perfect for a bit of escapism. The characters get pulled into a book portal. It's a light fun, standalone that's perfect for all ages.

Free with Kindle Unlimited

Click Here to Learn More

ACKNOWLEDGMENTS

I'd like to take a moment to thank everyone who helped bring this story to life. Without you, my dream wouldn't be possible. Thank you so much for your time and contribution.

Thank you to Charlee Garden for listening to me cry over this series on messenger as I slammed my face into the keyboard and yelled "Whyyyyyy?" late into the night.

Thank you to Kisha, Kevin, Nana, Mom in law, and Mom for being such passionate fans through this process.

Thank you to the YA Fantasy Readers group for chatting with me about books and keeping me sane.

Thank you to Lessa Lamb for reading over my sex scenes because I was too scared to publish them without a nod of approval.

Thank you to my beta readers Meg and Madeleine.

Thank you to my husband for making me a lovely home-office to work in and for listening to me talk about magic, Fae, and voices in my head for the last six months.

Copy Editor: Amber Richberger
Content Editor: Jami Nord
Heading Image Designer: Molly Phipps
Abilities Consultant: Trey Wilson
Blurb Writer: Charlee Garden
Book Cover Designers
Individual Books: Silviya Yordanova
Set Cover: Maria Spada

My Amazing Patrons:
Christopher J Canady
Jeanette George
Kellie Rivera
Michelle Curtis
Shelly Wilson
Kisha Wilson

Click here to become a Patron! Unlock exclusive content, prizes, and perks!

Printed in Great Britain
by Amazon